WHEN FLIES STRIKE

PREVIOUSLY BY PHILIP J. GOULD

Fiction

The Girl in the Mirror

The Sons of Gyges

The Whisper of Persia

Non Fiction

The Book of Alternative Records (Metro Publishing Ltd)

PHILIP J GOULD

When Flies Strike

First Published in Great Britain in 2018
Wildboar Publishing, Ipswich

A CIP catalogue record of this book is available from the British Library

ISBN 978 0 9934167 3 6 (paperback)

Cover Illustrations by Streetlight Graphics
Author portrait © Beth Gould

Dedicated to Janet Hackwith
Once upon a time, you were my mentor.
Although we went our separate ways, led different lives
and experienced new things
you have always been in mind when I write my stories.
This one is for you, Jan… let there be a fly revolution.

PROLOGUE

1

BRIGHT FLUORESCENT TUBES BURNED BRIGHTLY within the ceiling, making the already-clinical room appear pristine owing to the harsh white walls and reflective metal surfaces.

The room was set behind a wall of toughened glass ahead of a raised seating area. Like within a theatre, each row was elevated a couple of feet higher than the one in front, allowing unrestricted viewing. Despite the number of seats – at least one hundred – there were few spectators today; just a handful in suits and one prominent figure dressed in military uniform; the insignia on his arm and the medal ribbons attached to the left breast of his jacket indicated the man was a decorated general.

Within the laboratory, unfazed by the watchful eyes of the general or his cohorts – two captains, a major and the CEO of the facility – Dr Quisenberry continued on with his work. Dressed in a white lab-coat and looking serious, he peered down the twin lens of an optical (light) microscope. The specimen he studied was transmitted and enhanced for his audience on an LCD screen, the video capturing the image an arm's length from the scientific apparatus, as well as appearing on TV screens to either side of the glass wall outside the room.

Behind him, a lab technician – a young woman, similarly dressed in a white coat and wearing spectacles and a surgical face mask – shuffled about. Her hair was tied into a ponytail, bouncing a little against the top of her back. She carried a shallow metal tray upon which a number of capped test tubes containing oily-coloured substances chinked together.

"Are you ready, Doctor Quisenberry?"

The doctor made no signs to suggest that he had heard her, appearing deep in thought. Whilst scrutinising the magnified sample, the doctor used both his hands to manipulate a pair of knobs to the side of a sealed unit, within which the microscope was affixed and spied into.

"James?" the lab technician spoke with a little more urgency.

"Huh... sorry... I was miles away." Quisenberry didn't look up and sounded slightly distracted.

"Is everything all right? Are we good to go?" A tiny note of concern slipped into the young woman's voice.

Quisenberry sighed, removing his eyes from the eye-pieces and turned his head to his assistant. No one watching from outside could see the doctor's face, so they missed the look of uncertainty. His consternation wasn't because something was wrong; it was whether what he was doing was right.

"James?"

The uneasiness smoothed from the man's face as he forced a smile. "Sure. We're good to go," he said, reaching out for the metal tray and carefully laying it down on the table alongside the microscope. Before removing any of the test tubes, he quickly returned his eyes to the twin ocular lenses, checking the microscopic organism that was swimming about in the borosilicate glass petri dish like it was desperately seeking an escape route, positioned beneath the magnification machine.

On the TV screens, the enhanced image of the organism swam about; a small dot of movement with what appeared to be thousands of tiny hairs dancing about excitedly. Small flickers of bright light emanated from the dot like little sparks of energy.

With the general, none of the spectators had the first clue as to what they were witnessing. It could have been snot from an orangutan or pus from an ulcerated boil; it was anyone's guess.

"Okay… having removed the behavioural gene… all I need do… is… place the mutated replacement into the specimen…" With his right hand, he reached over to the metal tray and blindly sought one of the test tubes.

Pressing a button on the sealed unit beneath the microscope, a small door popped open, like that on an old tape deck. Quisenberry carefully placed the test tube into the opening and pushed it down with a small amount of force, hearing the seal on the test tube snap open as it became attached to the micro-scientific dispenser.

"I hope you guys know what you are asking me to do…" he said quietly to no one in particular. He pressed the button on the sealed unit a second time and the small receptacle, within which the test tube had been inserted, slowly closed.

Looking up from the microscope again, Quisenberry turned his attention to the computer station placed close-by. He typed in a command and hit enter.

On the computer monitor, a single word popped up: **EXECUTE?**

The doctor hesitated for a moment, looking painstakingly towards his assistant. She nodded reassuringly.

"Very well." Quisenberry pressed the return key on the keyboard and the word **EXECUTE?** was replaced with a whole sequence of numbers and letters, jumbled and incoherent. The sealed unit ahead of him began to make a whirring sound as internal parts, gears and pulleys became active.

On the LCD screen, the enhanced image still displayed the organism, though with the addition of something new.

Appearing from the left side, a long, thin needle skewered into view and continued further until it was pressing against the small dot. The edge of the dot appeared to bend slightly beneath the force and then bounced back into shape as the microneedle penetrated it.

Autonomously, the machine introduced the mutated gene, and after, swiftly retracted the needle; the organism changed to a bright red colour on the screen, though the electrical pulses that had flashed before continued at a more frenetic pace.

"What now?" the lab technician asked, doubtful, as though uncertain of what should or would happen.

"We wait," replied Quisenberry earnestly, "and see what happens."

2

Two months later.

"I can't believe all this... *hoo-ha*... for a load of bugs." An acne-riddled student-geneticist spoke in hushed tones to a female colleague sitting next to him. They were five rows up from the front.

Not knowing him, the black-haired young woman smiled politely but said nothing in response.

The theatre of seats looked down towards the laboratory, concealed behind a thick black curtain, all filled save for a smattering of empty places on the top row and a couple of orphan spots to the sides (though they too would be taken shortly after).

Taking up the front row were the VIPs. In the centre was the CEO of Biomargent Sciences, Tim Howlett; to his left was General Makepeace (a misnomer if ever there was one owing to his military profession); to his right was an old woman with a hard, gaunt face framed with thinning, wispy-white hair and who could easily have been Tim's grandmother. In actuality, she was a board member and one of Biomargent Sciences' majority shareholders. Completing the row were two captains, a major, and a mixture of personnel with an invested interest in that afternoon's demonstration.

Striding into the auditorium like a rock star was Dr Quisenberry, his white coat buttoned at the front, glowing bright beneath spotlighting. In one hand, he carried a thin pile of pale green cards which he had written a few prompts to help him address his audience; in the other was a small black device that looked like a presentation clicker. A clip-on microphone was attached to the lapel of his jacket, its wire disappearing within his clothing, plugged into a portable transmitter that was placed close to his spine and clipped to the belt at his waist.

Tapping the microphone caused a thumping noise to sound through the hidden ceiling speakers, which achieved the desired reaction.

The room suddenly fell quiet.

"Good morning. Thank you all for coming," greeted the doctor amiably, glancing at the top card. "Today," he continued confidently, "is the end of nearly two years of painstaking research here at Biomargent." He walked a few steps along, thinking the movement would add momentum to his speech. "For the past decade, we have been at the forefront of genetic and scientific advancements. We've developed cheap and effective vaccinations and found cures for diseases and cancers unparalleled by our competitors... the world over.

"Additionally, we've carried out scientific research in the genetics of many species at risk of extinction, in the hope of reversing their fate and restoring their fortunes. It's a procedure we've replicated in many animals, and indeed, countless plants – for the purpose of sustenance, productivity yields and nutritional supplementation.

"All this, we've achieved at Biomargent, for the sole purpose of improving life for the future." Quisenberry paused for a moment, subtly changing one of the prompt cards. "So, it was inevitable that our success and research would be of interest to others… those with *differing interests*." The doctor looked directly at General Makepeace. "What if we could use our scientific advances to better defend ourselves? Could we make a super soldier? How about a weapon even…? Something, perhaps which could give us the edge over our enemies, whilst at the same time eliminating the risk of death or danger to our men or women in the front line?

"That was the very question that was presented to me…" he went quiet and appeared solemn for a moment. "… and here we are," he perked up, "now at a place where I can stand here before you and answer that question. You are here to quite literally witness the birth of something truly great and exciting." Dr Quisenberry's voice failed to convey the feeling of euphoria he wanted to elicit. He walked across to the other side of the room and pressed a button on the small black contraption he carried.

A small motor whirred into operation and the black curtains that had been concealing the laboratory began to withdraw, teasingly-slow, to either side, like those coming apart upon the stage of a grand theatre. A sliver of bright light gradually appeared, stretching into the illuminance of sheer clinical whiteness as the laboratory, in its fully equipped glory, came into view.

Some members of the audience started to talk in hushed tones.

"So," Quisenberry turned his head so that his mouth was closer to the microphone. His voice boomed through the hidden speakers. Once again, silence descended and the doctor had complete attention. "Two months ago, we introduced a mutated gene into the DNA of a common blowfly, a housefly and a fruit fly… with different reactions.

"The fruit fly initially took to the genetic manipulation;

however, the results were sporadic and – if you can excuse the pun – turned out to be fruitless."

A few sniggers came from around the theatre, but hardly any laughs. It was like being in the audience of an ITV sitcom.

"*Phormia Regina*, or the blowfly, commonly known as a bluebottle – or a 'buzzing bastard' like I prefer to call them–" a few people this time did laugh, but the doctor continued, unfazed "–seemed to fair much better; as did the housefly. Not only did their DNA accept the mutated genes, they seemed to thrive on it."

On cue, two of Quisenberry's assistants appeared within the laboratory, each carrying with them a large, rectangular-shaped container. They placed them down flat on an empty workbench and stepped aside.

"Timed almost to precision; what you are about to see, in a few moments, is the birth of our third-generation mutated blowflies."

"Oooh, how exciting," heckled the acne-riddled student-geneticist sarcastically, not realising how good the acoustics in the room was. His comment echoed around the theatre. The black-haired woman next to him, joined by dozens of others, gave the youth a look of contempt.

"Actually – *Warren Anderson* –" he name-shamed, "it is." Dr Quisenberry's voice remained neutral. He turned to an intercom panel to the right of the laboratory's observation window and pressed a button. "Okay, ready when you are."

The two lab technicians busied themselves around the two metal containers, slipping free bolts and lifting up latches. In unison, they carefully lifted off the lids and placed them quietly down, hiding them behind the workstation.

"What you are seeing is fly pupae; approximately ten thousand of them! A normal blowfly lays around 250 eggs, which then hatch around twenty-four hours later. Ours can lay more than 500 – just one of the *enhancements* we've made." The metal containers were filled to half their depth with what appeared to be small, black, cylindrical-shaped husks that measured nine millimetres in length and three millimetres wide.

From the rows of seats, the contents just appeared to be a thick black mass; they could easily have been coffee beans.

A stray hand shot up from the audience. Quisenberry was disgruntled to see that it was the acne-kid five rows up from the front. "Can I ask you to save your questions for the end?"

"Sure," Acne said. He continued nevertheless. "I hope you don't think I'm stupid, but… flies are an abomination; there are enough of them around. Why would you want to give them a means to produce even more?"

Quisenberry smiled up at the inquisitor patiently, thinking how terribly stupid he is. "The reason, I will explain in due course. Now, where was I?" He looked momentarily confused. "Ah, yes," he continued, "enhancements. The common bluebottle isn't very intelligent; they're solitary creatures and appear, on the face of it, only interested in self-preservation and reproduction; they do things without thought or reason, with only the basic instincts serving their purpose." Behind him, there was a subtle movement within one of the trays.

A lab technician crossed the room to a hidden area, returning a moment later with a small video camera. On activation, the two television screens affixed to either side of the glass wall began broadcasting images, focusing in on the trays and presenting a much larger view of the test subjects.

A few murmurs followed from amongst the audience.

Quisenberry threw a glance over his shoulder, seeing what was distracting some of the people seated in front of him. "Thanks, Benny," he said. "Okay, on the other hand, in studies, we've found that the humble fruit fly seems remarkably intelligent for a creature with such a small brain.

"They seem to exhibit decision-making abilities and are much quicker in reacting to stimuli when presented with them; smells, sounds, movements – it's as though they can assimilate the best course of action, and then swiftly act upon it. Through lengthy research, it was discovered they possess something called a FoxP gene. Us humans, we have four FoxP genes; these genes are linked to language and cognitive development which allow us to learn intricate skills, like learning to play an instrument; type; paint; sew; play football. Be who we are. Without FoxP genes, there would never have been a David Beckham, a Michelangelo or a John Lennon; and, for a long time, it was believed only humans and primates had them.

"With the discovery of this FoxP gene in fruit flies, we experimented on other fly species, and found no others – not one – had it. They were unique! So, we introduced it, along with some other enhancements, to different species. I shan't bore you with too much science, but we introduced a longer life expectancy, –" all the time, the doctor was glancing at his cue cards, not wanting to forget a single point.

"–the ability to hear. A sense which was unique only to the small nocturnal yellow fly, *Ormia ochracea,* found throughout south USA and in parts of Mexico; slower metabolism, allowing for a more efficient and slower energy consumption; and something we've called 'thought receptors'." Quisenberry paused and exhaled theatrically, as though relieved. "In short, we've created a new species of fly – a super fly – and you were invited here, today, to witness not just their birth, but a presentation of their skills." The doctor turned and looked into the laboratory behind him, towards the trays of pupae where he spied a small amount of movement.

The television screens showed the activity much clearer. Dozens of the black pod-like cases were appearing to move, as though vibrating. Little cracks were starting to appear and the tips were breaking off to reveal a small bud of a head and a couple of thin black strands that could have been hairs, but were, in fact, legs.

"Ah, yes. This is great!" Quisenberry enthused. "You are now witnessing the birth of our flies. What you can see is the flies breaking free from their cocoons; it's terribly hard work for them," the doctor said, admirably. "This process does take a little time, so we'll leave them to it and I'll tell you a bit more about them."

On the television screens, more of the pupae were showing signs of activity and it wouldn't be long before they were all in motion.

"Of course, many of you are going to be wondering why you were invited here today. Surely, not just to watch a crazy man talk about mutant flies!" Quisenberry started to laugh. "No, no, not at all; that would be ludicrous, right? But you are here to see mutant flies, and more to the point, what they are capable of.

"Recall when I said, what if we could use our scientific advances to make a super soldier, or a weapon... something that would give us an edge over our enemies? Well... this is it."

Now, a significant portion of the hundred spectators began to talk; unfavourable comments were being shouted and words of disbelief filled the air. Only the front row of VIPs watched on impassively, as though party to foreknowledge, with the general the most subservient.

"Quiet down. Please. Please," the doctor implored. "Give me a chance to explain." The crowd simmered into silence. "Thank you."

In the laboratory, more of the pupae husks had split apart and, by now, several flies had wrestled free and were taking tentative steps around the tray and testing their wings.

"This new species of blowfly, with all the aforementioned enhancements, is our new weapon. With its increased intelligence, the ability to hear, and its inbuilt thought-receptors, we have ourselves a creature that is small enough to evade detection, clever enough to think laterally, and designed to think collectively. This is in addition to being able to hear programmable messages and instructions, I.E, under our complete control."

All the time Dr Quisenberry was talking, the trays of pupae were growing more active; now a writhing mass, magnified on the television screens for all to easily see. Almost all of the black husks were split open now, and a good number of flies had squeezed out. Some had taken to flight, buzzing around the room lazily. Naturally, the two lab assistants flapped and swatted at any flies that came too close, though very aware that they were being watched and laughed at from the gallery outside.

"We're nearly there, I see," the doctor was inferring the near-conclusion to the birth of his flies, "but before the demonstration, does anyone have any questions?"

A dozen hands shot up instantly. Quisenberry picked out a young woman from the centre row. She was blonde and wore designer glasses that made her look intelligent and bookish.

"You say they are under your complete control. How is that possible?"

"Programmable soundwaves; we've tailored a set of commands that the flies can hear and understand via their modified hearing and their inbuilt thought-receptors. Because of our genetic design, they can communicate amongst themselves – almost telepathically – a bit like bees or worker ants; this needs us only to communicate to one or very few to pass the message to all."

"It sounds great, what you've said an' all, about the mutations applied to the flies. But seriously, what benefit will they be to us, the military, or anyone? I mean... they're still flies." The black-haired woman received words and comments of support from many sitting around her.

"Which leads me, I think," Quisenberry turned to look into the laboratory behind him for encouragement, "to the main event. No more questions." The birth of all ten thousand flies were now complete and their buzzing, though subdued through the toughened glass wall, could be heard in the observation gallery. A thick cloud of black specks filled the void of the laboratory, making the brightly lit room almost appear drab and dark.

Quisenberry indicated for a trolley to be wheeled out to him, upon which was a laptop computer and an arrangement of electronic equipment with leads and wires plugged in at various points. Some were connected to a box that was indirectly linked to the back of the laptop.

Pressing a random key, the LCD lit up with a login screen. Before typing in the password, the doctor switched on the intercom into the laboratory.

"Okay, Benny... Tammy... I'm about to start."

"*Please do*," urged Benny from within the room. From the gallery, the audience could see that the flies were giving both lab technicians a fair bit of bother.

"Okay," Quisenberry thought aloud, stooping down slightly and tapping out a six-letter password, before hitting enter. The login screen changed, replaced by a new one that showed a command box, a control panel, and something that looked like an oscillator display, likely used for measuring sound frequencies. "Let's begin." He touch-typed a few instructions and then hit the return key. Standing, he turned about to peer into the laboratory.

To everyone observing, nothing spectacular changed or happened.

Quisenberry smiled. "Now," he said, "prepare to be amazed." He felt like a great magician as he typed a few more words and then gently tapped on an activation button on the keyboard, twisting his body ninety-degrees to watch the results of his actions through the toughened glass wall.

Many of the ten thousand flies were buzzing around the laboratory; others were resting or walking on any of the multitude of surfaces: the walls, the ceiling, the worktops, the apparatus, and the toughened glass partition separating them from the outside world. Nothing in their behaviour set them apart from any other fly.

Still tapping a button on the keyboard, the scene in the laboratory suddenly altered from wild, aimless abandon, to one of calm and order. The flies ceased dashing and moving and flying around the room, and fell to the floor in a sheet; the subdued buzzing stopped in an instant and the laboratory was once again brightly-lit.

"Now, watch this," said Quisenberry. He typed some more, before tapping down elaborately on another key.

As one, ten thousand flies lifted off the floor slowly, like a blanket wafted up to spread it out evenly; they ascended skyward in a controlled manner.

"What I am doing is keying in instructions that the computer then translates into a high-frequency signal, outside the range of human hearing. The flies have been modified to hear the sound, but, more importantly, understand it... As you can see, the flies are demonstrating this." To illustrate, Quisenberry typed in a command, instructing the flies to circle the room.

Immediately, the cluster of flies manoeuvred almost as a solid black mass around the laboratory. The viewing gallery, with its spectators sitting enraptured on the edge of their seats, began to whoop and cheer in glee and fascination at the spectacle. It was almost like being at a circus, witnessing a performing menagerie, rather than spectators to a scientist's bizarre experiment.

"Okay... somebody asked what use these flies would be to the military? Well, allow me to show you." The doctor speedily tapped a good many keys on the keyboard before theatrically raising his right hand and stabbing the enter key with his index finger.

The black cloud that had circuited the room a dozen times came to an abrupt stop and appeared to hover in mid-air. Through the toughened glass wall, a gentle, almost-melodic hum filled the air.

"Watch carefully." The doctor typed another instruction, followed again with an exaggerated action as he committed the command.

The flies reorganised themselves into a long phalanx and began flying around the room once again, this time, in the shape of an arrow. After completing the circumference, the flies changed course and headed towards one of the lab technicians standing quietly out of the way, finding sanctuary in the corner of the room. The other technician was sitting unobtrusively near to the room's exit.

"Doctor Quisenberry?" Benny, who had been watching like everyone else, spoke anxiously, his voice coming through loudly over the intercom's speakers set within the ceiling above the toughened glass wall. As the course that the flies were taking became clear, the lab technician spoke more urgently. "James!"

Dr Quisenberry watched the swarm of flies descend upon the lab technician. The young man was flapping wildly at the buzzing menace that flew at him suddenly from every direction; they turned about to recompose themselves and then attacked him again.

The performance was comical and the doctor couldn't help laughing. He turned to address the audience, who, by now, were whooping and cheering less and wearing expressions of concern or apprehension.

"Don't be alarmed," Quisenberry reassured, grinning. "I instructed the flies to harry and cajole Benny here, he's completely safe. But, I'm sure by now you can see their potential." The doctor returned to punching in commands on his keyboard.

Within the laboratory, the flies continued to fly at Benny, who slapped at his face and swiped at the air. The swarm fell upon him more doggedly, flying into his hair, kamikazeing into his face at full pelt, their sorties probing and punishing, inflicting pinpricks of pain against his reddening cheeks, and blinding him from aerially attacking his eyes.

"That's…" *peculiar*, thought Quisenberry, typing a little more urgently and smacking the enter key more desperately.

"Stop them, James! Enough… *Enough!!*" Benny was pleading. His arms were thrashing about, his feet jerking beneath him. He looked like he was doing a crazy old man dance at a senior prom.

In his panic, he walked face-first into a wall and knocked himself onto his back. The flies, seeing their target now on the floor, followed him down in a swoop, converging on his upturned face, carpeting every inch of exposed flesh, crawling into his clothing, and entering his nose and mouth.

"Doctor Quisenberry, I think you should end your experiment now," urged General Makepeace, appearing alarmed, standing next to him.

"What do you think I'm TRYING to do!" replied Quisenberry, seriously. Desperately, he tapped commands into the computer.

The flies within the laboratory continued with their attack, ignorant or deaf to the counter-demands being given. The second lab technician – Tammy – was now at Benny's side, buffeting flies with a metal tray she was using as a swat. "Help us, James. They're killing him!" she yelled, shrilly.

The general removed a handgun holstered at his waist.

"Seriously! You think to kill ten thousand flies with bullets!" The doctor stood up and abandoned the workstation. It was obvious that whatever control he once had over the flies, he had no more.

Sensing the scene was not part of the act, alarmed voices started to echo around the theatre, injected with whimpers, fearful utterances and demands for someone to: "Do something!"

"Help him, man!" shouted the acne-riddled student-geneticist from the fifth row. Horrified, a few show gazers were climbing to their feet and making their way towards the room's exit, appalled, sickened and unable to stomach more of what they were witnessing.

Tammy, meanwhile, was forced to deviate from attacking the flies to defending herself from them, using the tray as a shield, which she thrust outwards holding it by both hands towards the insects as they flew at her. With Benny unconscious, the ten thousand flies collectively altered their priority, taking up an offensive towards their attacker, an action that was intended to overpower the young woman in much the same way they had handled Benny.

Perplexed, the doctor couldn't help but feel admiration for his creatures. "Fascinating," he said.

"Do something, damn it!" the general grabbed Quisenberry by the lapels of his white jacket and barked in his face.

"Yea, you're right." Still slightly distracted by the spectacle within the laboratory, Quisenberry forced himself into action. Purposefully, he moved away from the trolley towards the left side of the room. Next to the glass observation wall, beneath a television (which continued to broadcast images from within the laboratory of the flies rushing around), was a small cupboard door that was locked. Using a small key on a bunch that he pulled out from beneath his lab coat, he opened the door to reveal a panel of switches and buttons, and a small electronic display screen.

"What are you doing, Doctor?" General Makepeace asked.

"I'm doing *something*," replied Quisenberry apprehensively. He flicked a couple of silver toggle switches, activating a number of LEDs at various places around the panel; a row of six white buttons began to glow brightly. He turned to face the general, an anguished look upon his face. "It wasn't supposed to be like that." Without hesitation, he pressed each of the six glowing buttons.

Immediately, an alarm bell began to ring, drowning out any other sounds that may have come from the laboratory. On the electronic display screen, a percentage figure appeared, starting at zero.

Inside the room, Tammy stopped batting the flies and turned towards the gallery, her eyes seeking out Quisenberry. As they clocked his, the dozen concealed sprinkler heads built into the ceiling above her head began to hiss.

I'm sorry, Quisenberry mouthed. Tammy directed her eyes to the ceiling, stark realisation terrifying her. Accompanying the hiss, the sprinkler heads dispersed a fine, slightly pungent smelling gas into the room.

"What are you doing?" asked the general, confused.

"The only thing I can."

Within the laboratory, the concealed sprinkler heads pumped the gas in increasing bursts, fumigating the void with a lethal, virulent mix that contained hydrogen cyanide.

The electronic display screen began to count upwards: 4%, 5%, 6%... This was the measure of toxins introduced into the atmosphere of the sealed laboratory.

Sensing danger, the flies abandoned their aggressive behaviour towards Tammy and averted their attention to the imminent threat and their desire to survive.

Spherically, the mass of insects flew towards the toughened glass window, the first hitting the lucent screen with a snap, its body crumpling to the floor, its wings broken from the impact. Others immediately followed, hitting the glass desperately hard, leaving a gooey-yellow residue upon colliding, and falling to the floor much like the first. With the precision of a drill bit, the flies flew at the same spot, one after another, in a long, thin line, pummelling the place, over and over, a single objective filling their thoughts:

Redemption.

Following the direction of the flies, Tammy staggered across the room, the effects of the gassy fog – in addition to making it increasingly harder to see – was beginning to subdue her. Coughing into her hands, she became suddenly alarmed to see thick globules of blood coating them. She screamed, overcome with pain and weakness. Sluggishly, she lurched forward the final steps and fell hard against the glass wall. The toughened glass banged beneath the impact. Desperately, she slapped the transparent barricade with the flats of her hands leaving bloody hand prints smeared in several places.

Help! She mouthed through the glass desperately.

The general watched on in horror.

The electronic display screen continued to present the percentage of toxins within the room.

57%.

Quisenberry turned away, unable to watch any more. The seats in the gallery were now almost empty with most spectators hastily making an exit through the fire doors.

The flies continued to hammer vigorously against a single spot in the glass wall, each impact resulting in a further death; the flies fell to a steadily increasing mountain of carcasses building up on the floor. After the six thousandth fly had smashed into the glass barrier, the tiniest chink, smaller than a pinprick, appeared in the glass.

A chink that was too late for Tammy. Her legs gave out beneath her weight and she felt herself slide slowly down the glass wall, her bloody hands leaving smeary red trails, marking her descent.

The electronic display screen now showed: 83%.

No sooner had the gas taken its toll on the laboratory assistant, the flies started to react to the effects of the lethal mix still pouring into the room; those towards the back of the spherical phalanx, longest exposed to the poison, unexpectedly dropped to the floor.

Like a row of dominoes, one-by-one, the flies succumbed to the grey fog. In their panic, the column pushed forward harder, faster, striking the glass ever more fiercely.

The tiny chink in the glass wall spider-webbed slightly; this encouraged the flies further. The pile of dead, broken, carcasses stood almost a foot high next to the wall; to the rear of the flying juggernaut, flies continued to drop, shrinking the strike force an inch at either end with every passing second. Although a small glimmer of escape appeared in the toughened glass wall, time was hurriedly running out.

Dr Quisenberry turned to look at the electronic display screen. 91% of the room's atmosphere was now filled with the noxious gas. "It's nearly done," he said tersely.

The flies were down to the last couple of hundred now, the

gas consuming them faster than they could hope to fly; chances of survival were beginning to fade, for Tammy, Benny and the remaining flies.

The spiderweb of cracks in the glass had grown ever-so-slightly beneath the torrent of protracted force; like a jackhammer, the tiniest of holes had appeared. But time was running out. In a final, impetuous push, the flies doubled up and flew at the wall in pairs, striking the fracture with twin force, synchronously dying and falling to the heap of bodies below.

The tiny hole grew slightly.

On the electronic display screen, the reading now measured 94%.

Now less than eighty flies remained from the ten thousand; each passing second resulted in six flies succumbing to the hydrogen cyanide mix, and a further four dying from the impact against the wall.

The hole was now big enough for an ant to climb through.

96% now appeared on the electronic display screen.

Sixty flies continued the battle to escape.

The hole was growing; now large enough for a fruit fly to pass through.

98%. The room was nearly completely filled with poison.

Thirty flies desperately persevered with the task.

99%.

Just twelve flies remained. Two more struck the glass causing some more tiny fragments to crumble free, death was swift.

The next two flies smacked the wall hard, the shock producing a nine-inch crack to stretch upwards like a beckoning finger and a hole slightly smaller than the size of a five pence piece.

Regrouping, the flies returned to single file formation, just as the last of the room's oxygen was replaced with poison.

100%

"It's over," said Quisenberry, satisfactorily.

A single fly squeezed out through the small hole, followed

promptly by another. Wasting little time, they flew skywards, heading for the ceiling, seeking a place to rest and take momentary refuge. A third fly crawled sluggishly over the lip of the hole and considered flying, before, with little choice, falling over the edge, dead from the effects of the gas pumped from the ceiling, falling to the floor.

"Well... not exactly what you promised, Doctor."

"No... not at all," he replied miserably. "I really don't understand... everything was going to plan... until..." Quisenberry completed the sentence in his head. ... *I set the flies on Benny*. "I can fix this," he said airily. "The next test will be conclusive."

"There won't be a next test, James," said the general brusquely. "I was stupid to believe anything you said. Programmable flies!" He shook his head, mystified at his own stupidity. "I'm pulling funding... this is over..."

"But... General, we're so close. Just a few tweaks, is all it will take. We'll take more precautions." Quisenberry sounded desperate. "Please!"

Ignoring the doctor, General Makepeace made a show of tidying the lapels on his military jacket before sweeping non-existent dust from his shoulder and turning to leave. The observation gallery was all but empty, except for him and the doctor. "I'll send a crew down to help clean up. Make sure you're here to greet them," he said ominously, just before walking out of the room.

CHAPTER ONE

1

I T WAS HOT, ABOUT 27° Celsius in the shade, and the sun was relentless as it baked the earth, heat thermals rising to the air giving everything a distorted, liquefied appearance; distant images wavering as though part of a dream conjured from a sleeper's untroubled mind.

It was the middle of an unseasonably warm, British summer. Two whole months of almost back-to-back, fierce sunshine, with only the occasional storm or flash flood interrupting – not that anyone was complaining, if you discounted the sixty-five million people living throughout the country.

Sean was alone in the room. His shirt was loose and untucked; the buttons undone. His smooth, bare chest was moist with perspiration and glistened as though coated with baby oil.

Out of the corner of his eye, he spied a very slight movement. It came from beneath the window in the living room.

Sean thought perhaps it could've been a fly, but wasn't sure. It might've been a wasp or some other insect. Nothing was certain in life and anything was possible. But most likely, it was a fly.

He stood up from the armchair, put aside the glass of ice-cold lemonade (which he had pressed against his hot forehead), and crossed the room to the music-system where he turned the volume down. Spandau Ballet's *"Gold"* was now playing quietly. Eighties music was his guilty pleasure. To the side of one of the music-system's speakers were a stack of CDs. Erasure; A-ha; Duran Duran; Eurythmics; Tears for Fears; Pet Shop Boys. There were even some Queen CDs and an album by Bros.

Walking to the window, Sean lifted the net and peered outside. From this vantage point, he could see nothing moving; no animals; no children; no prowlers. Not even a solitary bird, bee or butterfly. The space appeared serene and empty; nothing untoward or unexpected.

He allowed the net to fall back into place and returned to his seat.

After five minutes of sitting and listening to music – *"Gold"* had made way for *"Through the Barricades"* – the discordant ringing of the telephone sounded, jerking Sean from a pleasant daydream into action, his thoughts and imaginings becoming entangled as they dissipated.

"Hello?"

"Sean." It was Francesca, his girlfriend. She was his everything; the reason he got up in the morning, held down a job he despised and bothered to go to the gym six days a week, keeping in fine shape. He had the body that a Chippendale would have been proud of.

"Franny... how are you?" he asked excitedly. He hadn't seen her since Saturday. She'd been away on a conference and he was genuinely pleased to hear her voice.

"Oh, you know... tired," she sounded it. *"Listen, Sean... I have something I need to say."* The way Francesca spoke caused Sean to stiffen. Subconsciously, he knew something was wrong.

"How about discussing it when you get home? I'll cook your favourite meal and get us a bottle of wine."

"Sean." The way she uttered his name was dismissive.

Francesca sounded pained. "*Please, listen to me... for just a moment. I'm pregnant.*"

The air around Sean suddenly felt oppressive, almost stifling. For a moment, his vision swam away and he was staring at nothing but a bright light that filtered through the frosted glass of the front door.

"*Sean?*"

He found it impossible to speak. His throat closed up and his tongue felt like it had swollen to the size of an apple. He tried to think of something worthwhile to say; something that wasn't lame (like he always tended to do), grasping at many words that flooded his mind. He clawed at one or two sentences that flitted almost to his lips, like a family of gnats dancing about in a cluster, settling on: "Are you sure?" Not exactly the most inspiring response to finding out his girlfriend was now with child. Hearing it spoken aloud sounded stupid.

"*Yes,*" she said in exasperation. Sean could tell that she wasn't happy with his response.

"Well, that's marvellous... that's brilliant!" he backpedalled. "Just wait 'til I tell my parents the news. *Wow!* We're having a baby... I'm going to be a father..." A wave of exuberance flooded his senses making him feel giddy with excitement. He was overcome with immense joy.

"*Sean... don't.*" Francesca was struggling at the other end of the phone. Audibly, she swallowed; a loud clicking sound. "*There's something else...*" she paused, taking her time to either compose herself, decide whether to go ahead, or plumping for dramatic effect. "*It's not yours.*"

The line went quiet for a long moment. "What?" He couldn't be sure he heard her right. Maybe the feel-good endorphins rushing about his body had affected his hearing.

"*It's someone else's, Sean.*" To help him better understand, she rephrased it: "*I'm having another man's baby.*"

"Wha–"

She cut him short. "*Shut up, Sean, just listen for one moment! I'm sorry... but, this thing... it's bigger than us.*" Francesca allowed what she said to sink in. "*I'm sorry... it's over. We're over.*"

"Franny? What are you saying?" He didn't understand. On Saturday, when he'd seen her last, everything had played out as normal. They'd watched a film, drunk a bottle of wine and ended the night with an hour of foreplay and ten minutes of mutually energetic sex.

"*Didn't you hear me or do you always have to be this stupid?*" she sighed, adding softly: "*I've met someone else; someone with a bit more... passion.*"

"Passion?" Sean spat. "What about Paris last year? Or Vegas, the time before that? How about Majorca when we first started dating?"

"*I'm sorry,*" Francesca whispered. Sean could hear that she was crying.

"How... how long?" he asked desperately. "When did you start fucking behind my back?"

"*Does it matter? Goodbye Sean.*" Francesca disconnected, leaving Sean holding the handset, stunned, contemplative and in emotional turmoil. He sat like this, in momentary limbo, for twenty minutes.

Then, like an animatronic coming to life, Sean crossed the room and carefully replaced the handset into its cradle; deep in thought, memories of the woman surfaced like apples in a barrel of water; happy and blissful, un-cheating recollections.

Without warning, blind rage burst uncontrollably to the surface, surprising him with its intensity. He tore the phone from the wall and hurled it out into the hallway, watching it smash apart, spilling its guts and electronic components in all directions.

"Bitch!" Sean swore some more, his anger directing him towards the picture frame standing at the centre of the mantelpiece.

The photo was just a holiday snap, and not a very good one at that, but it held sentimental value. He picked up the frame and studied the two faces staring back. Him and Francesca on a catamaran whilst in Majorca, the first year they had started dating. She was in a tiny bikini that left little to the imagination, whilst he was bare-chested.

That had been three years ago.

"You bitch!" he screamed, punching the centre of the picture frame a dozen times, the glass cracking in a spiderweb. He pounded it a couple more times for good measure before noticing the dots of crimson spattering the shattered surface, leaking onto the photograph within.

"Oh... my hand," he sobbed pitifully, though his tears were more for the pain in his heart than the cuts to his knuckles.

His right hand was scuffed and bloody. Flaps of skin hung loose and the white of a carpal bone was clearly visible.

"Look what you've made me do..." he whined, miserably. The young woman smiled back up at him, a droplet of his blood crying from her eye. He wiped it free, smearing it across his face.

In the living room, the music ended, replaced by a distant, incessant drone. Sean thought it could've been a neighbour cutting the lawn, or maybe a motorbike, though dismissed it when the sound appeared closer, rising on its approach and falling as it moved away.

Sean walked from the hallway back into the living room, his eyes darting from one corner to another, his ears honing in on the buzzing sound, audibly searching.

Then it abruptly stopped, and he knew exactly what it was.

If there was anything on God's green earth he despised more than a fly, he hadn't yet met it. Wasps were a close second. Spiders and snakes he could handle. Bees? A necessary evil.

But flies?

What purpose did they have except for irritating and spreading their germs about? One minute they're walking on a pile of shit, the next they're making waves towards your lunch or dinner, or persistent in their attempts to land on your face or the lip of a beer glass.

"Where are you, my little friend?" he asked playfully, almost musically. There was a sign of madness in his eyes.

The fly buzzed in response, taking off from its place of rest or curiosity.

It was all that Sean required.

He crept up to the window, stopping just short of an over-sized cheese plant placed between the seventy-five inch Samsung 3D LED TV and an old leather armchair. On the arm was that day's *The Sun* newspaper. Slowly, he picked it up and rolled it into a baton. As he approached the window, he stopped. A bead of sweat made a trail down from his hairline, dripping with a stinging sensation into his eye. Another raced it down the left of his face making his skin crawl.

But sweat was a minor irritant compared to the buzzing fly. Sean could see it, flitting about pointlessly at the window, colliding with glass in its pathetic attempt to access the outside world, ignorant to the fact that it was an impenetrable obstacle, no matter how many attempts it made, hitting and ricocheting from the hyaline surface with cracks and snaps, like the tap of a dancer's shoe.

For a moment, the fly seemed to realise that flying *through* the window was a no-go, and settled down on the windowsill where it rubbed its forelegs together like it was having a wash or trying to make fire.

Sean focused on the insect and, for a split second, saw Francesca's face staring up at him. It wasn't the pretty cherubic features that he had fallen in love with; it was the evil-bitch-twin that she seemingly had turned into, straight after one phone call. Then she morphed back into the fly again; a nasty bloated bluebottle, its two large compound eyes watching and reading his every move.

"Okay... you little bastard," Sean uttered under his breath, thinking that speaking louder would alert the insect to his intentions.

Before the newspaper was set in motion, the fly had launched itself into the air and was buzzing from left to right in frenzied, evasive manoeuvres, darting this way and that, invariably hitting the glass window again in its frantic designs of escape.

"Ooooh, you're in for it now." Sean smashed the paper down on a spot he anticipated the fly would gravitate to.

SMACK!

The glass appeared to judder beneath the force and, Sean, taking out his frustrations on the insect, withdrew his makeshift swat expecting to see the mashed-in remains of the bluebottle, its blood and guts pulped against the glass.

As he lifted up the rolled newspaper, the sound of buzzing started up once again.

"You little shit! Make it easy for me, will ya?! You're gonna die anyway."

Sean flapped his newspaper animatedly from one side to another, like he was possessed – left to right, up and down – then suddenly stopping.

The annoying drone ceased.

Sean stooped down and scanned the floor in search of the dead or crippled fly; a fly with one wing and two legs trying to get away he imagined, or a fly on its back, legs cycle-kicking thin air.

He continued his search even after the sound of buzzing started up again, this time up close, taunting the man with daring kamikaze sorties close to his face, pinwheeling around his ears mockingly.

When it dawned on him that his search was in vain, he was back up on his feet, the newspaper weapon at the ready. He struck thin air like a baseball player; once, twice, then a third time, striking out.

"For fuck's sake!" The fly goaded him some more, landing on his ear. Sean slapped a hand to the side of his head, almost clipping the fly by accident. The fly took no further chances and flew off to the other side of the room.

With his weapon poised, Sean followed to where he spied the fly laying low. The buzzing had stopped and a quick scan of the area immediately presented him with his target; the pest was walking brazenly across the wall, close to the ceiling.

It knew what he wanted to do, the little fucker anticipated it. From the high point, the fly cleverly waited for Sean's attack; not only did the vantage point offer a panoramic view of the room a good two-feet above Sean's head, it allowed the fly to better use its perception of seeing movement and light four times faster than the average human.

"Come down from there," Sean urged, wrapping his hand tighter around the makeshift baton. Teasingly, the fly scurried along a few inches of wall, seeming to wiggle its butt in defiance.

Sean smiled, stepping forward on tiptoes.

He remembered a time when he was a kid. It was a summer, hot like this one; he used to hunt down the flies around the house and garden, mercilessly killing them for fun. Often, he pretended to be a soldier going into war – the fly his enemy. Some days he'd play Cowboys and Indians or Cops and Robbers, the fly always playing the antagonist. Armed with wooden rulers, rolled-up newspapers, fly sprays, and even a lighter and aerosol spray for one occasion; Sean would entertain himself for hours. The aim was always to destroy every last disgusting fly within range. He was never satisfied until all were gone, sometimes continuing his mission late into the evening.

He had kept a log book, tallying each kill like a seasoned

sniper. Ninety-six dead one day; ninety-four another. Once over a hundred!

When he ran out, or flies had started to avoid Sean's territory, Sean had ventured further, hitting the streets or a neighbour's garden, or tackling the fly population over at the local park. He had had an unhealthy obsession with them, one which he clearly wasn't over.

Sean slowly inched forward, raising the newspaper truncheon ever so slightly with anticipation.

"Now, stand still, you little bugger," he spoke quietly, hoping not to startle the fly or give the heads-up to his intentions.

With a deft flick of the wrist, the rolled-up newspaper descended upon the casually-walking fly, its guard momentarily down. The prospect of escape dissipated almost as suddenly as the primitive thought surfaced.

THWACK!

Theatrically, Sean whacked the fly, smashing the cudgel down with satisfaction, then again a third and fourth time, pulping the little crushed body almost into nothing.

"Yeeesss!" he whooped, dancing about the room ecstatically, the move completed with a Michael Jackson '*moonwalk*' and a '*push-pineapple, shake the tree*' manoeuvre. "That's what you get… you bitch!" It wasn't entirely clear who he was shouting at; the fly, or his cheating girlfriend.

It WAS clear that he'd taken out his anger at Francesca on the flying insect, whose remains were mashed into the paintwork.

In the corner was another blowfly, unobserved, minding its' own business. It sat in silence having watched the death of one of its four hundred brothers.

When Sean left the room, the fly made its escape, darting about in a zig-zag before hitting the glass of a window. A few fruitless attempts bouncing against double-glazing was rewarded when it struck thin air. It exited the house through the crack of a slightly-opened window.

Sean returned a moment later with a can of Fosters to celebrate, having washed the blood from his sore right hand, a bandage now fashioned across his knuckles. He crossed to the sofa and weightily sat down, leaning back against the headrest. With the ice-cold can, he gently caressed his forehead, easing the tension and the headache burning within. He cracked the beer open and raised it to his lips as a creamy-white froth bubbled up. It tasted refreshing and great.

Three-quarters into the Fosters, the anger Sean felt towards Francesca subsided, and the hateful feelings for the fly were suitably numbed. Five more cans later, washed down with half a bottle of Jack Daniels, the events of that day were at the back of his mind, just another fading memory.

The deed wasn't lost though, not entirely.

Although the human brain is conditioned to forget and bury memories – a sort of coping mechanism – the blowfly isn't so complex, not possessing such a luxury. For its entire adult life of thirty-seven days (on average), the blowfly remembers everything.

And forgiveness is just a trait found only in humans.

2

Sleep came instantly to Sean's alcohol-addled body. He lay fully-dressed across the centre of the double bed having collapsed; face forward, with his head just hitting the pillows. He was stretched out, arms by his sides, his legs slightly parted. His breathing was heavy, his teeth rattling occasionally as he crunched them together; each exhalation was accentuated by a noise that resembled that of an excitable pig watching as his trough was being refilled.

Throughout the house, lights burned brightly in every room.

Ignorant to his carbon footprint and a sky-high energy bill, Sean kept the lights on day and night, more as a deterrent for burglars, fearing the safety for his prized PS4 and large seventy-five inch Samsung 3D LED TV and the entertainment centre wirelessly hooked up to it. In addition to the lights, sound from said television echoed distortedly from downstairs. It was stuck on the channel last viewed; a rerun of *Two and a Half Men* where Charlie Sheen played on to an invisible audience.

For a 'fly on the wall', this was a regular outcome. Hardly surprising for a man whose girlfriend only lived with him on a part-time basis, and whose only real friend was the demon who lived inside a bottle; unlike the lamp, no Genie ever visited proffering wishes, just a raging hangover with its not-so-gentle reminder of the previous night's events.

If that wasn't bleak enough, an unpleasant puddle of partially digested food awaited clean-up at the foot of the stairs, just shy of the wooden flooring in the hallway, congealing into the 100% Pure New Wool soft heavyweight pile carpet – red – fitted to the stairs and bedroom landing.

Of course, Sean wouldn't need too much to jog his memory of what he did the previous night. If the headache and the vomit didn't remind him, the empty beer cans and the half-empty bottle of Jack Daniels would offer up more than a tiny clue.

Unknown and oblivious to him, the mess at the foot of the stairs and the discarded vessels of inebriation would never have to concern him.

Downstairs, in the living room, the Westminster mantel clock daintily chimed over the sound of the television, ringing in the final hour of the day: Eleven o'clock.

Sean muttered something shallow and meaningless before rolling over from one side to another, unconsciously trying to get comfortable. He turned fully over, settling onto his back. Deep in sleep, his mouth fell open, allowing his snores to slip from being swine-like, into deep grunts beginning from the depths of his stomach.

Outside, at the bedroom window, peering through a gap in the thin cotton curtains, a solitary fly examined the room. It could see the man recumbent across the bed, flaked out and 'dead' to the world; it could also hear his snore – loud that it was – through the glass.

Contrary to belief, some flies do have 'ears', including the one spying in. Found beneath the front part of the fly's thorax, the insect's 'ear' contains a tightly stretched membrane that reacts, much like the human eardrum vibrating when sound waves come into contact with it, and then transmitting the signals as 'noise' to sensory receptors.

The fly decided it had seen enough and took to the air, buzzing away into the night unnoticed.

3

At some point, Sean had vomited onto his pillow and was lying with his hair pressed into the unrecognisable regurgitated mess.

It was nearing six o'clock.

Outside, a milkman out on his early morning rounds, which was a sight growing rarer by the year owing to cut-price supermarkets and a change in buying habits. Obliviously, he drove by the row of houses, crates of milk bottles clinking together.

Across the road, a paperboy brought his mountain bike to a stop, brakes squeaking. He dismounted and dropped the bike to the kerb, picking out a newspaper from the bag slung over his shoulder, ready for delivery to number thirty-one at the end of the garden path he now sauntered towards.

Aside from this, the street was eerily quiet as dawn steadily crept in from the east, though signs of life blinked on and off as subdued lighting glowed behind curtained windows in upstairs' bedrooms and downstairs' halls.

At the bedroom window, the fly was back, watching and waiting.

Sean was completely still; his face in full view; flecks and patches of puke marked his face and matted his hair. He made a dry, gulping sound, grimacing at the foul taste that coated his tongue. He started to stir, and it was precisely then that the fly took off from the window and flew into the room, its buzz inordinately louder than normal.

It was almost time to begin.

The fly circled excitedly above Sean, its buzz resounding against the four walls of the bedroom, the acoustics of early morning making it sound all the more stronger.

Sean grinded his teeth together, then coughed a couple of times as though from a slight tickle, but remaining deep in his alcohol-induced slumber. For most of the night, his sleep had been void of thoughts; just black, empty, nothingness. The blow of Francesca leaving him followed by the torment of her admission to cheating never plagued his sleep at all, his subconsciousness sparing him the pain. However, as daylight began to filter into the room, Sean moved out from 'deep sleep' into the state of 'paradoxical sleep', more commonly known as REM sleep.

Cortical and Thalamic neurons within Sean's brain started firing, and suddenly, his subconscious sprung into overdrive, involuntarily producing a moving image within his head.

It was Francesca in an unfamiliar setting; she was sitting on a swing gliding up and down, back and forth. A carefree smile split across her face. She was laughing gleefully. The scene swiftly changed to another where she was laying on her front, her back arched so that she was facing him. She was naked and his active mind directed his eyes to the fall of her breasts.

"Sean... something is wrong. You need to get up."

"*I am up,*" he heard himself reply, a spectator in his own dream.

"*I'm serious!*" Francesca warned.

"*This is not real,*" he replied, unsurprised. Despite the vividness of the tableau, at some level, the rational part of Sean's brain could tell the difference between real and imagined.

Besides, Sean could tell that it was just a dream, for beyond Francesca's lovely form was a writhing mass of blackness undulating upon the wall; hundreds of flies were gathered together, watching like voyeurs at a Soho peepshow where £5.00 got you a peek and a promise, but nothing more.

Downstairs, in the kitchen, a blowfly gained access into the home through the vent to the rear of an extractor fan. It darted around the room and hovered below a fluorescent light – left on like all the other lights – before scudding out into the hallway, momentum and something akin to magnetism drawing it upwards towards Sean's bedroom.

Meer moments transpired and the fly was joined by another; this one slipping in through the crack of the slightly-open letterbox, the paperboy having dislodged it whilst feeding in that day's edition of *The Sun*. Then another fly appeared... before another, and another, followed by many more.

Within three minutes, the kitchen was alive with the electric buzz of three or four thousand flies, a sound not too dissimilar to that of an electric blender. Dashing and careening within the space between wall cabinets, the floor, and the Artexed ceiling; a throbbing cloud of swarming flies that almost subdued the overhead lighting.

Ten minutes later and the last fly filtered in through a gap in the extractor fan.

Immediately, the drone ceased, and like a sheet, the flies dropped to the tiles. The floor was covered with an undulating blanket of small hustling insects. As one, the carpet of flies advanced into the hallway, quietly drifting up the stairs in an impossibly orderly fashion, their wings inanimate; elevation was gained via the strength of their legs alone, hopping implausibly like a cricket, stealth their main aim.

Silently, the flies progressed towards Sean's bedroom, one stair at a time, swiftly reaching the landing and continuing towards the place they collectively knew they would find their quarry.

The bedroom door was closed, an issue had the creatures planning out the attack been bigger than the centimetre crack beneath the obstruction. Instead, the flies easily moved beneath the door, nudging and climbing over each other in eager anticipation. One or two buzzed in excitement, the urge to fly unabashedly near-to-overwhelming.

Restraint, a collective thought filled their tiny heads. It was almost the time, but the order was clear; the element of surprise was essential if history was going to be in the making. This would be the day jotted down in the annals, forever referred to as the start of when it all went crazily wrong.

When a lesser creature took it upon itself to stand up, against all odds and turn the tide; a true David and Goliath event.

This was indeed history in the making. This was the beginning of the revolution.

In his bed, Sean still had the pleasant dream of Francesca. Several times she had tried to warn him that something was amiss, but naively he just laughed her off dismissively.

"*Shoosh*," he heard himself admonish, wishing instead to enjoy the woman's beautiful form in silence – except, it wasn't silent. At some point, a gentle thrum had begun to fill the imagined room – constant, unwavering – a cadence emanating, for the most part, from the spreading patch of inky-black movement upon the wall across the dreamscape.

"*What the hell is that?*" he finally asked. For the first time, he wondered at its significance. Someone had once told him that dreams held meaning. For instance, he had learned that dreaming of death didn't actually foretell someone's demise; instead, it meant change was imminent. He made a mental note to look up on the internet what dreaming about flies meant.

Oblivious to everything happening outside of his mind, Sean murmured something incoherent and a dribble of saliva leaked from the left corner of his mouth, soaking into his pillow. An arm flapped up to swipe something invisible, and then fell back to the bed.

Ahead of the door, a black shadow advancing fluidly towards the bed, spilling in from beneath the barrier like dark water spreading from an overflowing bath.

Deep within his subconscious, Francesca stood up from the bed. "*I've got to go... before it's too late...*"

"*Too late? Too late for what?*" he replied, mesmerised by the full-frontal nudity appearing ahead of him. He was focusing on the patch of hair between her legs.

The buzzing in the background grew into prominence, no longer sounding just from within his dream, but from beyond it... as though...

... as though it were occurring externally, outside of his head and bed. Although starting to realise this, his brain wasn't quite ready to wake him up from his dream.

"*...for you...*" Francesca smiled and a fly crawled out from between her lips and took off to the air. It was big, the size of a small bird or a mouse.

A number of flies had gained access to the room via the window and were now flying spasmodically from one corner to another. But the main contingent made their approach in silence. Like a rolling tide, the jostling mass of flies reached the bedpost at the foot end, a stream of them quickening their pace to hurry past, heading for the opposite end, whilst others maintained order and steady speed, continuing with their journey upwards.

Thinking he would never wake up, Sean sat bolt upright and

started to scream, his eyes opening wide in terror. He started to pant, as though hyperventilating, and then, unaware of the approaching danger, started to calm down.

It was just a dream; only a dream; just a dream...

"Just a dream," he spoke aloud.

The flies that had been buzzing around the room hastily settled on walls, the ceiling and pieces of furniture, afraid of alerting Sean to their presence.

Inconspicuously, the thick current of flies continued to flow into the room from beneath the bedroom door. The first of the horde appeared at the top of one side of the bed frame, with others providing symmetry by appearing on the opposite side.

Sean shook the remnants of his dream from his head and closed his eyes. "Man!" he exclaimed, "that was crazy!" He sighed, falling back to the pillow, unaware of the puke beneath his head.

The blanket of flies dropped from the frame onto the bedclothes and bustled forward.

Sean felt something tickle his right foot lightly. He smiled at the gentle sensation, pulling his leg up towards his stomach. As a rule, he hated his feet being touched, but that slightest contact had almost been pleasurable, evoking a memory from when he was a small child. His father used to hold him by his ankle and tickle his feet playfully; he remembered laughing until he cried, his father not stopping until he had eventually wet himself.

It was a fond memory.

"I miss you, Dad," he said quietly, closing his eyes. Sleep came back easily, caressing his thoughts like a long, absent lover. Unfortunately, so too did the dream. Once again, Francesca was there. Like before, she was naked–

"*Hello, big boy*," she greeted.

–except, she *wasn't* naked. Something black, and evidently moving, clung to her skin, coating every inch and contour of her body with a strange living fabric.

In horror, Sean saw that they were flies; grotesquely big and hideously ugly.

"*What's wrong, Sean?*" Francesca asked in all seriousness.

"*Not again,*" he pleaded.

The black garment shifted and slowly fell from Francesca's body to the floor, first exposing the fullness of her breasts before revealing her nudity in its entirety. "*It's you that they want,*" she said, laughing. "*I'm not even here.*" Her laugh continued for a few more seconds before coming to an abrupt end in a fit of smoky coughing.

With a gasp and a sharp exhalation, a torrent of flies exited her mouth in a spray, spewing forth onto his bed, thousands upon thousands of them, all moving in one direction, specifically towards him.

"*No!*" Sean cried, waking mid-scream from his nightmare and sitting completely upright. His heart was racing and sweat coated his forehead.

He opened his eyes.

I must still be dreaming, he thought. Francesca wasn't there, but the flies were. They were everywhere.

"This isn't real," he asserted in disbelief. The flies had nothing to prove, so having been discovered, stealth was no longer necessary. As one, the flies not already on the bed, took to the air, filling the void above Sean with a droning buzz and a whirr of dark movement, gathering in a thick cloud.

Sean's arms flailed at the flies darting this way and that ahead of his eyes, his legs scissor-kicking at the ones crawling up his limbs and onto his body. The more resistant he became, the more frenzied the flies responded; flitting in and out of reach, shooting off at a tangent between one corner and another, the dawning light filtering through the gap of the curtains, blotted out by the swarm that was steadily increasing.

"What the hell's going on?" With his legs, he propelled

himself back against the bed's headboard, wishing he could melt or disappear through to the other side of the wall beyond.

He began to cry involuntarily and felt his body quaking in fear. He had never seen so many flies in his entire life. It was as though the entire world's population had decided to invade his bedroom.

Where in hell had they come from?

Then the rational part of his brain took control, leading him by the hand and making him ask a profound question:

What can a fly do anyway?

Still crying, Sean started to smile, and then to laugh; long, hard and gleeful, almost insane. With his mouth wide open, a fly saw its golden chance and communicated a simple command. A single thought:

NOW!

As one, the flies regrouped from their haphazard and disjointed 'toing and froing' fly about, into an orchestrated flying phalanx that first did a full circuit of the bedroom in an act of bold showmanship, before taking advantage of the opportunity.

Before Sean had realised the flies' intention, it was too late. The phalanx of flies swooped towards his head and attacked, cloaking his thrashing arms and jerking legs, washing over his face and becoming entangled within his ruffled, puke-matted hair.

No longer laughing, Sean cried out in alarm and slapped at his face, crushing dozens of flies with each swipe. His eyes were now covered with a writhing mass of wriggling insects. Sean clawed blindly at them, but it became clear there were too many, and he soon realised what they planned to do.

For every dozen he killed or brushed away, two dozen replaced them. For every two dozen stepping into the fray, a hundred others buzzed about close behind. In a matter of seconds, he felt movement bulge and burrow around and beneath his eyelids, and then the itchy scratching sensation began, irritating deep behind his eyeballs.

Sean rolled over onto his face, thinking he could dislodge or squash many of them against the pillow, but the little bastards were ready for this. The ones not up his nose flew up like a small mushroom cloud to avoid being flattened, reorganising themselves and joining a fresh contingent taking up the attack.

Almost immediately, Sean returned onto his back so that he was 'up-facing', finding the pillow just as prohibitive to breathing; his nasal passage was blocked by five or six flies wedged deep within each nostril; his mouth was once again wide open as his head burst up, as though out from beneath the surface of a swimming pool, heaving for air.

His long, laboured gasp was laden with one or two flies sucked in with the inhale.

Sean choked on the first one and spat out the second.

"Stop this... please!" he begged, as though there could be reasoning with the insects.

Ignorant to his wishes, the flies stepped up their assault.

Sean swallowed five flies with his next breath. With the help of two fingers, he stimulated his gag-reflex into promptly vomiting them back out. No sooner did he inhale again, a further half a dozen flies were heading into his mouth; in his attempt to belch them out, ten more saw their chances and defiantly flew in towards the back of his throat, followed by six others.

Sean flapped and clawed frantically at his throat as his airway became obstructed; it felt like a piece of food was lodged between the epiglottis and his pharynx. This was the point that usually required the Heimlich manoeuvre; a series of abdominal thrusts from behind to aid displacement of the obstruction. Unfortunately for Sean, this was not an option.

Sensing victory and wishing to get in on the action, all the flies within the room joined in with what would become the final attack. A thick column of bluebottles rocketed forward towards Sean's face, striking him hard against the nose and mouth.

Unable to breathe, Sean was forced to open his mouth wider, knowing already that the game was nearly over. A queue of flies took the advantage and streamed in, filling his mouth and continuing further down into the man's windpipe.

Sean opened his eyes wide in terror, the whites barely visible through the thick moving fabric of insects that covered his head like a ski-mask. Weakly, he clawed at his throat with one hand whilst the other flapped uselessly in a swat to the sides of his face.

He couldn't breathe and felt – rather than saw – darkness close-in around him as he slowly suffocated from the inside.

He felt very hot, stifling, like he was going to self-combust.

This is it, he thought calmly. He watched his life flash in front of him; his childhood; his family; past memories – good and bad –; images even of Francesca (and not the ones from his recent dream). So many thoughts tumbling and colliding for attention, whizzing in and out of focus, in and out of his mind. Beyond them all, he saw a small, fuzzy light, warm and welcoming, dancing invitingly at the end of a very long tunnel.

Accepting his fate, Sean relaxed his hands and gave up the struggle. The pain and suffering appeared to lessen. He focused on the small light and felt himself floating towards it.

With life slowly ebbing away, the flies reduced the intensity of their attack, collectively sounding a signal to retreat. As Sean died, they circled the room doing a victory lap in celebration, before coming to rest on the four walls of the bedroom, bringing a cessation to the boisterous, buzzing noise that neighbours would later report hearing.

After a minute's silence, seven hundred female blowflies sprung up in concert, flew aimlessly above the bed before settling on the exposed areas of Sean's lifeless body.

Within seconds, they laid up to five hundred eggs each. Once the business was concluded, the flies took to the air, joined immediately by their male counterparts. Buzzing emphatically, no longer coordinated, they flitted around the room in disarray, scattering to the four corners, as though blind, seeking a means of escape. Whatever mental link they had possessed, momentarily deserted them.

Aimlessly, the majority of the insects vacated the house via the bedroom window, billowing out like tendrils of dusky smoke; others crawling through cracks beneath skirting boards or floorboards, whilst some leaving by way of the gap beneath the bedroom door.

Upon exiting the house on Surbiton Close, the flies took to the sky, filled with elation and an urge – no, *need* – burning inside. Like survival and procreation was part of their genetic make-up, a new instinct spurred them on.

For years, the fly had been a scourge to society. Swatted into oblivion for just being present, sometimes hunted for pleasure or tortured and killed for no compelling reason. Cats toyed with them. Spiders caught them for food. All along, the fly was happy to play out its meaningless existence, accepting whatever pitiful ending life had in store.

But not anymore.

Now, the fly fancied – no, *craved* – a change. They had just killed Sean Wallace, and there had been others shortly before… and they had liked it. With each death, the dormant desire burned collectively within them. Now, they wanted to kill again. The bloodlust was strong. They wondered at the potential from carrying out future killings.

Were the mighty humans invincible? Could the tables be turned?

The possibilities to these creatures seemed enormous. There was no end to their imaginings.

Soon, man would live in fear of the fly, and never again would a fly be crushed upon the wall.

The revolution had begun.

CHAPTER TWO

D ETECTIVE INSPECTOR BAYLEM CALMLY STEERED the monsoon-grey Audi S3 into a quiet cul-de-sac that joined a slightly less dozy residential street, linking the more well-to-do area of Fulbarton with the less desirable council estate half a mile east.

Except, the cul-de-sac wasn't as peaceful as usual owing to the incident that had been reported less than half an hour earlier, and which the senior police officer was now heading towards.

Next to the detective was a woman in her mid-thirties. Her dirty-blonde hair hung to an inch above her shoulders, styled into a light feathery, almost carefree bob. Peering out through the side window, the sergeant quietly considered the neighbourhood.

Surbiton Close looked very much like any other throughout the town of Fulbarton, or indeed built uniformly across any number of suburbs across the UK. A row of non-descript semi-detached houses built from creamy-white bricks – now dirty-tan in colour through age – and topped with Tudor-brown pantiles tinged green with moss, hemmed in the closeted street.

The usually quiet surroundings were abuzz with a whole contingent of busybody spectators, a circus of media personnel standing excitedly behind white and blue police tape cordoning the area, and a multitude of uniformed and plainclothes police officers milled around in and outside an outwardly ordinary looking house, immersed in a range of duties consistently adopted when dealing with a fresh crime scene.

DI Baylem manoeuvred the Audi around the short, winding road, slowing down as he approached the taped barricade stretched across his path.

A pair of uniformed officers stood sentry in the centre of the road, watching as the senior police officer approached; recognising his car, the taller of the two untied the barrier and waved Baylem through.

The DI acknowledged the uniform with a subtle nod of his head and increased the car's speed.

"What do we know about this incident, sir?" Sargent Jayne McCardle reached up to the hinged sun visor, pulled it down from the ceiling and flicked across a small, rectangular sliding cover, revealing the mirror. She studied her reflection. The rings beneath her jade-green eyes conveyed her lack of sleep despite the makeup.

"Not much." Baylem pulled up behind a white Peugeot van. Blue and yellow markings decorated the centre of its sides and the insignia, *Crime Scene Investigation*, adorning one of the door panels indicated it belonged to the SOCOs. The road was narrow, so he carefully mounted the kerb before bringing the vehicle to a standstill. "Just... that a body was discovered this morning." He turned off the ignition and pressed the seatbelt release button. Unceremoniously, he climbed out of the car, flinging the Audi's door closed behind him.

From the boot of the car, the inspector removed a dark blue disposable coverall and a pair of lighter blue plastic overshoes, both from squished cardboard boxes. There was a carton of disposable latex gloves in addition to a container holding six half face masks close-by. He handed McCardle the coveralls as she joined him.

"Do you ever use those?" asked the sergeant, spotting the blue face masks.

"No, never," he replied as he picked out some protective clothing for himself. "But you never know. I like to be prepared."

Slipping into the forensic outfits, the police officers shuffled along the short distance towards their destination and stepped on to the garden path leading to number fourteen Surbiton Close. At the door, a plainclothes officer was waiting to greet them.

"Morning, sir."

Baylem twisted his wrist and checked his stainless steel chronograph watch. The time was just after midday. "Afternoon," he corrected mustily. "Tell me, what do we know?"

"A male body discovered this morning by the homeowner's mother; she identified him as her son, Sean Wallace. He was twenty-three; a labourer for a local building contractor. There are no signs of forced entry into the property, and no obvious cause of death, though Doctor Hamilton is with him now doing a preliminary."

"Thanks, Prior."

Detective Constable Tom Prior stepped to the left to allow the two senior officers admittance. "The victim is in the master room up the stairs, first on the left. Mrs Wallace is in through the kitchen."

McCardle smiled appreciatively. "Do we know that he is definitely a victim, Constable? Isn't it a bit early to say? He may have died of natural causes." Not waiting for a reply, she stepped into a hallway that ran eight feet in length and less than a metre wide.

Immediately to her right was a staircase and a little along, to her left, was a door that led into a living room. "Are *they* signs of a struggle?" she asked aloud, indicating the smashed remains of a telephone sprawled around the hallway. Joining it, less spectacularly, was a broken photo frame, tossed to the floor. Some shards of glass remained in front of a picture of an attractive woman wearing a bikini standing next to a bare-chested man. A smear of blood had recently been added.

"Could be," replied Baylem thoughtfully. "You speak with the mother; I'll take a look upstairs." Baylem backtracked to the staircase, the narrow hallway made it awkward to pass the sergeant without body-checking. She stepped out of the way over the threshold of the living room.

"Right you are."

2

The pathologist was stooped over the body when Baylem entered the room. A trigger-happy crime scene photographer was present, taking myriads of pictures, splashing flashes of light from his Nikon D810 DSLR camera around the room. He was taking particular attention to the body and the room's layout, that when uploaded into a special programme, could reproduce a 3D visual record of the crime scene.

"Afternoon, Inspector," welcomed the doctor, standing up. He was similarly attired to the newcomer. Both wore standard issue disposable blue forensic coveralls and overshoes. Although the outfits had elasticated hoods, neither man wore them.

"Floyd," replied Baylem informally. Both men were frequent acquaintances in their line of work, but were also known to socialise from time to time over a pint. They were clearly easy within each other's company. "What can you tell me?"

"Oh, I dunno. With confidence? The victim is male, aged approximately twenty-to-twenty-five; some superficial ante-mortem injuries to the knuckles of his right hand. Possibly from a fight..."

"Or, maybe from striking a picture frame downstairs?" Baylem ventured.

"Quite possibly. That could also account for the minute glass fragments found," Hamilton weighed aloud.

"Cause of death?" asked Baylem, not pressing the matter of the glass.

The doctor shrugged. "Nothing obvious, I'm afraid. Apart from the lacerations and bruising to his hand, there are no visible signs of trauma, and nothing to suggest there had been a struggle; could be asphyxiation. Then again, may just be a myocardial event. I can't speculate at the moment; you're going to have to wait for my report."

"Suspicious?" pressed Baylem.

"Unexplained," replied the doctor.

"Okay, what about the time of death?"

"I can't tell you anything conclusive, I'm afraid. I measured the body temp at roughly 21.5°C, which is the current room temperature... this tells me that he's been dead for more than twelve hours. There are no perceptible signs of rigor, which normally presents itself six hours after death, usually wearing off completely between thirty and forty-two hours later.

"Mrs Wallace indicated to the officer first on the scene that she spoke with her son two days ago on Monday, specifically in the evening... so that narrows it down a little. At a guess, I estimate time of death sometime between the late hours of Monday night – and the early hours of Tuesday morning; between eleven p.m. and five a.m. – give or take a couple of hours. Of course, I may be able to give you something more accurate once I've carried out the post-mortem."

"That's great, thanks."

"I'm not sure this is anything, but I've noticed something very peculiar. I don't think it's contributory to the cause of death, though."

"Oh?" Brayden raised an eyebrow quizzically.

"Yes, quite strange. All around the body, look–" Hamilton

stooped down and pointed to a spot on the bed. "–dead flies; literally hundreds of them! They're scattered all over the covers and on the floor; I even found some in his mouth and nostrils. Most peculiar…"

"Is that significant?"

"It could be. I don't know. I'll have them bagged up and sent over to entomology to take a look."

3

The town of Fulbarton was small with a population hovering around 30,000 (as of the 2011 census). Boasting enviably low crime statistics, Fulbarton was the place to go to retire or raise a family, a far cry from the rumbustiousness of other East Anglian towns and cities just a stone's throw away, like Ipswich, Norwich and Cambridge.

It was on account of the low crime rates that whenever there was an incident, a strong police presence would always turn out, no matter how insignificant or serious it then turned out to be.

Despite its good reputation, Fulbarton wasn't entirely without crime. Although not rife with murders, the annual average – based on a decade's worth of data – was 0.4 a year, which sounded less impressive than actually saying: there had been no suspicious deaths in over three years, with only four in the seven before that (all but one was committed by a jilted lover or persons known).

Back behind the wheel of the Audi, Baylem was wondering if that proud reputation was about to come to an end. Two minutes earlier, he had left the doctor to conclude his preliminary examination and left the scene for the SOCO's to carry on with their business. McCardle was seated next to him.

"What did the mother have to say?" Baylem started the car's

engine and manoeuvred out of the cul-de-sac, completing a turn that necessitated reversing into someone's driveway.

McCardle flipped open a small notebook, using a list of scrawled words as a prompt. "Mrs Wallace said that Sean called her Monday night, about half-nine. It was whilst she was watching *Silent Witness* on the BBC, which is how she can be so certain."

"Did he seem okay to her?"

"No. Apparently, he was drunk and very aggressive. Not in a good state. She said he'd been in a fight with his girlfriend, Francesca. Sean found out she had been cheating on him."

"Oh. Guess that accounts for the broken picture."

"Most likely. To be a fly on the wall," said McCardle, humourlessly.

"Which reminds me; did you see any dead flies in the kitchen?"

McCardle looked puzzled. It was an odd question. "No. Why?"

"Something a little strange, is all." He explained the hundreds of dead flies scattered around Sean's body.

McCardle closed her notebook, deciding there was nothing left to add from her conversation with Mrs Wallace. "Maybe they died from whatever killed Sean."

"Possible," he weighed up warily. It didn't seem likely.

"Or they could have been placed there."

"Possible," Baylem repeated. He sounded unconvinced.

"Like, in a ritual; perhaps as a calling card." She was thinking along the lines of a serial killer, though there were very few signs left behind to help accreditation.

"I think you read too much crime fiction, Jayne," Baylem was smiling. "How many cases do you know involved the leaving behind of dead flies?"

McCardle shrugged. "I dunno. None, but... there's always a first."

"In Fulbarton?" said Baylem incredulously.

The woman's demeanour hardened. She turned to look out

of the window, away from her boss. "There's no harm asking the question, though, is there? There could be cases from further afield."

The mirth left Baylem's face. "No, you're right. A good detective asks all the questions, no matter how trivial or farfetched they may seem." Despite intending to defuse the situation, he failed by allowing sarcasm to coat the comment. Noting his mistake by McCardle's continued cold-shoulder, further attempts at clearing the air were nullified by the abrupt interruption of the police radio.

"*Calling all units, B&E in progress at number sixty-three Claringdon Street.*"

"That's just around the corner from here, isn't it?" said Baylem.

"Leave it for uniform to deal with," replied McCardle tersely.

"Nonsense, we're in the area. We can respond..." Still driving, Baylem flicked a switch amongst an array of buttons on a central control panel set, where most cars have a CD player or controls for air con, and filled the air with the warble of a siren.

McCardle sighed in resignation.

At the front of the car, blue lights danced to the discordant tune from behind the Audi's grill (adjacent to the fog lights, just below the headlamps). The DI scooped up the handset. "This is DI Baylem. We're in the vicinity and responding, over." Returning the radio mic to its cradle, Baylem glanced towards the sergeant. "Makes life interesting, getting your hands dirty once in a while," he said placatingly.

In spite of being in the vicinity, Baylem and McCardle were not the first to arrive at Claringdon Street. A marked car was parked across a driveway in front of a house neighbouring sixty-three, the uniformed inhabitants nowhere to be seen.

Baylem drew up slowly alongside the police vehicle, peering in briefly before mounting the kerb opposite, bringing the Audi to a halt.

The front door of number sixty-three – a four-panel white UPVC door with a semi-circle window – opened and a female police constable stepped out. Baylem and McCardle climbed out of the car and walked purposely across the road towards the front garden from where the uniformed woman was now approaching.

"Sir?" greeted the constable, looking concerned.

"We were in the area. Thought we'd come and stretch our legs."

"Right." She spoke with a little unease.

"Control reports a break-in and entering. As you're first on the scene, PC Manning, what's the score?" There was a slight tone of annoyance in McCardle's voice.

"The neighbour reported hearing glass breaking to the rear of the house about half an hour ago, though said she didn't see or hear anything else. On investigation, PC Anders and myself located the source of the broken glass. A panel in one of the kitchen windows has been smashed. Upon checking the doors, both the front and back were locked."

"Okay," replied Baylem.

"We knocked, but no one answered. We asked the neighbour when she saw the owner last. She said not for a couple of weeks, which itself, was strange, but not out of the ordinary. The Jessops – the couple who live here – have gone away on short breaks a few times before, but not normally without saying something; the neighbour just thought that maybe they forgot and thought nothing more on it.

"Considering the Jessops haven't been seen for a couple of weeks, we took it upon ourselves to access the property, and forced the rear door."

"And?" Baylem quizzed.

"Nothing."

"Oh?" McCardle's interest went up a notch.

"Other than a broken window, there's no sign of a break-in or disturbance. There are loads of items of value on display, and nothing appears to be missing. Also, the window itself is too small to climb through."

"What about the Jessops?" Baylem asked casually.

"Nothing to suggest they've gone away," replied PC Manning.

"Any clues as to what caused the window to break?" McCardle took a turn to ask a question.

The constable shook her head. "No, but the force came from inside."

"Oh?" It was Baylem this time to show intrigue.

"That's not even the strangest thing," said Manning mysteriously.

McCardle raised an eyebrow.

The constable continued: "The kitchen is covered with dead flies… thousands of them."

Before either of the detectives could elicit a comment, the white front door to number sixty-three opened and PC Anders hurried out; not clocking the two plainclothes officers standing with his partner, he spoke excitedly. "Louise… you've got to see this. I think I know where those flies came from. It's gross."

CHAPTER THREE

"WATCH OUT." A BOY IN his early teens yelled, though he was seemingly too far away, too late and only mildly bothered. He stood a good distance but projected his voice clearly, which was unmistakably aimed towards the man sunbathing in the middle of a grassy expanse next to his girlfriend. There was no one else in close proximity.

Sensing danger more than hearing the warning, the man sat up and squinted ahead of him. A group of a dozen kids were playing cricket, two were running back and forth between two sets of stumps, the rest dotted around in fielding positions.

"Fore!" the teen hollered, not caring that it was a golfing term as opposed to cricket lingo. Its intended meaning was clear.

The man in his mid-thirties glanced up towards the sky just as the cricket ball came into view. With little thought, he cupped his hands, contorted his body, and snatched the ball clean out of the air a moment before it would have struck him in the face; the momentum forced him to do a small somersault backwards, ending with him landing on his feet in a flourish. He tossed the ball up into the air.

"Howzat!" he bellowed happily.

The group of teens whooped, clapped and cheered, adding calls of "nice one!" and "good catch, mister," his way.

"Are you showing off again there, Michael?" The girl, just two years Michael's junior, was looking up at him from the picnic blanket. She spoke with a soft Irish accent and was wearing white Farrah denim shorts and an orange high-neck tank top that concealed her breasts entirely but left everything below it completely exposed (including the belly button piercing – a silver lizard gecko sparkling under the sun). Concealing her eyes was a pair of tortoiseshell brown Ray-Bans perched on the bridge of her nose.

Michael grinned down at her. He looked handsome and majestic with model good looks and well coiffured brown hair. She smiled back up at him admiringly, watching as he pitched the ball towards the boy who had hollered the warning his way. The way he brought his shoulders back and hefted the ball made the muscles concealed within his grey Adidas T-shirt contort and ripple. It wasn't difficult to tell that he spent too many hours' bench pressing and curling iron in the gym.

The ball bounced ahead of the boy. He caught it off the rebound. "Cheers mate!"

"You're welcome." Michael sat down next to his girlfriend and reached over to a navy insulated picnic bag, the zipper-lid was unfastened and the neck of an empty wine bottle could be seen poking through the top. In a side pocket was a bottle of sunscreen lotion. He tugged it free and squirted a dollop into a hand, applying the white liquid to both his arms. "Do you want some?" he asked.

"Nah thanks. Defeats the whole point of sunbathing, don't you think?" she replied as she closed her eyes behind her sunglasses.

Michael didn't respond. She was right, but he had fair skin and a few suspicious looking moles up and down his body. She didn't care about the dangers of skin cancer or damaging her skin, but he did.

Kayleigh lived for the day, which was part of why he loved her so much and why he then reached into his trouser pocket and wrestled a small box out.

"Kayleigh?"

"Hmmm," she replied dreamily.

"I love you," he declared, full of emotion. There was nobody else in the entire universe who loved anyone more than he loved her.

"I love you too," she replied, light-heartedly. It sounded perfunctory, like she was speaking on autopilot.

"I mean it, Kayleigh. I've never loved anyone the way I love you," he gushed, kneeling in front of her. "I know we've only been together a year–"

"Ten months," Kayleigh corrected.

"–ten months. But I know that I want to spend the rest of my life with you."

Kayleigh sprung up into a sitting position. "What are you doing?" she asked soberly.

Ignoring her question, Michael reached towards Kayleigh's sunglasses and plucked them off her nose, placing them gently on the blanket beside her. "Kayleigh Diane Murray... will you make me the happiest man alive and agree to marry me?"

"Shut up!" she squealed, clasping a hand to her mouth, unsure whether she could trust herself to say the right thing. Her eyes misted up and her head shook slowly from side to side. After what seemed like a long time, the blonde woman's demeanour changed. A big, toothy grin split her face in two.

"Well? Will you?" Michael rushed, doubt in his tone. He was still holding the small box containing the diamond ring. Sparkles dazzled under the early afternoon sun from the gold band's apex; three 1/3 carat brilliant round diamonds were set impressively.

"Yes!" Kayleigh exclaimed excitedly. "Yes, yes, YES!!" she

screeched, throwing her arms around Michael's neck. She drew his face to hers, closed her eyes and planted her lips onto his. Eagerly, her tongue entered his mouth, caressing his lightly, and tasted the question that still vibrated on his lips; her tongue rolled further and explored the caps, contours and crevices of his teeth. Michael responded, equally as passionate, momentarily forgetting that he continued to hold the ring within his right hand.

Behind Michael, whoops, wolf whistles and cheers echoed around, immediately followed by lewd comments of: "Get a room!" The teens playing cricket had stopped to spectate the picnicking couple's amorous display.

Before Kayleigh had managed to unzip Michael's fly, Michael remembered that they were in a public park. Reluctantly, he withdrew from his girlfriend – his *fiancée* – and conscientiously pushed her probing hand away from the bulge that had half-formed at his crotch.

"Whoa. I want you to be my wife an' all, but I don't want to do this in front of an audience."

"Huh?" Kayleigh looked up and suddenly realised what Michael was implying. Her cheeks turned red. "Oh… how embarrassing."

"It could've been."

The heckling continued in the background; someone shouted, "Give her one for me," crudely. Michael ignored them.

"Here… I think this is yours." The man presented the small box towards Kayleigh, placing it in her left hand.

"Michael… It's beautiful." Kayleigh tugged the diamond ring from the black velvet cushion and slipped it on to the fourth proximal finger of her left hand. It fitted perfectly. "How did you know my size?" she asked curiously.

Michael smiled evasively. He didn't want to tell her.

"Tell me!" she chided. She made it sound like it was a big deal.

"Well," he started nervously. "One night, I kept myself awake to two in the morning." He started to laugh like it was a foolish thing. "Whilst you were sleeping, I used a ring gauge and measured your finger perfectly."

"What? Shut up!"

"It's true. It wasn't easy, I can tell ya! I thought I'd broken your finger at one point."

Playfully, Kayleigh punched him in the arm. Then relaxed. She held her hand out, fingers splayed as though drying nail varnish under a heat lamp. "Thank you," she said, overwhelmed. "I love it… and I love you."

They kissed again and Kayleigh felt Michael's hands climbing up her body, brushing the bare skin of her stomach beneath the bottom of her orange high-neck tank top and settling on her breasts, gently squeezing them.

"Oi Oi!" sounded from across the park as one voyeur observed the picnicking couple turning up the heat again. Followed by "Savaloy," as someone else joined in, finishing the rhyme. Laughter and playful banter followed.

It was Kayleigh this time that put a stop to things. Casually, she grabbed one of Michael's hands and pushed the other aside. "Let's go home," she suggested warmly, rescuing her breasts from ongoing fondling. "Unless you want a dozen wet-behind-the-ear boys seeing me get naked."

Michael didn't need telling twice. He was up off the blanket, scooting up items left over from lunch and placing them in the picnic bag and then shaking the fleece blanket free of dried grass, folding and then rolling it for transport.

Seeing that the couple were leaving, groans of dismay and words of objection followed; one eloquently exclaimed loud enough for the whole park to hear: "I'll have to put my tissues away now!"

Michael ignored what they were saying. He turned towards the group of friends and took a bow and casually waved goodbye. "Come on. Let's get out of here."

2

The red Triumph Spitfire was parked along a quiet road a short walk from Ainsley Park. Michael and Kayleigh walked towards it, hand in hand, the picnic bag bouncing against the outside of the man's left leg, glasses and the empty wine bottle gently clinking inside. The sun, now a quarter ways down the sky was still stifling hot and Michael was contemplating applying more sunscreen. He could feel the heat burning the back of his neck.

Arriving at the small old car, Michael used a key to unlock the boot. Unlike modern cars, the door did not open up on springs; instead, he pulled it upward by its edge, stowing the picnic bag and the blanket, which he had draped across its top between the handles. He closed the boot and walked around to the driver's side door. Also unlike modern cars, the Spitfire didn't have central locking.

Michael unlocked the door, climbed in and stretched across the passenger seat to flick up the unlock button, allowing access for Kayleigh.

"You're getting rid of this when we're married," she said matter-of-factly.

"Huh?" Michael feigned panic and a little alarm. He buckled up his seatbelt.

"I mean... a two-seater car is nice. But where would the children go?" Kayleigh reached up to the clasp of her seatbelt, pulled it down across her shoulder and inserted it into the socket to the right of her seat. The clasp clicked home.

Michael started to laugh, sounding nervous. He keyed the ignition and put the gear into first. The Triumph Spitfire required a bit of muscle to change gears, and the steering was heavy. Pulling away from the kerb was like manoeuvring a Chieftain tank, all fifty-six tons of it.

"This car is a classic... there's NO way I'm parting with it, honey. In many respects, this here IS a child," he tutted. "Uh-huh… no way!" he repeated. He meant it. The car had been a gift from his dad when he turned eighteen. It had been a clapped-out old banger then but, together, he and his pa had worked tirelessly for two years to restore it to its original glory.

It wasn't just a car; it had been a rite of passage. And since his father had died, the car – together with the memories of the time they'd spent rebuilding it – was all that he had left of the man.

For a moment, Kayleigh glared at him with a look of indignation. When the seatbelt buckle released of its own accord, the look changed to one that screamed:

Are you kidding me!

Forcefully, she pulled the belt back across her chest and snuck it home for a second time. "You need to get this fixed!" she said, turning away. Her features softened into a manner that many would recognise on the face of a woman. It was that 'I know something you don't' kind of look. She knew she would get what she wished; she just needed to be patient and use what she had to the best of her advantage.

"It's on my list of things to do," he replied dolefully.

Using the silver crank handle built into the door four inches above the stereo speaker, she wound down the window until warm air breezed in and buffeted her hair.

Michael drove away from the quiet park on to a busy street that took traffic directly to Fulbarton's town centre or away, allowing motorists a choice: forbearance or a chance of escape. Taking neither option, he took a right turn at the first roundabout.

A housing estate on either side of the road soon made way for the outskirts to an old village, the houses becoming well-spaced out with large parcels of land stretching long and expansive between. The landscape soon altered to include potato, rapeseed and wheat fields, and a chicken and pig farm, amongst the solitary houses dotted here and there and miles upon miles of bordering hedgerows. A small red airplane bumbled low in the sky, spraying a fine swirling mist behind it, dusting the crops beneath it.

Kayleigh could just make out the aviator through the windows of the small cockpit, comically dressed to look like one of those old World War 1 fighter pilots. She snickered to herself.

As the surroundings changed, the roads changed too, from broad to narrow, with some barely wide enough to allow two-way traffic.

Residential areas and roads with street lighting mandated a thirty mph speed limit. The long and winding road, with its tree branches hanging low, was neither residential or well-lit, and the national speed limit signs confirmed that Michael was right to push the Triumph to a death-defying speed of between fifty and sixty mph.

Every so often, a car, van, tractor or lorry 'whooshed' past on their right, causing the small two-seater sports car to rock and bounce on its axles.

Through Kayleigh's open window, wind gusted in but did nothing to halt the driblet of sweat that had formed on her forehead.

"You might want to shut your window," suggested Michael, barely heard over the noise of the wind and the roar of the old engine.

Splat!

An unidentifiable bug, its guts, and a small amount of blood marred the windscreen from where it had collided at speed. Michael pressed a button on the dashboard and a jet of screen wash gushed up from somewhere close to where the wipers rested. Immediately, the wipers began to swipe in arcs, one ahead of Michael and the other in front of Kayleigh. They effectively cleaned the mess free, though droplets of water runoff streaked in parts of the screen not reached by the wipers.

No sooner had the wipers stopped licking moisture from the screen, another bug butted the window.

Michael grunted at the mess appearing in the centre of his view. He activated the wipers again, causing the rubber blade to spread the gooey mess in a streak.

A further insect splattered the screen.

"Ah, fuck!" Kayleigh threw up a hand to her face, cupping her left eye. Beneath it, she blinked madly, feeling something moving beneath the eyelid. "Something's just flown into my eye!"

"I told you to close the window," said Michael smugly.

Still holding her eye, she used her right hand to crank the window closed. Slowly, like a portcullis in reverse, the gap decreased and the wind blowing in subsided.

"Are you all right?" Michael asked.

Kayleigh sniffed. "Yea. I think it's a fly. Bugger's in my eye." Unlike modern cars, the Triumph had no ceiling sun visor with a built-in mirror. Instead, she tried to see via the wing mirror fixed to the outside door panel to her left. She squinted through the glass towards the visual device, the sight from her left eye blurring.

"Can you see anything?"

In the mirror, she could just make out a small, alien object poking out from the fold of skin beneath her left eye.

Kayleigh made some noises of disgust. "Eww. I can't do this." Awkwardly, she was using the external mirror to guide her fingers. With the index of her left hand, she pulled the skin down from her eye to reveal the cause of her discomfort.

The fly was half-mashed into the ocular cavity, almost squeezed in beneath her eyeball. With the thumb and index finger of her right hand, she made to tweezer the fly out.

The Triumph Spitfire hit a pothole in the road. The car jounced on rickety springs and Kayleigh's right hand jerked sharply, the pincer finger poking her already sore eye.

"Aghhh! Goddamn!" Pain lanced through her head. Once again, her left hand was cupping her eye, caressing it, trying to soothe it. Because of the pain, tears were now streaming from both eyes.

"Babe, I'll pull over as soon as I can." The stretch of road Michael was driving was a single carriage with no parking spaces for at least two miles in either direction. "There's a pub up ahead. We'll park in there and sort your eye out," he asserted reassuringly. *Maybe get a drink whilst we're there*, he thought. His throat was parched and he felt a burning need to find a toilet.

"Blasted flies!" Kayleigh cursed. "I hate them."

"Now, now. I'm sure the fly didn't do it on purpose. It was probably just as pissed to have flown into your eye as you are." Michael steered the car around a sharp bend, his view of the road ahead momentarily obstructed by overgrown foliage.

Splat!

This time, a fly seemed to have flown into the windscreen of its own volition. It was a big one. Probably the biggest Michael had ever seen. Half of its body was pulped; the other half was completely intact and still alive. A wing batted wildly and a couple of legs seemed to bicycle wheel; it was as though it firmly believed there was still a way out of its predicament alive.

Straightening up the Triumph on the road, Michael couldn't help his focus drifting over to the dying fly sticking to the centre of his windscreen. The beating wings and kicking legs continued; he found them strangely fascinating.

"Michael!!" Kayleigh screamed. She had opened her eye for just a second, immediately seeing the danger.

A car horn blared from the other side of the road, long and loud, desperate and foreboding.

Jolting to attention, Michael saw that his Triumph – the car he and his father had lovingly restored – had drifted over the centre line into the path of oncoming traffic; specifically, on a collision course with a white transit van; double-glazing was strapped to one side with ladders; downpipes and fascia boards were bolted to the roof. Michael jerked the steering in Kayleigh's direction, bringing the vehicle back to the left side of the road just before impact was imminent.

The driver of the transit van glowered at Michael as he passed, gesturing rudely with his right hand.

Meekly, Michael held up a hand in apology, accepting fault.

"What's wrong with you, Michael?" Kayleigh was crying.

What was wrong?

Before he could answer, half a dozen flies smacked against the windscreen, followed by half a dozen more.

The bright sunshine suddenly disappeared, replaced by unnatural darkness. Michael leaned forward, peering up towards the sky to see why the gloom.

Where moments earlier he would have seen a blue sky, perhaps a couple of crisp-white clouds gliding lazily above, there was nothing but a shimmering black mass.

More flies collided with the windscreen. Michael activated the wipers, swatting carcasses to the sides and discolouring the screen further with muddy, bloody, pus-like gloop that obstructed his view even more.

"What's going on?" Kayleigh shrieked.

More flies rained down, no longer concentrated to the windscreen ahead, but falling steadily around them.

Tap... tap... tap... tap... tap... tap... like hailstones.

Flies thundered and bounced off the roof of the car.

Crack... crack... crack... crack... crack... crack...

Flies collided with the rear windscreen and the side windows.

Fwapp... fwapp... fwapp... fwapp... fwapp... fwapp...

Flies still careened against the front of the car, besmirching the windscreen and littering its edge with a black, gungy-residue soon becoming an inch thick.

Ignoring Kayleigh and paying as little attention as he could to the flies, Michael floored the accelerator and ploughed faster forward. It was now roughly a mile to the pub he reckoned; just a little further and they can stop, assess the situation and try to make sense of it.

The speedometer edged up from fifty mph to sixty mph, and then to seventy. He kept on applying the pressure, even after the car started to judder and the engine began to rattle. The Triumph wasn't used to such harsh treatment.

"Michael? I don't like this. What's happening?" The vibrations from the car caused her seatbelt to spring free again, retracting across her orange tank top. The clasp whizzed up back into its resting spot behind her shoulder. Fully focused on the weirdness of the situation and the pain continuing to itch and burn in her left eye, she ignored it.

Flies continued to fall, ever faster, striking and being struck, blotting the screen from sheer volume. The build-up of bodies grew steadily from the edge, creeping upwards to form a growing obstruction. The wipers were swishing back and forth at full pelt, but slowing under the weight of the ever-increasing numbers of flies converging on the moving vehicle, becoming useless with every revolution.

"Michael!"

"Oh God!" he cried out. He saw it a microsecond before she had; a pulsating inky-black mass that appeared to contract and expand, undulating smoothly like a balloon being inflated by an asthmatic.

It was something inexplicable and unimaginable; a dark patch hovering in the road a short way ahead.

A break in the fly-cloud above made the sunshine seem much brighter than it ought to have been, but the respite from the gloom was only transitory. Before either of them could comment, the interior of the car was unexpectedly submerged in complete darkness.

It was almost like a light switch had been depressed in a windowless room; one moment light, the next, sheer blackness.

The Triumph Spitfire plunged into the solid mass and Michael became blind to his surroundings. Feeling a change in the road's surface, he jerked the steering to his right. From memory, he knew that the road followed a windy route just before reaching the pub. A sharp left followed by a curving right before making a tight left again.

It was too farfetched to believe he could steer and drive the car blindly for the remainder of the distance to the pub, but he thought he could try. Michael felt the surface beneath the car return to being smoother, followed by a rumble as a front tyre rolled over a cat's eye in the centre of the road. Instinctively, he knew that he was driving on the wrong side of the road and made an attempt to rectify it.

Too late.

A car horn sounded distantly and the harsh shriek of tyres as the brakes were forcefully applied filled the air for an interminably long time.

Michael turned the steering hard towards Kayleigh – now screaming in the seat beside him – and felt the control of the car desert him.

The Triumph Spitfire spun a full 360° before its tail collided with an oncoming vehicle – a silver Ford Focus which had tried to brake and avoid the danger – the momentum causing it to flip.

CRASH!

Before the vehicle left the road, Kayleigh was propelled forward. Had the seatbelt still been in place, she would have been contained within her seat, but instead, her body smashed through the windscreen at fifty mph, disappearing beneath the Triumph as it rolled: once, the sounds of glass smashing and metal scraping and buckling: twice, the tyres exploded on impact like a four gun salute: then a third time, caving the roof in before crashing upright, head-on into a 300-year-old oak tree.

No longer recognisable, the red vehicle was a mangled wreck, concertinaed beneath the impact. Liquid gushed from the fuel tank beneath it, a couple of rivulets racing a line towards the road forming a puddle under a beacon of light where the sun filtered through an overhanging canopy of leaves from the oak tree.

Kayleigh's lifeless form lay across the road thirty metres back where the first of a multitude of road users came on to the scene, stopping their cars and hurrying out.

The driver of the silver Ford Focus – her car abandoned to the side of the road – staggered a dozen steps from where Kayleigh was. Oblivious to her own injuries – a gash above her right eye and a couple of broken ribs – she wanted to assist in some way. The accident was bad. She could tell by the way the body was stretched and covered in the road.

Covered? Who had covered it?

The driver of the Ford Focus didn't dwell on it. Unsurprisingly, her involvement in the road traffic accident meant she was the first on the scene, but she had her own injuries and, soon, something far worse to worry about. Crimson was dripping into one of her eyes, obscuring her vision. She rubbed it away with the heel of her right hand, improving things but only marginally. The cut was deep and was ebbing quickly. She tried to stem the flow by pressing a hand against it. Warm and sticky blood trickled between her fingers.

In the road, the black cover on the body appeared to move, ever so slightly, like it was draped loosely, shifting with the rise and fall of a chest.

The woman lurched unsteadily forward, close to the victim's side. Falling to her knees, she reached over to the cover, intending on pulling it aside to see for herself who it was, and his or her condition. Despite her own injuries, she hoped to offer some comfort and support before the emergency services arrived.

As her fingers came within a centimetre of the body, the cover shifted skywards, like a magician throwing a sheet up before using its camouflage to disappear beneath it; except, the woman realised it wasn't a cover or a sheet, but a body of insects gathered almost as one, cloaking the accident victim.

Flies, to be precise; big, fat, ugly flies that looked familiar yet strangely alien and somewhat bigger.

She recoiled in disgust and horror, taking a hasty step backwards, one that off-balanced her. She tripped over her own feet and landed on her backside, grunting from the impact.

Not stopping, she scooted backwards, using her feet to push away, feeling the gravel of the road wear and tear the seat of her light trousers, aware that the abrasion was taking a layer of skin from her bruising rump.

Now flying, the insect's wings produced a low humming sound, almost a drone, like a low note played on a hundred old Bontempi reed organs. No longer in a sheet, the flies flew disorderly, nebulously, like they awaited instruction, not dissimilar to children in a classroom prior to a teacher exercising authority.

In an instant, the thrum that filled the air settled on a rhythm that seemed organised, almost mechanical. The flies were no longer darting to and fro, no longer flying in a chaotic, agitated manner; no longer acting individually or against one and other. They flew as one, a cohesive unit, leagued together by some unexplainable force for some unknown reason or clear intention.

For a moment, the woman from the Ford Focus was curious, almost mesmerised by the display the flies were putting on. Using the distraction to their advantage, the insects casually drifted towards her, spreading out so as to encircle her. Before she knew it, they were completely surrounding her, the swarm dropping fluidly and caking her entire body from head to toe, leaving nothing exposed.

The woman thrashed around on the road, her arms flailing at the flying menace that now cocooned her entire body, and which had begun to direct its true intention upon her face, focusing particularly for her eyes, ears, nose and mouth.

Other drivers arriving at the scene watched on with mixed dread, confusion and macabre fascination. Some saw the woman lying on the road's surface, flapping about, clearly agitated, but none wise enough to understand the cause.

And no one got the chance.

The puddle of liquid that continued to leak from the wreckage of Michael's Triumph Spitfire was growing, spilling across the road like outstretching fingers, swelling towards other vehicles that were parked or just arriving; good Samaritans attending the scene to lend assistance. There was always one element that never surprised or ceased to amaze; the generosity and caring of others in the wake of a disaster or an accident. It was the single thing that made us human and the one thing that was certain; there was never a shortage of people on hand to help a fallen comrade.

Unfortunately, stupidity was equally abundant in humanity, and one such individual wasn't too bright as to realise the outcome of flicking his half-smoked cigarette into the road.

In a *WHOOSH!* the flammable liquid ignited, speedily chasing the point of its origin twelve feet, the flare following a course through brambles and dried grass – more kindling to the flames – and meeting the Triumph's fuel tank in less than two seconds.

BOOM!

What was left of Michael and the crushed remains of his vehicle exploded, sending flaming pieces of metal, engine parts, and body fragments fifty feet into the air, whilst leaving the shell of the car, along with the oak it had slammed into, a roaring orange and red fireball. Dense black smoke billowed into the clear blue sky, acrid and toxic.

Attendants, bystanders and those standing around watching, dived for cover or took refuge within their cars as the searing heat washed over them in a wave and burning debris rained down from the heavens.

The flies, vulnerable to the intense heat, abandoned the

struggling woman beneath their coordinated attack, taking off in parody of the undulating fumes that increasingly pumped heavenward. Their departure was barely noticed. Most witnesses only reported the scene of the conflagration and recalling the grim details of the accident; others who may have witnessed the peculiarity, dismissed the sight or distrusted their eyes, ascribing it to hallucination, heat stroke or a fatigued imagination.

Only the woman from the silver Ford Focus would talk of the flies and how she found the girl (later identified as Kayleigh Marsh) covered from top to toe in them. In her account, she recalled – before the Triumph Spitfire had clipped her car – seeing the oncoming car's screen obstructed with something dark and lifelike, something that was terrible and moving. Putting one and one together, she was, without doubt, concluding that it had been the flies that were responsible for the accident.

But nobody would listen, accusing her of being incoherent or mentally traumatised from the accident. Sedated, she was rushed off to Fulbarton's General Hospital for treatment and psychological evaluation.

Using the plume of slate-grey smoke as camouflage, the flies escaped into the afternoon sky, floating up to just less than six-thousand feet, close to the ceiling where the air temperature was too cold for insects to fly. Travelling in a southerly direction, the flies continued without rest for half an hour. Having failed to complete their execrable plan, it was imperative a replacement was quickly found.

In an ever-growing town like Fulbarton, they would not have to wait long. Unlike humans, they did not discriminate. It wasn't black or white, rich or poor, man or woman.

Religion or sexual orientation had no significance either.

The flies didn't need to be selective; they chose their targets without prejudice. On every corner of every street, in every town across the country and throughout the world, there were plenty of hosts to choose from.

CHAPTER FOUR

/

D I BAYLEM, DS McCARDLE, AND the police constable –
Louise Manning – followed PC Anders into the detached
house. The first thing to strike the Inspector was how
light and airy the place seemed. The walls were Swiss Coffee white,
adorned with paintings (mostly reprints) of landscapes by John
Constable and an occasional framed photograph of a young girl.
The curtains, ivory with an embroidered floral design in silver,
were open and held in place with white rope tie-backs. The carpet
was cream and thick pile, spongy underfoot.

There was little furniture; just a three-piece suite (also cream)
with a matching pouffe, a large screen television on a smoked glass
stand, a coffee table (also glass), and a nest of wooden tables set
aside tidily in a corner.

"It's this way," Anders hurried.

"What did you find, Constable?" asked Baylem, following the
man in the lead through to the kitchen.

"I think it's better for you to see for yourself, sir," replied
Anders. "It's just through here." The police constable guided them
across the kitchen towards a door that McCardle and Baylem
assumed led to a utility room or downstairs' toilet.

"See what I mean about the flies," regarded Manning off-hand.

"Oh, that's nothing," asserted Anders, opening the door and stepping through into a small room. The absence of a washing machine or other launder machines did nothing to dispel the detective's beliefs that they were entering a utility room. "You should see the ones down here."

"Down?" McCardle was puzzled, stepping deeper into the room, seeing the opening in the centre.

"I probably would've missed it had it not already been open. I guess normally it would've been concealed beneath that rug." Anders stood by the opening and pointed to a rolled up Tabriz medallion area rug – blue and cream coloured – that would easily cover the entire room. A hinged trapdoor was opened out, resting on the floor opposite it.

Walking to the edge where Anders was poised, Baylem could see the wooden staircase leading down. "What's that, a basement?"

"I didn't think houses along here had them?" stated McCardle. She guessed the estate had been built circa 1970, although you could tell that a modern extension had been added to the property more recently.

"Follow me. Watch yourself when you get to the bottom, there's a low beam I banged me head on. Be warned, you might want to take a deep breath before stepping in," Anders clambered down the stairs quickly and ducked upon reaching the bottom step.

Baylem, somewhat baffled, looked towards the woman constable.

"Don't ask," she said, "I only work with him."

Without hesitation, the DI stepped onto the top step and walked carefully down after Anders. McCardle and Constable Manning followed close behind.

On reaching the bottom, Baylem stooped as Anders had recommended, spotting the low beam almost as an afterthought; without the warning, he would have collided with it without a doubt. Ignoring the further suggestion of holding his breath, he walked in through a narrow doorway into an antechamber where Anders was waiting.

"It's through there, sir," the PC indicated an open doorway.

Before Baylem progressed, McCardle stepped off the stairs, tailed by Manning.

"Bloody hell, what's that smell?!" the constable scolded, cupping a hand over her mouth and nose.

Baylem knew the smell very well; putrescine, sulphurous, and methane-thiol – the fragrance of rotten meat and spoiled vegetables. Thick and cloying; the stink associated with decomposing flesh.

The aroma of death.

The DI braced himself for what to expect, mentally preparing for the scene beyond the door.

"Has someone died in there?" Manning walked towards the door.

"Don't," Anders grabbed his partner by the arm, halting her progress. "It's probably best you don't see."

Baylem disappeared through the doorway, followed by McCardle. Manning stayed back, fighting the urge to ignore her colleague and go after the senior officers, to have a look-see at the spectacle for herself. She wasn't a child, she mentally chided.

"Jesus, Mary, and Joseph," exclaimed Baylem, looking across the room towards the origin of the dreadfully fetid smell. The picture was worse than what he had imagined and consumed his attention. He didn't notice the small bed in one corner or the boxes of toys piled all around the room, or even the bookcase filled end-to-end with children's books by Roald Dahl, C.S Lewis, and even some David Walliams.

McCardle flinched and sharply averted her eyes. "Is that...?"

"The Jessops, we can assume," answered Baylem, guessing the direction of her question.

With her eyes closed, McCardle composed herself before

forcing another look. It was the worst thing she had ever seen. "What about the third body?"

So disconcerted by the scene, the DI hadn't registered that what he was seeing were three dead bodies. He had observed what looked like a man and a woman huddled together grotesquely, but completely missed what appeared to be a child, sandwiched between them.

The bodies were all in an advanced state of decomposition. Knowing a little thanatology, which is the study of death, Baylem could tell just by the appearance of the bodies that they had been dead for more than a week, probably over two. The exposed fleshy parts appeared dark in colour, between a deep shade of purple and a mottled black; their skin was a patchwork of blisters. Gas build-up within their bodies had caused bloating and a monstrous swelling, pushing their eyes completely out from their sockets, looking like ping-pong balls squeezed through a piece of elastic sheeting whilst their tongues poked out of their mouths, absurdly long and curling upwards. There were no distinguishable features to tell them apart, their faces unrecognisable; they were neither masculine nor feminine; the only way Baylem could hazard a guess was from the clothes they were wearing.

"Did the Jessops have a child?" asked McCardle distantly, the scene burning deep into her memory for future retrospection. It would haunt her dreams for years to come.

Baylem shrugged. That was a question they clearly needed to ask. "There's a photograph of a young girl on the wall in the living room. Maybe it's her."

"Anders wasn't joking about the flies. Look…" It sounded foolish in the scheme of things.

There were hundreds, possibly thousands of dead flies scattered around the room, heavily concentrated around the feet of the bodies.

"Most curious, hey?" Baylem was fascinated, but his voice

lacked enthusiasm. He crouched down. From inside his jacket, he withdrew a pen and used it to prod one of the flies. A fat, bloated specimen. A blowfly, the sort he knew fed and laid their eggs within rotten flesh.

"My serial killer idea sounds less farfetched now, doesn't it, sir?"

"Maybe," replied Baylem without conviction. He wasn't yet ready to admit that he was wrong.

"Of course, flies are often found near dead bodies," said McCardle, explaining the obvious. "Their growth cycle is frequently used to determine time of death." Not an exact science, but it helped set the parameters.

Baylem ignored her small talk. He teased a fly onto his pen and raised it up to within four inches from his face. He studied it closely.

"They look the same as the ones we found a little earlier with Sean Wallace's body." He was guessing as he hadn't paid much attention to them at that scene.

"I think these flies are important. They're a link to the other case."

The DI flicked the dead fly off his pen and stood upright, returning the writing instrument to his jacket. "Too early to jump to conclusions, Jayne, but you're probably right. I don't believe in coincidences."

2

Dr Hamilton stepped into the detached house a full hour later, just after 2:00 p.m. Like before at Sean Wallace's house, he was dressed in a blue coverall and matching overshoes. He carried in with him a black shoulder bag – like a sports holdall without any branding – which contained his tools and equipment.

Within the basement scene, crime officers were busy

photographing and analysing the area, dressed in disposable white coveralls and carrying all sorts of recording, inspecting, and criminology equipment.

DI Baylem was in the living room speaking on his mobile phone with Chief Superintendent Mills, pacing as he talked, forewarning his superior with regards to that day's affairs. He was now attired similarly to the doctor in protective forensic clothing.

DS McCardle and Constable Manning were carrying out door-to-door enquiries, enjoying the afternoon heat, glad to be away from the stench of decay and the sight of death inside the house.

"You do know that I am a practising GP, don't you?" griped Hamilton as he entered the room where Baylem was wrapping up his call.

"Dead people have no manners," said Baylem sarcastically.

Hamilton grunted. "I've not even had time for lunch," he further complained in unison with the rumble of his stomach.

"You won't want lunch when you come and see this," stated Baylem. "Follow me. It's downstairs."

"Down?"

"A secret basement. Access is through here," Baylem led the doctor through the hallway, across the kitchen into the utility room. The opening in the floor was exactly how PC Anders had discovered it. "The room was built beneath–"

"For what purpose?" Hamilton asked, cutting him off.

Baylem didn't want to speculate. "It's this way," he said, stepping onto the wooden staircase going down. He didn't warn Hamilton about the low-level beam at the bottom.

A young woman in white coveralls was busily taking photographs of the three bodies as the policeman and the doctor descended the stairs, moving lightly around the scene so not to disturb anyone or anything. She turned to acknowledge the newcomers as they walked in from the small room annexing it.

Dr Hamilton was rubbing a bump to the right of his head, wincing slightly beneath caressing fingers.

"Give me a moment. I'm nearly done," said the photographer, rapidly depressing the trigger of her camera, moving around the room with the agility of a ballet dancer. Flashlight dazzled the room in sharp bursts, creating shadows that made the scene even more sinister and macabre.

The DI and the doctor watched impassively. Silently, they took in the picture. Hamilton soaked up the view, focusing on the three bodies enfolded together; two adults embracing a much smaller figure, their pose almost protective. Baylem studied the personal effects placed tidily around the room in boxes and on the bed. Predominantly girls' toys; dolls, stuffed animals, some educational and learning games, the DI guessed the age of the child to be somewhere between six and ten.

On the wall were some paintings and drawings, clearly made by the room's inhabitant; and one who wasn't artistically adept. Some of the images could easily have been produced by a four-year-old.

"All done," said the photographer, half-smiling, half-relieved. "I'll get out of your hair."

Baylem acknowledged with a nod but said nothing. Dr Hamilton felt it polite to say something, offering up a "Cheers," by way of gratitude. It sounded out of place, like he was accepting a beverage at a Starbucks. The photographer disappeared in a hurry through the narrow doorway and clattered away up the wooden staircase.

"Perky little thing, that one," observed Hamilton, nodding his head towards the sound of the retreating photographer. He studied her jiggling rump until it vanished from sight.

"Hmm?" Baylem wasn't listening, instead, he was mulling over the tragedy in front of him.

"Never mind," sighed the doctor. He stepped ahead of the detective and crossed to where the bodies were seated or propped, his focus drawn to their faces; the eyeballs swollen from their sockets; the tongues impossibly long and distended; the darkness of their flesh and the flakiness of their skin. Body fluids expelled naturally from the bodies after death and had dried into an indurate, coagulated mess beneath the chair.

"Can you tell me how they died?" asked Baylem, hopefully.

Hamilton removed some latex gloves from a pocket in his coverall and stretched them onto his hands. He squatted down close to the bodies. "Not yet," he replied with a sigh, undoing his bag and setting about his work. "Come back in an hour. I like to go about my business without an audience."

Without a further word, Baylem left Floyd Hamilton to get on.

Twenty minutes later, Baylem and McCardle were sitting in the Audi parked in amidst a row of marked police cars. On their laps were take-out packaging opened out to reveal a carton of fries and a burger in a bun. Baylem went for a 'full house' comprising of bacon, cheese, egg, salad, and an unhealthy dollop of mayonnaise and ketchup between triple layers of beef patties. McCardle, on the other hand, opted for a light-bite of just a single burger and the merest hint of salad garnish, with no sauces or condiments. Disposable cups with lids were placed in cup holders – one set in the dash, the other built into the car's door. Baylem had coffee, white with sugar; McCardle tea, white, without.

"A hell-of-a day," opined the sergeant, plucking out a couple of fries and delicately placing them into her mouth.

"And there I was at breakfast thinking I'd be spending the day in the office planning my football season." Behind them, in the distance, the football stadium could just be seen above some houses and through a dense collection of trees. Fulbarton Town

Football Club had designs of Premiership glory one day but only narrowly avoided relegation from the Championship the season just gone. Many considered the building of a thirty-thousand seat stadium was a waste of money, but supporters believed it reflected the owners' lofty ambitions.

"What's to plan?"

Baylem ignored the mocking tone. "Oh, you know. What away games to go to. How much I need to put aside for ancillary costs." Changing the subject, he asked: "Did the neighbours have anything to say?" Requiring both hands, he picked up his full house burger and took a big mouthful, filling his cheeks. Strips of lettuce coated in mayo dropped down into the carton, narrowly missing his shirt and tie.

McCardle finished chewing. "Not a lot," she started. "No one has seen the Jessops around for a while. Maybe a couple of weeks… could be longer. They moved in a couple of years ago. The man worked in the city as a banker or a lawyer; the woman, no one seems to know what she did for work. She seemed to dress smartly and was out a lot. Quite unassuming, they kept to themselves and the neighbours likewise, though they were cordial enough to exchange Christmas cards and token gifts.

"I asked if the Jessops had children, and everyone says the same. No. If they did, they kept them hidden away." McCardle lifted up her meagre burger and took a small bite.

"Isn't it a bit odd that no one knows anything about these… *Jessops*?" Baylem queried, taking another large mouthful of food.

"Not really," McCardle replied. "Visit any street in any town across the whole of the country, you'll probably find the same story. You'd be surprised how little most neighbours know about each other. Ask yourself the same question: what do you know about yours?"

Baylem thought about it for a moment as he chewed his food. McCardle had a point. He knew one side was an elderly woman called May and the other, a couple in their mid-forties with two children, but other than that, he was clueless. He didn't even know their surnames.

"Our paths rarely pass," he replied, conceding, "we all work, we're all busy... we're never in at the same time. I can see your point."

McCardle felt smug for a moment. It soon passed. "The world is getting smaller because of technology, yet people are growing more distant to one another, becoming less humane. Fifty years ago, everyone would know your business; now, you'd barely get an acknowledgement in the street. Fifty years from now, it will be even worse. We will all be strangers... *familiar strangers*...but strangers nonetheless."

It was sad but true. It was less a society these days, more a co-existence.

Glumly, the two detectives ate the rest of their meal silently, with just the noise from the police radio for background punctuated by the sounds of their chewing.

A few minutes later, Baylem spied Dr Hamilton exiting the house, removing the coverall and other items of forensic clothing as he went. He was carrying his bag out with him.

"Let's see if he can give us some answers." Putting aside his food, the DI hooked open the Audi's door and stepped out. Reluctantly, McCardle followed.

"Don't waste your breath asking, Baylem," Hamilton hollered as he walked towards the policeman, anticipating his question. "I can't give you cause of death. It's not like you see in the bloody movies or on Midsomer Murders; I'm a man of science, not a magician."

"Okay."

"I'll need to get the bodies back to the morgue and do a full post-mortem first; toxicology tests and the ilk."

"Fair enough," replied Baylem, surprising the doctor by not pressing for a guess or speculation.

"As for time of death…" he deliberated for a second, "anything from two to three weeks."

"They looked like they could've been dead months," said McCardle, appearing at Baylem's side.

"Factoring in temperature and humidity, the speed of decomposition can be increased exponentially. Anyway, my interim analysis is complete. I've left instructions for samples to be collected and for the bodies to be moved to Fulbarton General Hospital."

"Is there anything you can give us?" asked Baylem, a hint of desperation in his voice.

"Not pertinent to their deaths, I'm afraid. There was something peculiar about the eight-year-old girl."

"Eight-year-old girl?" queried McCardle, sounding like an echo. She wanted to know how he could be precise about her age.

"Go on," pressed Baylem, a little impatiently.

Sensing McCardle's unasked question, Hamilton added: "I found a locket hanging on a gold chain from her neck, with an inscription; it said 'To Melanie, on your 8th Birthday… love, mummy and daddy'. There was a date on the back. June 20th… this year."

"Jeez," McCardle felt a wave of sickness as the image of the basement leapt into memory. She had been trained to disassociate herself from such scenes of shock and terror. By personalising it, the doctor had peeled a layer of resilience away like it was an onion. A hideously disfigured, decomposed child's face filled her mind, a gold locket hanging from her neck.

"That wasn't the peculiarity," continued the doctor. "I found the girl's wrists handcuffed. She was secured to the arms of her chair."

CHAPTER FIVE

"GOOD AFTERNOON, HINKLEY WALSH INSURANCE. How can I help you?" Justin Piper was slouched in his ergonomic office chair, the headset hanging lopsided from the side of his head, the mouthpiece hovering an inch below his mouth. In front of him were a keyboard and a flat, widescreen computer monitor. His desk, entirely clear of clutter, was decorated with 'good luck' confetti and banners declaring:

Sorry You Are Leaving.

There was also an aqua-blue see-through cup half-full with what appeared to be diluted orange juice.

"*I'd like to make a claim,*" said a frail old voice at the end of the call.

You all do, Justin thought to himself unenthusiastically. "Okay. Can I take your name please?" He spoke disinterested, his mind having already left three hours before he physically could.

Around the large open-plan office, more than fifty call operators sat at desks in bays of six, with low-level partitioning separating each into small impersonal booths and bright, milky-white lighting which beamed down from the ceiling. Justin didn't know what was colder; the lighting or the air blowing out of the air con units fixed at various points into the ceiling. Hanging around the room were caller display boards placed strategically so staff could see telephony data at a glance.

Queue information, handler availability, calls presented, calls abandoned, and average wait time, conveniently on view to 'help' operators manage their 'call' and 'after-call' time effectively.

After a couple of minutes running through a series of security questions, Justin asked the million-dollar question:

"What are you wishing to claim for today?"

"*I've had a slight mishap with my television,*" the caller said. "*I was carrying it down the stairs… when I lost my balance. The TV slipped from my hands and crashed and bounced down to the bottom.*"

If Justin had heard this cockamamie tale once, he'd heard it at least three thousand times… especially in the run up to sporting events, such as the World Cup or the Olympics, when watching such fanfare was made the more enjoyable on a flash new telly. That one and that old chestnut: a tin of paint being knocked off a ladder whilst decorating. Some people thought insurance was there to use to replace their old crap instead of help mitigate the financial burden after a genuine mishap or disaster.

He sighed. He was so glad that this was his last shift at Hinkley Walsh. No more TV claims. No more arguments or complaints with customers unhappy with repudiations or declinatures – although he secretly relished those (often doing a moonwalk across the floor to celebrate).

And no more practical jokes. They would be sorely missed by him. There had been a lot of laughs, mostly at others' expense (especially Sonia's, who had been the brunt of most of them).

Tomorrow… a fresh start.

A brand new job looking after the family and a new beginning.

But first, one last gag; *a final hurrah to remember me by*, he thought. Though, that would be for later.

After five minutes, the claim was registered and the caller rang off. Justin peered over the top of the partition towards Steve, a veteran of the claims department having worked there nearly three years. "Don't you just love this job?" he gloated.

"Fuck off Justin," Steve was in the middle of handling a loss adjuster report in respect of a flood claim. He was busy raising payments and appointing suppliers and contractors to replace and repair substantial areas of damage. Despite the rebuke, he was Justin's best friend. For the moment, he looked a little stressed.

Taking no notice of Steve's request, Justin continued, "Yea, I think the job would be a lot easier if the customer knew how to claim properly. I mean, if they cut out the bullshit, our lives would be better..."

"Your life will be better tomorrow... when you don't have to deal with this crap anymore," stated Steve irritably.

"True, but I'm thinking about you... and my friends. The ones I'm leaving behind. I think I might write a book... 'How to make the perfect claim', I'll call it. I'll give helpful hints and handy tips on making claims... a 'dos' and 'don'ts' guide. Blast away some of those myths and highlight the easiest claims to make."

"Sounds like a guide to being fraudulent to me," asserted Steve with little reflection.

Justin ignored him. "I mean, for instance... why do people always knock an entire tin of paint over to make that 'carpet claim'," he raised two sets of fingers to accentuate the word. "A simple bottle of nail varnish would do the same damage," he started to laugh. "You know... the easiest claim to make is an accidental loss of money."

Next to him, Steve tossed aside his work, giving up on the loss adjuster report for a moment. When Justin got started, nothing would shut him up, not even an admonishing glare from the team leader or a quiet word from Elaina, the department manager.

"You just go to a cash machine, draw out as much cash as you want... *or can*, and remember to request a printed withdrawal advice at the end. Then, call your local police station or phone them a couple of hours later and report that your wallet is missing; say that you think you may have dropped it, pleading stupidity. They'll log your loss and give you a reference number. Armed with these two bits of information, call up your insurer and tell them you've lost your wallet. They'll register your claim no quibble and ask for substantiation, which you will already have. Once they have that, claim settled. Bosch! Even if they suspected something, how can they disprove your claim?"

"Ingenious," Steve meant it.

"I know! I have others too… freezer food… loss of luggage whilst on holiday… vet fees…"

"Vet fees?" Steve was sceptical.

"If you want to know more, you'll have to buy my book."

"I think we'll have to keep a careful eye on any claims you might make!"

Justin laughed, "No fear. I'm insured somewhere else. Never piss in your own pond, I say." With spying Elaina Banham heading their way, Justin trundled his attention back to his desktop and hit a button on his phone, accepting a new call.

2

As six o'clock flashed up on the caller display board, whoops and sighs of relief could be heard across the floor. One or two people were up out of their seats and immediately heading for the exit.

"There goes Shergar, first out of the stalls," muttered Justin loud enough for Steve to hear next to him. A skinny, ratty-faced woman with lank, mousey hair hastened for the door. Her weakest characteristic, and the one she was remembered for, was her raucous laugh; a cross between a cackle and a siamang gibbon's mating call, heard throughout the day, but predominantly in the afternoon as clocking-off time approached. "She doesn't realise that the saying 'last in, first out' applies mainly in the context of hiring and firing, and not the order of attendance."

Steve said nothing and just laughed. Unlike Shergar, his cachinnation did not draw any attention.

Swiftly, the open-plan office emptied of staff until only Steve, Justin, and the claims manager remained.

"Are you coming to the pub?" asked Steve, turning off his PC and straightening up his desk.

"Yea, in a bit," replied Justin. "I've arranged to meet everyone around seven. I've just got a couple of things to do first."

"Okay, matey. See you shortly," Steve buttoned up his jacket and flung a backpack onto his shoulder. "Night Elaina," he called up the office as he headed towards the exit.

Elaina Banham was standing over her desk preparing herself to leave. "Night Steve," she replied in a sing-song happy voice.

Justin watched Steve swipe his cardkey and bow out into the corridor where there were two elevators and doors leading to male and female toilets, and another to the stairs. When Steve disappeared, Justin returned to his work.

"I hope you aren't staying much longer Justin… after all, you're not being paid now it's after six." Elaina, who was tall for a woman – made taller by her red stilettos –, bore an uncanny resemblance to the British TV actress, Sarah Parish. If that wasn't striking enough, she had enormous breasts that Justin often found his eyes drawn to; the top three buttons on her blouse were always unbuttoned, revealing an enviable cleavage deep enough for Olympian Tom Daley to dive into.

"Nearly done," Justin replied. "I just wanted to finish off my work before I left. I won't be long."

Elaina smiled warmly. "That dedication will be missed," she said wistfully. "Good luck in your new *career*…" she wrinkled her nose at the word. "If you ever want to come back, just let me know."

"Thank you, Elaina," he meant it.

"Don't forget to hand your cardkey into security... oh, and can you close the window behind you before you leave." With that, Elaina turned her back to him, taking big strides towards the door.

"Will do," Justin said quietly. He watched Elaina go, his eyes following her beyond the exit, tracking her as she left the floor.

Behind him, the vertical blinds, half-closed, swayed back and forth, disturbed by a gentle breeze that came in through the window he had opened earlier that afternoon. He made a mental note to close it as soon as he carried out his plan.

Elaina disappeared through the door at the end of the short corridor, taking the stairs down.

When he was certain she was gone, Justin quickly finished working on his final claim and powered off the computer. From a window overlooking the road leading in (and out) of the carpark beneath ground level, he observed Elaina's yellow Mini Cooper whip up the road and turn right at the junction.

Satisfied he was alone, the practical joker set about the task he had remained behind to do.

From beneath his desk was a sports bag, a Head Retro Monte Carlo holdall, black and red. He unzipped it, immediately releasing a terrible smell which, surprisingly, had been contained within since nine that morning. He gagged and fought back tears from the strong odour assailing his nostrils, overcoming the urge to retch whilst reaching into the bag with both hands.

Partially wrapped in an orange Sainsbury's shopping bag, the five-day-old haddock no longer seemed like such a great parting gift to the claims handler. At just over forty-five centimetres long, the fish had been purchased from a market stall, especially for the occasion.

Taking the bag, Justin walked away from his desk towards the centre of the room, to where a black refuse bin was placed. From the single surveillance camera, anyone watching, or eventually reviewing video footage, would see what appeared to be the last worker going to the bins to get rid of some rubbish and then disappearing out of shot.

What they couldn't see were the drinks or snacks machines set around the corner from the bins or the water cooler with its inbuilt cup dispenser, the overhead dome camera's range only able to view ahead, behind, to the left, and to the right of its axis – not around corners. Confident that nobody was now watching, Justin leapt up onto a vacant desk. Still holding the orange bag containing his fish, he stretched up towards the ceiling with his right hand (the fish in his left) and jabbed at one of the ceiling tiles. Dislodging it a little, a small amount of dust fell onto his face. From somewhere, he could hear a gentle hum as though from an electrical source, possibly the elevator.

He wrinkled his nose and then sneezed, *ACHOOO!*

He stepped back a moment, allowing the tile to fall back into place. Rubbing his nose, he composed himself and steadied his hands. Reaching up to the tile a second time, this time he poked the polystyrene with a bit more force, directing the tile slightly away to fall to the side, revealing a section of crawlspace big enough for a small animal to roam about in, but not wide enough for a man. It didn't matter; he had no ambitions to get up there.

Sniggering to himself, Justin reached into the Sainsbury's bag, mentally recoiling from the feel of the haddock (which was by now warm and sweaty) and pulled it free. Not wishing to touch it any longer than he had to, he tossed the fish through the square gap in the ceiling, hearing it land with a satisfying 'thud' atop a few tiles closer to the centre of the room, near to the wiring and pipework leading to an air con unit.

On tiptoes, Justin poked his head up through the gap; warm,

stale air washed over him. It was hot above the ceiling and the humming sound seemed louder than before.

Thinking nothing of it, he squinted in the dinginess, urging his eyes to adjust to the gloom, to see where the smelly haddock had landed.

Too dark, he reached into his trousers' pocket for his phone, activated the torch function and brought it up into the space in the ceiling.

The bright luminance picked out the fish lying across a joist and two tiles. Feeling pleased with himself, he started to laugh at the likely outcome of his 'leaving' prank. The smell was already godawful; he dreaded to think how bad it would be in the morning after a night broiling within the stifling crawlspace.

He wondered who would discover it first. It wouldn't be Brian, the security guard. He'd overheard him telling someone once that he had no sense of smell, a result from having had nasal polyps when he was a child.

No, it would likely be Sonia, the butt of most of his practical jokes; this one would be the one she would remember him by.

The thought of Sonia logging into her phone first thing with that rotten stench filling her nose; her gagging as she answered her first call… the image brought a fit of giggles fighting its way to the surface. Quite meek, she would likely suffer in silence until Elaina came in… usually half an hour later.

Justin lowered his mobile phone, stooping down from the gap in the ceiling. Fumbling with the loose piece of polystyrene that had been pushed aside, he was about to pull it back over into place when he thought he saw movement from the corner of his eye. The narrow crawlspace was completely dark, so the likelihood was slim, but intrigue teased his mind.

From somewhere, the electrical hum continued to drone, perpetual to the point that it was barely noticeable, comingled with other, desensitised sounds (like taps dripping, wind blowing, birds chirruping, etc.) the brain habitually blocked out.

He raised the phone up, the torch function still in play and boosted his height by standing once again on tiptoes. Like background sounds, he no longer noticed the heat.

His eyes fell upon the haddock and then scanned to the right of it, towards where he thought he had seen something.

The low hum, which Justin thought was the elevator, cranked up a notch, ever-so-slightly, the change gradual and barely noticeable. In much the same fashion as a live frog doesn't grasp that it's being cooked in a pot of water on a gas burner, Justin didn't hear the buzzing.

Slowly, he followed his gaze with the aim of his phone's bright light; rotating his wrist to guide the beam in a swath in the general direction he thought he'd seen movement.

He sighed. "Must be imagin–" cutting the sentence short, a black, obscure mass billowed forward from deep within the crawlspace, propelled by a force that Justin was unprepared for. Instinctively, he dropped down from the ceiling in a flinch but not before the amorphous dark entity had funnelled out through the gap alongside him.

FLIES!

Thousands of them converged on Justin. He dropped his mobile phone, which clattered and then bounced off the desk. In a panic, he began flapping and backhand-swiping at the swarm that encompassed him.

"Go... get away! Shoo!" he heard himself screaming, like it made a difference. If he hadn't noticed the buzzing before, he was more than aware of it now; the drone drilled into his head almost as irreverently as they manoeuvred and harried him.

Forgetting that he was standing atop a desk, the ground literally moved from beneath his feet as he stepped blindly backwards and for a long moment, he felt like he was falling into a deep, dark cavern.

The flies that clamoured around, and more specifically behind him, parted as one to form a wide berth, momentarily giving off a disorganised appearance and flying haphazardly, allowing the man to fall the distance to the floor without crushing any of them beneath him.

As soon as the danger had passed the swarm of flies restored order and capitalised on Justin's prone, confused form; swooping down in an arc after him.

"What the hell is this? Help!" On his back within the space between the empty desks and the vending and water machines, Justin thrashed about, his arms flailing, his hands tearing at the flies which he came into contact, or landed on his face. Hundreds settled upon his body and many more aimed to land on his head, crawling into his hair, flying into his ears, nostrils, eyes, and mouth. Vigorously, he clawed at the insects entering the small orifices leading into his head, absently raking more out of his hair with his fingers and desperately batting others buzzing close-by away from his eyes.

Still, the flies advanced with reinforcements continuing to swell their numbers, flowing in a never-ending current from the square gap in the ceiling.

Rolling onto his front, Justin anticipated the flies' intentions, a sudden feeling of composure overcoming him and clarity filling his mind.

All I need to do is shield my face, and I'll be okay, he thought. Tucking his head down and hunkering up from the carpet onto his knees, he started to crawl, stopping every foot to skim flies away from his mouth and nostrils, but powerless (it seemed) to halt them amassing over his eyes. No sooner did he brush them aside, more converged, blocking out his vision. Blindly, he crawled some more, stopping again when a few flies managed to infiltrate his mouth with an inward breath, one making it down the back of his throat.

Justin coughed noisily. In the panic to dislodge the fly and spit it out, he inhaled five more. Angrily, he chewed down on them, mashing their small bodies between molars, crushing and pulping them, their texture and taste inexplicably disgusting, but he had worse things to worry about. He spat the carcasses out, all whilst continuing to flap, slap, flail, and thwack at the unceasing onslaught.

Crawling, inch-by-inch, Justin was doing enough to survive. He knew it. The flies sensed it. Although they had the numbers to their advantage and some clear biological enhancements that empowered them to mount such an audacious attack, these did little to counteract the fact that the man was doggedly-determined to defend their advances and vitally protect his air passage.

Spurred on by instinct alone, Justin edged closer to the main aisle that ran the length of the open-plan office, and more importantly, the area covered by the dome surveillance camera (which he had advertently put himself out of view from). Flies swooped down on him forcefully, raining blows against the side of his head and to the centre of his back.

Ignoring the pain, Justin shifted nearer to the opening.

Flies desperately burrowed into his eyes; others fruitlessly attacked his nose (which was blocked with squished fly bodies) and his mouth (which he kept firmly shut until the burning in his chest from holding his breath became too much).

Momentarily conceding, Justin screamed from the hurting and the itchiness that stung and irritated behind his eyes and the feeling of insects tunnelling into his head, towards his brain. He gasped for air, using a hand to shield his mouth from an unceasing, frenzied attack of bugs coming at him in a pressure spray. The constant shot blast of insects impacting his face caused welts, sores, and blistering to appear.

Forcing himself to ignore the discomfort and torment that the flies continued to bestow upon him, he inched nearer to the aisle. He knew, once out there, Brian would likely see him on the security VDU and come to his rescue.

That was if he wasn't out back smoking a cigarette (which he was often found to be doing). Or in the toilet doing whatever it was that kept him holed up for half an hour or more at a time.

Not your common house variety, the flies knew what Justin's intentions were. Seeing that their bombardment was not working, a simultaneous thought entered their tiny heads.

The mass of flies dispersed into a buzzing fog. Moments later, they formed two columns; one returning immediately to attacking Justin, barely allowing a moment's respite; the other, moving away purposefully towards the wall, flying just above the vending machines, particularly interested in the hot drinks machine that stood just an inch inside from where the aisle began, where Justin was now sidling past in his attempt at salvation.

The second unit of flies gathered at a place below the topmost edge of the vending machine's back panel, creating an orderly line half a dozen flies deep, filling the entire width of the cabinet. With the foundation laid, more flies joined the party, efficiently landing atop the first row, adding another layer, followed by more, then another, line after line, row after row. At fifteen flies deep, the gap between the vending machine and the wall was bridged. Still, the flies assembled, squeezing into the fray, applying pressure between the two objects; one immovable and the other anchored only by a cold water pipe and an electric cable, both attached at different points in the wall.

Simple physics explains that two solids cannot occupy the same space; with every extra fly taking up position, space had to be obtained from somewhere. Collectively, the insects knew that if they held strong, used momentum and focused wholly on an idea, the desired outcome would be realised. That outcome required the use of a device to act as a weight-bearing jack, like a hydraulic rescue tool that firemen used to force open car doors in accidents; something that would push with enough force to create movement.

That weight-bearing jack was none other than the flies themselves, one after another flying into place, compressing and sacrificing themselves between the wall and vending machine, little by little causing the drinks cabinet to lean forward; the bottom edge, towards the rear, lifting ever-so-slightly from the floor.

Bolstered by the barest movement, flies flew in ever-faster, increasing the angle with which the machine was now leaning, gravity still favouring an upright balance, but not for much longer.

Now only a couple of inches away from the aisle, Justin was feeling exhausted. The fight to keep the flies out from his mouth and the effort in crawling away, despite the distance being barely four side-steps, was taking its toll. He clawed at the carpet, digging his fingers into the fibres for traction, hoping to drag himself the final steps. One or two nails bent back from his finger, ripping free and starting to bleed.

The column of flies harrying Justin deserted him, giving the man a glimmer of hope. They ascended to the ceiling, turned sharply in a reverse 'L' and joined the tail end of column one, augmenting the swelling numbers that were pushing the vending machine so that it was now leaning precariously forward. The only thing keeping it up was the water pipe, the hose pulled taut, almost beyond stretching point.

Spying the tip of Justin's finger – all bloody and missing a nail – stretching out into the aisle, the remaining flies gave up an order and threw themselves into the final assault. In a giant fist formation, the flies hurtled towards the back of the leaning vending machine, exacting more combined force than a bullet discharged from a Smith and Wesson Magnum.

Two things happened.

The first, under the strain caused by the sheer number of flies against the back of the vending machine, the hose connecting it to the water supply split in two, creating a jet of water to burst out in all directions in a frothy spray.

The flies' second and final objective, saw the vending machine topple completely over, crashing heavily on top of Justin.

Before he was able to exert one final push, the weight of the drinks machine had crushed his vertebrae, knocked all the air from his lungs and pinned him to the floor. Still conscious and paralysed from feeling any pain, Justin slowly turned his head to where the vending machine had once stood. With sore eyes and blurring vision, he saw the remnants of a very bad dream.

From floor to ceiling, concealing the wall in its entirety was a blanket of twitching, undulating, blackness.

The flies watched… and waited.

"H-e-l-p!" Justin croaked.

In response, the flies issued a single, buzzing sound. It echoed mockingly, almost like a laugh, though abhorrent and evil.

Justin lowered his head to the floor in defeat.

The flies allowed him to take a couple of shallow, carefree breaths, before telepathically communicating the order to finish it.

En masse, the insects leapt from the wall and floated down towards Justin, falling onto his weeping, pustulated face, crawling unimpeded into his mouth and any other opening leading into his body, including a nasty wound to the side of his face adjacent to his upper jaw bone.

Swiftly, the former Hinkley Walsh claims handler blacked out from lack of oxygen, relieved that the horror was finally over. For all tense and purposes, he was dead, but clinical death wouldn't follow for a little over four minutes when all brain function had come to an end.

Knowing that he was still alive – although barely – the flies took pleasure in concluding their enterprise. The males took a feast from the cadaver, the females laid their eggs.

Within minutes, they were finished and, one by one, they

departed, retreating from the scene individually and inconspicuously, rather than the vast swarm they had arrived in. Flitting about the room, they headed towards the only discernible exit; a window at the far end of the office, open just a crack, highlighted by the rattling vertical blinds. Slipping through the half-closed slats, the flies escaped into the mild summer evening, floating into a warm current.

Despite their discretion, a bystander outside the insurance building would later report seeing something strange. He would claim seeing what he thought was a smoky substance billowing out through a window from the third floor. At first, he thought nothing of it... but the shape of its movement, rippling haphazardly in an unpredictable fashion, it reminded him of starlings, how they flew in a swooping mass... referred to as a murmuration. He watched for a couple of minutes, mesmerised by the manifestation, before shrugging off his fascination and going on his way.

3

At the security desk, Brian glanced at his digital watch.

6:30 p.m.

Only half an hour before clocking off time, he thought.

In front of him were three flat screens; one displaying a grid split into six, broadcasting live images from surveillance cameras placed strategically around the building; another provided a visual of all personnel in the building at any time in a list, including what floor they were on; and the final screen was hooked up to the insurance company's computer network, allowing the security guard access to the internet and secretly, to Netflix which he covertly watched films or episodes of Orange Is the New Black.

It was around the time he would begin his final building check, where he would visit each of the four floors, turn off all the lights, check the toilets, and lock the doors before setting the motion detectors and intruder alarms.

As he was about to start his rounds, he checked the staff tracker, which the HR manager referred to as 'employee management' software. Triggered by an employee's cardkey once swiped into the building, the programme registered all the rooms visited and how long staff was in there. The cynics amongst Hinkley Walsh's ranks believed it was just a tool to check how often – and how long – individuals spent going to the toilet.

Not expecting to see any names registering, Brian was surprised to see Justin Piper's was appearing; the only person (apart from him) apparently still in the building. He was still checked into the third floor, the claims department.

"You're working late," Brian mumbled, which he found surprising as he knew it was Justin's last day. He had a note somewhere to remind him to collect the claims handler's cardkey at the end of his shift (which he had forgotten until now after seeing the man's name on the screen). "Guess we'd better gee you up," he said. "It's time to go home."

Collecting his own cardkey from the desk and a bunch of keys from the top drawer, Brian made for the gap between the high reception desk and the wall, but not before scooping up a heavy-duty rubber torch. Although he never used it, and being at the height of summer didn't require it as dark fall wasn't expected for three more hours, Brian liked the feel of it in his hand, thinking it made him look more authoritative, like it were a truncheon. In America, he reflected, he would have had a gun strapped to his waist.

Swiping his card to open the turnstile barrier, Brian stepped through to the area in front of the pair of elevators.

He pressed the 'up' button.

Immediately, one of the elevator doors opened. The security

guard stepped in, pressing the '3' on the control panel. The doors closed behind him as he circled round to face the front.

Slowly, the elevator ascended, passing the first floor and then the second. After twenty seconds of travelling, the number '3' appeared on the red LED panel, followed by an electronic *BING!*

The doors opened and Brian stepped out into a short corridor. To his right were the doors to the stairs and toilets, to his left the entrance to the open-plan office. Using his cardkey, he opened the door and walked into the claims department. The door closed slowly behind him.

Turning right, he walked to where he knew Justin's desk was located, made easier to spot by the 'Good Luck' and 'Sorry You're Leaving' banners festooned about the man's workspace.

Of Justin, there was no sign.

A strong smell of fish assailed his nostrils before he had the chance to see Justin's bag on the desk, forcing Brian to step back and cover his nose with a hand. The window behind him was open, the vertical blinds rattling against the wall and clanging the radiator beneath.

"Jeez... what the..." he didn't finish the sentence.

Peering up the office, the security guard could see that something wasn't right. Just ahead of the wall to his left, which extended around a corner (approximately at the halfway point of the room), he could see part of the drinks machine lying in an impossible position, fallen just over the threshold of the aisle, and a pool of spreading water.

Brian ran the distance; his torch held ahead of him like it was a pistol. "Oh my God!" he exclaimed as he located Justin Piper, crushed beneath the vending machine. But something about the way he looked didn't make sense.

And the drinks machine, how could that have fallen in such a way?

Involuntarily he vomited, bending over and turning at the

same time so not to projectile onto his shoes or clothing. The taste, comingled with the strong smell of old fish made him retch again, bringing more puke and watery eyes.

Staggering to the nearest phone, the security guard lifted the receiver and pressed '9' for an outside line. With the dial tone burring in his ear, he punched in '999'.

"*Emergency. Which service?*" a female operator immediately filled his ear.

"Err, um... there's been a..."

What? An accident?

"...An in-in-incident," he heard himself stuttering.

He tried to calm down, took a deep breath (which was a mistake as the rancid fish smell made him want to vomit again). He spoke slower, articulating each word. "Someone is dead... or at least hurt real bad."

"*What's happened, sir?*" asked the operator.

Brian backhanded spew away from his mouth, absently wiping it on the outer thigh of his trousers.

"I don't know," he said.

He didn't.

"It's one of my co-workers... Please send someone quick! I haven't a clue how... but he's lying flat beneath a drinks machine."

Chapter Six

/

Fulbarton General Hospital, located to the north-east of the town, was spread over three floors across two large buildings. On turning into the grounds, a roundabout was placed in the centre of a wide road, directing traffic to the left, right or ahead, depending on what department or entrance was sought and which carpark had available spaces.

Baylem was alone having left Jayne McCardle at the station to pursue other lines of enquiry. She was more suited to the desk job, whereas he hated being confined within four walls.

He steered the Audi ahead in the direction of the 'Accident and Emergency' department. Despite the vast carpark, there were very few spaces for visitors. Baylem took the car to a space designated for Dr Patel in orthopaedics and keyed off the ignition.

The clock built into the dashboard displayed the time: 07:11 p.m.

It had been four hours since Dr Hamilton had finished his preliminary examination of the bodies at sixty-three Claringdon Street and almost seven since attending the scene of Sean Wallace's death on Surbiton Road.

Heading into the hospital, DI Baylem couldn't help showing

his distaste for the place, turning his nose up at the sick and injured he passed. The smells associated with hospitals made him absently stifle his nose with the thumb and index finger of his left hand. Purposefully, he walked through the double-doors leading in, turning left towards a dingy corridor beyond a small, empty waiting area. To his right was the accident and emergency department which, from the sounds emanating, appeared to be inordinately busy.

A short walk down the corridor was an internal set of double-doors, beyond which were stairs leading up and down; architects would describe the type as 'L-shaped'. Upwards were the second and third floors where various wards, including intensive therapy, could be found; a two star hotel for the sick and dying. Downstairs was a contradiction. Less a hotel, more a storage place for inanimate things, including the dead. The hospital's morgue was located amongst a number of rooms and it was the course which Baylem was headed.

The DI pushed open one of the doors and hurried through, taking the steps down two at a time. Without realising, he whistled a tune, nothing recognisable, just a melody of his own making.

At the bottom of the 'L-shaped' stairs, Baylem pushed through another door and entered a cold, dimly-lit corridor that was wide enough to push a hospital ward bed down with space either side for a couple of passers-by. It ran the entire length of the hospital. On the wall was signage highlighting the various departments that occupied the floor, chief support services that required little or no visitors.

Amongst them were supply management, filing, storage, hazardous waste disposal (the incinerator) and office space for training and seminars. Most significantly was the mortuary, a place where the dead were discretely taken, the departure lounge to their final destination.

It was where the detective now headed.

Although the basement wasn't a frequent place for civilian visitation, there were occasions – rare in Fulbarton – when bodies required identification. Out of necessity, the morgue could be found close to the floor's main entrance; an easy passage for any unfortunately stepping on to this floor. Baylem only needed to take half a dozen steps before he was standing at the threshold.

Sensing the DI's arrival, Dr Hamilton appeared at the double-doors, pulling them open theatrically. "There you are, Baylem. You're just in time for the main event... this way." Garbed in surgical scrubs, a matching cap containing his dark hair and a plastic apron streaked with gore, he looked menacing. All that was missing was a blood-stained cleaver and he could have walked straight off the page of a Richard Laymon novel.

Following the doctor in, Baylem entered a short corridor off which a couple of doors stood closed and one, a little way along, that wasn't. The nearest set of doors Baylem knew was the room where all the bodies were kept for storage. Within were three chrome mortuary cabinets, each front loading with space for six bodies, all refrigerated. It was commonly referred to as the meat locker.

Hamilton strode past towards the door that was open, the bright light spilling out cold and uninvitingly.

"I have all the bodies from Claringdon Street laid out in here," declared the doctor ostentatiously, stepping into a large operating room. "I've done most of my work." Four autopsy tables were spaced out within the room; each was stainless steel with a small sink built within at the end. Each supported a dead body.

Baylem reluctantly followed him in. No matter how much preparation, you could never be prepared for the sight of an autopsy room, especially one in the throes of a post-mortem.

"I finished on the chap from Surbiton Close a little while ago. He's over there," Hamilton nodded in the direction of the furthest table. A white sheet had been settled neatly over Sean Wallace's body. "Very interesting," he said, prudently.

"Really?"

"Can you close the door behind you?" asked the doctor, not adding anything further regarding the first body recovered that day. "You can grab some protective clothing from in there," Hamilton pointed towards a large metal cupboard. "These things can get terribly messy... but not half as bad as working on a live one."

Baylem flashed a look which the doctor interpreted as curiosity.

"No arterial circulation," he explained, "so no blood sprays."

The DI trotted across to the cupboard, pulled open a door and saw three boxes containing surgical gowns, disposable coveralls, and aprons. He helped himself to a green coverall and stepped into it. From the waist up, he secured the plastic studs all the way to his neckline. He wished he could carry on up and over his nose. The smells from the bodies, mingling with the clinical aroma of the hospital and an undertone of formaldehyde was overpowering.

Hamilton didn't look affected by the stench at all. He instead walked about, breathed and talked unrestrained, desensitised to the sight and smells associated with death and decay. "Dental records were easily procured with regards to the two adult bodies we removed from Claringdon Street," he said. "Without question, they are the Jessops. Tobias and Julie. Forty-four and forty-one, respectively."

The doctor walked between the two tables, the naked bodies of Mr and Mrs Jessop either side of him; owing to decomposition and the state of being in mid-autopsy, if it wasn't for genitalia, they would have been indistinguishable from each other. Both of their chests had been cracked open and flesh had been flayed apart to reveal internal organs from the stomach up to their necks. He turned to face DI Baylem, "I doubt you want to hear all the boring stuff." Hamilton was, of course, referring to the weights and measurements taken of body parts from each corpse. He reached down to a clipboard which was hanging from a hook on one of the metal tables.

"Yea, spare me the fine detail," Baylem confirmed.

On the clipboard were a couple of sheets of paper. The topmost one was a diagram of the human body. The doctor had scrawled down notes and measurements all around it. "Okay, nothing untoward regarding their internal organs," he started. "The spleen, intestines, and the stomach are all in quite advanced stages of decomposition. The kidneys, liver, and heart... they're a bit hardier, though also in quite a bad shape. You can tell the bodies have been dead for a bit, just by the colour of the flesh."

Baylem had come to that conclusion in the basement of the Jessop's home earlier that day just by smelling them.

"Gaseous by-products from the breaking down of cells cause anaerobic bacteria to convert haemoglobin molecules into sulfhaemoglobin. It's the presence of this molecule settling within the blood that gives the flesh its greenish, purply-black appearance... that almost marbled-effect."

"Does it help with time of death?" Baylem hazarded a guess of around three weeks.

"Factoring in environmental temperatures–" it had been stifling in the room below ground level "–I'd say the victims died about eleven days ago."

"Okay. What about the cause of death?"

"Well, that's the million-dollar-question, isn't it?" Hamilton replied without humour. "There are no visible wounds or signs of trauma from what I can see. Had there been just one body, one could easily attribute death to a myocardial infarction, and we'd focus our attention on that; but three? It's not likely. Also, the way they were found; the adults were sitting in a protective manner, ahead of the child. It's like they were trying to shield her from something.

"When there are no clear signs of cause of death, we then

consider asphyxiation. Sometimes accidental asphyxiation occurs, especially in confined spaces. Lack of oxygen and a build-up of carbon dioxide often results in a very swift death but this is unlikely in this instance, especially in view of the condition of the bodies. And there's also the presence of so many flies to consider."

"I was going to ask about that," interposed the DI.

"If the room was void of oxygen, then the flies would not have been able to live in there either. So, we can rule out accidental death."

"Couldn't the flies have died in there with them?"

"No," Hamilton replied without hesitation. "And you'll see why in a moment."

Baylem made a long, explosive sigh as he came to terms with what that entailed. "The Chief Super is not going to like this. There hasn't been a murder in Fulbarton in three years."

"I'm not entirely sure murder is the cause, either," said the doctor cryptically. "Come and take a look at this."

Baylem took a few steps, matching the doctor for pace as he followed him to the head of the table.

From an instrument trolley, Hamilton picked out a sterilised scalpel and towered above Tobias Jessop's body. "I hope you weren't planning on eating tonight," he said.

"I doubt I'll ever eat again," he muttered in response.

Hamilton pretended not to hear. "Now, asphyxiation was my gut instinct and this I can prove. Take a look at his eyes." The ping-pong balls were still pushed out of their sockets. Where Baylem had shied away from them before, he was now more attentive.

"Are they bloodshot?"

"Bingo! All three bodies are the same."

"What caused it?" asked Baylem.

"No signs of a struggle; no environmental oxygen deprivation. It had to have been caused by something quickly and something which the three of them saw coming... hence the way we found the adults, posed in that protective stance."

"Do you know or are we dancing around in circles?"

Hamilton smiled patiently and nodded slowly. Confidently and with steady hands, he placed the scalpel on Tobias Jessop's neck and cut an incision line three inches downward towards his chest. Putting aside the cutting instrument, the doctor used both hands to prise an opening just beneath the man's throat, revealing a compressed black mass.

"Jesus!" exclaimed Baylem, raising a hand to his mouth and pressing it tightly. It was either to suppress any further utterance or to retain his stomach contents which had been threatening to bubble up his oesophagus since entering the room.

"Flies... hundreds of them, compressed in so as to cause a tight and effective blockage, creating what we would call in the business, 'a foreign body airway obstruction'. Against my better judgement, I'd say the cause of death was asphyxiation due to a very swift introduction of these insects entering into their mouths and nasal passages. Loss of consciousness would have been rapid."

Baylem regained composure and lowered his hand from cupping his lips. "Were the flies forced into their mouths?"

Hamilton shook his head, "I don't believe so." Picking out a long-handled instrument with a small, spoon-like end, he leaned over the deceased and poked it into the dissection. "Here... look at this." Gently, he scooped out one of the flies like he was picking out a piece of chocolate from an ice cream sundae. It was fat and bloated and appeared to be in good shape. The doctor lifted the surgical spoon up so they both could inspect it closer. "If the flies had been manually forced down their throats, I would imagine they would have been crushed in the process. By the looks of this fella, you can see that's not the case; he's dead but in perfectly good condition.

"Also, there's a question mark with regards to the flies scattered around the floor of the bodies."

Baylem remembered seeing them all over the place. McCardle had argued that their presence added credence to her serial killer theory.

"I found trace evidence of organic matter belonging to the flies on the flats of both Mr and Mrs Jessop's hands. Comparatively, the fly samples I swept up from the floor show signs of injury from impact – as from blunt force impact, or in other words, likely resulting from the act of being swatted."

"Are you suggesting the Jessops were attacked by flies?"

"Farfetched, isn't it just? But that's my explanation for their deaths. The girl's, too, I'd add."

Baylem turned his head slightly towards the furthest autopsy table. The small girl was spread out and arranged in much the same way as Mr and Mrs Jessop. An image of her small body, cuffed to the chair, filled his mind. "Is there anything you can tell us about the girl?" he asked morosely.

Hamilton walked casually away from the table supporting Tobias Jessop and moved towards the fourth table, upon which the small girl was laid out like a butchered animal. "She's eight years old and shares the same blood type as Mrs Jessop. I've sent for a DNA profile to determine parentage, but I think it's obvious she was their daughter."

"Why was she handcuffed to the chair?"

The doctor shrugged, "You're the detective, that's your department. However, it could be a strange way of dealing with her condition."

"Condition?"

"Yes. It appears she had an underlying medical problem. Cerebral palsy from the looks of things. Further tests will confirm this. Maybe it was a coping mechanism or perhaps the girl was aggressive or liable to harm herself... or others. I don't think it is conducive to her cause of death."

"Nonetheless, it's a mystery that requires solving," Baylem thought aloud.

"Maybe."

"Why would a parent cuff their child to a chair and hide them away in a secret room?"

Hamilton shrugged, making no offer of an explanation. "All I can add is, although she was locked away, there are no signs of physical abuse, sexual or otherwise. She could have been locked away for her own good."

"Well, that's what perverts and crazy people say to justify their actions," replied Baylem, brusquely. "But, with the Jessops dead…" he sighed, "somehow I doubt we will ever know." He turned away from her, parking that line of enquiry for a moment. "What about the body we picked up from Surbiton Close?"

"Sean Wallace?" replied Hamilton. "Yea, I finished up with him first. That's what makes this whole thing the more interesting."

"How so?"

"He died in much the same way as the Jessops; the same species of fly clogging up his throat, the same asphyxiation, and the same outcome. The only difference, he put up a little bit more of a struggle."

2

Baylem found DS McCardle in the incident room back at Fulbarton Police headquarters forty-five minutes later. Half her attention was focused on an article she had Googled filling her computer screen, the other half was teasing noodles from an aluminium container onto a plastic fork. It was becoming a habit eating take-out food, however, her slim figure and low cholesterol level belied this. Alongside the tray was a greasy paper bag half-filled with chicken balls. A polystyrene cup nearby was open, brimming with an orange sweet and sour sauce that had dripped on the desk.

"What did Hamilton have to say?" she asked as Baylem crossed the room and slipped off his jacket. She forked noodles and fried vegetables into her mouth.

The DI crossed the small office to his desk. In addition to McCardle's, there were three others; two belonging to detective constables and another, no longer used (though cluttered with files and loose papers).

"The damnedest thing," Baylem replied, settling into his leather executive chair. He stretched his legs out ahead of him and placed his hands behind his head as he leaned back. "The damnedest thing," he repeated softer, almost a whisper.

"Well?" pushed McCardle, finishing her mouthful.

Baylem straightened up in the chair, crossed his arms, and leaned across his desk. "You were right," he said. "The flies are important, and appear to be a link to both these cases." The DI proceeded to brief his sergeant with everything he had learned from Dr Hamilton.

"So... am I getting this straight?" said McCardle. "All four victims were killed by flies, forced into their airways, causing death by asphyxiation?"

"It appears that way, yes."

McCardle shook her head in disbelief. "Who does that? And how?"

"Not sure anyone did! I called into forensics on the way back and there's no signs of forced entry into either of the properties; no evidence of an intruder or third-party involvement in any of the deaths. They dusted for prints... nothing. They found plenty of flies though; all over the place. All evidence seems to indicate that the insects entered the houses of their own free will and attacked their victim's respiratory systems voluntarily," Baylem chuckled mirthlessly. "I've never seen anything like it; Hamilton neither.

He cut open each of their throats to reveal the flies – hundreds of them – tightly compressed together in a fashion that made an airtight obstruction. It was like opening up a Fray Bentos pie, though not as appetising. The obstruction was very effective."

McCardle started to laugh. "Nothing you are saying makes any sense," she said. "Flies aren't intelligent creatures. They don't go around killing people... that's absurd!"

"I know!" Baylem's chuckle turned into a hearty laugh like McCardle had just cracked the funniest joke he'd ever heard.

"What about the girl? She was handcuffed. Who is she and how does she fit in?"

Baylem hadn't forgotten about her but how she was linked seemed like a footnote, almost an irrelevance. He couldn't find a reason to think there was a link to how she died. Sure, there was something untoward going on there with regards to her and the Jessops, but the manner of her death with which they were investigating seemed to stand apart from her specific story.

He took a long moment to think up a response. "I think she was their daughter," he eventually said, "who they didn't want anyone to know about. They kept her imprisoned in the basement beneath the floor. Why? We may never know. It's sad but unlikely pertinent to the case. For the time being, let's focus on her death and that of her parents, and Sean Wallace. I'll get an analyst to look at their past history in due course."

"Flies?" the sergeant's voice was saturated with sarcasm. She had barely heard another word Baylem had said after his assertion.

"Yes... flies."

"To do what you've suggested," reflected McCardle, full of doubt, "would not only require the flies to work in conformity, they'd need to somehow communicate with each other." It didn't just sound nonsensical, it sounded ridiculous. "What about the broken window at the Jessops'? Isn't that evidence of a break-in?"

Baylem shook his head; his laughter was long-forgotten. "No.

The glass was smashed from the inside… and as crazy as this sound, all evidence directs us once again to the cause also being from the flies. I don't understand the science of it but apparently, it's all down to velocity and concentrated effort."

"Meaning?"

"The flies flew fast at the same spot on the glass, one after another, over and over, like a tiny hammer-drill, bang-bang-bang; though many died in the process of the cause. It answers the question why we found all those dead insects scattered around the kitchen."

"What about the dead ones on Sean Wallace's bed?" queried McCardle, picking holes in the theory.

"All died as a result of Sean fighting them off. Hamilton found trace evidence of fly DNA on and about his hands. On studying the dead flies, he deduced they had perished from a swat or crushing."

"You do know it all sounds like crap, don't you?" McCardle was direct and no longer amused by her superior.

"You're right, Jayne. It sure is a mystery," Baylem replied honestly, drawing his hands together in a clasp and resting his head on them, as though deep in thought.

"The chief is not going to buy it."

"I know. I might not tell him."

As though hearing an invite, Chief Superintendent Mills appeared at the door, entering like a ninety-mile-per-hour gust of wind. "Baylem… my office." It wasn't a request and he disappeared almost as fast as he had arrived to avoid any protest or signs of insubordination. Blink and you would've missed him.

"He's working late," observed the sergeant.

Unmoved, Baylem shuffled in his seat. "Anyway, what have you been up to? Not just stuffing your face with Chinese?"

"Researching," McCardle said, "serial killers… and flies. Oh, and something else that may be interesting. But it all can hang until you get back. You'd best not keep the chief waiting…"

CHAPTER SEVEN

T HE TOWN HALL, PLACED WITHIN the heart of Fulbarton's town centre, was built in 1870 in a grandiose Victorian style. A magnificent tower taking pride of place at the centre of a gabled roof housed an illuminated four-dial turret striking clock which was commissioned from the makers of London's Big Ben. A still functioning bell rang on the hour up to midnight, starting again at seven a.m.

As Edwin Carslake's chauffeur-driven black Jaguar pulled up outside, the auspicious timepiece clanged eight times, ringing in the hour. The town's elected Member of Parliament climbed out of the vehicle, met at the kerbside by a grey-haired man wearing bifocals, an off-the-rack charcoal grey suit and a red scarlet checked tie. Draped over his shoulders and hanging opulently across his chest was the mayoral collar.

"Mr Carslake... how fine it is to see you again!" greeted the mayor, Dennis Matthews. He took the MP's hand and, whilst pumping it, he faced a photographer, booked for the occasion by the local newspaper.

"You know me, Dennis... always happy to lend my support to such a worthy cause."

Flashes of light dazzled the two men as the photographer took shot after shot. Mayor Matthews grinned like it was his wedding day.

After a long minute, the photographer thanked them and then returned his camera to a shoulder bag.

"I hear there's been some troubles locally... a number of unexplained deaths?" The mayor spoke casually, as though making conversation.

"Oh, it's nothing, Dennis. I've been assured by the Police Commissioner that nothing untoward has happened; nothing that will blemish Fulbarton's crime statistics at any rate. Accidental deaths on all accounts."

"That's reassuring. Of course, a strange coincidence if you ask me. What d'you make of the flies?"

"Who told you about that?" challenged the MP. As far as he was concerned, this information was classified.

"I have my sources," he replied diffidently, half-smiling. "Shall we?" Ending further discussion, the mayor gestured for the MP to follow him up a flight of steps at the front of the building. Leading across a wide entrance foyer, they entered a grand function room through a large double-door entranceway, to the front of which was a stage. A podium had been installed and behind it was an arrangement of musical instruments; drum kit, guitars, and keyboards. A line of microphone stands stood to attention at one side.

"How many tickets did you sell?" asked Edwin, more for small-talk rather than genuine interest.

"Five hundred," replied the mayor. "Mostly business leaders and people of exemplary reputation. We're hoping that a good many will make some generous donations this evening, and that their generosity will encourage others in the community to follow suit."

"Yea, well. I'll do what I can to get the ball rolling. Tell me, who's the headline act?"

"Oh, some American girl... *Makayla* or some such. She was our benefactor's favourite artist. Apparently a big pop star, but I've never heard of her. The record company is donating her time, thinking the publicity will be good for her image."

"I think she had a number one album last year," the MP endorsed. He kept it to himself, but he secretly admired the music starlet.

"I wouldn't know," persisted the mayor, leading the politician towards the centre stage. "Anyway, if you are happy to get things underway, I'll introduce you."

Two minutes later, the grand function room was full and the MP was standing beneath a warm spotlight behind the podium, a microphone propped in front of him.

"Ladies and Gentlemen, thank you for coming to support the Daryl Figgis Cancer Trust fundraiser," he started, his voice booming through the PA system. "With your generosity, we are hoping to raise enough money to build a specialist child cancer clinic in Daryl's name.

"Most of you will know that Daryl battled an inoperable brain tumour courageously earlier this year. He captured our hearts with his unceasing positivity and unwavering bravery. We followed all the 'ups' and 'downs' of his tragic illness, through the magic and intrusion of social networking; his daily blogs and hourly tweets were a source of encouragement, and surprisingly of immense enjoyment." The MP paused to take a sip of water from a glass left in front of him.

"During his short battle, Daryl himself set up the Daryl Figgis Cancer Trust, selflessly putting others ahead of himself. Not to detract from the treatment he received locally, but it was his intention to see improvements in cancer care for young people, seeing and experiencing first-hand the inadequacies and budget constraints the local NHS trust are under, a travesty you will know that I laboriously campaign against. Improved waiting times, better screening procedures and enhanced cure and recovery rates

– these were his aspirations, highlighting a maturity far ahead of his seven years.

"He knew it was too late for him when he created the Darryl Figgis Cancer Trust, but he wasn't willing to give up the fight, directing the remnants of his energy to help others – a legacy that I want to play a small part in honouring. With your help, and following Darryl's spirit, I'd like for us fortunate to be here today to help see Daryl's ambitions realised."

Around the grand function room, the audience broke out into a thunderous applause. It reminded Edwin of the time when he had taken the stage at his first Conservative party conference in Brighton four years earlier, warming up the audience before the PM was set to take the stand. He had championed the government's austerity programme of cuts, had spieled his 'the future's golden' speech and promised that he would do 'everything in his power' to return the 'Great' back to 'Great Britain'. Inevitably, his address overshadowed the prime minister's, inveigling many in the audience to hail him as the future of the party, some touting him as the next Tory leader.

Edwin Carslake waited for the noise in the hall to die down before bringing his address to an end. "Thank you, thank you," he said in recognition of his audience's veneration.

Silence descended the room.

"Politicians are often accused of saying things more over doing them. So…, I'm going to break from tradition–" a few people laughed in the audience, "–by pledging the first donation." Slipping a hand inside his jacket, he withdrew a chequebook, which he opened out and placed on the podium. "I am writing a cheque for fifty thousand pounds." He quickly scrawled on the pad, elaborately pulling it free from the perforated stub and holding it up to the audience for inspection. "The target is for two million pounds by the end of the night. I've told our headline act… MAKAYLA–" a few people cheered at her mention, "–that she should only come out when that figure has been reached."

Playful boos echoed around the function room.

The MP had a giant grin on his face. "Get those chequebooks out, ladies and gentlemen. You know what to do! I'll pass you back to the mayor of Fulbarton." He stepped away from the podium, stopping briefly a little distance towards the stage exit where mayor Matthews had appeared. The mayor put on a show of thanks by shaking his hand and accepting the man's cheque, a moment captured once again by the photographer for the local press.

"Ladies and gentlemen, give it up for our esteemed parliamentarian." Obeying the mayor, a deafening roar of claps, whoops, cheers and whistles filled the air.

Before disappearing backstage, Edwin took a bow towards the audience.

"Thank you, Edwin, and thank you for your donation of fifty thousand pounds!" The mayor held it up high for inspection. "Now, you don't have to give quite as much as that... but, of course, don't let me stop you! If you can make cheques payable to the Darryl Figgis Cancer Trust, and post them into the letterboxes we have placed around the room, we'll give you a running total as the night wears on.

"Now, despite Edwin's assertions that we need to raise two million pounds BEFORE Makayla comes on stage, she will, in fact be here – LIVE – in just half an hour's time." Once again, on the mention of the American starlet's name, cheers followed and the noise level within the audience swelled. "Get yourselves a drink and write those cheques whilst you wait!" The mayor stepped away from the microphone and left the stage.

2

Makayla was diminutive at just under five feet in height. With long, brunette hair, a heart-shaped face and azul-blue eyes, she was by far the best looking woman in the room.

Wearing little more than a bow knot white lace negligee more suited to the bedroom than centre stage at a pop concert, the singer revealed too much flesh that made the male members of the audience very hot and the women cringe with embarrassment or disgust. Strutting around barefoot, the American paced energetically from one side of the platform to the other, a cordless microphone held up to her lips.

Over the course of an hour and a half, Makayla changed her costume eight times (nothing less revealing) and performed songs from her first album and hits from her second. She also performed a rendition of *Mrs Robinson*, the song by Simon and Garfunkle, which she substituted the 'Mrs' with 'Mr', intending (it seemed) to tantalise and titillate the men in attendance, a play on film *The Graduate*'s theme of an older woman seducing a younger man, but in reverse.

"*Coo, coo, ca-choo, MR Robinson, Jesus loves you more than you will know... wo, wo, woooo...*" Makayla sang seductively into the mic, leaning towards a sweaty-faced bald man sitting at a table closest to the stage, gifting him a sizeable portion of cleavage and a lascivious look that would give him pleasant dreams for years. "*God bless you please, MR Robinson,*" she continued, directed deliberately towards the bald man, "*Heaven holds a place for those who pray... hey, hey, hey... hey, hey, hey.*"

When the song finished, Makayla waved elaborately to the audience and left the stage. The spotlights dimmed, steeping the room in darkness. Concertgoers in the audience started to bellow "More!" screaming and whistling for the show to continue.

Makayla didn't disappoint. She returned to the stage wearing an ermine cloak that hung to her waist and a crown, masquerading as a barelegged queen.

"Do you want this?" she bellowed to an ecstatic audience.

"Yes," as one, came the reply.

"Are you sure?" she teased, using a tone of uncertainty.

"Yes," returned the audience ardently.

"I can't hear you!" she screamed, half-laughing.

"YES!" screamed the crowd, quivering to her needs.

Raising an arm with the microphone still in hand, she commanded the room to settle. It did. Just one or two coughs spoilt the silence. She closed her eyes and waited for the opening chords to her final song, the obligatory encore. *One Last Wish* was Makayla's biggest hit to date, and it was no surprise that she left it to the end.

Rather apt, thought Edwin Carslake, standing in the wings to the right of the stage. Darryl Figgis' last wish had been for his charity to raise enough money for the children's cancer unit. The song wasn't very good, he reflected. Lyrically it was lacking, and instrumentally it was simple and repetitive. The fact it was a huge hit wasn't surprising, owing to the star quality of its performer and the simple minds of her target audience.

When the song came to its conclusion, the mayor entered the stage, clapping and gurning appreciatively. Holding a microphone of his own, he addressed the turnout. "What about that!" he bellowed. "Ladies and gentlemen... everyone... give it up for..." he glanced at a pen mark on his hand, a scrawled reminder, "...Makayla!"

The audience cheered frenetically. Makayla waved in all directions of the room, blew kisses and took a bow, this time placing a hand subconsciously across her chest. "Thank you!" she said, emotionally. "Remember, everyone... there's a little boy up there," she pointed skyward, "watching down right now, who made this all happen. Thank you!"

A bigger cheer erupted which was soon followed by: "Makayla! Makayla!" chanted, over and over.

The diminutive figure of the young singer blew a final kiss to her admirers before stepping off stage, walking towards Edwin Carslake, MP.

"Fantastic performance Miss... um... Makayla," Edwin gushed like a schoolboy.

"Thank you," she replied, making to move past him.

The MP blocked her off. "I especially liked your version of that Simon and Garfunkle classic."

The nineteen-year-old had no choice but to stop. She took a moment to study the man, noting that there was something familiar about him. "Most men your age do," she almost purred. "Do I know you from somewhere?"

Edwin smiled coyly. "Maybe TV," he said. "I'm often seen with the prime minister in the news. I was also in GQ magazine a couple of months back. I'm a junior minister in the government."

"You're an important person?" she queried. "Someone with power, maybe?" She was young and had no clue about British politics.

Edwin laughed. "I like to think so," he bragged, his stature seeming to grow an inch.

"I like that," she whispered. "Would you like to go somewhere with me, to get a drink?"

"Yes, absolutely," Edwin replied excitedly.

Makayla beamed. "Great! Let me throw some clothes on and I'll be right with you, *Mr Robinson*." The American starlet scampered off down a short corridor and turned into a room that had been set apart for her.

Creeping up behind the MP, Mayor Matthews spoke, startling him. "What's that all about?"

"Pretty little thing, isn't she? She's asked me to take her someplace for a drink."

The mayor grunted. "Aren't you married?"

"Not tonight," he replied, slyly, adding a wink.

3

Makayla fumbled for the cardkey, blindly swiping it through the slot in the door's handle whilst continuing to kiss and grapple with the forty-seven-year-old pressing up against her. An internal mechanism clicked and a small lime-green LED glowed on the base of the handle, indicating that it was no longer locked.

Sensing, rather than seeing (or hearing) the unlocking of the door, the brunette elbowed the door open and clambered into the hotel room.

Disentangling from the petite young woman, Edwin Carslake pushed the door closed behind him, hearing the automatic lock engage.

In the room, a wall mounted air conditioning unit whirred, pumping and circulating cold air. Engrossed with each other, neither of them noticed or saw the line of small black insects clinging to the underside of the cooling appliance, silently waiting and evaluating.

"Where were we?" asked the MP playfully. Before he had closed the gap, Makayla answered him with actions, taking his tie in one hand and tugging him forcefully towards her, mashing her mouth against his and forcing her tongue between moist lips, probing. Reciprocating, he explored her mouth with the tip of his tongue, brushing over the smooth enamel of her teeth and tasting the sweetness of her breath along with an undertone of alcohol.

Giving into his urges, spurred by the excitement of having not only a nubile woman in his grasp, but a promising young pop star, he pulled open her black leather gothic waist-cincher basque corset top, exposing her small but pert breasts, the areole dark pink behind a slightly lighter erect nipple.

"Oh, *Mr Robinson*... you naughty boy!" she purred, her hands tugging at the zipper of Edwin's trousers, one delving deep between the gap to grapple with his stiffening, suffocating member through the fabric of his silk boxer shorts.

Lending assistance, the MP unbuckled his belt. The trousers snagged at his knees before further intervention helped them to gather at his ankles. He hastily stepped out of them as he manoeuvred towards the king-sized bed taking up the centre of the penthouse suite, dragging Makayla, whose hand was wrapped around his shaft, with him.

A solitary fly, doing a sortie, violated the airspace around Edwin's head. Distractedly, the MP swatted it away. With a youthful leap, he propelled himself 'Fosbury' style onto the centre of the bed, disengaging from the American's grip. He bounced on the soft emerald-green covered mattress, springs creaking and groaning beneath him.

Slipping the black leather corset free from her shoulders, she shrugged the garment to the floor, where it fell a foot away from Edwin's trousers, her breasts gently jiggling. Seductively, she peeled her Karl Lagerfeld black sequinned leggings from her legs, and then teasingly rolled her pink *Betty Boop* printed knickers from her waist and over her thighs, letting gravity take them to the floor. Uninhibited, she stood completely naked in front of the forty-seven-year-old.

Embarrassingly, Edwin realised he was dribbling as he imbibed Makayla's perfect form, seeing her pubic area groomed tidily into a neat landing strip. Nervously, he sucked in the saliva, the sound and the scene slightly grossing the pop starlet out.

"Forgive me," he whispered. "It's seeing your heavenly body…"

"Shush!" Makayla climbed onto the bed. "You'll spoil the moment." One hand drifted towards his boxers, the other to his face. She placed a finger on his lips as she tugged free his hardness, releasing his stretching underwear, the elastic almost garrotting his testicles. Seeing a look of pain on the man's face, she swiftly relieved him. Requiring both hands, she lopsidedly pulled the boxers off his legs. The execution was awkward and unsexy.

Edwin didn't notice.

"I'm hungry, Mr Robinson," the nineteen-year-old breathed, crawling on all fours towards him. "Satiate me."

The MP gulped as Makayla straddled him and gasped as he

felt his erection slip into the hot, juicy cleft between her legs; for the moment, the tip taken just a little way in.

Makayla moaned. "Do you want this?"

"Yes," Edwin replied automatically.

"Are you sure?" She lowered herself a little further, taking an extra inch of the MP's shaft.

"Yes," he responded with more emphasis, mentally willing her to continue, almost needing her to complete the affair.

"I can't hear you!" she screamed blissfully. It was like she was addressing her audience again at the concert, her vagina dropping a further inch closer to the base of his phallus.

"YES... YES... YES!!" he shouted. Edwin desperately wanted it, and his throbbing cock appeared to want it even more; he could bear it no longer.

Feeling the MP's despair through the conduit squeezed between her labia, she relinquished her control, allowing him to enter her completely, his seven inches of slick, unrestrained muscle taking the full journey, only stopping when his thick tangle of pubes enmeshed with her neat rectangle of hair.

Slickened from the first ride, Makayla raised herself up, Edwin's shaft slipping half out of her. Before completely emerging, she thrust herself down. A couple of strokes later, she found her rhythm. Like a piston, she seesawed on his central pole, momentum causing the desired friction that would bring both of them to climax.

On the precipice of an orgasm, a fly buzzed around Makayla's face. She would have ignored it had the pesky insect not darted into her mouth. Spluttering and gagging, the fly was caught at the back of her throat. Stopping in mid-thrust, Makayla noisily hacked up the fly like she was clearing phlegm.

"Are you all right?" asked Edwin, which the American interpreted as *hurry up and continue*.

"Yea," she said, starting to ride, finding the rhythm once again.

Up and down.

Up and down.

Up and down.

A few more strokes and Edwin felt the intensity in his groin begin to form; a sensation that needed nurturing if it was to be fully realised. Grabbing hold of Makayla's buttocks, his arms moved with her, slowly taking control of the young woman's momentum, directing her to go faster, faster, impelling her forward, encouraging her to expedite the conclusion, and importantly for him, his ejaculation. "Are you... ready?" He was almost at the point of eruption and his voice was dripping with expectation.

"Not yet!" She jounced harder, feeling her own fire stoked and building, a tingling sensitivity beginning at her clit, spreading throughout her body, causing her to tremble. "Yes!" she screamed, her point of no return met. Grinding her hips, she thrust down hard, feeling her slit tighten around Edwin. "Yes!" she shrieked in pleasure, drawing herself up again.

Edwin had held the dam for as long as he could. Now, as Makayla lowered herself again, his restraint dissipated. "Ahhhhhhhhh," he cried out as the volcanic build up exploded deep into her.

He may have won the race, but the brunette wasn't going to be left behind. Despite the man's groans and bucking beneath her, she carried on riding him, pumping his spent penis for all its worth, feeling the tingling sensitivity expand into a roaring burst of pure ecstasy.

"Ohhhhh, yes.... FUCK YES!!" she cried, her eyes closed. Her back arching as a million neurons exploded inside her brain and endorphins flooded her body. Significantly slower, like she was on a carousel ride coming to its end, she continued her ride, multiple orgasms racking her body, explosions of the purest euphoria. Her face was a contradiction of emotions; pain, joy, fear, happiness, elation, sadness. Her mouth was wide open. "Ahhh, yes," she groaned, shuddering, bringing her rhythm to an end.

Edwin sighed, wistfully and regretfully. Not regret because he had cheated on his wife; that didn't bother him. This wasn't the first time (although it would be the last) he had screwed a young woman in a hotel room. No, it was the fact that it was all over with, even if the American pop star still had him deep inside of her. He wondered if he would be able to manage another round after a break.

He hoped so.

On top of him, Makayla groaned some more, prolonging her coital enjoyment. Edwin closed his eyes. *You go, girl*, he thought, wishing he could experience an orgasm that would go on and on.

Makayla made some gasping sounds and began jerking about on top of the MP again, this time, less in rhythm, more chaotic. The movement wasn't unpleasant and Edwin was surprised to find himself beginning to feel aroused again.

"Uh-uh-uh-uh-uh," spluttered from the young woman's mouth, her wriggling was getting more frantic.

"Okay, Miss, I–" *think you've had enough*. He didn't finish his sentence. He couldn't. As he opened his eyes, shock and confusion stilled his tongue. What he was seeing couldn't be real. It didn't make sense.

Makayla was clutching at her throat. Only, it didn't look like the American singer from the earlier fundraiser, not anymore. Where her face had been was a black, moving mass, like a horror mask comprising of hundreds, if not thousands, of flies. What he had thought was the sound of her orgasming was, in fact, her struggles to breathe. Edwin could see that the flies had entered her mouth and coated her tongue and lips. Where the nineteen-year-old managed to exhale or cough, flies billowed out between her teeth in a small cloud, like a puff of vapour on a cold day.

Still writhing on top of him, the MP tried to scooch out from beneath the young woman, realising that in her panic, her muscles had tensed and were contracting, including the *bulbospongiosus* around the wall of her vagina. He quickly discovered that he was pinned beneath her, and even worse, held captive *inside* of her. His tool of pleasure was gripped vicelike by the same pair of muscles that had played an essential part in his earlier joy of sex, contributing to Makayla's clitoral erection and climax.

Before Edwin was able to attempt forcing himself out from beneath the American, she made a harsh, gasping, sucking sound, something like that made by a plughole consuming the dregs of water from a sink, both gurgling and reverberating air together. Her twisting and struggling suddenly ceased and her body that had rocked and swayed a moment before, slumped forward, collapsing into Edwin's arms.

The MP jerked his head to the right, moving just enough so that her head hit the pillow next to him. Her body was draped diagonally across his torso. From his peripherals, he could see the flies – a moving, rippling ski mask on Makayla's head – crawling over each other, completely coating every inch of her countenance and blending in with her long brunette hair.

"Oh God!" he exclaimed, unable to contemplate the sheer horror of what was happening to the woman on top of him.

With a backhand, he slapped at the flies, crushing some against Makayla's face. A small swarm of insects floated up and landed on Edwin's hand.

"Ahhhh! Fuck!" Unexpected and uncharacteristic, the group of flies bit him causing a concentrated dart of pain to shoot up his arm. Reactively, he punched out at the flies, landing a fist against Makayla's right eye socket. For a moment, the place became clear of insects and he could see an azul-blue eye staring out at him, wide and pleading... but not for long. Like scavengers, a deployment of flies replaced those Edwin had scattered.

Rubbing the back of his hand, the pain subsided, though a red mark comprising of twenty pinpricks in a circle the size of a milk bottle top was evidence that he hadn't imagined it.

Desperately, he tried pushing the diminutive American off him, an act that should have been easily accomplished. Except, it wasn't; it appeared to be hopeless. He managed to raise her a couple of inches away from him, but only her top half was amenable. Her death-grip on his genitalia was uncompromising, like the jaw of a snapping alligator turtle, which, when clamped on its victim, either continues its bite until flesh has been rent free or its head is decapitated.

Giving up, he allowed Makayla to fall back onto his chest, her head once again dropping to the pillow, this time her face contiguous to his, at almost kissing distance.

A soft drone from the end of the bed dragged his attention away from the abomination close to his face.

"Oh God," he whimpered in understanding, wishing he hadn't looked.

More flies had joined the party, landing on both the American's feet. Like a shroud, the mass of teeming insects washed up and over the contours of her body, some falling onto Edwin as other flies muscled past them in a survival of the strongest display.

Despairingly, the MP turned away to look for something – *anything* – that would help him escape.

"My phone!" he exclaimed in a 'Eureka moment', the sudden outburst startling a dozen flies which buzzed about his face in agitation but made no attempt to land on him.

His LG mobile was in a pocket within his trousers.

A disheartened thought sprung to mind. His trousers were on the floor, halfway across the room where he had left them in his passion.

Edwin wriggled and tussled beneath Makayla's weight, reaching for the side of the mattress with his left hand, his intention to use it to pull him to its edge.

He managed to slide three inches before elaborate movement at his side caught his eye.

It was the flies and Makayla.

He didn't want to look but felt compelled. He relaxed his hand from the mattress' edge and turned back to face the grotesque visage lying on the pillow next to him.

Her head was swelling from the influx of bloated flies that converged on her face, seeming to expand like a slowly-inflating balloon. The black, moving shroud continued to glide up her body from the bottom of her bed, now shifting fluidly over her buttocks and progressing up her back, as though cloaking her for the purpose of decency.

Nothing had changed since before. The flies were there. Makayla was still dead. *I imagined it*, he thought, studying her lifeless, insect-infested appearance. Unconsciously, he re-reached for the mattress' edge. Before his fingers made purchase, the American's eyes popped open; the action seemed autonomous, dispatching the flies occupying her eyelids and the surface surrounding them to buzz about in agitation.

Edwin gasped in shock.

"Er...gla...er...gla..gla...er..mer...gla..." The noise seemed to emanate from the young woman's mouth.

"What are you... saying?"

The woman made some more noises but they were too low to hear. Although repulsing him, Edwin leaned closer, inclining his head very slightly so that his ear was closer to her mouth.

Makayla said nothing more.

Edwin turned so that he was again opposite the fly-infested face. Her azul-blue eyes were still open; the place where her lips had quivered inarticulate words, were hidden behind the living yashmak of pestilent creatures.

"What are–" *you saying?* The politician didn't get to finish his sentence. Makayla belched a jet of flies the short distance into his wide-open mouth, causing him to begin retching, gagging and choking.

Powerless to react, Edwin accepted the flow of insects as they gushed incessantly into him like water from a power-spray, filling and probing his mouth as effective and as effortlessly as Makayla's tongue had, just a short time earlier.

Attempts of resistance, of fighting and fending the insects off were met with hordes of angry bloated flies nipping and biting at the flesh of his hands and arms.

The geyser of small creatures flowed ceaselessly into the man's mouth, clogging his airway and depriving him of essential oxygen. In no time, the struggle was over. The light of the room faded to nothing, replaced by the deepest, blackest darkness he'd ever experienced. This was followed by a sudden 'pop' inside his head, like the built-in amplifier within his brain had blown a fuse; nothing but sheer silence. Last to desert him was his awareness of being.

Edwin Carslake MP, slumped to the pillow he was sharing with Makayla, breaking the train of insects flowing from the woman's mouth into his, sending the tide to spout skyward like an oil gusher, the force of their ascent continuing unabated until hitting the ceiling with a hard crack. His blistered left arm slapped down atop the American singer's back with a meaty thump, resting across it in a limp parody of an embrace. His eyes glazed over as he died and a line of blood trickled from his mouth, soaking into the white pillowcase beneath his face.

Following what was becoming their *modus operandi* once the kill was achieved, the females laid their eggs on their latest hosts.

After a couple of hours, as dawn fast approached, orders were telepathically communicated among the fly population within the hotel room. As they had been given just a simple language, the transmission received was facile and confined to one word, but adequate in its simplicity.

Retreat!

As one, the insects took to the sky in a haze, their work

complete. They vacated the room via the vent of the wall-mounted air conditioning system, taking the flexible ducting pipe that drew fresh air into the cooling machine that serviced all the rooms within the luxury hotel.

4

The Portuguese cleaner rapped her knuckles against the door. "Housekeeping!" she called out, loud enough to be heard through the solid penthouse suite door. She waited a moment – long enough for an inhabitant to answer – and used her master cardkey to unlock the door, swiping it through the slot close to the handle. In the corridor ahead of her was a trolley laden with her cleaning tools, toilet rolls, refuse sacks and piles of fresh linen for bed changing and clean towels.

The sound of the internal latch clicked free. It was followed by the sight of the small LED lamp on the handle beginning to glow lime green.

A glance at her watch confirmed she was making good time with her rounds. It was half-nine, and most of the guests had checked out by eight. The cleaner was humming a tune to herself as she entered the room. Immediately, she saw the naked limbs of a man and a woman, straddled together. The rest of their bodies were obscured from view by a chair and her inattention.

"Oh, *com licença... com licença,*" *excuse me, excuse me,* she said embarrassed. Using a hand to cover her face whilst averting her eyes, she turned to leave.

Except, something stopped her in mid-stride; her experience led her to expect a room's inhabitant to jump up in alarm when intruded upon in such a manner, especially when naked. Usually, they scrabble for bedcovers to make themselves decent. These two made no attempts at covering up.

Perhaps they are asleep, she pondered. "Hello… housekeeping!" she hollered over her shoulder, heavily accented. She waited a long moment for a response or a sign that she had been acknowledged. A sideward glance, using her peripherals, she noticed no movement.

Odd, she thought.

With a mind to leave and come back later, she stepped towards the door, a hand reaching for the handle.

A mobile phone began to jingle behind her, slightly muffled, as though stifled from being buried within clothing. The ringtone was a song she recognised, something by Coldplay. She didn't know the name.

With still no signs or sounds of movement, curiosity edged way for concern. Tremulously, the cleaner turned back and tentatively stepped forward into the room, slowly walking towards the bed.

The naked limbs were in full view. She could see by their shapes and definition that a man was lying on his back and a young woman, lying prone, was on top. As she stepped closer, more of their nude profiles came into sight. Nervously, feeling like a voyeur, the cleaner allowed her eyes to slowly wander up their bodies.

By the way they didn't move she knew something was wrong. Before her gaze passed their shoulders, she heard herself scream; long, loud, shrill and terrified. Guests heard her across that level and the one below.

Inevitably, her eyes settled on the couple's faces, their features contorted in fear, their mouths stretched open in an eternal rictus. If this hadn't been bad enough, their mottled, blotchy complexions compounded things.

This time, the cleaner's scream would be heard throughout the entire hotel, from the reception on the ground floor, to the leisure suite at the top; it was a long while after before she stopped.

CHAPTER EIGHT

/

"RESEARCHING," SAID McCARDLE, "SERIAL KILLERS... and flies. Oh, and another thing that may be of interest... But it all can hang until you get back. You'd best not keep the Chief waiting."

Baylem grunted, his face contorting to show contempt, disapproval and reluctance all at the same time. The prospect of meeting up with the Chief Super and the manner and tone used in his summoning perturbed him. Without a word, he sprung up from his chair as though jet-propelled and scurried out of the office. *Better to get it over with*, he concluded.

Smiling to herself, McCardle returned to her computer, tapping a few commands into the search engine, thinking to look into whether there had been any other fly-like incidents occurring.

A couple of heartbeats later and a news article flashed up on her screen. A local journalist – Emily Herrington – had written it for the *Fulbarton Evening Herald*. It appeared in yesterday's edition.

The headline made the hairs on the back of her arms stand on end and caused a tingling sensation within the pit of her stomach, which she initially put down to wind.

She read the headline aloud:

"When Bugs Attack: Insect Swarm Causes Fatal Road Accident."

Enthusiastically, McCardle proceeded to speed-read the article, only to sigh vociferously in disappointment at the end. Factually written, the news story gave details of an accident occurring on the outskirts of Fulbarton. Two cars involved, resulting in the deaths of a driver and a passenger of one vehicle, and the hospitalisation of the driver of the other. The cause of the incident was being investigated, though there was an unsubstantiated report from an eyewitness claiming that a swarm of flies had been seen close to the scene. No further elaboration or imputation was forthcoming. And no one else corroborated the statement.

"Sensationalism," the sergeant deplored, shaking her head dismally. *What reporters do to sell a story!* Accompanying the headline and news item was a photograph that captured the scene: a burning vehicle, dozens of bystanders milling about, emergency vehicles, police officers and the sight of a body in the foreground, respectfully covered with a white sheet. McCardle was about to disregard the article – her index finger poised to close the browser page – when a gut-impulse stopped her.

Emily Herrington's piece ended with a paragraph calling for any witnesses of the incident to call PC Mark Carrigan. His FIN (collar number) and a local phone number, which McCardle recognised as belonging to HQ, was included.

Impulsively, the detective sergeant scooped up the handset of her desk phone and pressed a button.

A voice immediately filled the earpiece. "*Fulbarton Police Head Quarters, how may I help you?*"

Foregoing any pleasantries, McCardle replied: "PC Mark Carrigan please."

"*Hold please*," said the switchboard operator, just as bluntly. With no hold music, the line appeared dead. Pressing the handset firmly against her ear, McCardle could just detect a faint whistle of static. For what seemed like an age, she sat twiddling her fingers around the coil of wire connecting the phone with the cradle and beginning to daydream about extraneous things and what to feed her cat.

"*Hello, this is PC Carrigan.*" The handset was held loosely in her hand and the sudden resonance caused her to jump. The phone receiver clattered to the desk.

"Ah, shit," McCardle unconsciously blurted, quickly gathering up the phone. "Evening, Constable," she amiably greeted, settling the handset to the side of her face. "This is DS Jayne McCardle."

"*Oh, hello,*" he greeted cheerfully.

"I was wondering if you could help me," she didn't wait for assent. "Yesterday, you attended an RTA involving two fatalities."

"*Yes... that's right. Gruesome business. A lass not wearing her seatbelt; broken neck. And her partner, the driver; burnt to a crisp.*"

"Sounds awful." McCardle spoke disinterestedly, almost condescending. "Tell me; was there anything unusual about the cause of the accident?"

"*Not that I could tell, no. Of course, collision investigators are currently involved, and–*"

McCardle interrupted him. "It's been reported that a swarm of insects might have precipitated the accident."

The police constable at the end of the line started to laugh. "*I wouldn't believe everything you read in the local rag, sergeant, but...*" he said mirthfully, "*the other driver, the one from the second vehicle... she did mention something about seeing hundreds of flies at the scene, but the point is, nobody else did. We put it down to shock, possibly delusion.*"

"Delusion?"

"*Yea. We found prescription medications in her handbag. Olanzapine and lithium. Drugs usually given for bipolar or other mental disorders. Based on this information, we didn't think we could take her comments too seriously.*"

"Oh, okay. Thanks."

"*You're welcome.*"

"Before you go, what's her name and where can I find her? The driver of the second vehicle, I mean?" McCardle intuitively found a pen and readied to write on a shorthand notepad, a clean page opened out ahead of her.

The constable didn't immediately respond. Shuffling noises filled her ear as he riffled through papers aggressively. With a start, his voice returned. "*Adele Pettit, aged thirty-seven. She lives to the west of the town. Number fourteen Backhouse Lane. Currently at Fulbarton General Hospital recovering from injuries sustained.*"

"Thank you, officer Carrigan."

"*Most welcome,*" he replied.

2

Baylem was in a dark mood when he reappeared a quarter of an hour later. With his forehead furrowed and his eyes mere slits, he wore an expression that the sergeant interpreted as suffering; from what, she couldn't second guess. It was a look she'd seen before, most often after an encounter with the Chief Superintendent, and sometimes when inflicted with one of his 'headaches' which frequently pained him.

Highlighting his affliction further, Baylem raised his right hand and caressed his temple.

Twisting around in her chair to face Baylem, McCardle asked: "Was it that bad?"

"Worse," he replied, cryptically. He crossed to his desk and sat heavily in his executive chair. Slouching down, he placed his hands behind his head, entwining his fingers together. "He wanted an update on today's discoveries, about Sean Wallace and the Jessops." The DI sighed in exasperation.

"And?"

"I told him that their deaths were not natural and that they were tenuously linked. I explained the facts, nothing more. What we found at both scenes. What Hamilton discovered in post-mortem. Huh!" Baylem lowered his arms, shaking his head in agitation. "The Chief Super laughed at me! He told me to forget about the flies, they weren't 'pertinent' to the investigation. He told me these cases were closed."

"Not pertinent?" the sergeant queried, raising her voice. "How can they not be?"

"Oh, he knows he's talking out his arse," related Baylem. "He's just not bothered. Modern day policing has nothing to do with solving crimes or catching criminals; it's about 'statistics' and 'manipulated' information.

"We've gone more than three years without a murder or a suspicious death; the Chief Super doesn't want to concede that record now, not when his best-buddy, Edwin Carslake 'MP', is using local crime figures in his plot to inveigle his way into government; his sights are on one day reaching number ten Downing Street."

"Christ, that's balmy, sir!"

"Balmy?" Baylem smiled. He hadn't heard the use of that word since he was on the playground at primary school. "I told him straight that I thought it was bullshit," he said.

"How did he take that?" McCardle was bemused.

"Did you not hear me? The cases are now closed." In frustration, Baylem scooped up the papers sprawled across his desk into an armful, half-swivelled in his chair, and dumped them above the metal waste bin close-by. The fact that much of what he was disposing of had little to do with the two cases they had been investigating and more to do with his expenses claim and course-work for a forthcoming 'health and safety at work' exam, did not bother him.

"Um, that might be a little premature," advised the sergeant, referring to the matter of closing the cases. "Whilst you were with the chief, I came across a report in yesterday's newspaper." McCardle had printed off the article and held it up towards her superior.

"'When Bugs Attack: Insect Swarm Causes Fatal Road Accident'. Is that genuine?"

McCardle shrugged. "I spoke with the officer handling the case. He thought it was bunkum, but there's no harm speaking with her."

"Well... that's not strictly true," Baylem was implying the chief super's direct orders. "The cases are closed regarding Sean Wallace and the Jessops."

"Yes, I know. But our enquiries will be strictly to do with the RTA."

"Oh? And how do we explain us getting involved? We can't just assume roles in someone else's case."

"Let's just say I received an anonymous tip-off regarding the cause of the accident being deliberate; perhaps the suggestion the brakes had been tampered with. It would give us credible reason for involvement."

Baylem gave McCardle's suggestion some thought which did nothing to lessen the headache which was steadily worsening. "That might work," he said, optimistically. "But," he checked his left wrist. The watch indicated the time was closing in on ten p.m. "It's getting late. We'll focus on that in the morning. I need to get to bed. My head will burst if I do much more thinking today. You should get some rest too, Jayne."

"Right you are, sir."

Before either of the detectives made moves to leave, there was a knock at the door followed by the immediate appearance of a familiar face.

Uninvited, PC Anders stepped into the office.

"Anders... twice in one day! Didn't your shift finish four hours ago?"

The constable ignored DS McCardle's attempt at conversation, his attention seeking out the senior officer in the room. "Sir, I thought you might be interested to know that there's been another death."

A look of dismay filled the DI's face. "Where?"

"Hinkley Walsh Insurance, in the High Street. A fella was found by a security guard, trapped beneath a drink's machine. They thought it was an accident."

"Sounds like an accident to me," asserted McCardle, shutting down her computer and reaching for her handbag beneath her desk.

"Except, the drink's machine was somehow pushed over with force... and... this you'll find interesting," said Anders excitedly, "... more flies; dead ones again, this time, thousands of them."

McCardle and Baylem shared a look, intrigued and disappointed. Between the two, they had wordlessly agreed they wouldn't be going home anytime soon. For the benefit of PC Anders, the DI spoke:

"Okay, we're on it. First, does anyone have any Migraleve?"

3

"When d'you think we can clear this all up?" A tall, thin woman, casually dressed in jogging trousers, trainers and a white silk camisole, took big strides as she charged the length of the office to where DI Baylem was standing alongside Dr Hamilton. There was no doubting she was a person of importance within the world of Hinkley Walsh Insurance.

Baylem inclined his head towards the approaching woman, swiftly assessing her. Judging her to be in her late-forties, he noted that she wore little makeup and was naturally very attractive. Despite her visual appeal, the manner in which she had spoken rankled with him a little.

Dr Hamilton was talking animatedly as he worked around the body. Baylem returned his attention to the scene, blotting out the approaching woman for a moment.

A young man was pinned to the floor beneath a drink's machine, exactly how PC Anders had said. Additionally, there were thousands of dead flies spread around the place; with quite a few mushed into the decedent's mouth and nostrils.

"Excuse me? Are you supposedly in charge here?" Before the woman reached the Inspector, DS McCardle stepped in front of her. She had been questioning the security guard at a desk a short walk from the aisle.

"I'm DS McCardle... and you are?"

Slightly perturbed by the obstruction, the woman turned her attention to the plainly-clothed police officer standing in front of her. "I'm the manager of this department," she said haughtily. "Elaina Banham. When can this be cleared up?" she asked again, dismissively.

"Mrs Banham–"

"MISS BANHAM!" the woman corrected.

"–Miss Banham. This is currently a crime scene. Nothing can be touched or 'cleared up' until forensics and the doctor have concluded their preliminary enquiries." Trying to pacify the department manager, she added, "It shouldn't be much longer."

Elaina Banham's tough exterior melted, as though a huge burden had been lifted. "I'm sorry to come in all guns blazing," she said. "I have over sixty staff depending on me, my boss on my back and a number of business targets to meet; with hefty financial penalties should I fail. Despite this... *situation*, it's BAU."

"BAU?" McCardle didn't know the abbreviation.

"Business as usual," Elaina replied. "At eight a.m., our phone lines will open on the dot and customers will be ringing us up to make claims, or chasing payments or decisions. We need to be ready half an hour before then for the staff arriving."

The sergeant made a face to show she understood. "We'll do our best."

"Thank you." Elaina Banham meant it.

"Do you mind answering some questions?"

"No, not at all."

McCardle directed the department manager away from where Baylem was still conferring with Dr Hamilton, towards a bank of desks. The security guard who had made the grim discovery was sitting at a desk nearby, his back to them.

"Tell me. That smell... is that normal with dead bodies?"

At first, McCardle didn't know what the woman meant. She sniffed in deep and wrinkled her nose. Though not as strong here as it was around the body, the odour was still present and very unpleasant. The DS could only describe it as ammonia-like; fetid and rotten. It reminded her of the time she found a dead seal washed up on the beach at Hunstanton during a childhood holiday, fishy and decaying. "Can you believe I hadn't noticed it," she said. "No, that's not how dead bodies smell. That's something entirely different."

"Well, it wasn't here before."

Changing the subject, Sergeant McCardle produced her notebook and a pen. "The deceased worked here, I believe. Justin Piper."

"Justin? Oh God... how... awful." Elaina's eyes glazed over.

"What can you tell me about him?"

Elaina Banham shook her head. "How awful," she repeated.

"Did he work here long?"

"Today was Justin's last day," Elaina replied, composing herself. "I was the second-to-last person to leave – Justin was the last. He was one of our best claims handlers. Hard working. Conscientious. A bit of a laugh, too. He was always playing practical jokes and making wisecracks. I was going to miss him... are you sure it's him?"

McCardle nodded her head. "We checked his ID... and the security guard confirmed it."

"Oh dear... poor Jo. What will she do?"

"Jo?" McCardle quizzed.

"His girlfriend. She'd just had a baby. A little girl. He was giving up his job to become a full-time parent so that she could go back to work. She's a lawyer or something in a high-powered job. He didn't need to work, and he fancied the role of primary care giver."

"Do you know if anyone would want to do Justin any harm?"

Elaina laughed. "Hurt Justin? Absolutely not! Everybody loved the man."

"All the same... Drinks' machines don't fall over by themselves."

Elaina Banham glanced to where she could see the toppled vending machine. She hadn't seen Justin's body beneath it but could imagine how it might appear, crushed and bloody. DI Baylem was concluding his conversation with the doctor still completing his preliminary, and was looking her way. Her face reddened guiltily. "That's true," she said sadly.

It was too late to go back to the office, and although tired, Baylem felt the importance of running through the latest event and exchanging information with McCardle before retiring for the day.

The publican of The Rose and Crown on the corner of Norwich Road was about to call time when the police officers stepped through the door. The bar was empty, except for the busty blonde-haired maid in her early twenties who was collecting empty glasses and cleaning tables, and the barkeeper himself, a portly fellow who went by the name of 'Keith' and was easily recognised by his facial hair; long, fuzzy sideburns that merged into his moustache. Bereft of beard, it gave him the appearance of an old admiral from the 1800s.

"I guess you'll want the usual?" Keith asked, automatically gravitating towards a T-style draught beer tower behind the bar, picking out a pint glass from a shelf beneath and placing it under one of the five taps. He flicked a lever and caught a steady flow of dark liquid into the glass. Although perceived to be black, Guinness was in fact a very dark shade of ruby. "I'll bring them over."

"Thanks, Keith." The DI led McCardle towards a table in the farthest corner of the room, sitting in a fitted burgundy seat designed for three that backed against the wall.

McCardle took one of the matching upholstered lounge chairs opposite – the end one – placing her handbag on the empty middle one next to her.

Clinking a handful of empty glasses, held by their rims, the barmaid sauntered past, heading for one of a pair of doors adjacent to the bar, behind which was the kitchen. The other door led into the men's toilets.

"Here you go, detectives," Keith said cheerfully, placing the pint of Guinness on a beer mat in front of Baylem, and a glass of white wine ahead of McCardle.

"Any chance you could rustle up something to eat? I've not had time to eat since lunch."

The barman gave a pained look, like he was wrestling with his conscience. "The kitchen closed at nine," he said reluctantly.

Baylem's face dropped pitifully. As though well-rehearsed, his stomach growled noisily, validating the need for food.

"I'll see what I can do," said Keith, turning away in resignation.

"One of your steak and kidney pies would go down a treat!" Baylem called out happily.

Keith harrumphed as he vanished into the kitchen, leaving the DI and DS in the bar to themselves.

"So," started Baylem after taking a mouthful of the Irish stout, "five bodies in three different locations. Nothing linking them except the nature of their deaths and the abundance of dead flies we found at the scenes."

"Are we assuming our latest victim died in the same manner?" asked McCardle. She ran a finger around the rim of her wine glass creating a very subtle sound to resonate.

"Not assuming, no. Floyd examined Justin Piper's mouth and nose. He found flies… many of them. Enough to block the man's airway twice over."

"What about the vending machine?"

Baylem shrugged. "It definitely took a lot of force to topple it and it played its part in Justin's demise." The detective took a deep pull from his pint. "From the looks of it, the weight of the machine ripped the connecting pipes from the wall; untethered, the machine fell on the man as he attempted to crawl away, pinning him to the floor."

"Crawling away?"

"There's evidence to confirm this."

"Oh." McCardle imagined the scene in her head. Nothing made sense. "What caused the drink's machine to fall on him?"

Baylem shrugged his shoulders. "He was laughing at the time, but the good doctor suggested it was the flies that did it."

The DS started to laugh herself, stopping to accept a deep swig from her wine glass. Baylem noticed that half of its contents were gone when McCardle returned it to the table.

"What did you find out from the security guard?"

The woman cleared her throat. "Very little," she complained. "He discovered the body just after seven p.m., whilst on his final rounds before closing up."

"And the highly strung woman you were interviewing?"

"The Claims Manager, Elaina Banham. She was the last person to see Justin alive, around a quarter-past six."

"So, the time of death was between six-fifteen and seven

o'clock. What about surveillance footage? Did the security guard not see anything on CCTV?"

"Brian said he didn't notice anything untoward; however, he admitted not being at his desk for much of the time after Elaina had left. He spent a while in the toilet and a bit of time out front smoking a cigarette.

"As everything is recorded digitally, he offered to send me surveillance footage from the floor for the time in question; though doubted it would be of any use. I'll review it later tonight or in the morning," the DS contemplated. "Brian said the area where Justin was found isn't captured by the dome video camera, which is convenient."

"Very. But not a coincidence. It appeared that Justin was planting a nasty surprise in the space above the ceiling. Floyd and I were despairing at the atrocious smell."

"I observed that. I guessed it wasn't from the body."

"No," said Baylem. "I noticed the ceiling tile that had been set aside and climbed up and took a look. I found a half-decomposed fish up there. Brought tears to my eyes and tested my gag reflex."

"Miss Banham said Justin was a bit of a practical joker," said McCardle. "Looks like this was his leaving present."

"I guess the last laugh was on him," replied Baylem dolefully.

Hearing the kitchen door clatter open noisily, the detectives fell silent.

"Here you are, your Lordship," Keith presented sarcastically, "one steak and kidney pie." He placed a hot plate in front of the DI. Accompanying the pie was a deep mound of fluffy creamy-white mashed potatoes and a puddle of baked beans in tomato sauce. "Enjoy."

"You do know he microwaved that?" McCardle asked playfully in a low voice.

"And?" queried Baylem. "Isn't that how all dinners are cooked?"

CHAPTER NINE

/

S TARING BACK FROM THE MIRROR was a face McCardle barely recognised. The dark rings circling her eyes reminded her of a raccoon, and her complexion appeared blotchy; a reaction from too much wine consumption. She looked terrible and along with her headache, felt much worse.

After brushing her teeth, she stepped into the bath, drew the diamond-patterned curtain and took a long shower beneath the unit affixed to the side of the wall. She hoped the hot spray would revitalise her. Failing that, she would settle with its soothing relief and being cleansed. The grim discoveries the day before had left her feeling dirty, and she believed the putrid smell of rotten, decaying fish, had somehow transferred to her, settling onto her clothes and coating her skin. Every so often, she caught a whiff of the mephitis, strong and nauseating.

Completely washed, she stepped out of the bath, dried herself and wrapped the towel around her body. Walking into the living room of her apartment, she used a remote to activate the TV.

BBC news filled the screen, along with the pleasing image of a handsome male presenter. In the bottom left-hand corner, the time was displayed digitally:

06:18 a.m.

With the remote, McCardle turned up the volume.

"*...the government have announced plans to cut further funding to public services in its attempt to plug the ever-widening national debt...*"

"Great," the DS muttered, knowing full well that further cuts would soon be announced to policing locally and likely to her department. The force was already undermanned; it was just fortuitous that Fulbarton's crime rates were low comparative to other towns across the country.

Well, were, she mused, thinking fleetingly of the three crime scenes she had attended the day before. She returned the remote to the arm of her chair and used a smaller towel (which had been fashioned around her head) to ruffle dry her hair.

The telephone on a charging cradle began to ring. Occupying the centre of a side table beside the three-seater sofa, McCardle hurried across to it and snatched it up before the answering machine would kick in, which was set for after three short rings.

"Hello?"

"*Jayne? It's Baylem... Have you seen the paper?*" The DI was referring to that day's local newspaper, *The Fulbarton Chronicle,* the sister paper of the *Fulbarton Evening Herald.*

"Mornin' sir," she replied flippantly, before adding, "no. Not yet. I've only just got up... I didn't get to bed until after two." After two more glasses of wine at The Rose and Crown, where the sergeant summarised and theorised further on the events of that day, she went home intending to go straight to bed. Instead, her hand had settled on the DVD copy of the CCTV footage Brian – the guard at Hinkley Walsh Insurance – had given to her. Wishing to see for herself what little the surveillance dome had captured, she had spent a good hour scrutinising the recording. The time had been mostly wasted.

McCardle heard Baylem grunt down the phone. "*Front page headline: FULBARTON RESIDENTS LIVE IN FEAR!*"

"Seriously?" exclaimed McCardle.

Baylem continued. *"Some hack has written a piece about the unexplained deaths we discovered yesterday, speculating that they are linked to two other similar incidents."*

"Two?" queried the detective sergeant.

"Yes. One, you've already stumbled upon; the car accident on the outskirts of Fulbarton... the one which we briefly discussed last night before the events at the insurance office; the other; a small dairy farm on the outskirts of town. Situated about a mile-and-a-half from where the car accident occurred. The reporter doesn't think it's a coincidence.

"An entire herd of Montbeliarde cows were found dead (or dying) a week ago. Fifty-three animals in all destroyed. A local vet who did a post-mortem had been baffled by the cause of death, though the reporter quotes him saying: 'there was a significant number of flies discovered on the scene and couldn't rule out an extreme case of myiasis... more commonly known as Fly Strike'..."

"I had a rabbit when I was a kid who died from that," interjected McCardle ponderously, adding sadly, "flies laid its eggs in and around her anus. When the maggots were born, they ate her from the inside out. It didn't take long for her to die."

Ignoring the sentimentality, Baylem continued. *"It's possible these two cases ARE linked to the ones we found yesterday, but I wish the press had spoken to us first."*

"Why? What would we have said? No comment..."

Baylem grunted again. *"Well, the Chief Super is not at all happy, especially after the orders he gave me last night. I had him call me at quarter-past five this morning, chewing my ear off. He now says it's imperative that we investigate, if only to reassure the public so not to cause a panic. He also wants me to make a statement."*

McCardle sniggered.

"You know how much I hate public speaking!"

"What's the plan, sir?" she asked. The BBC news programme continued to play out on the television. A middle-aged reporter filled the screen, standing in front of a familiar building.

"*We need to eliminate or establish links to the dairy farm and the RTA in corroboration with our ongoing enquiries. If they are related, maybe it will help us make better sense of what the hell is...*"

McCardle's attention broke away from her superior at the other end of the phone. She honed in on the reporter taking up the space on her flat screen TV.

He was young, wearing a grey suit and a matching tie. "*... at least seven unexplained deaths this month in the small East Anglian town of Fulbarton, with eyewitness accounts and local reporters claiming a deadly swarm of flies are to blame...*"

The reporter was replaced by the news presenter back in the studio. "*Is that likely though, John?*" asked the handsome man sitting behind his desk. "*Are the people in Fulbarton right to be worried this morning?*"

Ignorant to anything further Baylem was saying, DS McCardle interrupted him: "Sir, you better switch on the BBC... there's something you should see."

John Harriman showed no emotion as his image returned to the screen. McCardle slinked around the sofa with the handset pressed to her ear and sat on the edge of the centre seat.

"*Well, pathology reports are not conclusive,*" John Harriman started, "*however, the fact of the matter is, all these deaths have flies in common. An anonymous source told me that the airways of Sean Wallace and the three bodies belonging to the Jessops were all obstructed by foreign objects, lodged in the back of their throats. Those foreign objects were found to be flies... hundreds of them compressed together.*"

"*Oh, bloody hell!*" bellowed Baylem into McCardle's ear. She guessed he was now watching the same programme as her. She didn't respond, choosing instead to continue watching the news piece.

The presenter in the studio was back on the screen, an anxious look upon his face. "*Do we know what type of fly caused this, John? Are they your everyday, garden-variety type, or are they something else?*"

"*There's been no official word regarding the flies, or indeed whether they actually ARE the cause of the problems here in Fulbarton. But a community is waking up this morning in fear and there are many questions that need answering, along with the need for reassurance that these deaths are not going to continue."*

The picture turned back to the studio. *"I understand Fulbarton Police are going to be issuing a statement a bit later this morning?"*

"Yes, that's right. Detective Inspector Baylem is the officer in charge of the investigation. We're expecting him to make a public announcement sometime around nine."

"Thank you, John."

"Did you see all that?" shouted Baylem through the phone. *"Bollocks!"*

"I guess the Chief Super won't be able to sweep this under the carpet now, sir."

"Guess not," Baylem replied uneasily, going quiet for a moment, reflecting deeply.

When nothing else was said after twenty seconds, McCardle spoke up. "Sir, are you all right?"

"I'm going to grab a bite to eat and a coffee on my way to yours. Do you want anything?"

"No, sir, I can make my own."

"Very well. I'll drop by to pick you up in twenty minutes."

"Twenty minutes? It takes me that long just to apply my makeup. I'm not even dressed yet!"

"Bloody hell, Jayne, you're not on annual leave! I'll give you half hour."

2

Not a second later, DI Baylem arrived exactly thirty minutes later at five-past-seven. Parking up the grey Audi S3 alongside the road in a marked bay, the policeman climbed out and sauntered across to the contained apartment block. To the side of the entrance was an electronic intercom panel with numbered push buttons. He punched number three and waited.

The speaker crackled on. "Come through," reverberated McCardle's voice, followed by a long buzz.

Baylem pulled the handle on the door as the lock mechanism disengaged, allowing entrance. He hurried through and breezed along the short corridor towards where he knew the sergeant lived. Her apartment was one of four on the ground level; the one furthest along on Baylem's left. He rapped his knuckles against a white, solid door, behind which the sound of shuffling was soon heard.

Upon opening, DS McCardle stood just inside. Wearing a matching charcoal grey blazer and skirt combo, with a light blue and white pinstripe blouse, the collar was open at her neck. Her dirty-blonde hair had that warm-air-dried, flyaway look, hanging loosely just above her shoulders.

"Come in," she said. "I'm nearly done." She indicated her hair by combing a hand through it. "Take a seat; I'll be with you in a min." Baylem followed the detective sergeant into the apartment. When she veered right into a bedroom, he continued into the living room. BBC news was still running on the TV.

"I meant to ask; did you find anything on that CCTV recording from the insurance place?" Baylem spoke loud enough to be heard in a neighbouring property.

"A little, but nothing conclusive," McCardle replied from the bedroom. "I'll show you in a minute once I've done my hair."

After three minutes, the woman came into the room looking fresh and tidy. The dark rings around her eyes had subsided through the magic of makeup; her hair was now styled into an almost natural, carefree bob. It had more body and was less flyaway.

"I went through the entire footage," said McCardle, crossing the room to where her laptop was resting atop a dinner table that appeared to be used more as a depository for books, papers and household clutter. She picked up the red laptop and moved purposefully to the sofa, taking a seat next to the DI and placing the computer on her lap. Opening up the screen, the laptop flickered into life. "At six-twenty, Justin can be seen walking the length of the office, then disappears around that corner; that's where the vending machines are."

Baylem watched the office worker do exactly as McCardle had said.

"I'll zoom into that part of the video," with a finger, she lightly tapped the screen where Justin had disappeared from view. "Although you can't see much of anything... there is a bit of shadow in a few minutes." She used the fast-forward icon to speed through the footage. "There!"

Studying the screen, DI Baylem stared at the place where McCardle was pointing. A dark umbra subtly appeared across the carpet ahead of the hidden area where Justin had vanished moments earlier, it was amorphous and unidentifiable. "What is it?"

"I think it's our killer... or killers. See the shape of the shadow and how it swirls and thickens before thinning out and dispersing? Now watch this..." The DS sped through a bit more of the recording, stopping abruptly. "There! See it?"

Baylem squinted.

McCardle rewound the playback. "Watch carefully." She selected play and used the zoom feature to hone in on the area of shadow.

The dark patch on the carpet swelled abruptly to form a solid, rectangular strip.

"Is that the vending machine?"

"Yes... but that's not it... just a little... longer... *there!*"

"I'll be damned," uttered Baylem in disbelief.

"That's what I thought, sir." She pressed the pause button, freezing the frame. On the display, a shapeless dark mass had strayed into view, appearing solid. "That's what killed Justin Piper."

"What is it?"

"I asked myself the same thing," replied McCardle, "so, with a bit of computer magic..." she tapped a few keys on the flat keyboard and watched the frozen image grow. The shapeless mass now filled the entire screen, but owing to magnification and the low resolution of the recording, the picture was indistinct and fuzzy.

Baylem groaned, growing impatient.

"Just need to do a bit of jiggery-pokery," she said, tapping a key lightly, using a combination of editing tricks to enhance the picture. In a quiver, the freeze frame morphed into something distinct.

"That's amazing, is that a fly?" Baylem asked.

"Flies, sir. Plural. There are at least a hundred in the picture, just from what we can see. It's likely there are thousands more. Maybe tens of thousands; must've been to overpower a grown man."

"AND a family of two adults and a child," reflected Baylem, thinking back to the Jessops. "Shit... I was hoping that Floyd Hamilton would be wrong?"

McCardle closed the laptop. "None of this seems right to me. Flies killing people? That's not a normal behaviour."

Baylem stood up from the sofa. "None of this makes sense. Why would these flies act in such a way? Where are they coming from? Where are they going? Are they indigenous to Britain, or are they foreign invaders?"

McCardle took her laptop back to the dinner table. "All good questions, but where do we start? How do we get answers?"

Before Baylem could consider a response, his mobile phone began to ring. He pulled it from his trouser pocket. "Baylem," he said, pressing the iPhone to his ear.

McCardle could hear a small, indistinct voice through the earpiece of Baylem's phone, but nothing of what was being said.

Turning to McCardle, Baylem raised an eyebrow. "When and where?" he asked his caller. There was some response, which

Baylem reacted to with: "Okay. Tell the officers on the scene we're on our way." He disconnected the call and returned the iPhone to his pocket.

"Not another death?" asked McCardle, apprehensively.

Baylem sighed. "No, thankfully. Despatch has just responded to a call from a woman claiming to have fended off a swarm of flies attacking her infant child."

"Seriously?"

"Apparently... Though, it could be a hoax. Amazing coincidence that a little over half an hour after the BBC broadcasts a report speculatively linking the deaths of yesterday to 'fly attacks', someone calls emergency services claiming to have survived such an assault."

"It might be genuine," said McCardle optimistically.

Baylem grunted. "Come on, let's make it fleeting. I have a press conference to prepare for."

3

At quarter-to-eight, Baylem and McCardle stepped through into a house on Rosslyn Street, a small two-up, two-down affair nestled in the centre of a terrace that looked plain and unassuming.

A uniformed woman police constable stepped aside in the narrow hallway to allow the plainly-clothed detectives admittance. She followed them into a cluttered living room, where toys were strewn across the floor and laundry was piled crumpled and untidily on a sofa and one of the armchairs.

A young woman stood in the doorway leading into a back room. She was rocking a baby in her arms. "Hello, Mrs...?" greeted Baylem, walking deep into the room so that he was standing face-to-face with her.

"Megan Pritchard... *Miss*."

He was old-fashioned and tended to assume women over a certain age, or ones with child were married, a mistake he often made. "I'm DI Baylem. This is DS McCardle. Would you mind telling us what happened?"

Megan continued to rock the baby gently in her arms, the motion more to calm herself than the child, who appeared close to sleep, sucking on a clenched hand. Although dressed in a white bodysuit, Baylem guessed the sex of the baby as being male; not by any physical characteristic, but by the gender-specific toys scattered around; blue cuddly toys, plush Thomas the Tank Engine and Micky Mouse.

"Would you like a cup of tea first? Or coffee? I'm making myself one."

Baylem shook his head. "Thanks, but no."

"Here... would you mind?" Megan offered the baby towards McCardle to hold. "Just for a moment, so I can put the kettle on."

Awkwardly, the DS accepted the infant child, like she was accepting a motion-activated bomb. Nervously, she cradled the baby, an alarmed look on her face. "How old is he?" asked McCardle nervously. The baby was no longer close to sleep. His bright blue eyes were wide, staring up at the policewoman, studying her.

"Harry's two months old," replied Megan from the kitchen. "He's a little small for his age coz he was born a bit early... thirty-six weeks. He's a hungry little fella, so he'll soon catch up. You sure you'd not like a tea or something?" The sound of a kettle being filled up could be heard.

"No, that's quite all right. Thank you," answered McCardle.

A moment later, Megan returned from the kitchen and held her arms out for McCardle to pass Harry back.

"Miss Pritchard, what happened?" Baylem asked for a second time. "You reported that flies were attacking you. Can you tell us precisely what happened, from the beginning?"

"You're going to think I am crazy," she replied, a tremor in her voice.

"If it's the truth, you've nothing to worry about," reassured McCardle.

Megan laughed doubtfully. "We'll see," she said. She walked across the room to a small seat-like bouncer, laying Harry into it and securing him with straps around his waist. "Today started as normal," began Megan, standing back up. "Scott – my boyfriend – got up at six for work, and I got up a little later, showered and had breakfast. At quarter-to-seven, Scott went off to do his thing, leaving me here with the baby.

"I was sorting the linen–" Megan gestured towards the clothes scattered over the seats, "–when Harry started to cry. I carried on with my chores for a little longer, letting Harry strengthen his lungs as I was told it doesn't hurt a baby to cry a little; when his crying turned to a scream – terrible screaming – I knew something was wrong. I stopped what I was doing and ran up the stairs to his room.

"I near-screamed myself! It was awful." Megan's face was filled with shock and horror, her eyes wide, like she was reliving the moment. "At first, I couldn't believe what I was seeing, and couldn't move... but then Harry stopped his cries and seemed to be choking." The young woman was shaking and tears were forming in the corners of her eyes. "They were killing my baby! It was the fear of losing him that made me do what I did. I reacted, rushed over to Harry's cot, pulled him out, and through a fog of flies, I ran from the room, closing the door behind me.

"Quickly, I swept the flies off Harry's face, off his head, and more off his body. I found loads in his mouth and used my fingers to pluck them out, clearing his airway. In no time, he was screaming again, which was fine; he was breathing. But that wasn't the end of it. The flies which were clinging to Harry's body, or which I hadn't killed, started going berserk and attacking us.

"I didn't know flies could bite! These ones could. They kept flying at us, aiming for our faces, our eyes, our mouths! I kept hitting at them, knocking some away, but more would come back at us. They were persistent, never giving up. In the end, I took Harry into the bathroom and climbed under the shower. Flies don't like water so much, and the ones that continued to cling to our clothing, our hair or our faces, were soon drowned. A good many more died in their vain attempts at getting to us, heedless to the danger the shower presented them.

"What seemed like a long time later, when the flies had stopped coming, the bathroom was now filled with steam thick as smoke, I climbed out of the shower. Dripping wet, carrying Harry still crying, I searched the house, checking to make sure it was safe. It was. The flies were gone... or I had killed them all."

"What happened then?" asked McCardle, like a child enthralled by a Brothers Grimm fairy tale.

"I called Scott and told him what had happened. He told me he'd read something in *The Fulbarton Chronicle* and said that I should call the police... and here you are."

"It sounds like quite an ordeal, Miss Pritchard," said Baylem, who had listened carefully to the young woman's account.

"Tell me about it. I can't stop shaking." Megan raised an arm out ahead to show that her hand was quivering. "I'd have a stiff drink if I weren't breastfeeding... which reminds me; Harry is due a feed in a minute."

Without realising, Baylem found his eyes straying towards the young woman's chest. He mentally admonished himself. "Can you show us the baby's room?" he asked.

"Yes, it's this way." Megan Pritchard led the two detectives out of the living room, across the short hallway to the stairs, and up. Harry's room was the second room along the landing, the bathroom being the first. The room opposite was the master bedroom. "It's just through there," she opened the door and nudged it forward. She made no movement towards entering herself.

"Thank you," said McCardle, stepping into the room. Baylem clicked on the overhead light. A Winnie the Pooh shade hanging from the six-inch pendant light fitting glowed warmly.

The room had been decorated entirely with the Winnie the Pooh theme, with wallpaper, curtains and matching bed linen completing the nursery. Walking casually towards the cot, Baylem could see evidence of the fly attack all around.

Scattered on the floor, in the cot, on the bed linen, and everywhere, countless dead insects flung or fallen. Some crushed; others showing little signs of trauma. Baylem stooped down. From inside his jacket, he withdrew a pen and prodded one of the dead flies around his feet.

"Looks to be the same as the others," he said.

"How did they get in?" asked McCardle.

Baylem stood up and surveyed the room. Something caught his attention, but he ignored it for the moment. The Winnie the Pooh curtains undulated gently at the window. He zigzagged across the room, careful to avoid standing on any of the flies. At the window, he drew the curtains open to reveal a view of a well-kept garden. "The window is open a crack... I'd guess the flies entered through here."

"Is that wide enough?" asked the DS. "These flies... they look quite bloated to fit through it."

"You'd be surprised how small a gap they can squeeze through," Baylem replied. "Tell me, Miss Pritchard. When did you open this window?" He raised his voice, not knowing whether the young woman was just outside the room or if she had returned downstairs.

Megan Pritchard was waiting on the stairs' landing and appeared almost immediately. "It's been open for weeks," she replied. "It gets really stuffy in here during the summer... especially in the afternoons and evening when the sun faces this side."

"Have you been aware of an increase in fly activity in your house over the past few days?" Baylem retraced his steps back to the entrance of the room, where the young woman had appeared.

Megan shrugged. "No more than normal for this time of year. One or two in each of the rooms; they usually come and go."

"What about in this room?"

Megan shook her head. "Until this morning, I can't say I've seen any flies in here. Spiders, definitely... but not flies."

"Okay. Just one last question: that camera set into the ceiling..." the DI pointed towards a bullet camera positioned in the corner on the external wall side, "does it work and is it attached to a recording device?"

"Yes... that's the brainchild of Scott. We have a camera in every room – except the bathroom – and two outside, for security. Plus it allows us to keep an eye on Harry when he's in bed. You can't be too careful these days... not with all the immigrants coming over."

Actually, McCardle was about to point out, *most house burglaries in the UK are committed by white, British men*, but then thought there was little merit in doing so.

"It's hooked up to a video recorder downstairs."

"Was it on when the flies attacked?"

Megan nodded. "Yes."

Baylem's expression brightened. "I'd like to see the video, if I may?"

The young woman turned and left the room, followed by Baylem, with McCardle at the back. They clambered down the stairs. In the living room, the constable was where the detectives had left her. She was playing with the baby.

Megan Pritchard led Baylem and McCardle into the kitchen. "We keep the system in the cupboard, hidden behind tins of beans and boxes of teabags," she said. "Scot says that burglars often sabotage the systems by turning them off, or even taking them with them. He thought it was a good idea hiding it somewhere less obvious."

Baylem saw the sense in it.

"It's in here," said Megan, opening up a built-in cupboard that took up space between a recess where a fridge freezer had been installed and the doorway leading out to the garden. She reached in to remove some carefully placed tins, to reveal the surveillance system. "There." On the top of a thin, black box, was a ten-inch monitor affixed to a black plastic stand. The young woman pressed the small button on one edge and watched it boot up. A few seconds later and the image of a split screen appeared; six small pictures within a grid. Most of them appeared fixed like photographs, but two – the living room and the kitchen – displayed movement; the police constable and the baby in one, and the backs of the detectives and Megan in the other.

"Is it easy to rewind the video... and focus on the recording from one camera?" asked McCardle, peering into the cupboard. On various shelves were packs of dried food, cereals, biscuits, tinned produce and sundry other items.

"Fairly," she replied. "Here." She stabbed a finger at the touch-screen monitor, touching the image from the camera broadcasting from Harry's room. The picture filled the screen, together with a playback bar at the bottom and icons for pause, rewind and fast-forward. "You can either swipe the bar to move the picture back and forth. Or tap these buttons."

"Thank you. Is it okay...?" *if we take a look on our own?* Baylem was edging past the young woman.

"Absolutely," Megan replied. "If you don't mind, I'll leave you to it. I need to feed Harry anyway."

"Cheers," said McCardle, filling the space vacated by Megan, moving up close to the DI.

Baylem was rewinding the video, the speed was 'x2', and was very slow. Meddlesomely, McCardle brushed Baylem's hand aside and tapped the 'rewind' symbol a couple of times; each touch doubled the speed – 'x4', 'x8' – so she jabbed it some more until the picture was backpedalling almost at a blur.

"Stop!" snapped Baylem. "There. Look. Miss Pritchard picks up Harry."

McCardle tapped the play button. "My God… he's covered. You can barely tell that there's a child beneath." The video was showing Megan pulling her baby up from the cot, hastily flapping at the flies, and hurrying from the room.

"Let's go back further to see where the flies came from."

The sergeant moved the recording back ten minutes… the flies started dropping down from somewhere in small, disorderly groups, whilst others buzzed in solo from around the room.

"Can we see where they are coming from?" asked Baylem again, staring at the show.

"No… not clearly. They seem to be arriving from various points, from all around the room. But look, the flies aren't landing on the baby yet. They're gathering on the cot."

"Go back further… keep an eye on the window. I have a gut feeling that is where they came in."

McCardle took the recording back deeper into the night. An hour before the attack, the flies stopped coming. The room was gradually darkening as the sun went back down, night time replacing it. The colour image had changed to black and white with a green tinge. The clock wound back through the minutes, then the hours. Harry was asleep in bed; moving occasionally.

At midnight, Scott walked backwards into the room, picked up the baby, and walked backwards out of the room. The bright patch of light spilling in from the stairs' landing blinked off.

"Where did the flies come from?" asked Baylem impatiently. McCardle pressed the 'rewind' symbol again to speed things up. The playback moved back ever faster. Soon, darkness gave way to light and the comings and goings of both Megan and her boyfriend, Scott, were telecast, as they entered the room, opened the curtains, went to the wardrobe, came in for something else, went back out again, the time counting downwards through eight p.m., seven p.m., six p.m., five p.m....

"Stop," Baylem saw something, "let it play for a moment."

McCardle pressed the 'play' symbol on the screen.

Appearing small on the display, an insect arrived through the gap at the window. Hesitantly, it jerkily-crawled over the frame into the room and appeared to look around as though checking the way was clear, before taking off, flying unwaveringly – completely un-fly-like – in a straight course across the room.

"Where's he going?" asked Baylem quietly to himself, following it with his eyes.

McCardle saw it first. "Up there," she said, pointing a finger towards the wardrobe. Initially, Baylem couldn't see what it was she was indicating.

Then he noticed. The top of the wardrobe was a throbbing, coagulating, carpet of agitated insects, so many gathered in such proximity that climbing over each other, and attempting to exist in the same space, was unavoidable.

"That's not natural," he said. "There must be hundreds of them."

"More like thousands," McCardle revised, "maybe tens of thousands." Voluntarily, she started rewinding the footage again. One by one, flies began to drift backwards across the room to the window, disappearing over the edge into the afternoon sunshine, then clusters of more than half a dozen, and groups of twelve to fifteen. Like rippling smoke but in reverse, the flies flew backwards to the windowsill, bobbed about like they were contemplating something, and then disappearing through the crack into the afternoon sun.

"Did you see them?" Megan Pritchard appeared in the kitchen

behind them, almost startling Baylem. She was holding Harry over her shoulder, tapping his back gently, trying to get some wind.

Baylem turned from the surveillance station to face the young woman. "In a manner, yes," he said. "I don't suppose there is a way I could get a copy of some of this footage?"

4

The press room had never had so many journalists, photographers, newscasters or television cameraman in situ. The eight rows of fifteen chairs weren't enough to seat everyone, so many stood around the sides of the room or at the back.

Baylem entered via what he referred to as the tradesman's entrance, the door closest to the back offices, where only police personnel were admitted. The press had arrived in force through the civilian entrance, to the front of the building. McCardle was at his heels behind him, following like a rock star's groupie.

A woman in a dark-blue suit and a sharp collared white blouse stepped up from the side on to a small stage. A little along to the centre was a lectern, the Fulbarton Constabulary logo printed on the audience-facing side, and a gooseneck microphone was affixed into it, positioned at speaking level. "Ladies and gents..." she said, moving in front of the microphone. The room swiftly fell silent. "In a moment, Detective Inspector Baylem will make a statement. Please hold off on asking questions until the end, when the DI will be happy to answer one or two."

The woman stepped away from the microphone as Baylem strode confidently up to the stand. "Thank you, Barbara," he said, addressing the PR rep employed to manage press enquiries and releases.

She stepped down from the podium and took up a spot close to where McCardle stood watching.

"Thank you, everyone, for coming at such short notice." He made it sound like he had personally invited the media to come at his bidding. "In the face of growing public concern and the frivolous reporting in the press and on the TV today, I thought it provident that I share with you the facts surrounding the deaths occurring in Fulbarton yesterday.

"Police were called to a residential address in the morning, where a man was found dead lying in his bed. There were no signs of breaking or entering, and the cause of death was unknown. Later that day, reports of a break-in were received at another residential address. Upon investigation, the house in question appeared undisturbed, except for the breakage of a small glass window. It was after a full search of the property that we discovered three bodies, in an advanced state of decomposition, in a room at basement level. There was no evidence of a struggle and no clear indication of the cause of death.

"Late last evening, I was called to an incident at Hinkley Walsh Insurance, where a man was found dead on the third floor. A vending machine had toppled over onto him and appears to have played a significant part in his demise. Now, we are treating each of these deaths as unexplained, but we are NOT ascribing them to anything sinister. We are not treating them as murder, so our town's exceptional crime statistics remain unblemished, and we are not considering outlandish ideas such as 'fly attacks', 'zombies' or 'alien abductions' as causation." A few people laughed in the audience.

"Let me reassure the public. These deaths, though tragic and the causes still unknown, are not linked in absolutely any way. It's just a sad, terrible coincidence that they occurred so close together, in strange, unexplainable, circumstances, in a town unaccustomed to such events.

"Our condolences go to their families at this difficult time and our enquiries will continue as we endeavour to ascertain the cause of death for each of these victims, and we'll communicate our findings as and when, once next of kin have been notified. That's all I have to say on the matter... for now." Baylem looked around the room, noticing hands shoot up skyward. He turned to face Barbara who nodded for him to carry on. "Okay. I have time for a couple of questions," he said, sounding reluctant. "You," he pointed to a woman in her thirties, who, unbeknownst to him, worked for the *Fulbarton Evening Herald*. She had raven-black hair hanging loose and framing her oval face and an understated beauty with barely any makeup. Behind the red rectangular full-rimmed glasses were brown eyes.

"Emily Herrington, *Fulbarton Evening Herald*," she started. "What can you tell us about reports that there were an unaccountable number of dead flies found at each of the scenes; AND is there any link between these deaths, and those dead cows found at the dairy farm and the road traffic accident the other day, where eyewitnesses claim to have seen a swarm of fly-like insects leaving the area?"

DI Baylem cleared his throat. "Well... firstly, it is commonplace to find flies where dead bodies are found. Blowflies lay their eggs in the flesh of the deceased. We often use the growth cycle of the larval stages to pinpoint a time of death. Though I can confirm there were an abundance of flies at all three of the scenes, we must stress this isn't uncommon, especially, if you take into consideration the very warm, humid temperatures we're currently experiencing.

"To answer the second question, my department has no involvement with regards to the dead cows reported as being found at the dairy farm. My understanding is a local vet is investigating that. Also, the road traffic accident on the outskirts of Fulbarton; the witness providing that account with regards to seeing a swarm-like number of flies at the scene could not be corroborated by anyone else in attendance, and was given even less credence is the fact that this witness suffers from a medical condition where delusions are commonplace."

"So, are you saying there is no link at all between these occurrences?" pressed Emily Herrington, jumping in before the DI could move on to another question.

Baylem glowered at the local report. "I think my answer clarifies the position, yes."

Calls of "Inspector," echoed around the room. Hands shot up like children desperate to answer a teacher's question.

"No more questions," said Baylem, stepping away from the lectern.

Dissatisfied journalists stood up and waded forward hurling questions and demanding answers, crowding around the DI as he made his escape through the tradesman's entrance. McCardle followed him out as three uniformed policemen stepped up to the doorway to bar any unauthorised access. Shouts of dissent followed them deep into the building.

The DI hurried down the corridor, stopping after a couple of turns.

Out of breath, McCardle bounded up behind him. "Sir, are you all right?"

Baylem was smiling and seething at the same time. "The Chief Super should've done that. He's used to talking out of his arse. Plus, public speaking was never my passion," he said. "Well? How did I do?"

"I thought it went well, sir," she said, unconvincingly. "But, after this morning... how long do you think people will believe it for?"

Baylem started walking again, this time with less haste. He headed towards the stairs that led to his office. "If I was a betting man, I'd say until lunchtime, at the latest," he said with conviction.

CHAPTER TEN

D R JAMES QUISENBERRY WAS AT the breakfast table spooning cornflakes into his mouth from the Kellogg's *Frosties* bowl. In front of him, Tony the Tiger was on its side declaring with great enthusiasm "Gr-r-r-eat!" within a speech bubble. It reminded his fiancée, Gemma, of his lighter side, even though it was rarely on display these days.

The kitchen-diner was spacious and tidy. Along one side was a stainless steel double-oven, hob and an extractor hood built-in above it, all spotlessly clean; opposite was a built-in fridge freezer, and joining the two sides between uninterrupted worktops was a sink just beneath the window overlooking a well-kept garden, a dishwasher and a washing machine. Filling the space between were matching wall units and cupboards hidden behind expensive oak doors.

The dining area was separated from the kitchen by a breakfast bar which offered a natural partition within the room; four tall padded stools were tucked in beneath it. Quisenberry was sitting with his back towards the kitchen. To the right of him, along the length of the wall, was a mahogany sideboard; two bowls (one filled with fruit), and an array of photographs were placed symmetrically atop a white linen table runner that overhung at either end. Resting in the second bowl were loose change, a mobile phone and a bunch of keys.

Standing on the other side of the kitchen doorway, her back turned to face the television hanging from the wall, Gemma stroked her swollen stomach. Her pregnancy was near to term at thirty-eight weeks and she was good to drop. The humidity of the summer and the discomfort associated with carrying a child made the experience insufferable, one which caused James no end of an earache. She watched the early morning news whilst nursing a cup of lemon tea, occasionally blowing a thin stream of air towards its deep-amber surface in an attempt at cooling it down.

"*There have been at least seven unexplained deaths this month in the small East Anglian town of Fulbarton, with eyewitness accounts and local reporters claiming a deadly swarm of flies are to blame...*"

"James, are you hearing this?" Gemma asked over her shoulder.

"What?" replied Quisenberry between chewing cereal.

"*Is that likely though, John? Are the people in Fulbarton right to be worried this morning?*"

"The news, James. There's something about flies... there have been some attacks. They're nothing to do with you, are they?"

Quisenberry stopped eating, dropped his spoon in the half-empty bowl of cornflakes, stood up hastily and joined his partner to watch the television.

"*Well, pathology reports are not conclusive,*" started the reporter. Quisenberry recognised him as John Harriman. "*However, the fact of the matter is all these deaths have flies in common. An anonymous source told me that the airways of Sean Wallace and the three bodies belonging to the Jessops were all obstructed by foreign objects lodged in the back of their throats. Those foreign objects were found to be flies... hundreds of them compressed together.*"

"Did he say where that is?" asked James, ignoring the accusation he had noted within her voice, a slight note of apprehension in his.

"I dunno… some place in Fulbarton, I think."

"Here in Fulbarton?" he asked anxiously.

Gemma turned to her fiancé, seeing the furrowed lines of his forehead and the alarm in his eyes. "James?" The way she spoke his name was laden with an unasked question: *what's going on? What's wrong?*

"*Do we know what type of fly caused this, John? Are they your everyday, garden-variety type, or are they something else?*" continued the television, the picture changing efficiently to the outside reporter. "*There's been no official word regarding the flies, or indeed whether they actually ARE the cause of the problems here in Fulbarton. But a community is waking up this morning in fear, and there are many questions that need answering, along with the need for reassurance that these deaths are not going to continue.*"

Quisenberry turned towards Gemma and forced a smile. "I'm sure it's nothing," he tried reassuring, "just a coincidence."

The television broadcast continued with the presenter back in the BBC studio ongoing his long-distance interview. "*I understand Fulbarton Police are going to be issuing a statement a bit later this morning?*"

Quisenberry turned his attention back to the screen on the wall.

"*Yes, that's right,*" continued the reporter, "*Detective Inspector Baylem is the officer in charge of the investigation. We're expecting him to make a public announcement sometime this morning.*"

"Detective Inspector Baylem," repeated the doctor to himself, like it might be significant. He said it again to ensure that it was retained, this time, inside his head: *Detective Inspector Baylem.*

"What's going on, James?" Gemma repeated. "Is this some-thing to do with your… *project*?" She was starting to panic. There was nothing she didn't know about his scientific work at the lab; the confidentiality agreement he had signed had evidently not ex-tended to her. James Quisenberry trusted her with all his secrets;

it was how she put up with his long absences and late nights and knew that he was a brilliant man.

He was a geneticist at Biomargent Sciences, a company infamous for its research using animals, much to the condemnation of animal rights activists and members purporting to belong to *PETA*. No creature great or small was invulnerable to study, in this case, erring towards the latter end of the size scale.

Her fiancé ignored the question.

"I thought you said the programme was finished, that you were done with those bloody flies!" Gemma snapped, sensing a potential threat to the father of her unborn child.

"I am," Quisenberry asserted sternly. Impulsively, he snatched up the TV remote and turned it off. "Something must have happened prior to the study's end." He started to pace, his thoughts travelling to a couple of months earlier, to the time of his demonstration.

That had gone terribly wrong.

The flies were all destroyed... he told himself. Two people had died, and as a result, General Makepeace had pulled the plug.

But were they all dead? Doubt filled his head and he caressed his temples with one hand, as though attempting to ward off a migraine. He walked across to Gemma and stopped close-by. "Gem... don't worry about it." He kissed the pregnant woman on the forehead and laid his right hand gently on her bump. "I'd better go." He moved away towards the dinner table and snatched up his navy blue, single-breasted blazer from the back of a chair.

"Already? You've not finished your breakfast."

"I'm stuffed!" He blew out emphatically, rubbed a distended belly, and then slipped on the jacket, fastening one of the buttons. "Listen... I love you, Gemma... and little Morton," he said earnestly, indicating the unborn baby. "No matter what happens, remember that." Without a further word, he about-turned, scooped up his mobile phone and keys from the bowl on the sideboard and left the house, taking the rear exit; French doors set into the side wall of the kitchen-diner. He slid it open a gap, sidled out like a crab, and then closed it behind him.

2

Listening to Ed Sheeran in the car helped him relax. For the forty-minute drive, Quisenberry couldn't stop worrying about the news item regarding the incidents occurring in Fulbarton.

Were his flies truly responsible?

They couldn't be, he reasoned. His flies were all dead. General Makepeace had insisted upon it, threatening Biomargent Sciences with financial repercussions if James Quisenberry did not comply with the kill order and the fly programme was not terminated.

Even so, he had to make sure.

A light drizzle had started to fall. Ordinarily, the doctor would have noticed, especially as the summer had been exceptionally dry and hotter than normal, with several days in July already hitting 30°C and half the month to go. The respite from the heat was more than welcome.

The dual carriageway was quiet as he drove along, and soon, he saw the signage placed to the side of the road marking his exit. He flicked the left indicator and manoeuvred his white Ford Edge on to the ramp, positioning the vehicle into the lane marked for the turn ahead.

The single carriage was lined by thick foliage and tall trees, the fields and buildings beyond purposely hidden from view along with the high perimeter fencing topped with spirals of barbed wire; elaborate security measures. For the next five minutes, Quisenberry drove, ignorant to the light rain and not noticing the deathly silence as the last track on the CD finished, ending Ed Sheeran's singing. A sudden break in the umbrage revealed the narrow lane that wound for half a mile towards the facilities where the doctor worked.

A security barrier was in place as the driver of the white SUV approached. A man in military greens stepped from a small brick building carrying a clipboard, walking to a place just ahead of the blockade as Quisenberry slowed his car and then stopped. A press of a button set into his door activated the electric window. It wound down gingerly. The guard stepped down from the pavement and stooped into the car, spots of rain entering with him.

"Good morning, Doctor." The guard had a London accent.

"Craig," greeted Quisenberry distractedly.

"Nice day," he said sarcastically.

The doctor grunted.

"D'you have your pass, sir?"

"Oh. Yea. Sure." Dr Quisenberry slipped his right hand into his blazer and produced his ID card, holding it out for Craig to inspect.

The guard took it, gave it half a look, and then handed it back. This was a daily performance – a routine that every employee of Biomargent had to endure. Security was paramount. The contrivance was not to check that staff were authorised to visit – not entirely – but to ensure that staff had their requisite passes to gain access to the labs and buildings beyond. "Very good, sir." He handed the card to the doctor, stepped up to the pavement and pressed a button on the yellow barrier cabinet; the six-meter boom (the metal bar obstructing the road) began to rise. "Have a great day!" bade the guard.

Quisenberry waited a moment for the barrier to open fully before setting the car forward. In the rear view mirror, he watched the guard disappear back into the small building and reach for his telephone.

3

"You wanted to know when Doctor Quisenberry arrived. He's now here, General."

"Thank you, Craig," replied General Makepeace from his desk. Set ahead of him was that day's edition of *The Fulbarton Chronicle*, the headline: FULBARTON RESIDENTS LIVE IN FEAR!

In the corner of the room, affixed on a cantilever bracket to the wall, was a thirty-two-inch flat screen television with the BBC news on. The sound had been muted, but the general could see what was being said by the subtitles flashing across the bottom.

His mood was dark. Darker, it felt, than the sky outside. It was raining; droplets were 'pit-patting' against the floor-to-ceiling windows that filled one side of the room. Like baby's tears, they trekked thin lines down the glass. The weather was reflecting his disposition, for he felt no joy for what he was being forced to do. The handset of the phone was still in his hand from speaking with the guard. Craig had done as asked, calling him to advise when the geneticist, James Quisenberry, had arrived.

General Makepeace lifted the phone's receiver to his ear, his other hand punching the three numbers of an extension into the telephone's number pad. The ringing tone sounded for a couple of heartbeats, before being replaced with the telltale signs of an open line: subtle background noises and the faint whistle of air and the sigh of breathing.

"He's here. Meet me at his office in ten minutes."

The recipient of the general's instructions said nothing by way of acknowledgement. The line continued to hum with activity before crackling, as if from amplified movement, and then nothing, dead silence. Makepeace replaced the handset in its cradle and puffed out his cheeks. Slowly, he expulsed air through closed lips.

He glanced at the newspaper and the name of the reporter assigned to the story taking up most of the front page.

Emily Herrington.

"She knows too much," said the general to himself, adding ominously: "that ought to be remedied."

The phone began to ring stridently, line one on the digital

display began to pulsate. The general swept up the handset and jabbed the button flashing. "Hello."

"*General? It's J-James. James Quisenberry. Um...*" It was clear that the caller was nervous. "*... I think we have a problem.*"

"You think." Distractedly, he picked up the newspaper and held it in front of him, the headline glaring up. He looked straight through it.

"*It could be a coincidence...*" Quisenberry said, "*... if not, I can fix it.*"

"Fix it? How? Can you 'un-kill' people?" General Makepeace tossed the newspaper across the room. "Fuck!"

"*Trust me, sir,*" implored Quisenberry. "*If it's our flies, I can track them and bring them to heel.*"

"You told me they were all destroyed."

"*They were! I dunno what happened. Maybe some escaped.*"

"Escaped? You assured me that could NEVER happen!" the general yelled. "At least five people are dead! DEAD! There could be more; no, there WILL be more!"

"*You don't know that!*"

"You say you can track them if it's our flies? How?"

Quisenberry went quiet, as though he was considering a response to a tricky job interview question.

"You still there?" pressed the general impatiently.

"*Radio waves,*" blurted the doctor. "*My flies were genetically enhanced with the ability to receive information through radio waves... that was how I was manipulating them during the demonstration.*"

The general recalled the doctor's demonstration debacle. Two lab technicians had died during the presentation; panic had spread among the hundred-strong audience before the flies had been destroyed and order restored.

"If I remember, that didn't go too well," downplayed the general.

"*True, but that's not my point. The flies not only receive information; they unconsciously transmit it, too; it was one of the fail-safes introduced in the event we lost control of them."*

"How insightful," lamented the general.

Dr Quisenberry pretended not to hear him. *"Using three or four strategically placed antennas, we may be able to locate them by triangulating the source of transmission."*

"Seriously, would that work?"

"Well. Not with a small number of flies, as the wavelengths would be too long. But with a great number – an optimal figure of say, ten thousand – this would transmit a strong enough signal.

"We would soon find out whether – somehow – they're our flies. To do what is being reported would require a lot of insects working together... that many would definitely generate enough of a signal to establish origin."

"I don't know," pondered the general. "How are you sure it would work?"

"Well, it's simple," said the geneticist. *"If we can't find a transmission, we can safely assume it's not our flies to blame. We can take a deep breath and live the rest of our lives."*

"Except, these fly attacks, if that's what they are, will continue."

"Not our concern," replied Quisenberry insouciantly.

"And, if we find a transmission?"

The line went quiet again. Pensively, the doctor replied: *"There's going to be a shit load of explaining to do and a damnable amount of damage control needed."*

James Quisenberry was at his desk when General Makepeace stepped in a couple of minutes later. No sooner had the call been terminated, the army officer must have left his goldfish bowl and set forth for the geneticist's laboratory on the other side of the compound. He was flanked by two Military Policemen, and a little further behind him was the CEO of Biomargent Sciences, Tim Howlett, looking flustered and a little distressed.

"General?" a puzzled look filled Dr Quisenberry's face, turning to concern, followed by fear. He sat upright, his legs positioned in readiness to spring up, preparing for fight or flight. "What's the meaning of this?"

"James, I've given what you said a bit more thought. Do you have the frequency the flies would be transmitting at?"

"Yes, here," he gestured towards his computer with a wave of his hand, "but–"

"Then, your work here is done. For your own protection, we need you to go with these men. Officers, take him into custody."

The two MPs sidestepped past General Makepeace and towered over Dr Quisenberry. "Doctor, please come with us," one said, stretching out a hand like he was offering support or help.

"You can't do this," replied the geneticist. "Tim?" he implored the CEO to step in and help. "For fuck sake, we grew up together. Do something!"

Like a timid animal, Tim Howlett shrunk back, his face ashen-white. "I can't," he said feebly. "I have what's best for you and the company, to think about."

"For me? For the company?"

"It's like what you said," declared General Makepeace, "there's a damnable amount of damage control needed... starting with you."

With little sign of James Quisenberry getting up from his chair, the MP who had politely asked him to come with him, grabbed hold of the geneticist's arm and pulled him to his feet. With more fight than was anticipated, the second MP stepped in with handcuffs and wrestled one loop into place, forcing both the man's arms behind his back and securing the second restraint.

"Take him somewhere safe... make sure he's comfortable. When the time is right, we will have further use for him."

The first MP nodded.

"What about Gemma?" Quisenberry pleaded, desperately. "Our baby is due any day now. She needs me! AARON needs me!" He emphasised the name. The security guards were pulling him up from the chair.

"Is that your baby's name?" General Makepeace asked. There was a twinkle in his eye. He appeared to be enjoying the encounter.

"Yes," the doctor lied. *It's Morton, you prick*, he thought.

"I'll make sure they are looked after," replied the general, sinisterly.

"Stay away from her!" James warned. Heavily, he was dragged across the room towards the exit.

General Makepeace said nothing, a knowing smile spreading across his face.

"You won't get away with this!" screamed the geneticist as the two MPs roughhoused him out of the laboratory, dragging him kicking and screaming down the corridor. "I'm not the only one who knows!"

"I figured that," muttered the general for his own benefit, adding ominously, "which is why I've taken steps… for her protection, of course. Goodbye, James."

The laboratory door closed behind them, though the seal did little to blot the sound of "Bastards!" being hollered as he went.

The general turned to face the CEO. "An unfortunate necessity, I'm afraid," he smiled wanly. "It's just a matter of containment. He's too valuable and he knows too much." He manoeuvred around the room to position himself behind Quisenberry's desk, "Now. Let's see if I can make sense of these radio frequencies."

5

Whilst her fiancé was being hauled from his laboratory in handcuffs towards a holding room beneath ground level, Gemma was returning from an early morning walk to the local Tesco Metro, two blocks away, nestled between a hairdressers and a hospice charity shop. Gently swinging at her side was a shopping bag with a loaf of bread, ham, a bunch of bananas, a pint of milk and that morning's edition of *The Fulbarton Chronicle*. She had scowled at the paper's headline, fear and foreboding causing her heart to triple-beat. Looped over her shoulder was a small handbag, just big enough for her purse and mobile phone.

Despite the early hour – it was ten-past-seven – the sun was already warming up, but not fiercely hot like it had been these past couple of weeks; this was a factor in her choosing to venture out before most people were barely out of bed. Gathering around the sky were some dark clouds as light rain was forecast, but for now, she was grateful for the sun's rays caressing her skin as she had left home without an umbrella.

A milk float hummed by and a paperboy on a mountain bike whizzed past on the opposite side of the road. There was little other traffic on the street, just an occasional car moving by in either direction.

The pregnant woman slowly crossed the road at the zebra crossing, halting a solitary vehicle; its driver appearing a little impatient in contempt of her condition. She acknowledged the driver, waving a 'thank you', stopping on the other side to rub her swollen belly.

"Nearly home," she whispered to her bump. The unborn child appeared to give a kick in response, Gemma smiled. Nothing in the world was more satisfying or rewarding than carrying a baby, she thought. On the other hand, the acid reflux, the swollen ankles, and the haemorrhoids were an entirely different (and completely unwelcome) matter.

At the end of the road, she turned right at the junction on to The Avenue, and crossed the road to the other side. Her house was now just a block away. One left turn, then a short walk past a block of flats and twelve semi-detached houses, their gardens long and narrow, was all that remained.

She was in no hurry, though the screeching of tyres behind her startled her. She stopped to glance over her shoulder and watched as a black Land Rover Discovery entered the road a little too fast, followed closely by a silver Renault van.

The manner in which they moved appeared purposeful, as though on a mission. Sensing danger, she turned her head slightly, away from the road, hoping to avoid seeing the drivers of either vehicle or the passengers, and them from noticing her. Gemma waited for them to pass before continuing her jaunt, dismayed to learn that they were turning left, taking her road. More screeching tyres followed.

Curious, the pregnant woman quickened her stride. It wasn't easy and the pace soon caused a stitch to stab at her side, dull and throbbing; she gritted her teeth and persevered. There was a nagging suspicion about those two vehicles, a strong instinct that something was amiss. She knew she wasn't psychic – didn't believe in it – but often experienced such sensations, like she had a sixth-sense. It was a gut-feeling. She called them the *heebee-jeebies*, which wasn't the literal meaning of the slang term, although often the sensation *was* intertwined with trepidation.

A feeling she was now experiencing.

Gemma stepped around the corner, and stopped–

–dead ahead, the Land Rover and the Renault van had come to a halt. A stream of men dressed all in black, wearing ski-masks, helmets and armed with assault rifles, hit the concrete, running.

Gemma gasped and was close to hyperventilating. The handles of the bag in her right hand slipped free from involuntarily loosening her grip, clattering to the paving. Transfixed, she watched as eight serious-looking soldiers charged down the path towards her home, followed by a bald black man; she assumed, just by the absence of battle-dress, he was in charge. Beneath a Kevlar bulletproof jacket, he wore a suit.

Casually, the man entered her front garden and turned his head her way, looking straight at her. If he realised she was his target, he did not acknowledge it; instead, he followed his men, who had split up and were now positioned at the front and rear of the property, preparing to storm in.

"Shit," she exclaimed. Hastily, she picked up her bag, grateful that nothing had spilled out, and about turned, retreating around the corner. Unsettled as she was, she moved only slightly faster than a steady walk, her bump and the burgeoning need to pee preventing her from moving any quicker. Every so often, she threw a glance over her shoulder, fearful that those entering her home would redirect their attention and start giving chase.

After six nervous peeks, a couple of corner turns and arriving at the front of a coffee shop a short way from the Tesco Metro she had shopped in quarter of an hour earlier, Gemma shuffled between a seating arrangement set on the forecourt by an employee – a spotty youth – who was still in the midst of setting and wiping tables. The door into the coffee shop was propped open. Without any drama, she walked in, glad to be shielded from traffic and any pursuers.

"Is everything all right?" The barista perched on a stool behind a serving counter looked up, concern filling his face, noting the woman's 'condition'. He was in his late-fifties, dressed in white with a blue pinstriped apron tied around his waist. His white-blond hair was long and neatly fixed in a tail at the back of his head.

She hadn't noticed how breathless she was. Catching some air, she forced a smile. "Yea... I'm desperate for the toilet."

On one of the walls, a TV was on. A twenty-four-hour news channel played out, the volume turned low. Subtitles flashed across the screen.

The barista matched her smile. "You're welcome to use ours… though it'll cost you a purchase. Toilet's out there." He pointed towards the back of the room where a door with 'Toilets' was clearly marked.

"That's no problem. I was going to order something. Do you do lemon tea? If not, a cold diet coke with plenty of ice will be fine."

Gemma locked the 'Ladies' door behind her and was soon perched on the wooden seat of the toilet, relieved to release the pressure on her bladder. Baby Morton gave a kick in gratitude, as though pleased with having more space to roam inside. She pulled her knickers back up and crossed to the sink. A mirror behind it reflected her rattled appearance. Her face looked hot and blotchy, and her long brown hair was matted and damp. Running the cold tap, she palmed a handful of water over her cheeks, repeating the action several times. Suitably refreshed, she used paper towels to dab herself dry.

Returning to the coffee shop, the barista had set her drink – lemon tea – down in a place facing the television on the wall. Gemma walked steadily in and placed her bags on a chair alongside one she eased out to sit upon. Settling down, she fumbled her mobile from her handbag. Pressing a hotkey, she dialled James' number.

The ringing tone played for ten seconds before being replaced by a recording of James:

"Hi, this is James Quisenberry. I'm sorry I can't get to my phone right now, but if you leave your name and number after the beep I'll get back to you…"

Ahead of the beep, Gemma disconnected the call. Before she had time to think of what to do next, the handset began to ring. The barista recognised the tune as the theme from an old TV detective series, *Van der Valk*.

The screen flashed up the caller's identification as: JAMES.

"Hello, James?" relief filled her head. It was short-lived.

"*Afraid not,*" said an unfamiliar voice. "*This is General Make-peace. Your boyfriend… is… how do they say? … Indisposed.*"

"Oh? Where is he?" she asked, fearful and worried. "Is he okay?"

The general didn't elaborate, instead moved on: "*Where are you, Gemma? I sent someone to collect you. You're not at home…*"

Alarm bells rang inside her head. An image of the Land Rover and the Renault Van flashed into her mind; the armed soldiers piling into her front garden, followed by the bald black man who had looked her way but seemed not to see her.

"I…" she desperately clawed for something to say, "… had to go out for a walk," she said, settling on a lie. "The baby was giving my uterus merry hell this morning. I couldn't get comfortable."

The general laughed breezily at the other end. "*The joys of childbirth,*" he said, as though he had experienced such a thing himself. "*James said Aaron was causing you some problems.*"

"James said that?" asked Gemma, seeking clarification. "He told you our baby's name?"

"*He swore me to secrecy, but yes. He said you'd settled on Aaron.*"

"James would never say that," she denounced. "You're lying. What have you done with my fiancé?"

"*I'm not the only one lying, Gemma. You're not out for a walk, are you? You're at a coffee bar on Shaftesbury Road!*"

Gemma flinched; dropping the handset like it suddenly became hot, the mobile breaking apart upon impacting the floor with a clatter, the back and battery bouncing away.

"You sure everything is all right, Miss?" The barista had been quietly observing the woman from behind the coffee bar.

"No," she replied gravely. "I'm in danger."

"Danger?" It sounded too melodramatic for the barista. He decided not to say as much.

"Is there a backway out of this place?"

"Yea, sure," he replied breezily. "It's through here." The barista indicated behind the coffee bar, willing to entertain the young woman's anxiety.

Gemma reached into her handbag and pulled a five pound note from her purse. "Here. For the lemon tea." She handed the money to the man. "Keep the change."

"If you are in danger, wouldn't it be better to call the police?"

Gemma was tempted, but the sound of tyres screeching in the foreground woke her up to reality. It was too late. "I'm out of time," she told the white-blond haired man. "They're here. Stall them... *please*... for my baby's sake!"

The barista looked down at her sadly. He nodded. "Come." He stepped aside, allowing the woman through. "At the back of the kitchen, you see that door. It leads to an alley. Follow it; it will take you out on to Earl Common." Whilst talking, he was scribbling down a number on a piece of paper within his order pad. "If you need somewhere to stay, or help later... when things are settled... call me."

"Thank you." Gemma accepted the slip of paper, knowing she wouldn't use it, before disappearing into the kitchen and racing across to the back door. The barista followed her out. The door was unlocked and opened easily. Outside, it had started to rain.

"Hey, what about your stuff? Your phone?" asked the barista, catching her attention as she stepped out of the kitchen.

"Hold on to it for me, or throw it," she said with indifference, facing him for a final time. "I have no use for them now." She looked scared and was holding her stomach like she was holding something in. Baby Morton wasn't happy, she could feel it.

Turning away, she closed the door behind her and was gone.

CHAPTER ELEVEN

/

THE THIRD-FLOOR CORRIDOR OF THE Alexandra Hotel and Country Club was richly decorated with crystal chandeliers and prints of famous art works spaced along either side of the walls and situated between most of the rooms.

Shortly after half-ten, DI Baylem stepped out of the lift closely followed by his sergeant. With them was the hotel's manager – a slight man of Bangladeshi ancestry – following one step behind; he was smartly dressed in a black suit, red tie, and black shoes that were polished to an immaculate sheen. Downstairs, they had passed two attending paramedics on their way out, their demeanour and downturned faces telling them all they needed to know: their callout had been grim and pointless.

A uniformed constable was standing sentry outside a door ahead. He straightened his posture as he saw the senior police officers arrive.

"So, other than yourself and the cleaner, no one else has visited the room, and nothing has been touched or disturbed?" Baylem was moving briskly; keen to see for himself the identities of the two bodies discovered dead on the bed earlier that morning.

"That's right, sir... to the best of my knowledge. Of course, ambulance men came, and that policeman there... but no one from the hotel."

"Thank you, Mr Malik. I think we're okay from here." Baylem arrived outside the room and the constable on guard duty stepped aside and used the cardkey to unlock the door.

"Please, call me Jamal," he said. "If you need anything... anything at all, just let me know."

Baylem nodded appreciatively. "My sergeant here will want to speak with both you and your cleaner shortly for a statement. Also, with anyone else who may have been on duty and came into contact with these two guests."

"No problem. I'll be downstairs at reception."

Through the doorway, Baylem stepped into the spacious penthouse suite, recognising it was clearly not cheap accommodation. The red carpet was thick and bouncy beneath his feet and there was a burgundy leather sofa and armchair taking up a sizeable portion of the room, a casual distance ahead of the bed. A mahogany coffee table was set with a bowl of fruit in the centre of the seating arrangement. Built into the wall overlooking the room was a very large television that might have looked less conspicuous within a sports bar.

Clothing belonging to the room's inhabitants had been removed in a hurry and lay strewn across the floor, crumpled and forgotten. On the king-sized bed, their bodies were naked and entwined together, joined literally at the hip.

Glancing at them, McCardle could see that they looked to be in mid-coitus, the woman straddling the man; her legs positioned in a 'w' either side of his outstretched lower limbs. She was slumped over, her body twisted awkwardly so that her head was on the pillow; face turned inwards, gazing almost lovingly towards that of the man's. "Any idea when Doctor Hamilton will be here?"

Baylem circled the bed, mentally noting the scene. He focused on the two bodies, ignoring the fact that they were naked. "Floyd should be here soon," he said sadly, studying the face of the man turned his way. "It is him," he determined, adding some tuts. "Edwin Carslake, MP. I didn't like him." He sighed. "I guess the Chief Super won't be so concerned about us investigating these deaths now his buddy has been killed. Crime stats are going to be shot to hell. Who's the woman?"

"She looks familiar," replied McCardle, but couldn't identify her from looks alone. "Very attractive," she observed, stating what Baylem had already established for himself. She scanned the floor for something that could help with yielding her name. Beneath a pair of black sequinned leggings was a small leopard-print purse. "Aha. I might've found something." The sergeant picked it up and studied it curiously, trying to gauge the owner's character just by its look and feel. Getting nothing, she opened it. Inside were a small phone, some cash and a Californian Driver's licence. "Makayla Rose... name's familiar... isn't she that pop star, or something?"

"Yes... I can just about recognise her. Not my kind of music. She was performing at a fundraiser at the Town Hall last night. Must have been how the MP managed to hook up with her... lucky bastard."

"Lucky? He's dead, sir."

"Well... lucky, in the sense that he managed to end up in bed with her in the first place. Look at him; hardly God's gift is he?"

McCardle ignored the salaciously inappropriate comment.

"D'you think they're linked to the deaths from yesterday?" McCardle asked, changing the topic.

"Yes, without a doubt. And the incident with the infant this morning. It's too much to be a coincidence. Besides..." he slipped a pair of latex gloves on and leaned across the left side of the bed. Delicately, he picked up something from beneath the woman's shoulder, dropping it into the centre of his palm. It was a fly, fat and grotesque. "...this confirms it." There were plenty more of the insects scattered around the bed clothes. "My guess: cause of death... hypoxia, most likely from a fly invasion, blocking the airwaves. I'm betting, the same M.O as the others. If we cut their throats open, I'm sure flies will spill out like the innards of a Chicken Kiev."

Trying not to picture that, Sergeant McCardle stood to the right of the bed, peering down at the victims' heads; the man's was turned away from her, but the woman's was facing with her eyes wide and mouth agape. "But how? How's it possible? How on earth can flies do this? Who's ever heard of flies working collectively and cohesively?"

Baylem shrugged. He flipped his palm over and dropped the fly back to the bed. It landed after a bounce. "You saw the security footage earlier from that bedroom attack yourself. There's no denying that those flies were clearly intent on killing that child. It was only luck and quick thinking that the mother got to him in time."

The door into the room opened with a bit of force, startling the plain-clothed police officers. The pathologist, Dr Hamilton, charged in. "Baylem... McCardle," he greeted. "This is getting to be a bit too much of a regularity." He placed down his bag and proceeded towards the victims. He was already wearing forensic coveralls and latex gloves, and was ready to begin preliminary examinations. He walked around the bed, peering down at the intertwined bodies. "I guess this encounter didn't exactly end the way they had hoped."

"Clearly," replied Baylem. He skirted past the pathologist, allowing him better access.

"Any thoughts as to who they are and what might have happened?" asked Hamilton whilst peering in close towards the heads of the deceased.

"Edwin Carslake and Makayla Rose. I might be going out on a limb, but I think they were in the middle of interco–"

"Yes, yes, yes... I can see that. I'm talking about their deaths!"

"Isn't that your job?" asked McCardle.

Hamilton ignored the remark.

"From the looks of things, same causation of death to those investigated yesterday. A distribution of blowflies can be seen around the bodies, and, if I'm not mistaken, traces of them can be found inside their mouths." As DI Baylem talked, the doctor was examining the bodies, nodding his head.

"Yea," agreed Hamilton. "Your assumption appears to be correct, although I can't be certain until I've carried out the full autopsy. Any thoughts on how the flies gained access to the room?" A quick survey proffered no clues. The windows were plate glass, floor-to-ceiling design, with no means to open them.

McCardle was inspecting the room, her eyes scanning around, settling on the wall-mounted air conditioning unit set into the wall. Without a word, she crossed over to it, her eyes locked on.

"No, not yet," said Baylem. He hadn't even started thinking on it.

"Sir... I think I found it," interrupted McCardle. She dragged the burgundy leather armchair to the wall and climbed atop it. From her raised position, she craned her neck to study the air con unit more closely. From inside her jacket, she produced a black biro pen and used it to poke between two slats of the vent at the front. Dragging it across the slit from one side to the next, she knocked free dust, a puff of which fell into her mouth, causing her to recoil and expectorate noisily. Whilst distracted, something small and black fell to the floor.

"You all right, McCardle?" asked Hamilton, looking up from where he was exploring the victim's mouths.

"Yes," she confirmed, wiping her mouth with the back of her hand. Baylem crossed to her side, mistaking his approach as chivalry. As she held out her hand for him to take, to steady her balance as she stepped down, she realised he wasn't there at all for that. Ignoring her, he dropped to his knees and fixed his eyes on the fly that he had watched drop to the floor. McCardle half-fell off the chair.

Unlike all the others Baylem had encountered, this fly was alive. It walked lethargically across the carpet, zig-zagging drunkenly away from the policeman's prodding finger. A couple of times it attempted to fly, bounced up, and then dropped back down again.

"Is that?" Hamilton left the question hanging.

"Yep. A live one. Do you have anything in your bag of tricks that we can keep him in?"

Dr Hamilton crossed to his surgeon's bag and unbuckled a pair of straps, opening it up. From deep inside, he retrieved a sample pot with a translucent lid, the sort usually used for gathering liquid or secreted evidence. "This should do." With the point of a pair of scissors, he stabbed a few air holes into the lid and then handed it over to Baylem.

Baylem pulled free the top and lowered the pot in front of the staggering fly, laying it on its side. With the lid, the DI encouraged the fly from its rear, nudging it into the pot and then sealing it. "There," he exclaimed triumphantly. "Good work, McCardle," he said, standing up. "That's answered the 'how'. All we need is the 'when'?" The DI turned to Hamilton. "Any ideas of the time of death, Floyd?"

The doctor considered the question. "I can't give a definitive answer; at a guess... approximately sometime between one and three a.m."

"Okay... that just leaves us begging the question: why? What's making these flies act so uncharacteristically? Why are they attacking people? And, why now?"

Hamilton shrugged. "Not my area of expertise," he confessed. "Entomology might be able to help. I'll give my contact a call... I sent him some samples yesterday, so I can see if he can shed some light on these as well." The doctor stepped back towards the bed, returning to examining the bodies.

"Great. I'll leave this for you to deal with," the DI held up the pot towards Hamilton, "here." He placed it on the coffee table.

"Thanks. By the way, inspector; saw you on TV this morning... very evasive," said the doctor, sounding impressed. "Not sure anyone will be buying your statement that these incidents are unrelated; especially after this. An MP... and isn't she a pop star?"

"Yes, she is; the American. I'm half-expecting as much, though will do my best to avoid causing a panic. You know what Joe-public is like..."

"Try as much as you like, but goes with the territory; it's human nature. And I doubt Emily Herrington will be too bothered one way or another; as long as she gets her story. Even so, if we get many more of these deaths, I think I might begin to panic myself!"

Baylem laughed nervously. "Let me know when you're done with the autopsy, Floyd. I'll drop by later." He turned to his sergeant. "McCardle, let's leave the doctor to his work and speak with the staff. Then, we have some lines of enquiry needing to be marked off the list."

"We do, sir?" McCardle looked momentarily confused.

"Let's satisfy ourselves that there is no link between these cases and that RTA you were so keen to mention last night; not to forget that dairy farm incident..."

2

Exiting the hotel building half an hour later with statements from the manager, the cleaner and a night porter, the detectives were met by a pack of slobbering journalists standing outside the entrance doors, shouting questions over one and other, barging and bustling for attention. They crowded Baylem and McCardle who responded with "no comment" over and over as they pushed their way through towards their vehicle, parked half-on and half-off the pavement. Marked police cars were positioned either side of it.

Seeing Baylem and McCardle in the thick of what resembled a baying mob, uniformed policemen waded in, forcing a human barrier that allowed the plain-clothed detectives easier passage.

Surprisingly disconnected from the throng, Emily Herrington was standing in the background, a distance from the clamouring journalists. Not moving, she waited a moment; the path between her and the detectives was clearing as disappointed journalists quietened and dispersed.

Sergeant McCardle was climbing into the passenger side of the car; the detective inspector had walked around the Audi to the other side, avoiding a steady stream of motor vehicles passing along the road.

Emily stepped forward. "DI Baylem, I have some information that might interest you; about the flies and where they are coming from..."

Initially, Baylem ignored her, opening the door of his car and stooping to climb in.

"My source says her partner created them; that they're not here by accident, but by design," blurted the reporter, halting Baylem just as he was about to disappear into the car.

The detective stood upright, peering towards the woman over the roof of the Audi. He remembered her from the press room earlier that morning.

Seeing that she had his attention, the reporter took a slow, measured approach.

"Miss Herrington, I have no time for your games."

She smiled. "I'm serious, Detective Inspector. What I've been told will explain all these deaths. It's in your best interest, I assure you."

"Miss Herrington," Baylem acknowledged frostily. "Why do you persist with linking these…" he tussled for the right thing to say, "… deaths… to flies?"

Emily was now standing close to the car. McCardle had stepped back out and was obstructing her from progressing any nearer to the DI.

"Because, the flies caused them," she asserted confidently. "I know it and you know it. They're only going to get worse. And I now have someone who has proof of it."

"Oh?" exclaimed McCardle, curious.

"Proof? Why are you telling us this? Why not just print your damnable story?" denounced the DI. "What's in it for you?"

Emily scowled at the senior policeman's disdain and disrespect for her. "I want all the facts, with permission and exclusivity to publish a full account in today's edition of the *Herald*, and any follow-ups. In exchange, I will give you my source and everything she knows."

"And if I say no?" quizzed Baylem.

"Well," said Emily. "I will print my *damnable* story, filling in the blanks with educated guesses and sound reasoning, and you'll get nothing in return. No answers and more deaths."

McCardle peered over the roof of the car towards Baylem, raising an eyebrow. Ignoring his partner, Baylem stared hard at the journalist. Her features looked homely and her regular presentation neglected and unkempt. Despite the dishevelled appearance, her demeanour was confident and her brown eyes, magnified by the red rectangular full-rimmed glasses she wore, were filled with an intensity that made the DI almost quiver at the knees.

Baylem came to a decision. "Okay."

"Do we have an agreement?" Emily wanted firm clarification. "Yes."

"Excellent." The raven-haired woman climbed into the rear passenger seat without invitation, a smile balanced on her lips.

Smugly, she glowered through the window towards others from her profession wandering around forlorn outside the hotel as she closed the car door behind her.

"Get in," he muttered sarcastically, seeing the reporter making herself comfortable in the back. "Jayne, this might be a fool's errand," Baylem said over the roof of the car. "There's no point us both being bogged down with it. Go find PC Anders, he's here some place. Go together out to the dairy farm. After, head over to the hospital and meet with the RTA witness, I'll try to catch up with you there as soon as I can. See if there is any substance to Miss Herrington's journalism."

"Right you are, sir." She closed her car door, turned around and moved away towards a small group of uniformed officers standing in front of the hotel.

Baylem climbed into the Audi and buckled his seat belt. He twisted in his seat, half-facing the reporter. "Where to?" he asked.

"Across town; Meadow Croft Crescent. I have a house there."

They found her sitting on a grey fabric and brown leather three-seater corner sofa, her legs propped up on a stool placed ahead of her. The television was on, *This Morning* with Philip Schofield and Holly Willoughby filled the screen. Daytime television didn't normally interest her, but today was different. She had hoped to watch something engaging to distract her from worrying about her fiancé. Instead, she had settled on a programme which was exploring the very subject that she was trying to avoid.

The presenters were interviewing a guest, a proclaimed expert in pest control and the study of insects, a subject that was at the forefront of her mind and the majority of people across the country it seemed. Fulbarton was in the national news, and reacting to the headlines and reports of a number of deaths in the town, *This Morning* was running a piece the hosts hoped would help address the growing fears beginning to grip the country.

Gemma turned away from the TV to face Emily and her companion. She could tell from the way he was dressed that he was a policeman.

"Gemma, this is Detective Inspector Baylem."

"Hello," said Gemma cautiously. Her eyes darted back to the television. The pest control man was talking animatedly about the humid weather being partly responsible for the increased fly population.

"*...what about the behaviour of the flies in Fulbarton? Is that normal?*" asked Holly Willoughby earnestly. "*Can we do anything to protect ourselves?*"

"*No, this is not a common behaviour of flies; in fact, I'd bet anything that the deaths in Fulbarton are not as a result of flies at all; however, yes... if it is flies, you can protect yourselves easily. A good fly spray can be purchased from a DIY store or supermarket...*"

"Afternoon, Miss Warren." Baylem ignored the television; though saw the pregnant woman's attention was focused on it.

"Call me Gemma," she replied distractedly.

"Gemma... Miss Herrington here tells me that you may be able to help with my enquiries."

Gemma tore her eyes away from the flat screen and looked up at the DI. "Is it true? The flies are killing people?"

"Well... I don't know... not for definite," replied Baylem, unconvincingly. He took a seat next to the woman. Emily sat down in an armchair that matched the sofa opposite, alongside the television. "I am investigating a number of deaths which bear similarities to one another. Flies appear to have contributed, but how and why is a bit of a mystery. They appear to be working cohesively and have a number of different characteristics to the common fly. Emily says you may know something about them. She also said you believe you are in danger because of it."

"Yes," replied the woman, adding nothing further. She winced from a spasm occurring between her legs. The sensation had started a day earlier but was now happening more frequently.

"Emily said your boyfriend created the flies. What did she mean?"

Gemma puffed out her cheeks and blew out a stream of air. "They'll kill me for this," she said.

"We'll protect you," offered the policeman. "I can have you placed into witness protection or, at the very least, protective custody."

"Okay," the woman decided. "I'll tell you everything I know, on the condition that you not only protect me, you find James Quisenberry... bring him back to us, and protect him also."

If James Quisenberry WAS responsible, Baylem would be hell-bent on finding him, and not just to appease the pregnant woman. It wasn't a lie when he said: "I'll do everything in my power. I promise."

The young woman reached for the TV remote, turned *This Morning* off and composed herself. "James – my fiancé – works for Biomargent Sciences. Heavily funded by the military, they develop, amongst other things, weaponised pathogens, artificial intelligence and the study of genetics.

"For the past three years, James has headed a small team looking at genetic enhancements, manipulating the DNA in various animals, improving their senses and abilities; mice, apes, dogs, birds... and flies. You name it."

He didn't. "Why?" Baylem asked, "For what purpose?" It didn't make much sense to him.

Gemma stroked her stomach. "For the good of the country, that's what James always said... to justify the things he did. He called himself *Frankenstein*, for much of his work involved dissecting animals and sewing them back together again; well, not literally; most of his work was done under a microscope, splicing genes and mixing DNA." She paused for a moment, a sharp pain making her flinch. "They were creating weapons… for the army.

"Of course, much of what James did failed, especially in the early days. But then he had a breakthrough. With DNA manipulation, he discovered he could change things at a cellular level. I don't quite understand the science of it all, but he told me he had made cross-breeds; creatures with traits unique to one species, merged with the abilities of another. He called them *chimeras*. There were orangutans with birds; dogs with bears; even humans with leopards. For all intents and purposes, they were monsters, and the outcomes were horrific and predictable. One of them escaped and somebody died, and that was the end of that, so I thought naively.

"Then James had the idea about flies. It sounded crazy and farfetched, I never liked it as I don't like insects and I told him as much. But he sold it to General Makepeace, though, who saw the benefits and the havoc these small creatures could cause an enemy."

"What was special about these flies?" asked Baylem, curious. From the corner of his eye, he watched Emily produce a notepad and a pen.

"James wanted to create a superior fly, one with enhanced intelligence and other modified abilities; hearing, cognisance, telepathy and communication."

"Communication?" he asked, amusement slipping into his voice. "You mean they talk?"

Gemma laughed at how absurd that sounded. "No… not in the literal sense. James told the general that he would be able to communicate with them, on a very basic level, and they would be able to respond. Also, in much the same way as bees, they would be able to connect with other flies to share thoughts and make decisions collectively. It was supposed to make them more efficient." Another spasm rocked Gemma's body and she jerked, arching her back.

"Jeez." Baylem ignored her discomfort, his mind straying to earlier that morning. The video footage of the coordinated fly attack on Megan Pritchard's baby played out in his head, dissolving into another; an imagined depiction of an attack on one of the victims he'd tended during the past twenty-four hours.

Although Gemma could tell the DI's mind was momentarily faraway, she soon had his attention back. She continued, the pain subsiding: "James spent the best part of two years playing God with his bloody flies. He lived and breathed for them, and then one day, out of the blue – this being four months ago – he brings some home with him, in a jar!" She laughed at the absurdity of it. "All excited he was, like a big kid wanting to show mummy his school work. Using his laptop and a small amplifier connected to it, he removed the lid from the jar and released the flies.

"At first, they darted around the room like... well, like flies. James then goes to his computer and does something, hits some keys and turns on the amp. A weird sound comes out of the speaker and the flies do this strange, but amazing, thing. They stop in mid-air, as though frozen in time. James changed something and a different sound was emitted from the amplifier. The flies buzzed about the room a couple of times, then grouped together.

"I'd never seen anything like it. As one, James made the flies move around in a formation; it was like watching an air show, a bit like the Red Arrows, only in my living room. After half an hour, James did something on his computer and the flies returned to the jar and he closed it with the lid."

"Wow... sounds..." Baylem couldn't think of the word to describe his feeling. He just added: "Wow."

"I know. I still didn't like the flies, but I could see benefits to them. I couldn't help but be amazed."

"So," said Baylem, coming to terms with what the young

woman had just said, and what was being implied, "are you claiming these flies are controlled? That the deaths occurring in Fulbarton are not by some strange phenomenon, but by design and intent?" *Was it murder after all*, he added to himself.

"I don't know, Inspector," said Gemma, honestly. "Two months ago, James carried out an experiment in front of an audience of a hundred or so people. Using ten thousand of his flies, he put on a performance similar to the one he did for me in my living room, only, it went wrong." She went quiet, her mood darkening. A wave of discomfort flared in her groin again.

"What happened?" pressed Baylem. Emily was silently scribbling notes on her pad.

Gemma took a deep breath and slowly exhaled. "The flies stopped following James' orders," she said solemnly. "There were two technicians inside the lab, and the flies attacked them. James said he tried everything to bring the insects back on line, but it was no good. Both the technicians died and James had no choice but to destroy the flies."

"The flies were destroyed?"

"Yes," replied Gemma.

"All of them?"

She nodded, closing her eyes. "James had wanted to continue working on them and told me he could fix the problem, but General Makepeace ordered him to stop. The enhanced flies lost their appeal to the general and the programme was forcibly ended. And that was the end of it."

"Except... it isn't the end of it, is it Gemma?"

The young woman flinched, a stab of intense pain taking her by surprise and doubling her up. Baylem misinterpreted it as a reaction to his question. She knew that it was something else; a strong contraction.

"What else are you not telling me?" Baylem wanted to wring every morsel of information from her before entertaining her demand for protection.

The contraction subsided and Gemma took a deep breath.

"Are you all right?" asked Emily, breaking her self-imposed vow of silence.

"It's just... the baby," she said to the journalist, dismissively. She turned back to DI Baylem. "I don't know anything else. James never kept anything from me," she insisted. "He told me his research into the flies was over, and I believed him. Except... I don't know..."

"What is it?"

"On the telly this morning, we saw the newsperson talking about the deaths and James went all strange. He skipped breakfast and rushed off; said he had to go to work early. He looked worried... and scared."

"Where is he now?" Baylem asked.

"At work, I think. I don't know. I tried calling him, but he didn't pick up. After a couple of times trying, his phone was answered by General Makepeace. He told me he had sent someone to 'collect me'. To go where, I don't know. I didn't stay on the phone long enough to find out. I knew I was in danger and had to get away. That is when I went to Emily, and she's kindly kept me here ever since."

"How did you know you were in danger?" Baylem couldn't make sense of why the heavily pregnant woman had jumped to the conclusion that she was under threat.

"Because the general lied to me," she told Baylem about the baby name mix up. James had given General Makepeace the wrong name; a deliberate mistake meant to alert his fiancée. The DI wasn't convinced, the whole thing sounded weak. "Also, moments before, I had watched armed men arrive at my house. I was on my way back from an early walk to the shops. I saw soldiers carrying rifles charge up my garden path."

"Are you sure?"

"Of course I'm bloody sure! They weren't Jehovah's Witnesses,

I can tell ya! I didn't imagine it. They arrived in a hurry, some in a car, but most in a van. And didn't you hear me? They had guns!"

"Okay. Okay." Baylem had no further questions. "Sounds all very…" he didn't finish the sentence.

"You don't believe me, do you?!" Gemma's voice went up an octave. "You think I'm making this all up, that I am a stupid pregnant woman? Well, I'm not… here." From around her neck, she tugged at a chain, pulling free a small key that had nestled between her ample breasts.

The DI caught himself glaring at her cleavage. He forced his eyes away.

"It's to a safety deposit box. Inside it you will find everything. James's research and a recording of his disastrous demonstration; all the proof you'll ever need." She lifted the chain over her head and handed it over to the policeman.

"Thank you. Where is the safety deposit box?"

Gemma told him. "I hope it helps," she added. "Now, what about the protection you promised me?"

"If Miss Herrington doesn't mind, could you stay here for the moment?"

"I don't mind," replied the journalist, happy to be a part of a story that was continuously unfolding in front of her.

"I'll send a unit over to collect you in a short while. If, by some miracle your boyfriend makes contact, be sure to let me know. If what you say is true, it's imperative we find him…"

"Um… *Detective Inspector*… I don't think that's going to work," said Gemma apprehensively. "I think my waters have just broken."

"Are you ready to admit that these deaths in Fulbarton – all of them – are linked?" The journalist stepped up beside the DI at the road's edge. Together, they had helped Gemma Warren out to the ambulance and now watched as the vehicle pulled off, followed closely by a marked police car. "Come on, Detective Inspector. We had a deal?"

"Off the record? I don't want to cause a panic," he replied.

Emily Herrington nodded hesitantly.

"Okay. I don't expect to read this in tomorrow's chip wrapping," said Baylem seriously. "And if I do, I'll never deal with your paper again."

"You have my word."

"All the victims appear to share a common cause; death by hypoxia, induced by blockage of the airways. Shall we go back inside? I could really do with a cup of something liquid to drink."

"Tea?"

Baylem followed the journalist into the house. From inside his pocket, the DI's mobile began to ring. "Hello? McCardle?" He closed the front door behind him.

Emily disappeared through a doorway into the kitchen. The sound of filling a kettle up and teacups tinkling together soon followed.

"*Baylem... I've just finished at the farm. It's those flies, all right. Luckily, the vet who the farm manager called was still on site. I spoke with him. An autopsy was carried out on several of the cows, and guess what the vet found?*" it was a rhetorical question, "*flies! Their throats were crammed full. Speaking with the farmer – Tom Lavery – he is still at a loss as to how it could've happened. Whenever the animals have been spooked in the past, they'd make a lot of noise, and not just mooing! But, the farmer said he heard nothing. We checked CCTV footage... and the damnedest thing... I've never seen anything like it; so many flies, all attacking at the same time.*"

"How many cows were killed?"

"*Fifty-three.*"

Baylem's phone double-bleeped in his ear. "Just a sec, Jayne..."

he checked the screen; a further incoming call. He recognised the number as his mother's.

What are you doing calling me at work? His mother never ever called him, not even when there'd been an emergency; like the time when his dad had suddenly been taken ill. She hadn't called him with the news until after his shift had ended, by which time it was too late and his father had died in hospital.

The DI returned the handset to his ear. "I have another call; can you hold for a moment." Not giving his sergeant a chance to protest, Baylem pressed a button and then readied himself to speak with his mother.

"Mum?"

"*Oh, help me, August?*"

Baylem cringed to hear his Christian name. Only his mother ever called him it as he kept it a close-guarded secret. Whenever someone had asked for his name, he had always answered 'Baylem', never August. He couldn't even fall back on a middle name, like so many others invariably did when burdened with such a heinous moniker, for his parents cruelly gave him a girl's name, and not even one which suitably served both sexes (like Jesse). A subject of so much ridicule and torment as a child, his dad exonerated himself by claiming it gave his boy 'character' and helped 'toughen' him up. It inexplicably did neither.

"What's wrong?" a tone of panic crept into his voice.

"*There are flies coming into the house... hundreds... maybe thousands of them!*"

"Don't panic, mum... lock yourself in the downstairs' toilet, and put a towel down along the bottom of the door. I'm on my way!"

Just before the line was disconnected, the sound of glass breaking filled his ear. "Oh, no!" He quickly toggled over to the other call. McCardle was hanging on at the other end. "Jayne?"

"*I'm still here.*"

"It's my mother... She said there were flies coming into her house... then the line went dead."

"*Oh, Christ!*

"Call for backup and meet me there."

Emily Herrington appeared at the kitchen door carrying a tray with two steaming cups and a plate of biscuits. She could have been entertaining friends.

With a pained look, Baylem returned his phone to his pocket. "Sorry, Emily, I have to dash. Duty calls."

CHAPTER TWELVE

MACKENZIE HARDWICK, A HAPPY-GO-LUCKY NINE-
TEEN-YEAR-OLD, crossed the wide space that greeted
shoppers entering the Castle Tower shopping centre,
built in an area once occupied by a Norman keep that was destroyed around the time of King Stephen during the civil war of
1139 – 1154. Some foundation stones were all that remained of
the castle, an insignificant pile of rubble to the rear of the shopping centre that often played host to gatherings of bored youths
with nothing better to do other than congregate and smoke suspicious homemade cigarettes.

The mall was well-lit and aggrandised with a number of big
chain retailers, like Boots, Iceland, River Island, HMV, Waterstones
and John Lewis, to name but a few; plus a number of smaller
outlets dotted between them boasting a host of wares and services
including mobile phone unlocking, key-cutting, speciality foods
such as Polish and Indian, jewellery, build a plush toy, and an array
of clothing and shoe stores aimed at customers of all shapes, sizes,
creeds and orientation.

Mackenzie happily glided past the various shops, giving most
a wide berth as she headed towards the centre of the building

where a double escalator dominated, one set travelling up whilst the other brought shoppers back down. Alongside this was a row of metal doors, behind which three lifts were in different stages of movement as they carried customers between the ground floor and any one of the four upper levels, the top being the food hall.

Stopping in front of the lifts, the nineteen-year-old punched one of the buttons, registering her desire to travel upwards. An LED panel above one of the three doors flashed up and slowly counted down from four to zero.

Impatiently, Mackenzie tapped her feet and nervously bit her lip.

"Doors open," an electronic, effeminate voice sounded as a lift arrived, a metal door drifting smoothly aside. A woman wearing a hijab pushed a stroller out of the escalator with a small boy of three or four strapped in. He looked up at the young woman and poked his tongue out at her.

Mackenzie reciprocated by thrusting out her own tongue and scrunching up her face.

"Kaba Kadin!" *rude woman*, said the woman behind her hajib, misinterpreting Mackenzie's action and hurrying her child away.

Mackenzie didn't understand the woman's words, but could tell by her fleeting disappearance that she wasn't happy.

Smiling, the nineteen-year-old stepped into the now-empty lift and reached for the panel of numbered buttons. Before doing so, she studied her reflection in the mirrored wall to the back of the elevator. Her face was pale, framed by golden blonde hair which was tied into a tail at the back. Fleetingly, her slate-grey eyes assessed the rest of her appearance.

Her frayed denim shorts looked small, barely covering her bottom and revealing a lot of both legs. Her soft-peach long-sleeved blouse was buttoned up to where the shirt collar fell open, just above the rise of her small breasts. *Not too slutty*, she thought.

She returned her attention to the control panel, stabbing the topmost one. Number: '4'. It was nearly lunchtime and hunger pangs prodded her insides, reminding her that she hadn't eaten at all that day, despite her mother's protestations and offers of frying up a breakfast.

"Door closing," the effeminate voice declared an instant before the doors skimmed shut. A small motor whirred and gears and pulleys began to groan slightly as the elevator car began its journey. Quietening with momentum, it effortlessly ascended towards the top floor.

A small LCD screen above the number panel counted up from zero, passing floor '1', and then '2' five seconds later. Before '3' flashed up, the lift began to judder and groan noisily. The fluorescent ceiling light flickered on and off a couple of times and the speed of the lift's ascent momentarily slowed before picking up pace again.

"That's weird," whispered Mackenzie.

The LCD displayed '3' as the lift passed the third floor and the nineteen-year-old's thoughts moved on to the problem of what food she was likely to order.

BANG!

From above her head, something exploded in the lift shaft. Reflexively, the nineteen-year-old dropped her head and clasped her hands over it, expecting the ceiling to cave in on her.

It didn't, but she couldn't see that. The lights had gone out, enveloping her in thick, impenetrable darkness that caused alarm and panic to engulf her. It was so dark that she couldn't tell whether her eyes were open or shut.

Immediately, the lift car jerked to a halt. The twang of a metal cable snapping followed by the sudden feeling of weightlessness caused Mackenzie to fear the worst and her stomach to lurch seemingly up to the back of her throat.

The floor beneath her feet fell away.

"Ahhhhhhhhhhhh!!!" she screamed as the lift plunged back

down towards ground level. A split-second later, brakes began to shriek and the downward momentum was halted abruptly. Mackenzie's body slammed into the lift's ceiling and then fell hard to the floor. She landed with an: "Oomph!" and a scream.

A bell began to ring, long and monotonous. An alarm, signifying warning or giving a distress signal.

Dazed and confused, the nineteen-year-old tried lifting herself up from the floor and found that she couldn't move. One of her legs was bent awkwardly beneath her weight and the slightest twitch of a muscle caused a spasm of pain to blast through her body.

The young woman cried out, tears leaking from the corners of her closed eyes.

A heavy, metallic thud echoed through the elevator car, as though something had fallen against the roof.

Beneath Mackenzie's crumpled body, she felt a subtle vibration, almost like an electric thrum.

More bangs and clangs above the ceiling, and the sound of metal grating, like two edges scraping against opposing forces.

Maybe I'm being rescued, Mackenzie considered, not realising that only twenty seconds had passed since the lift had ceased travelling.

"Hello!" she called skyward, like she was hoping to converse with God.

Miraculously, a small voice responded. The built-in panel speaker next to the numbered buttons crackled into service.

"Hello? This is Castle Tower security... if you can hear me, don't panic. The lift has broken down, is all. We'll have you out in a jiffy..."

"Thank God!" Overcome with relief, she momentarily forgot the noises from the other side of the ceiling and relaxed against the floor. Knowing that rescue was imminent helped soothe the panic, despite the feeling of claustrophobia clawing in her mind and the hurt she was feeling from the fall.

The emergency trapdoor above her made a slight, metallic

scraping, followed by a multitude of raps, sonorous taps and more clangs. Someone (or something) was definitely shifting around up there.

"I'm impressed at how quick you're getting to me," said Mackenzie in a raised voice which she directed skyward, automatically assuming the continuing noise above the ceiling belonged to a would-be rescuer. "You should know," she continued, "I think I've... broken... my leg..."

Mackenzie thought nothing of the fact she received no reply. Beneath her body, the vibrating sensation continued; ameliorated, she ignored it, choosing instead to imagine the appearance of her knight in shining armour. She pictured a young rugged fireman in the shape of Channing Tatum hanging from a fast-rope, secured at the top of the elevator shaft by four other firemen, suave and burley; in her mind, all members of an amateur stripping dance troupe, bare-chested and slick with oil. Her fantasy was influenced by the fact that she had recently seen Magic Mike XXL on TV. The thought helped ease the pain throbbing in her leg and the claustrophobia of being confined within the small lift car, exacerbated by the sheer blackness.

Creeeaaakk!!

The emergency trap door fell open on a pair of slick hinges, swinging hard against a side wall with a clash of steel.

CLANG!

Mackenzie recoiled in shock, relief swiftly replacing the sudden scare the noise caused. Her mind formed the expectation of seeing torchlight and a pair of boots appearing within the opening; however, after what seemed like half a minute, nothing emerged (except a draught of stale, stuffy air).

"Hello!" she called upwards. Through the breach in the ceiling, she heard her voice echo within the cavernous shaft.

Hello...lo...lo...

No one else replied. All noise had ceased. Only baleful quietude met her ears; even the clanging, banging sounds had stopped.

In complete darkness and in total silence, Mackenzie started to feel panic take a grip in the centre of her chest.

What's happening?

With nothing changing, she began to hyperventilate. The temperature within the lift was stifling and every breath Mackenzie took seemed heavy and diminished of oxygen.

Calm down, she told herself. Closing her eyes, she tried to imagine something good, something relaxing. Her yoga instructor had taught her a number of techniques to combat anxiety, which she now attempted to draw upon. She forced herself to take a deep breath.

Easier to think than do; the air was definitely getting harder to breathe.

Her lungs were beginning to burn and her head was pounding. Mackenzie had read somewhere mountain climbers' experienced similar feelings at high altitude. *But*, she reflected, *I'm not on a mountain. I'm in a shopping centre, stuck in a lift. This can't be happening.* Even so, the sensation continued and she knew she was in danger of losing consciousness.

Whilst struggling for breath, Mackenzie hadn't noticed the subtle change to her surroundings.

It was still overbearingly dark, and she continued to be trapped inside the lift. But something had changed.

It was no longer completely silent.

A small buzzing sound appeared within the elevator car, darting from one side to another, quickly joined by another.

Jolting her head, Mackenzie honed in on the two droning sounds, momentarily forgetting the labour of breathing. She recognised them as flies.

"Great," she murmured. "All I need is a couple of bloody flies to pester me."

The two flies zoomed in and around Mackenzie's head, purposefully irritating her. She blindly flapped at one half-heartedly, missing the insect by a clear foot. Immediately, the hum of the flies grew in pitch, like an *accelerando*. Initially, she thought they were agitated by her attempt at thwarting one, but then realised, after a minute, the sound didn't abate. She knew that now there were three flies within the small enclosure.

Very soon, there were four. Then five... six... seven... ten... twenty... thirty... fifty...

With more flies entering the elevator car, the drone of the insects increased in volume. The hum, so constant, reverberated around the small box-room, so loud that the soundwaves caused the walls of the lift to vibrate. The nineteen-year-old could feel it in the floor beneath her.

Within the eye of an insect tornado, Mackenzie clapped her hands over her ears and drew her head towards her chest. Ignoring the pain from her broken leg, she tried to make herself smaller, dragging her limbs into her stomach.

She couldn't see it but sensed the number of flies within the elevator had grown from just a couple into a vast number. In fact, more than five hundred were with her now, circling her transfixed body, and increasing steadily as a cataract of insects cascaded through the emergency trap door.

A series of pops and clangs sounded over the din of buzzing insects, emanating from above the elevator car within the shaft, followed by a:

"Ding!"

The lights in the ceiling flickered on, which Mackenzie could just about see through her closed eyes; a subtle change in the tone of blackness.

Daring a look, she opened her eyes a slit–

–flies detached from the swirling twister that continued to ring her and propelled towards her face.

She closed her eyes back up.

Too late!

One of the flies darted into the corner of her eye and burrowed down beneath the orb, circumnavigating around the pressure of her lids towards the back of the ocular cavity, following for guidance a sinewy strand of nerves that led into the woman's brain. At a fleshy wall of resistance, the fly started to bite savagely, digging an entry into the frontal lobe.

"Ahhhhhhhhhhhhh! My ey–!" Mackenzie's scream of pain was stifled by the arrival of more than two hundred flies funnelling into her mouth in a breakaway surge from the cyclone that continued to swell around her.

"–erg-gherr… *pleh!*… erg-gherr…" Mackenzie was choking and gagging; she managed to spit out a mouthful of insects, to no avail. More and more fell onto her face and poured into her mouth in a way that she was powerless to stop. It was akin to an absurd style of waterboarding, substituting water for flies, and interrogation for unceasing punishment.

The intolerable pain inside her head was nothing compared to the burning agony that expanded inside her throat, spreading to her lungs and chest. Mackenzie's eyes were wide and bulging out, and a thin streak of blood leaked from the one the fly had burrowed under as she clawed weakly at her neck, gasping for breath like a fish plucked from its bowl.

With little more fight, the light of the elevator car faded as consciousness slipped away. Before oblivion took her, she was just able to detect a slight change in the lift's standing; it was moving. As darkness filled her head, she just made out the LED above the number panel flicker from '3' to '2'.

The lift was going back down.

Mackenzie slumped to the floor, her limp arms dropping to her side. The flies continued to enter Mackenzie – hundreds or possibly thousands of them – filling her lungs and intestines, causing her body to swell like she were a balloon inflating, her blouse expanding around her stomach, the buttons pulling taut and threatening to pop free.

2

"Doors open," the electronic, effeminate voice sounded as the middle lift finally arrived. It had been half an hour since security personnel within the shopping centre had communicated with the sole occupant. Engineers had been on site working to apply a temporary fix to the faulty elevator, but firemen had arrived and were waiting on standby. Mackenzie would have been impressed.

A small congregation of shop workers and emergency service staff (two firemen and a volunteer police officer) waited as the door of the shopping centre lift glided smoothly open.

Before the doors had completely revealed the insides of the elevator car, a woman in her forties emitted a high-pitch scream that chilled the bones of everyone who heard it throughout the four floors of the building.

"Oh my God!" exclaimed a fireman, walking from behind the small gathering of shop workers, pushing through to the head of the throng.

Inside the lift, a young woman was sprawled out on the floor, her legs bent awkwardly beneath her, her face turned away. Her head was completely covered in a black cloak of shuffling insects everyone could tell were flies.

To the onlookers, she appeared to still be alive. Her chest and stomach were moving, like the rise and fall of breathing.

"Mick," the firemen said over his shoulder. "Go get the paramedics."

Mick, a small sweating man, fully garbed in firefighting regalia, wheeled about in a hurry and jogged off towards the shopping centre's exit/entrance.

"Are they the same flies the news said killed those people?" asked the woman who had screamed, now completely composed, standing next to the fire crew manager. A note of fear was still in her voice, but fascination and intrigue kept her rooted to the spot.

The lead fireman said nothing. Tentatively, he stepped into the lift and began to crouch down, a hand reaching towards the prostrate form lying across the floor. Before his hand made contact, a button on the woman's soft-peach blouse popped free and the material fell aside to reveal her extended stomach, bulging close to the point of bursting. The fireman recoiled, initially from shock, but quickly he recovered; he leaned in to get a better look.

Beneath the surface of the girl's bloated stomach, the fireman could see something – or some *things* – moving about. Rippling, marble-like activity could be seen, pulsating, contracting and retracting under the skin.

"What is it?" asked the woman.

The fireman stared at the girl's abdomen, not sure how to answer the question. He was just about to say: *I don't know*, when a small hole appeared in the woman's stomach just above her bellybutton, cut (or chewed) from inside. He leaned in closer, curiosity getting the better of his judgement.

"Pwooo!" a small expulsion of air, followed by a thick geyser of insects exploded from the young woman's stomach and hit the fireman square in the face. Propelling backwards, he fell out of the lift into the small gathering of people, knocking the woman who had been quizzing him over, and landing on the volunteer police officer who had been passively watching. The stream of flies flowed towards him in an upward trajectory, fixated on entering his mouth and nasal passages. With such force, the long hawser of insects discharging incessantly from the nineteen-year-old's stomach caused the lead fireman to collapse to the floor beneath the impact.

The woman who had screamed, picked herself up and started

bellowing, "Run!" and "Get away!" at the top of her voice, adding insanely: "It's the flies!" Her warnings were effective, mobilising many others in earshot, causing a stampede as shop goers began to panic, not necessarily convinced of the reason, but buoyed by the hysteria and terror affecting others. Like sheep, they followed en masse, many of whom now screaming or crying. She scurried away towards the exit, almost running into Mick, who was returning with a blanket from the fire engine parked up outside.

Bemused at first by the woman in her forties, his merriment soon transpired upon seeing the rush of people charging towards him; beyond them, his superior, lying on his back, was entangled with the volunteer police officer, and what looked like black smoke pouring into his face, but which he already knew was something much, much worse.

"Oh Christ," he said, hearing himself repeating the fleeing woman's alarmist words: "It's the flies."

CHAPTER THIRTEEN

AT THE OTHER END OF Fulbarton's town centre, in an area known as the 'restaurant district', a man and an older woman entered a small Italian restaurant called Fat Mama's House, placed in amongst a variety of diners catering for all tastes, stretching either side of the road.

"Are you sure about this place, Barney?" asked the woman. "I mean, it doesn't look very special." She was twenty years the man's senior and wore dowdy dark clothing; a black skirt that hung to her ankles and a cardigan which was buttoned all the way up the front despite the warm weather. Her curly black hair had flecks of grey in it, and the horn-rimmed glasses resting on her large nose made her eyes look too big for her face.

"This will do, ma. You said it was 'my choice'." said Barney, a thirty-something with a round, pudgy face that made his age indeterminable. He was taking the lead by walking towards a floor-standing message board, upon which a sign stood proud, stating: *Wait here to be seated.* "Besides," he added with enthusiasm, "they do the best pizzas in Fulbarton."

"Huh!" the man's mother huffed. *I don't like pizzas,* she thought, *it's just glorified cheese on toast,* but restrained herself from voicing any protest. An Italian waiter dressed immaculately in black trousers and a black short-sleeve shirt (the restaurant name and logo was printed on the pocket) appeared from behind a service bar towards the back of the room. To the right of it the kitchen could be viewed.

"Table for two?"

"Er, yes. Please," replied Barney.

"I am Gianni, your waiter... please follow-a-me."

Still ahead of his mother, Barney stepped past the 'Wait here' sign and sauntered after the waiter through a narrow corridor between empty tables, towards a dining suite set for two along the farthest wall.

Barney and his mother were the first diners of the lunch period.

"Here?" suggested the waiter serenely, smiling pleasantly. He pulled out a chair in a gentlemanly fashion for the lady.

"It'll do," she said haughtily, taking the proffered seat by plonking herself heavily down and causing the chair to creak alarmingly beneath her colossal weight. She dropped her handbag under the table, close to her feet.

Barney sat down in the chair opposite. "Thank you, Gianni."

"This is the lunchtime menu." The waiter handed a leather-bound binder to each of them. "Can I get-a-you something to drink?"

The woman ordered a white coffee. Barney felt the occasion deserved something stronger, something more refreshing. He settled for something entirely different, playing it safe. "Lager, please."

"We have bottles of Peroni... or Carlsberg on tap."

"A bottle of Peroni will be good. Whilst in Rome... do as the Romans... Thanks."

Gianni feigned understanding and disappeared to the bar to get their drinks, leaving Barney and his mother to study the menu. The woman turned her nose up at everything, giving a withering look towards her son. "We should have gone to Wetherspoons," she said, disgruntled. "Hark at the prices!" she hissed, adding a few tuts whilst shaking her head in further disapproval.

"As I said, they make the best pizzas in town. Look behind me," he turned his head slightly towards the direction he intimated. The kitchen could be seen behind a serving counter, and sitting impressively in the centre of the preparation area was a large industrial-sized kiln-style oven, brick-built, beneath a wide stone chimney breast that disappeared into the ceiling. "A Stone Bake, wood-fired pizza oven. They cook them fresh in the kitchen here, not the reheated microwave rubbish you get in a pub."

"I don't like that," she grumbled, looking past the oven. "I prefer not to watch my food being cooked; takes away the mystery. Spoils the whole ambiance of the place."

Barney tutted to himself.

Gianni returned a couple of minutes later with a tray. "Here-a-you go, madam." He set down a white cup and saucer in front of the woman. "And... for you, sir." Putting the tray down on a neighbouring table for a moment, he poured the bottle of lager into a Peroni-etched Italian beer glass, placing the tall glass and the bottle down in front of the man. "Can I get-a-your orders?"

"Um," Barney turned to his mother, unsure.

"I'll have the tagliatelle carbonara," she said without suspense.

The waiter produced a small notepad. "A good choice! Served with our finest prosciutto... a beautiful ham that compliments the dish." He jotted down the order. "And for you, sir?"

"Um... I'd like to order the Fat Mama's Special pizza."

Consisting of a cheese-stuffed crust base, an authentic Italian tomato sauce produced on site, mozzarella cheese and topped with ham, spicy beef, pepperoni, chorizo sausage, bacon, onions, and red and green peppers (all in good measure), the Fat Mama's Special pizza was the menu's *pièce de résistance*.

"You're a man from-a-my own heart. Very good; any sides to go with those?" The question was to both seated at the table.

"Ah, no… thank you, Gianni." Barney answered, knowing his mother wouldn't want to shed any money for extras.

The waiter smiled and closed the small notebook. He toddled off towards the kitchen, shouting a smattering of commands in Italian which prompted a man – Barney presumed was the chef owing to the pristine whites worn, including a *toque blanche* (cooking hat) – to jump up from inactivity to begin preparing food.

"You'll be amazed at the food," said Barney, lifting his beer glass to his lips. His mother said nothing, just stirred sugar – spoonful after spoonful – into her coffee. By the look on her face, no amount of praise or ballyhoo would appease her mood.

The chef started singing an Italian song in the background whilst preparing pizza dough. The waiter moseyed back to the bar where he could be seen wiping glasses into a polish.

Glancing over his shoulder, Barney watched as the chef began tossing the dough about his head, slamming it down to his worktop, kneading it some, before flipping it up again, in part to show off his skills.

Barney was marvelling at the finesse being employed by the chef, how dexterous he was. Watching him work was a thing of beauty, smooth and elegant, a bit like a ballet dancer. So absorbed, Barney didn't hear the fly buzz in from above, a lone insect that sallied around him and his mother, ducking and diving, testing the airspace by flying in zigzags and figures of eight. Once or twice, Barney's mother backhanded it, causing the fly to dart here and there in frenzy. Occasionally, it landed, and now teasingly, it gravitated towards the rim of Barney's beer glass.

"Shoo!" reprimanded Barney's mother, flapping aggressively towards the fly as it barely settled.

"Ma?" Barney twisted back to face her, discombobulated at her sudden outburst.

"A fly," she replied in defence. "Bloody thing keeps buzzing about; just landed on your glass."

Noticing it for the first time, Barney watched the fly hovering about close to the ceiling before setting off across the room.

"Ignore them... that's what I do," reckoned Barney. "They don't hurt."

"No? What about the ones in the news and the papers this mornin'?" she queried. "Supposed to've killed half a dozen people, apparently."

"I doubt that," dismissed Barney. He didn't pay any notice to the news and never bought a newspaper. "Sounds a bit daft to me."

The Italian continued to sing in the background, loving the sound of his voice. Between tapping a tune on a saucepan, he chopped up meat and vegetables, some of which he used on Barney's pizza.

Barney spied the chef cross to the big pizza oven with a metal pizza peel (a flat oven tray on a thirty-one-inch wooden handle); laden with a pizza topped to almost overflowing with a variety of meat and vegetables, the Italian shoved it in like he was feeding coal into a steam-powered locomotive.

"Daft or not," interposed Barney's mother, "that fly is back... It looks like he's brought a friend with him."

Now there were two flies swooping around the space above their heads, putting on an aerial display that frequently involved mid-air contact. As they dropped to a level close to Barney's head, he swatted at it with a drinks' menu.

"I thought you said you 'ignored' them?" ridiculed his mother, smiling toothlessly.

"I do... as a rule. Can you believe it!" he exclaimed, watching the flies soaring about. Where there had been two, there now were three. "It's like they are multiplying!"

From the bar, Gianni noticed Barney and his mother's agitation. Casually, he walked across the room, draping the tea towel over his shoulder. "Is ev-ery-thing, okay?" he asked politely.

"These blasted flies," answered Barney's mum, beating him

to the reply. "They keep buzzing around our heads. It's not very hygienic," she remonstrated.

"No, madam, you're absolutely-a-right," the waiter replied. "I shall do what-a-I can to get rid of them for you…"

"Do you always have a fly problem?" continued Barney's mother, unappeased by the waiter's assertion.

"No, no, no… not usually; it's the weather. Very hot. More flies for the time of year…" Without warning, the waiter snatched up the tea towel and whipped it skyward towards the three insects dancing about. The cloth connected with one of the flies and dispersed the other two.

A fly dropped into Barney's Peroni lager and swam about on the surface, moving desperately around in a circle.

Gianni watched the two surviving flies take towards the ceiling, using the cover of height to their advantage. Unperturbed, the Italian mounted a chair positioned behind a neighbouring table and plucked out his small order notebook. Giving no hint as to what he was about to do, he lunged towards a fly that had momentarily settled upon the wall, mashing his notebook forcefully towards it.

Barney's mum flinched.

The waiter withdrew his hand and the notebook to inspect the fly's carcass.

"Piccolo bastardo!" *Little bastard*, lamented Gianni, seeing the absence of a dead fly; somehow it has managed to escape. Goadingly, the pair of flies now danced around his head.

"Che cosa è la questione con voi?" *What's the matter with you?* called out the chef from behind the serving counter.

"Mosche insanguinate!" *Bloody flies*, replied the waiter, flicking the tea cloth ahead of him towards the ceiling, doing nothing to hurt the insects other than disturbing their flight path.

The chef disappeared for a moment and entered the restaurant via a door marked: PRIVATE. In his hand, he carried an aerosol spray.

"Come down from up there," demanded the chef, reverting to English for the benefit of the two diners. The waiter continued to flap about above him. "Gianni! Scendere!" *Gianni, get down!*

Reluctantly, the waiter jumped down, superseded by the chef who thrust the can of fly killer ahead of him. With the barest movement, the chef activated the aerosol spray and administered a jet of mist towards the two flies that merrily bobbed about in the sky above his head.

Nothing seemed to happen. Obliviously, the flies buzzed about brazenly, impervious to the effects of the fly repellent. Adding insult, a third fly appeared from nowhere and joined the pair of insects flitting around the chef's head.

The chef sprayed a further jet of poison towards the offending creatures. This time, one seemed to succumb, spluttering like a spitfire downed by the Luftwaffe during the Battle of Britain, plummeting to the floor in a vertical drop and bouncing against the carpet.

"Yea!" celebrated Gianni, an over-the-top performance.

"Oh, give me strength," muttered Barney's mother under her breath. "It's like they've just gone and won the World Cup again!"

"Ma!" hissed Barney in admonishment, slightly embarrassed at her comment, recognising the racial slur undertone.

Neither the chef nor the waiter noticed.

On close inspection, the fly on the floor was not dead. Stunned, it staggered jerkily in a stop-start fashion. Before it could recover, the waiter brought the heel of his black Oxford shoe down on it, crushing it beneath was a satisfying crunch.

DING!

A bell sounded from the kitchen, alerting the chef that the pizza was ready. Indignantly, he jumped down from the chair landing on both feet, abandoning the two insects merrily flying about above his head. He hurried back to the kitchen, disappearing through the door marked: PRIVATE, and reappearing behind the serving counter.

With his back towards the restaurant, he grabbed hold of the long wooden handle of the metal pizza peel and removed the pizza from the large oven, placing it down on a large metal table with a noisy clatter.

"Che è dispari," *That is odd*, he exclaimed, moving in closer to get a better look. He reverted to English: "I only left it for a few seconds."

The pizza appeared burnt, completely black, except... *that can't be the case, could it?*

His thoughts were full of doubt. Before he was able to inspect the Fat Mama's special, the black coating shifted and began to emit a sonorous hum.

Buzzzzzzzzzzzzzzzzzzzzzzzzzzzzzzzzzzzzzzzzzzzzzzzzzzzzz.

In a blur, the black pizza topping drifted up as a solid mass, and then, like an illusionist's levitation trick, floated slowly towards the chef. Mesmerised, he watched the amorphous object approach him, not sure what to make of it or whether he could trust his eyes. A sideward glance towards the table where the metal pizza peel still remained showed the Fat Mama's special appearing as he had expected it; cooked to perfection.

He uttered under his breath: "Che diavolo..." *What the hell...*

Before the chef could dwell on the phenomenon any further, the brick chimney breast above the wood-fired oven began to rumble and clang; vibrating as though the Flying Scotsman was thundering past close-by. Plaster dust puffed down from the ceiling in flurries, dislodged from a sudden, unseen force; the metal grill shelf at the centre of the oven jangled against brick runners.

A thin curl of smoke fanned out from the topmost edge of the oven, dark-grey and wispy, like a long, skeletal finger, it stretched towards the ceiling before increasing in density as a puff of soot billowed into the kitchen.

Edging away from the oven, his retreat was obstructed by the serving bar behind him; unperturbed, he sidled slowly towards the exit door leading into the restaurant, the feeling of fascination and fear competing within him.

Gianni, his attention still on the two flies dodging his floundering attempts at swatting them, glimpsed his colleague in the kitchen, backing away from something. The way he moved alarmed him.

"Fabrizio? Are you okay?" he called across the room towards the kitchen and the chef's back.

"Forse sí forse no," *maybe, maybe not*, came the reply. Beyond him, a droning/whistling sound, low in pitch but growing in tempo could be heard, and he watched a smoky-haze slowly coalesce towards him.

"What?"

Before the chef could expand his answer, the room filled with a thick black, undulating brume disgorging in like it were pumped from a gas or air compression unit, with the speed and brashness of a sandblast.

"Dio mio!" *Oh my God!* Fabrizio could see what they were.

Flies!

Thousands, if not hundreds of thousands of them, swarming together tightly like nothing the Italian had seen before. He backed into the exit door, a hand snaking behind him for the knob. As his fingers curled around the protuberance, the dark, thrumming swell surrounded him from floor to ceiling and as dense as concrete; smoothly, it closed in.

"Mamma mia!" *My mother!*

In the restaurant, Barney's mother stared at the black fog filling the kitchen, her eyes widening in fear.

"Ma?" Slowly, Barney turned to peer over his shoulder. "Oh

shit," he exclaimed, standing up, forcefully knocking his chair over behind him. He knew what the growing hum and the mass of darkness converging on the chef was. "Ma, we're getting out of here."

The blood-curdling scream from the chef halted them in their tracks; long and piercing, but over almost immediately. It was replaced by a stifled choking, gurgling sound.

"Fabrizio!" The waiter hurried towards the kitchen, stopping short of opening the door, the sight of the smoke and the black mass of insects freezing him to the spot.

Unmoving, Barney's mother sat glued to her chair.

"Ma!" Urgently, Barney grabbed hold of the older woman, only then did she react to his frantic demands. She stood up and allowed her son to lead her towards the restaurant's exit/entrance.

"Wetherspoons sounds like a much better choice now, Barney, doesn't it?" Galvanised, the older woman spoke unaffected and stuffily.

"Yea, ma."

Before either customer made it to the door leading in/out of the building, the infestation redirected its focus, directing three channels of flies like extending limbs over the serving counter into the restaurant, moving purposefully and independently towards the three occupants within the room. The first branch descended upon the waiter, smacking him hard in the face, promptly overwhelming his airways with little or no resistance. The waiter collapsed to the floor, his face completely covered in bloated, bigger-than-average bluebottles.

The second and third appendages spreading from the still-burgeoning blanket of darkness filling the kitchen had designs on Barney and his mother, and fell upon the fleeing duo a mere second after the waiter had succumbed without protest to the first insect attachment. Slipping to the immaculate clean tiles, Barney's mother was jostled hard to the floor and dragged back, pulled forcefully from Barney's grip.

"BARNEY!" she screamed.

"Ma!" The moment's hesitation was the difference between living and dying. Watching his mother disappear beneath a blanket of flies was the last thing he saw. The third attachment of insects blasted into his face like a sandstorm. He danced about, flapping his hands and arms to the side of his face, clawing and slapping at the insects landing on his hair, coughing and spitting at the few that passed through his lips into his mouth. Unperturbed by the resistance proffered, the flies upped their attack by dispensing reinforcements from the kitchen and their already dead victims. In no time, Barney's head was encased at the centre of a swarm of flies four feet thick. Cut off from oxygen, the man, who minutes earlier had been looking forward to eating a Fat Mama's Special pizza with all its mouth-watering toppings, dropped to his knees and slumped forward onto his face.

Barney was barely alive, but taking no chances, a thick column of flies marched steadily into the man's mouth.

Outside Fat Mama's House, a husband and wife, together with their two young children, stepped up to the entrance. The man laid a hand gently on one of the brass pull handles set into the frame of the glass panelled door. On the opposing side, a fly buzzed up and landed on the 'open' sign displayed through the glass. It was watching keenly.

The husband, wearing a tight T-shirt that accentuated his muscular torso, turned towards his family. "Are you sure you lot want pizza? I mean, we could go to MacDonald's if you'd rather…" In truth, it had been his decision to visit Fat Mama's House.

"Yea… yea… yea, MacDonald's, MacDonald's… please, dad!" One of the children – a boy, and the eldest by two years – replied. His sister, just four years old, eased over to her father's side, peering into the Italian restaurant.

The girl turned fast, as though afraid and reached up to her father. Without hesitation, he scooped her up and held her in his arms. "Can we go to MacDonald's?" she asked timidly.

"Sure, sweetie," he said, removing his hand from the door and turning away from the Italian restaurant. "But, I thought you wanted pizza."

"I know," she replied, full of regret. "I just don't like the look of the flies..."

Puzzled by her comment but not wishing to explore what his daughter meant, the father casually led his family away down the road.

CHAPTER FOURTEEN

/

THE COMMUNICATIONS ROOM TOOK UP most of the third floor of the Fulbarton Police HQ building. Laid out impressively with eight rows of six desks, spaced adequately for privacy and comfort, each workstation was set up with dual computer screens, sophisticated telephony and radio equipment and operated by a team of staff who handled upwards of five hundred emergency calls a day. Ordinarily, no two calls were ever the same; one minute an operator could be taking down details of a stolen vehicle, the next a domestic disturbance or a report of a missing person.

The variety of the role is what Tina Jacobson enjoyed, and the fact that she was the first port of call from a person in need of help or someone in distress was even more rewarding. Tina just loved to help people, even if the subject matter could sometimes be deemed as harrowing or terribly distressing.

Like most call centres, the telephones didn't ring, chime or sound an electronic tune; instead, calls were announced via a small warning bleep in the operator's ear and answered with a flick of a button.

Tina glanced at the clock on her phone as a call buzzed through to her headset. She accepted it.

"Fulbarton Police, how can I help you?"

Sniffling was all that could be heard.

"Hello? Can you talk? If you can't talk and it's an emergency, make a noise or cough… or press 'five' twice…" Tina glanced at the caller ID panel. A mobile phone number was displayed.

More sniffling.

"I'm sorry," continued Tina, "I'll have to terminate this call if you do not respond."

"… *I'm sorry…*" a small, female voice filled Tina's ear. "… *my baby is dead…*" She sounded utterly distraught and terrified.

Tina shuddered. "Did you say your 'baby is dead'? What's your name and address, Miss?"

"… *my dog is dead…*" the woman on the phone continued.

"Miss? What's your name and address please?" Tina was hitting the keys on her computer. Quickly, she recorded the caller's phone number.

"… *he was only out of my sight a minute… now he's gone…*"

"Miss? Are we talking about a baby or a dog?"

"… *Oh, no… no, no, no… they're coming back… they're coming back!*" The woman sounded hysterical at the other end.

"Miss? Who's coming back? Tell me where you are and I'll dispatch a patrol car to you…"

"… *the flies!*" shrieked the woman. "… *the flies… they killed my puppy… now they're coming to get me… help me… please… HELP ME!!*"

The call ended abruptly.

Tina checked the number she had recorded on her screen and quickly dialled it.

The ringing tone at the end of the line began to ring. Tina listened to the digital tone for more than thirty seconds before a voice cut in, requesting she leave a message after the tone.

Tina slipped the headset off her head and stared anxiously at her computer screen, thinking on what to do next. She stood up and crossed to a tall, skinny man in his thirties with thinning hair, a gaunt face and sunken-in eyes. He was sitting at his desk typing up a report using just the pads of his index fingers. Tina thought he looked ill or seriously malnourished.

"Jamie? I just had a call cut-out on me. A woman seemed to be in distress; said something about flies 'coming to get her'. Could be related to those cases we were briefed on earlier..." *and which were featured in the news*, she further thought.

Before he could reply or give advice, another operator stepped over, interrupting. "Sir, I've just sent a response team to Castle Tower shopping centre... there's a reported fly attack. A young woman, said to have been trapped in a lift, was found dead, and an attending firefighter has subsequently been killed..."

"Jesus!" exclaimed the team leader. He tapped the fingers of both hands nervously against the top of his desk.

"Sir... they have evacuated the shopping centre, but people are panicking; some were hurt getting out. They say the flies are still in there. Is there anything else we should do? Like, call pest control?"

Jamie was about to reply when a guy with a crew cut and tattoos stepped up. A small queue was forming behind him. Despite his tough-looking appearance, he spoke quietly. "I don't think you're gonna want to hear this," he said, "but I've just ended a call with a paramedic attending an emergency at a house out on Cambridge Drive... a small boy, pronounced dead at the scene. There's evidence of flies..."

2

Bedlam.

That was the best word to describe the communications room thirty minutes later and the one Chief Superintendent Mills used to describe what he found upon entering the third-floor office. The caller display wallboards were flashing red, alerting operators and the leadership team to the fact that they had a queue of callers (unheard of during the day), currently fluctuating between thirty-five and forty, with an average hold time sitting in the region of eleven minutes.

Without prompting, the duty team leader, Jamie Day-Hewitt, stood up and greeted the Chief of Fulbarton's police station. "Sir... it's chaos. I've never known anything like it. We had a busy morning... but this," he indicated the hubbub of noise, of flustered conversations and panicking operators; "this is unheard of."

"Are they all...?" Chief Superintendent Mills left the question hanging.

"Yes, sir... we're calling them 'fly strikes'."

"Fly strikes?" The senior police officer thought it sounded a little melodramatic. He didn't add any comment. "How many?"

"So far... thirty-eight reported incidents, and counting. Some are hoaxes, but many are not; at least a dozen dead; likely more. There are a lot of worried or scared people out there..."

The Chief Superintendent shook his head, unable to grasp the full extent of the problem and completely at a loss on how to solve it. Fulbarton Police were more accustomed to dealing with shoplifters, burglaries, cybercrimes, missing persons, rapes and social disorders. On the rare occasion, they handled murder cases – but none for some considerable time – these were clear-cut and straightforward. Never had they investigated attacks by pests or flies before, and certainly nothing of such magnitude or scale.

"What are we dealing with?"

Although it wasn't required as he had an eidetic memory, the team leader picked up a clipboard from his desk and flicked through some A4 sheets of paper which he had hurriedly scrawled upon. He began to reel off a number of examples: "A fly attack at Castle Tower shopping centre where a woman and a firefighter have been killed, flies observed in large numbers close to the victims; a child was found dead in his bedroom, flies were seen crawling over his face; a woman called to say that her dog had been killed... also by flies, before her line went dead; a dental patient, heavily sedated, was found unresponsive after being left alone for just a couple of minutes... again, flies were seen leaving the scene," he looked up. "Do you want me to continue?"

Chief Superintendent Mills shook his head. "DI Baylem is the investigator in charge of these... *fly strikes*. Do you know where he is?"

"No, sir... last I heard he was attending the MP, Edwin Carslake's crime scene; he's not reported in since this morning. We've put a call out, but he's not responding."

"Where is he?" Mills muttered to himself. "Okay. Keep trying. I need him here. We need to issue another statement to the press... before all hell breaks loose."

CHAPTER FIFTEEN

D ETECTIVE SERGEANT MCCARDLE WAS COMFORTING Baylem's mother when the DI arrived, breathless and out of sorts when he charged in through the front door. Sweat coated his face like he had run the sizeable distance from Emily Herrington's house on Meadow Croft Crescent instead of making a dash from his Audi parked on the other side of the road.

"Mother, are you okay?!"

The frail old woman looked up from beside McCardle, her eyes rheumy, her cheeks moist from crying. "Oh, August," she sobbed. "It was awful... I thought they were going to get me." She raked a shaky hand through her thin white hair. "I saw the news this morning and what happened to those poor people. Then a little while ago, I saw those flies... buzzing around in here... and more outside... I thought: this is it..." She started to cry.

"Don't worry, mum, you're safe now," placated Baylem, like he was addressing a small child spooked by an imagined boogey man during the night. He placed himself down in an armchair, settling on the edge so that he was sitting upright with his feet flat on the floor.

PC Anders stepped into the room from the kitchen. He shook

his head. "Apart from the one fly I found in the living room when we arrived, I haven't found any others."

Baylem's mother looked up towards Anders, a wild look upon her face. "I never imagined them," she said with certainty. "They were here. Hundreds of 'em... I saw 'em."

"How about a nice cup of tea to settle your nerves, Mrs Baylem?" asked PC Anders brightly, changing the subject.

She nodded slowly. "Yes... Quite..."

"Then I'll get a dustpan and brush to clear that up." The uniformed officer indicated the remnants of a shattered glass, knocked over or dropped, its contents soaked into the carpet. He disappeared from the room into the kitchen.

Must've been the glass breaking sound I heard, Baylem recalled, just before his mother's call had ended. "Where were they, mum?"

She looked confused.

"The flies?" clarified Baylem. "The ones you saw. Where were they?"

Gradually, she became lucid. "Oh... they were everywhere. One minute at the window... then in the corner... and then flying around the lampshade. They were all over the place... most terrifying."

"When did you first notice them, Mrs Baylem?" asked McCardle softly.

"Well," the old woman started, as though beginning a lengthy tale, "I was watching *This Morning* with Philip and Holly... like I do every day, and I saw you on it giving your statement – I was so proud – and they were soon talking about the deaths here in our very own town; they were speaking with someone local highlighting the apparent fear here, and then interviewing a so-called fly expert who was spouting loads of big science-y words.

"This was all after they broke the news that our MP, Edwin Carslake, and that American pop singer he was with at the time were found dead this morning; horrible stuff. Anyway, they were saying things like, 'make sure your windows and doors are all secured shut' and 'tape up your air vents', and telling us to get a 'survival kit' of fly killer sprays, repellents and to stock up with a week's worth of water and tinned foods and some such. Scaremongering, I first thought, preparing us; like we were getting ready for a war.

"And then I saw them with my very own eyes. They were flying around the room, taunting and goading me. Every step I went, they were there... When I saw the second and third fly, I panicked. And then I saw hundreds of them, flying all around me. That's when I phoned you..." She was speaking directly towards her son. "I knew you'd take care of me..."

McCardle stroked the back of the woman's hand, nodding knowingly. Baylem sat impassively, deep in thought.

PC Anders returned with a cup and saucer. Hot tea threatened to flow over the cup's edge as he placed it down on the small coffee table set within the centre of the room.

"Mum. The sergeant here and I are going to take a look around out back for a moment. PC Anders will look after you..." Baylem stood up. "Jayne, it's this way." He led the sergeant out of the room, through a very short hallway into the kitchen. The exit door was just two strides across lime-green linoleum situated between built-in cupboards, one side housing a washing machine, the other a sink and draining board. A plastic drying rack held a couple of plates, a saucepan and a selection of cutlery.

Closing the door behind her, McCardle followed Baylem around to the side of the bungalow.

"Your mother was lucky," said the DS.

"She was never in any danger," asserted Baylem. "I should have realised. My mother can't help it. She has an anxiety disorder and suffers from the early stages of dementia. She takes medication for both; I should have asked if she'd been taking them. If she misses a few doses, she's apt to suffer with delusions."

"She seems convinced, though."

"I'm sure she was. To her, she was in genuine danger and the flies were real. Most likely, she saw one or maybe two flies and, coupled with what she was seeing and hearing on the television, her fear or worry caused her anxiety threshold to max out and her brain conjured up the imaginary attack."

"Your poor mother."

"Yes," replied Baylem sadly. "Things have been steadily declining since my dad died two years ago..."

McCardle gently laid a comforting hand on the DI's arm.

"I'm okay," he said reassuringly. "Now, let's get back to the dairy farm, and then I'll brief you on my time with the journalist; did you find out anything else? Anything useful or interesting? Are you sure it's our flies responsible?"

McCardle gave Baylem a withering look and slowly withdrew her hand. "Without a doubt, it was the flies that blighted his cattle... I've bagged a handful of samples for analysis, but they looked the same as the ones we swept up yesterday and again this morning. I didn't learn anything else, other than what I already told you, and which was reported in the papers; the dairy farm was completely wiped out. As I said in my call, he showed me CCTV footage of the incident. It was scary shit," she didn't need to elaborate. "Tom Lavery was peeved we hadn't taken him seriously when he first reported the incident."

"I can understand that. On the face of it though, cattle being attacked by insects is hardly a criminal matter; it's something DEFRA is more likely to deal with."

Further discussion was interrupted by DS McCardle's mobile phone ringing. Impulsively, she answered it. "McCardle."

"*Detective Sergeant...*" a female voice filled McCardle's ear. "*I have Chief Superintendent Mills for you.*" A beat later, she was replaced on the line by the commanding officer: "*McCardle... where the hell is Baylem?!*"

"He's here with me, sir," she replied unpretentiously.

"*Tell him to answer his bloody phone... we've been trying to get hold of him for nigh on an hour... it's pandemonium here.*"

"What's going on, sir?"

Baylem raised an eyebrow imploringly towards McCardle.

"*The end of the bloody world, that's what's going on. I don't care what you are currently doing; get yourselves back to HQ... pronto! I need Baylem to give another statement, and someone to tell me what the hell is going on!*" Giving no room to protest, the call was ended.

"That was the Chief Super," said McCardle, returning her mobile to her jacket. "He needs us back in the office. He sounded a bit fraught. And said you need to answer your phone."

"Okay... we'll head on back. First, we need to collect something."

"Collect something?" McCardle repeated, parrot-like.

Conjuring a small key from his pocket, Baylem held it up for inspection. "Emily Herrington's contact – Gemma Warren – gave this to me. It's to a safety deposit box. Inside it, we'll find out everything apparently."

2

For more than an hour, a spike of calls entered the communications room at Fulbarton Police HQ. Operators logged a never-ending series of reported 'fly strikes', triaged the cases in order of urgency and dispatched police units to locations most needed. Stretched to breaking point, it came as something of a relief when calm descended upon the station, conveniently just as DI Baylem stepped into the building.

McCardle was at his side.

Chief Superintendent Mills appeared within the corridor, blocking passage. "Ah, just the man," he greeted, adding: "and woman."

"Chief." Both spoke in unison.

"Though, you took your time," he griped. Baylem offered no explanation and Mills continued. "I've scheduled a briefing for half-two, which I'd like you to lead." He was speaking to the DI. "And a press release half an hour after."

Baylem groaned silently. "Oh?"

Mills continued. "I've set up an incident room for you. It's time we got a handle on the situation. No doubt you saw the press build-up outside. These bizarre insect attacks are gaining a lot of attention, locally, nationally, and worldwide; especially with the deaths this morning of Edwin Carslake... and that American singer. I think I saw a crew camping outside from CNN! Can you believe it?

"To make matters worse, we've been inundated with reports of further fly strikes since lunchtime; at least a dozen dead, many others injured or traumatised."

"We've not been idle, sir," said Baylem, churlishly.

Mills ignored him. "Come. The Home Office have sent a representative to help manage additional resources. There have been offers of support from forces across the UK, and there's been a suggestion of using the army, who I believe are on standby."

Baylem raised his eyebrows.

"Needless to say, the prime minister is urging us for a speedy resolution to the... situation. He's deeply aggrieved by the death of one of his MPs... Carslake was apparently a golfing buddy with a bright future."

Baylem grunted at the useless information.

"Here we are." Mills led the two detectives into a conference room that had been hastily transformed into the incident room. "You can have whoever you want... I've set the ball rolling; I've called in DI's Randall and Hardy to lend a hand; along with their teams. Doctor Hamilton has also called in a forensic entomologist from the Natural History Museum in London. He should be here shortly."

"That might be useful."

"Yes, well, Hamilton seemed to think so." Mills checked his watch. The time was close to half past one. "You have approximately an hour... I'll leave you to prepare for the meeting."

3

An hour was no time to prepare for a taskforce briefing, but between Baylem and McCardle, and enlisting help from Constables Anders and Manning, things were more or less ready when Chief Superintendent Mills returned with the representative from the Home Office. Already present was DI Randall, an officer in his fifties with receding hair and a thick black moustache that overlapped his top lip. Using a handkerchief, he mopped sweat from his forehead. It was hot and his sleeves were rolled up to his elbows and his grey tie was pulled loose at his neck.

"I see you've made it your home," said Mills as he walked across the room to where Baylem was standing. In a glance, he had seen photographs tacked to the walls, a map of Fulbarton pinned to a notice board and a PowerPoint slide projected onto a large white screen affixed to the brickwork facing the room.

"Quite," replied Baylem, not turning. He was standing close to a desk working on a laptop that was hooked up to the overhead projector. Busily, he tapped at the keyboard.

The Chief Super walked towards the detective inspector. The room was partitioned, half was set out with an arrangement of chairs placed 'assembly fashion' ahead of the projection screen, the other half was crowded with desks and tables, most decked out with computers and telephones, and all complimented with office chairs designed for practicality rather than comfort.

"This is Annabelle Herman, special advisor from the Home Office," introduced Mills. Baylem stopped typing and looked up.

Annabelle Herman was a tall woman; at least six feet, even without the red stilettos on her feet. Her auburn brown hair was centre-parted, hung parallel to her chin and framing a heart-shaped face. Baylem saw she was holding her right hand out towards him; the left clutched a black leather Barbour briefcase. "Hi," she acknowledged, smiling.

Baylem accepted her hand and gave it a long, gentle shake. "Pleased to meet you," he said smoothly.

"Annabelle is with us for as long as this emergency continues," overstated the Chief Super.

"I'm sure we could get along fine without outsider help," said Baylem, not discourteously. "No offense…"

"None taken," she replied. "Strictly, my role here is twofold. I'm to find out what's going on and report back to the home secretary and the prime minister, and to offer whatever help or support the police department needs to combat the issue affecting the town."

"Shall we?" Mills was directing the Home Office advisor towards a seat at the side of the room.

With the time now edging closer to half-two, the room was slowly filling up with people. Despite the seating, almost everyone was standing. Excluding Baylem, McCardle, the two constables still helping with setting up the room, the Chief Superintendent and Annabelle Herman, there were fifteen people so far in attendance. More were dribbling in all the time. Baylem spotted Floyd Hamilton conversing with a British Indian with short white hair and a white goatee beard. He was dressed smart but casual.

"Can I have your attention," said the Chief Super breaking away from Baylem and Herman, marching to the front of the room. All conversation suddenly ceased. "Please take seats. DI Baylem is the lead in dealing with these…" he didn't know what to classify them as, so settled with: "… incidents, and will in a moment like to address you all."

One or two pockets of people baulked at Baylem's mention, notably around the two other DIs in the room; Randall and Hardy. Neither of them – both ranked Baylem's equal – batted an eyelid, though Hardy, a woman who had been in the force since the mid-eighties, felt she was the more experienced officer to handle such a case of public interest.

Swiftly, those in attendance gravitated towards the chairs set out in five rows towards the front of the room.

"Thank you. Hopefully, between you all, you can get to the bottom of what's causing the flies to behave in such a way and devise a plan to put a stop to them. Detective Inspector... if you don't mind?"

Reluctantly, Baylem shuffled to the front of the room, bypassing the police chief at centre stage as he went. For support, McCardle moved with him, stopping a short distance to the side.

Chief Superintendent Mills took a seat at the side of the room close to where he had directed Annabelle Herman.

"Where to begin..." Baylem started, thinking aloud. In his hand, he held a remote presentation clicker. "Okay, so you've all seen the dailies, watched the news and read today's papers. Some of you may even have watched *This Morning*... Holly Willoughby was looking especially lovely today." A few people sniggered at the offhand comment. The DI crossed the room to a side wall upon which a number of photographs had been displayed. "Sean Wallace," he said, pointing towards a portrait in the midst of scene photos, showing the dead man in better health. "Found yesterday. Cause of death, asphyxiation. Cutting open his windpipe during his autopsy revealed literally hundreds of flies compressed from the back of his mouth and down for a considerable way into his trachea." Baylem moved a foot along to a second set of pictures.

"The Jessops: Tobias and Julie and an unidentified child approximately eight in age. All found dead a short time after Sean," he didn't expand on the mysterious circumstances surrounding the little girl handcuffed to a chair in the basement. "Same M.O. Time of death… approx twelve days ago." Baylem moved along to a third set of photos, pinned up similarly to the previous two exhibits.

"Last night, Justin Piper, found dead at Hinkley Walsh Insurance. It was his last day, in more ways than one. He was found pinned to the floor beneath a vending machine; cause of death… crushing you might think, but no; by, you've guessed it… asphyxiation… flies found again in the throat." Baylem had seen Hamilton's autopsy report a short time earlier whilst preparing the incident room. It was a carbon copy of the four prior victims.

The DI moved along some more, this time to the wall facing the room, the projector screen was placed centrally.

"This morning, McCardle and I attended a report of a fly infestation. A young mum – Megan Pritchard – found her infant child, Harry, in his bedroom covered with flies." The picture on the wall was a still taken from the CCTV footage recorded. "Luckily, Miss Pritchard got to her child in time. Using initiative, she climbed into the shower with him. Turns out, these flies don't care much for water. The tragedy was averted and we got our first break." Using the remote, Baylem clicked a button and flipped through a couple of slides on the PowerPoint presentation being projected onto the screen beside him. "This is CCTV footage taken at Miss Pritchard's house." The black and white video began to play silently on the wall. "It's given us the first look at what we are up against."

A muttering came from parts of the audience as footage showed the arrival of a fly through the gap at a bedroom window. Eyes followed it across the room, disappearing at the top of a wardrobe.

"If you look carefully, you will see literally thousands of flies moving about on the top there," The DI used a laser pointer to highlight where he meant. "This image was taken several hours BEFORE the flies attacked the baby. I've had the video spliced, cutting out everything until the moment of the attack. What you are about to see is the flies working in their full glory."

Exactly as promised, the picture changed and showed a black cloud of insects float up from the top of the wardrobe and swoop down towards the cot. A minute later, a young woman appeared at the door. At first, she stood stock-still, clearly shocked at what she was seeing. Then she moved, pulled out the baby from the cot and rushed from the room.

"Once it was clear the flies had failed to achieve their objective, they quickly vacated the property." Baylem pressed the button on the remote clicker and the video slide skipped back to the title page. He walked across the floor to the other side of the projector screen. More photographs were stuck up; some were familiar as they had been downloaded off the internet, others once again taken by police photographers from a crime scene. "Edwin Carslake, MP. And... the American pop singer, Makayla, over here for a fundraiser held last night at the Town Hall. Found dead this morning in mid-coitus within a hotel room by the cleaner." He craned his neck to look across at the pathologist. "Floyd... have you had the chance to complete the autopsy yet?"

Dr Hamilton shuffled in his seat, uncomfortable with the sudden attention. He cleared his throat. "Um, yes."

Baylem waited for his old friend to expand upon his answer.

"Cause of death is identical to that found in all the others. Flies crammed into their airways, cutting off oxygen causing total hypoxia. Death was swift in both victims."

"Thank you." Baylem moved on to another set of photographs. "These pictures are around a week old, from a dairy farm on the outskirts of town. An entire herd of milking cows were killed, cause of death... ditto as before. And if that's not enough to get us all excited and frothing at the mouth, there are claims of a swarm of flies causing the fatal road accident reported in the local press two days ago." Using the remote clicker, Baylem flicked a button to produce an image of the front page of the *Fulbarton Evening Herald*. The headline:

When Bugs Attack: Insect Swarm Causes Fatal Road Accident.

"We've not had a chance to substantiate that claim as of yet, however, having spoken to the constable who attended the scene and perused through statements taken, I am led to the conclusion that this incident is linked... without question. That brings us up to where I am at with regards to this case and the death total currently sitting at nine victims..."

"What about the dozen or so fatalities occurring over lunchtime?" asked DI Randall seated at the front of the audience. "Do we have details on them? Are they not to be included in your tally?"

Baylem sighed and appeared to be giving the question a moment to consider. He'd read through the reports and reviewed the call transcripts during the hour since arriving back at the police station but hadn't had time to properly ingest them. He shook his head in dismay. "No. Not yet." *But we will*, he thought. "We have police units and SOCOs attending each incident as I speak. As soon as we are done, DI's Randall and Hardy will assist me by sharing the site visits and coordinating enquiries. Doctor Hamilton will examine the dead as quickly as he is able and orchestrate the removal of the bodies where he will carry out post-mortems. Once the cause of death has been verified, then we will add them to our death list."

Annabelle Herman was sat on the second row. She raised her hand tentatively like she was in school and needed the toilet.

"Yes?"

"Do we know where these flies have come from, or why they are attacking people?" she asked.

The DI clicked through a couple of slides on the projector to display a photograph of a man in his mid-thirties lifted from his Facebook page. "James Quisenberry," he said without introduction.

"He's a geneticist at a company called Biomargent Sciences. I met with his girlfriend a short while ago. The man himself is missing. She says he created them for the military, splicing their DNA or something, making them more intelligent and more formidable... amongst other things."

"That makes sense!" a voice exclaimed from alongside Dr Hamilton on the second row. "I'm Doctor Monroe Malhotra, entomologist with the Natural History Museum. Dr Hamilton has been sending me samples of the flies from your crime scenes... he invited me here," he started to laugh nervously, "I have to admit, I was not sure what in hell I was looking at."

"Can you explain?" asked Baylem.

"Well, I've never seen anything like it, sir. On the face of it, these flies bear an uncanny likeness to the *Calliphoridae*, more commonly known as the 'cadaver fly' or 'blow fly'. Taking a look at their cell structure though, I found that, genetically, they couldn't be any more dissimilar. In fact, I was starting to believe we were looking at a new species entirely, made up completely from the best bits of other insects. I did wonder if some mad scientist had created it in a test tube, and now, here you are confirming it."

"You say they've been made up from the 'best bits' of other insects, what d'you mean?"

"Well, sir. There's the presence of a gene called FoxP, which is found in fruit flies, as well as in human beings. It's believed to be linked to intelligence. Also, I found the DNA of other species of insects interweaved within, which I couldn't understand on the face of it, but now, with your assertion, makes perfect sense. Flies... bees... ants... creatures which have unique strengths, be it reproduction, aggression, telepathy; on their own pivotal to the originator's survival and completely non-lethal, but synthesised together... makes for something entirely more interesting."

"So, without dressing it up, what are we dealing with here, Doctor Malhotra?"

"Flies like no other. It's going to sound OTT, but super flies if you may permit me to call them such. They are stronger; they communicate and work as a single unit, and appear to reproduce at an accelerated rate, hence why there is so many of them, and counting. And I don't think they've completely finished evolving."

Chief Superintendent Mills stood up, his face taut with concern. "What can we do to stop them?"

Dr Malhotra looked solemn. "Are you religious?"

Mills laughed, lacking humour. "No."

"Pity. Me neither. I think a good prayer is needed about now."

"Maybe James Quisenberry's research will help us come up with an answer," suggested Baylem, taking the lead again. From inside his jacket pocket, he retrieved a small USB key. "We need to find James urgently, but in the meantime, I've been given this. James kept it safe in the event something untoward happened to him; his girlfriend indirectly gave it to me." Baylem walked forward and passed the small storage device to the entomologist. "See if you can make anything of it."

"I'll get straight on it, sir."

"Everyone else, let's crack on."

Bodies stood up from chairs as detectives, constables, analysts, Dr Hamilton, Dr Malhotra, and others, including Annabelle Herman, reorganised themselves.

"Annabelle, a quick word?"

"Sure, Inspector..."

"Do you know anything about a General Makepeace? It's been suggested that he undertakes work within Biomargent Sciences, and may know the current whereabouts of Doctor Quisenberry."

The Home Office advisor shook her head slowly, though her eyes seemed to betray her denial of knowledge. "I have contacts within the Ministry of Defence. I'll see what I can find out."

CHAPTER SIXTEEN

G ENERAL MAKEPEACE WAS SEATED AT the head of a large table within the boardroom of the Biomargent Sciences administration centre. Protruding from his left ear was a Bluetooth earpiece linked to a radio receiver set ahead of him.

To the general's right were four company people: Tim Howlett and a large woman of indeterminate age – a director within military research. Next to her were two other Biomargent stakeholders; one a majority shareholder (an old woman with a hard, gaunt face framed with thinning, wispy-white hair), the other a lawyer with the firm. On the opposite side, balancing the table, were military personnel with ranks of major, captain, and lieutenant (which there were two).

The time on the wall clock placed to the centre of the farthest wall was five-past-three, a sweeper hand silently brushing off each passing second. Beneath it was a large flat screen television that filled up half the plain white stud wall.

"James Quisenberry maintains his innocence," said Tim, voluntarily defending the incarcerated geneticist currently locked within a basement room doubling as a makeshift prison. Armed guards patrolled outside key-locked doors. "He says he shut the programme down as ordered, and I believe him."

"We still don't know that these fly attacks are anything to do with us," asserted the large woman. The security pass hanging from her neck identified her as Carmel Martins. "Plus, he's signed a confidentiality agreement. Even if he were guilty, there's no way he'd talk."

Makepeace shook his head. "I know he's innocent. I had him confined for his own good… but it doesn't matter. We've bigger concerns." Using a small remote controller, the general switched on the television. It took a moment before an overhead image of Fulbarton and surrounding areas appeared, approximately ten square miles of it in vibrant high definition.

Tim Howlett looked puzzled, not understanding the significance of what he was seeing. He held his tongue, knowing that an explanation would be forthcoming.

"These are live pictures being broadcast from an MQ-9 Reaper I've requisitioned, equipped with state of the art surveillance capabilities." The MQ-9 Reaper was an unmanned aerial vehicle, more commonly known to most as a 'drone'. It was one of a dozen the RAF used for covert and surveillance operations. "It's currently flying at an altitude of twenty-thousand-feet above Fulbarton. Carmel was right when she stated that 'we still don't know that these fly attacks are anything to do with us'. But I think they are, and I'm going to use this to set the record straight."

"Are you expecting to see the flies from so far up?" queried the old woman, a hint of contempt in her croaky voice.

"Yes, I am," replied Makepeace, "in a manner." Smoothly, he touched the earpiece in his left ear. "Garvey. Ready when you are." At the other end of the radio was the drone pilot, stationed 140 miles north at RAF Waddington.

Words and numbers flashed up on the large screen television before the image flicked from colour to dark-grey. Lighter grey –

almost white – outlines mapped out roads and landmarks. A timer began counting down in the top right corner from sixty.

"It takes a minute to initialise the software," explained Makepeace, addressing the room. "Then, if any of our flies are out there, we'll soon know."

"How's that possible?" asked the captain, identified as Dodd on his military uniform.

"It was Quisenberry's idea, actually. He told me the flies emitted radio waves... a failsafe he bred into them so that we could keep track. On their own, it would be hopeless; a bit like looking for a needle in a cornfield. But in large numbers... and I'm talking the volume capable of doing what we're seeing in Fulbarton, they'll light up like a fire in a gunpowder factory. All we need is to trace their signals via a suitably placed receiver; in this case, a radio telescope, which we've attached to the Reaper."

The timer seemed to tick down slowly, now thirty seconds until initialised.

"Jesus, it's like waiting in for a delivery..." The earpiece in the general's ear crackled then began to talk. For the benefit of those around him, he repeated what he heard: "So the Reaper will go off-line for a few seconds as it switches broadcasting to radio waves... okay Garvey, copy that."

The timer was now down to single figures.

9... 8... 7... 6... 5... 4... 3... 2... 1...

The picture on the screen flickered off and on twice, went off for a long moment, and then flashed back up.

The dark-grey image of Fulbarton was back in place, together with the lighter grey outlines of landmarks and roads as before, but now with a contrasting difference; there was the addition of a vibrant red colour in dots and patches spattered all over.

"Oh, sweet Lord," said Makepeace, visibly rattled. Slowly, he shook his head.

"What is it?" asked Carmel in ignorance.

The general ignored her, turning away slightly. He pressed the button on the earpiece. "Garvey? Maintain position and see if we can get some close-ups; then revert to standard mode... see what you can make with any live visuals." He plucked the comms link from his ear and dropped it to the table. "Fuck... that's not good. Not good at all."

"I take it that those red splodges are radio waves. How are we to determine what the flies are, and what are from other sources..." Tim spoke pragmatically, suffering none of the unease or anxiety expressed by the general.

"Other sources?" scoffed Makepeace. "The flies emit a unique frequency. What you are seeing belongs to one source, and one source only."

"But–" started Carmel, a mask of fear slipping into place.

"Oh," uttered the CEO, sinking down into his chair.

"Yep... my thoughts exactly. They're our flies... this confirms it... no doubt about it."

"But how?" croaked the old woman. "Our programme was shut down. Quisenberry said so..." Her protest went unanswered.

"What are you going to do, General?" Tim asked nervously.

"What are WE going to do, you mean?" Makepeace reached towards the drinks tray set on the table alongside a cake box crammed with an assortment of Krispy Kreme doughnuts and poured a glass of water from a serving jug. Ice chips rattled against the edge. "It's out of my hands," he said, adding dismissively: "This goes way above me. The prime minister is holding a COBRA meeting as we speak. It was inevitable... after all the news reports and the *This Morning* show." He sipped at his water. It was refreshingly cold. Before he could elaborate, his mobile phone – placed atop a small pile of dossiers – began to vibrate. With no apology, he snatched it up. "Yes, hello?"

"*General Makepeace.*"

The general recognised the female voice and felt his resolve melt very slightly. "Yes."

"*I thought I'd give you the heads up. Fulbarton Police knows about you, sir; and about Biomargent and James Quisenberry being responsible for the flies.*"

"Oh. How do you know that?" asked the general, his tone neutral. He stood up from the table, turning his back on his colleagues and subordinates.

"*Because the Home Office assigned me to them. I'm here now, assisting DI Baylem and his incident team.*"

General Makepeace expelled a lungful of air in exasperation.

"*We have a big problem, sir,*" the woman continued. "*They have a flash drive with all of Quisenberry's research. They also know of your involvement...*"

General Makepeace turned around and returned back to the table. The major was tapping out a text message on his smartphone. Tim Howlett was talking softly with Carmel and one of the lieutenants; small chitchat, nothing of substance. They quietened as the military leader glowered angrily at them.

"Don't worry about the flash drive, Annabelle, or what they know about me. I am well connected and besides, it's too late for that now; I doubt the drive will be any use to them anyway, not with the time they have left."

"*What d'you mean?*" asked the Home Office advisor, "'*time they have left'?*"

"The flies," he replied too quickly, adding no further explanation. "Listen, I can't say anything more at the moment, except we are beyond the point of taking preventative steps. There will be further attacks, and worse still to come. We can't stop it; it's now all about containment."

"*Containment?*"

"We'll need to confine the problem so it doesn't become a pandemic or cause nationwide alarm. I'll call you later when I have specifics." Makepeace disconnected the call and sat back down.

140 miles north, Garvey flicked a switch and the overhead

radio telescope broadcast of Fulbarton changed back to normal HD video mode, the lens zooming in on an area that had moments earlier appeared densely red.

A row of terraced houses fell into focus and with them, their dark slate roofs, vaguely similar to others close-by, though shimmering with a rippled, shuffling, moving-effect.

"Jesus... there must be thousands of them," proclaimed one of the lieutenants to Makepeace's left. He was leaning forward, getting closer to the broadcasted image.

"Hundreds of thousands I'd guess... ready and waiting," said the general. "Maybe even millions, if you factor in all of them... many are lying low, or gathering... like a well-disciplined army. Just waiting..."

"Waiting for what?" asked the CEO.

"For their orders. For the next phase of attacks."

"Next phase?" queried the old woman.

The general ignored the majority shareholder. Just because she bought her place at the table didn't earn her his trust or respect, or obligate him in any way.

"What are we working with here, General?" asked Tim, small and whiney, his eyes glued to the blanket of flies crowded together upon the roof. The surveillance drone focused on other, neighbouring properties to reveal similar infestations. "Can we stop them?"

Makepeace turned to his military council, speaking directly to his appointed number two, Major Broadbent. Without thinking, he plucked up his phone from the table. "Major, whilst I'm speaking with the prime minister, have someone fetch James Quisenberry from the basement. Somehow he's got us into this mess; he can help get us out of it." Without further word, the general stood up and exited the room.

Tim Howlett sat forward in his chair, making ready to address those sitting around the table with a serious look on his face. "Did any of you want that chocolate doughnut?" he asked bluntly, pointing towards a chocolate iced glazed ring doughnut sandwiched between a sugared cake and a pink iced doughnut with sprinkles within the cake box in the centre of the table.

2

Prime Minister David Humphries spoke to the general on speakerphone. Members of his cabinet could be heard in the background through the small speaker of his smartphone, occasionally adding comment or joining in the conversation. Having attended COBRA meetings before, Makepeace could picture the set up. Like disciples seated around Jesus at the last supper, they would be sitting around the British leader at the large table filling the room. COBRA was the acronym ascribed to emergency meetings held at Whitehall, named after the room where such gatherings took place: Cabinet Office Briefing Room A.

"*So, General Makepeace, what conclusions have you come to?*" asked the prime minister. "*These pesky flies are causing merry ding-dong over there in Fulbarton,*" he said casually. It wasn't every day the leader of the United Kingdom held a crisis meeting to discuss an invading army of insects. "*Do they pose a significant threat to neighbouring towns, or to the rest of the UK?*"

Makepeace had retreated to a vacant office a short corridor away to make his call and had closed the door behind him, not wishing to be overheard. Even with the privacy, he couldn't help the pervading feeling that he was being watched or listened-in to.

"It's a ticking time-bomb, Prime Minister. I've ascertained that the flies responsible for the attacks are characteristic to those manufactured at Biomargent Sciences during research. Using a surveillance drone, I've also been able to pinpoint their exact positions, as well as the size of the infestation we are dealing with."

"*That sounds great!*" the prime minister exclaimed. "*So, if we know where they are... can't we just send in a team of exterminators to eradicate them?*"

"It's not that simple, sir. From what I can tell, the whole town is overwhelmed with these flies, and we're not talking our common, every day, buzz-about-the-kitchen, piss-you-off and want to die, kind of housefly. From what I know, we're talking genetically enhanced, super-intelligent, micro-killing, bad-ass mother-fucking flies that plan shit out, work in conjunction and are intent on a killing spree. These things will up the ante if provoked."

"*What are you suggesting, General?*"

"Firstly, we treat Fulbarton like we treat an outbreak of a highly contagious disease or contaminant. We place the whole town in lockdown; nothing in, nothing out. Then we set a quarantine zone, with a ten-mile circumference."

"*How do you propose doing that? These flies are not going to stay put just because you put a few boundaries up.*"

"There are ways, Prime Minister." Makepeace didn't augment his assurances. "But, you don't need to worry about the minor detail," he added confidently. "The next step will be to lay down a trap, something that will tempt the flies and draw them all into one, easily identifiable location."

"*Sounds intriguing. How do you propose to do that?*"

"Fulbarton Town Football Club. With seating for twenty-three thousand people and pitch space for several thousand more, we could get every inhabitant of Fulbarton in the one place, all at the same time."

"*Okay, go on.*"

"The flies take the bait and whilst engaged with their all-you-can-eat buffet, we take them out."

"*Take them out?*" challenged the prime minister.

"Yes, Prime Minister. A couple of 'Storm Shadows' should do it." Storm Shadows were laser-guided missiles, launched from the air by RAF Tornados and extensively used in combat, most notably during operations in the Iraq war. It was the most advanced weapon of its kind on the planet.

"*Won't that result in catastrophic losses of people, Prime Minister?*" interjected an unidentified voice somewhere behind David Humphries. "*It's a huge cost... and they are our people.*"

"It's called collateral damage, sir," interposed the general as though it was a trifle matter. "I assure you, these are acceptable losses in contrast to the potential risk the flies pose to the country as a whole. If we don't contain the danger now, our way of life and the very fabric of humanity as a whole is in jeopardy. It's a small price to pay, I assure you."

"*A bit extreme...*" said a woman closely seated to the prime minister.

"*That's as it may, General. But, such a sacrifice...*" Humphries was almost at a loss for words. "*... I don't think I'd be able to sleep at night... and it's an election year coming up.*"

"Prime Minister... it's your decision, I know, but... this is our one real shot to nip this thing in the bud. Look at what they did to Edwin Carslake... he was a friend of yours, wasn't he?" Makepeace didn't wait for affirmation. "That was bad, but I know what these flies are more capable of; I helped design them. This is likely our only chance."

"*And what are they capable of?*" asked Humphries loftily.

"Complete annihilation: They invade, they kill, they feed and they breed. If we let them take one town – and believe me, they will – nothing will stop them taking them all..."

Tim Howlett was halfway through eating a second doughnut when General Makepeace exploded back into the boardroom. Startled, he over-chomped on the fried dough confection causing raspberry jam to spurt from its bottom and spattering his white shirt like blood squeezed from a small animal.

Major Broadbent was standing to one side of the room glaring out through one of the large glass panelled windows. The view was terrible; just industrial buildings with chimneys pumping out thick white smoke and warehouses with little or no clues as to what they housed. A stack of haulage containers six levels high and twice as long and three times as deep increased the ugliness of the immediate surroundings. Separating these, in a field of grey, was concrete parking crammed with cars in a variety of colours shimmering beneath a radiant sun that had burnt away all of the earlier clouds. A storm had threatened, but came to nothing, delivering only an hour's worth of rain that was over before most people had ventured out from their beds. Hearing the general return, he jerked himself around. "Sir..." He was about to make an announcement but the general threw up a hand to silence him.

Makepeace saw the look of angst on the major's face and noted the air of nervousness around the room. Whatever was on their minds could wait, he thought to himself. He lowered his hand. "I've just spoken with David Humphries," he began, omitting the man's title.

The major swallowed his urgent disclosure and shrunk back, leaning against the window behind him.

"I briefed him on what we've discovered," continued Makepeace, "and gave him my prognosis on how I think things will play out. I outlined our options, but gave him very little to choose from. He didn't like it, but, nonetheless, ultimately gave me his blessing.

"We're to set things in motion, as outlined in The Civil Contingencies Act, under the subsection relating to disease control. Operation Remedy is a go..."

"My God, General," said one of the lieutenants apprehensively, understanding instantly the general's intent. The captain and the other lieutenant looked straight ahead impassively.

"Operation Remedy? What does that mean?" asked Carmel, beating Tim to the crunch.

"In simple terms, it means we're to neutralise the problem. Think of it as this: Fulbarton is a cancerous tumour, and not one of the good, easy to fix ones like Hodgkin's lymphoma, oh no. To ensure it doesn't spread, we need to act quickly and decisively. To continue with the analogy: we've identified the bad cells, now it's time to plan our strike."

"Jesus, Phil," started Major Broadbent, shocked. "That's tantamount to genocide. Those are OUR people!"

"Seriously!" disputed the CEO.

The old woman two places along sighed resignedly but wore a look of acceptance. In silence, she supported the general's intention.

"I wish it didn't need to come to this," said Makepeace without remorse, "but needs must. Plus we have a duty to protect our interests. How long do you think it'll be before word gets out that Biomargent are responsible for these flies? I'll be fine, but d'you think you'll all get off scot-free?"

Sheepishly, Tim nodded. He was a reluctant participant, but a participant all the same.

"No, if that gets out, you'll have more to worry about than the price of our stocks and shares. Now, where's that sorry sack of crap Quisenberry?"

Still standing, Major Broadbent straightened in false confidence. "He's gone, sir," he said reverentially. "I radioed down for guards to collect him, but when they unlocked the basement, they found the room empty..."

General Makepeace glowered angrily.

"We have no idea how he managed his escape, there are no other exits; no ways in or out. It's like he just vanished."

Makepeace slammed his fists down onto the table. For a

moment, he appeared in turmoil, struggling to contain his anger. He waved a fist towards the major. "Find him," he said, forcing himself to relax straight after. He lowered his hand. "But, first... start stage one of the Civil Contingency Act. We can't afford to be complacent."

"Isn't that a bit extreme?" asked Tim feebly, earning a reproachful look for daring to utter in protest.

"The more extreme, the better..." replied the general playfully.

CHAPTER SEVENTEEN

/

"I T'S LIKE WHAT YOU SAID; *there's a damnable amount of damage control needed... starting with you.*" General Makepeace's comment played over-and-over inside Quisenberry's head.

The two military policemen had dragged him out of his office along a seemingly endless corridor, down two flights of stairs and then through three sets of double-doors, the last of which led into a wide antechamber. Brightly lit and serving little purpose, the small room acted only as an entrance to a much larger basement storage facility; a pre-room.

Without care, the MPs opened the solid wooden door, activating the overhead lights with motion sensors. As the fluorescents flickered into life, they propelled Quisenberry through the doorway and laughed as he fell awkwardly and skidded a few feet before stopping, scraping a couple of layers of skin off and tearing corresponding holes at the knees of his trousers. Before the doctor had time to sit up, the MPs had disappeared through the door and closed it with a bang behind them.

The sound of a key grated within the old lock, followed by

further laughter. Bolts clacked home with a little shrill protest, securing the door and the room's prisoner.

"Perfect," he muttered under his breath. "Fucking perfect..." He stood up from the dusty black floor and backhanded filth from his trousers. The tubes of light fixed into the ceiling settled all around him. Further assessment revealed that dirt marred the sleeve of his jacket where he had skidded and marked his black shoes. "Well..." he walked with a shell-shocked gait, meandering the short distance to the door. Half-heartedly, he tried the handle, unsurprised to find it locked. "Shit!" He slammed his fists against it, the bang resounding in the enclosed room.

Turning away from the door, the geneticist considered the space that surrounded him.

There was an old office chair stowed beneath a table pressed up against the wall close-by. Quisenberry crossed over to it and dropped down forlornly; pressing his head into his hands and feeling his body rock back and forth from the hip, the chair creaking noisily beneath him. Hopelessness was overwhelming and he felt tears prickle his cheeks and an unbidden sob escape his lips.

After an hour and all cried out, the feeling of despair lessened and Quisenberry picked himself up from the chair. "I can't stay in here," he muttered. He wasn't concerned about his own wellbeing, but feared for the safety of his girlfriend, Gemma.

Despite the phosphorescent light spilling down from the ceiling, the room felt gloomy and dispirit. Industrial metal shelfing filled much of the room from floor to ceiling, with narrow aisles between. Box files and sundry items were crammed onto each, with nothing seemingly of interest or any value.

Quisenberry moved his attention towards a section of the basement which was kept clear for maintenance. He moved ahead slowly. A couple of large water tanks took up most of the area, plumbed into the floor with pipes leading out of it in a network that led throughout the building; fixed into the wall, adjacent to them, were a multitude of levers, glowing buttons, LCD screens, instrument panels and a confusion of wires that spider-webbed into the ceiling and every other direction. A large yellow warning sign indicated danger with a bold, black lightning bolt striking a prone figure, was affixed prominently at various points around the servicing area.

"Being electrocuted isn't going to solve anything," muttered the geneticist, turning away dejectedly. He made to move and then stopped.

"But..." Had he spied something else? He had a sudden thought. He turned back and walked slowly to within a foot of the big industrial water tanks, each hulking drum containing 15,000 litres. Sandwiched between the two cylindrical barrels was a set of metal steps braced into the wall and floor for stability, providing access to the service hatches that Quisenberry could see bolted shut at the top of the tanks and ahead of them, embedded into the concrete, was the object he had subliminally identified.

A dark grey manhole cover, made from iron.

"Hel-lo," said Quisenberry, unable to contain his excitement. In less than a second, he was down on his knees, his fingers probing the cover's edge for a handhold. Fumbling around its border entirely, he realised that there was no way to prise it up using his bare hands.

Inspecting the cover, he could see a pair of holes designed to be used with a D-handle manhole key. With a grunt, he stood up and began to search the area for the required tool. With more luck than he believed possible, he noticed what he needed hanging from a hook on the wall behind the metal steps.

There were two of them, both black with T-shape handles and D-shaped ends. They looked like the world's smallest shovels.

Quisenberry hurried across to behind the steps and pulled the two keys down. In no time, he was squatting over the manhole cover, inserting the two 'keys' into their respective holes and turning them half a degree, until they turned no more. With a bit of effort, he pulled the iron manhole cover up an inch, his muscles screaming in protest, unused to the strain. With a heave and an expulsion of air, the geneticist banged the cover aside.

Peering down, Quisenberry was pleased to see that the hole was wide enough for a body to pass, and that it led to an underground services tunnel that the geneticist guessed led north or southwards, depending on which direction was taken. Furthermore, a stepladder descended towards the tunnel, affixed to one wall just beneath the opening. Pipes and wires could be seen beneath and disappearing into the tunnel and the sound of flowing water could be heard in an echoed-distance.

"Hold on, Gemma... God, I hope I'm not too late," Quisenberry whispered, twisting the two D-handle manhole keys from the cover and tossing them aside. Dropping to the floor, he dangled his legs over the opening of the hole, scooched his butt to the edge, and then set a foot onto the second rung of the stepladder. Swiftly, he climbed down until his head was just poking out, reached across to the manhole cover and dragged it with a lot of effort over the hole above him, scraping it noisily against the black, epoxy resin flooring. Hurting his fingers and grazing his knuckles in the process, the doctor pulled the cover down after him, hearing it bang into place with a satisfying:

CLANG!

With the sound of flowing water now louder and the basement room closed off behind him, Quisenberry clambered down the ladder, bypassing the last rung to drop nimbly to the tunnel's floor.

The walls and ceiling of the tunnel were horseshoe-shaped and white-tiled. Pipework ran the entire length, from one end to the other, connected – so Quisenberry thought – to the water tanks in the room above. At various points, the pipes disappeared into the ceiling. There were also thick black cables like uncoiled snakes, intertwined with thinner wires, bunched together with ties and affixed to the wall with clips and metal brackets.

Although below the average height for a British male, the geneticist was still tall for the tunnel standing at just under five-foot-nine inches. Stooping into an almost perfect Quasimodo stance, Quisenberry began walking fast northwards. The tunnel was dimly lit with safety LED lighting placed every five metres built into the arched ceiling.

Quisenberry soon discovered that the tunnel travelled a good distance further than the length of the building, and a number of tunnels joined or branched off from it at various turns. Not wishing to get lost or find himself trapped – like the fabled minotaur in Daedalus' *Labyrinth* – the geneticist decided to follow the sound of running water, shortly coming to an access point where the noise was loudest, and which dropped down into a dark, shadowy cavern that he easily guessed was the sewer.

His suspicions were soon confirmed when, upon dropping down from the service tunnel, he landed within two feet of liquid putrescence, the smell of which turned his stomach and forced him to regurgitate what little breakfast he had consumed earlier that morning into his mouth.

He swallowed it back, finding it took all his resolve not to completely vomit up. The taste leaking into his mouth was both acrid and sweet, a mix of bile and cornflakes. The combination, along with the stink of raw sewage, was repellent.

"Oh God," he whimpered, pushing up the front of his suit jacket to block his nose. Although the thought of travelling within a confined space, up to his knees in excrement, repulsed him, the notion of returning to the locked basement seemed worse.

Barely suppressing the fetid stench permeating the thick, sharkskin woollen suit, he started wading forward through the inky-dark passage, much narrower than the service tunnel he'd just vacated and dreadfully darker without any overhead lighting. He wished he had his mobile phone, on which was a torch function; it had been on his desk when Makepeace had ordered his restraint.

For what seemed like an hour, but, in fact, was only twenty minutes, the geneticist reached a junction in the tunnel and faced a dilemma.

"Now which way?" he asked aloud, his voice reverberating into an echo within the T-intersection.

The sound of crashing water emanated from the tunnel continuing to his left, whereas nothing discernible could be heard from the passage to his right. Standing stock-still, Quisenberry could see the flow of the sewage water from the tunnel he stood and the one to his right, coalesce into the passage to his left. On close inspection, he watched lumps of waste he didn't care to linger on float on by, and a little after – even more disturbing for the man – the sight of two rats swimming past, travelling in the same direction.

"My dad always said: if you find yourself trapped, keep an eye out for rats. They'll lead the way out... or eat you." Humourlessly, he started to laugh, taking the left turn. Splashing noisily, he followed the rats and the flow of water, the rodents appearing to be racing each other as they put some distance between themselves and the doctor, disinterested in his presence and unconcerned that he was following them.

Five minutes later, the tunnel swerved right and the near-total darkness gradually faded away as light spilled in from the outside, along with a refreshing breeze that dappled his skin. Quisenberry lowered his jacket from his nose and mouth to test the air, taking in a deep breath through his nostrils.

The sewer smell was still terrible, only slightly improved. He trudged through the water twenty metres, finding the tunnel came to an abrupt end, the water and waste flowing over in a short waterfall into a further tunnel that began below him, continuing to transport the runoff in a different direction towards the treatment plant. Ahead, across a gap a metre in width that separated the tunnel was an overflow pipe, slightly narrower than the passage he had been traipsing, but wide enough to pass through.

Amazingly, the two rats Quisenberry had been following were on the other side, noses twitching as they peered over the overflow-pipe's rim. Either they were sniffing the air for danger or looking skyward for divine intervention. Whatever it was, the rodents came to a decision fast and dropped over the edge like lemmings, now out of site.

"If you guys can do it, so can I!" declared the doctor bravely, taking a standing-leap across the void and landing easily on the opposite side, three metres from where the pipe led out into hazy sunshine. In a half-crouch, he shuffled along and peered over the lip of the outfall conduit, relieved to feel and breathe in the outside air. There was no longer any sign of the rain from earlier that morning, like it never happened. He paid it no further thought. "I guess that's not so bad," he said, indicating the size of the drop.

Below him, two feet down, was a calm river bordered by a bank green with wild plants, bushes and trees. On its surface, white lilies could be seen amongst patches of dense leaves floating serenely. Quisenberry recognised the river, could even see the footpath along the opposite side. He had walked it abundant times, more so as a kid bunking off from school between lessons, which was just half a mile away across a dual carriageway, via a gentle walk through a recreation ground and a field of allotments.

The rats were nowhere to be seen and with less circumspection, Quisenberry jumped feet-first into the river, landing with an almighty splash! The water consumed his legs to just below his groin. Unlike the filth he had waded through within the sewers, the river's water was cleaner, icy-cold and caused him to involuntarily shiver. Taking large strides, he was soon scaling the other side of the stream and casually wringing out water from the legs of his trousers. With shoes squelching underfoot, he started walking in the direction of the town centre. He checked his watch.

12:40 p.m.

Wishing to put some distance between him and the Biomargent Sciences complex, he soon found his walk develop into a jog and gradually turn into a run.

It was close to four-and-a-half miles to the centre of Fulbarton, but Quisenberry was desperate to find out something else first. Leaving the river path fifteen minutes later, he bounded through underbrush that hemmed in a short clearing and gravelled carpark. Slowing to a walk, he stepped onto crazy paving of various coloured stones winding a gentle route through a small garden lined with tables with parasols and chairs. There were signs of recent occupation with empty glasses and a used ashtray placed towards the centre of one table, but whoever they were, they were long gone.

The Black Swan public bar and restaurant was an old village pub, boasting fine ales and home cooked meals. Set within a Victorian building, The Black Swan was one of only a handful still in business on the outskirts of Fulbarton.

Quisenberry glanced at his watch as he stepped into the bar area.

12:56 p.m.

A short, dark-haired woman looked up from behind the bar, approximately mid-thirties and wearing a white tank top that had two black handprints suggestively placed in alignment with the modest rise of her chest. Quietly, she assessed his appearance, noting that he was dressed smartly in a suit, shirt and tie combo, but the look devastated by the sodden trousers and the dripping wet shoes on his feet.

The bar and restaurant was quiet, with only half a dozen tables filled with diners and a couple of guys feeding money into fruit machines. The air was filled with the sound of jukebox music, easy listening fare made up of pop tunes and classic rock.

"Had an accident?" asked the barkeeper, slightly concerned. Moving forward, she wore a look of mild interest on her face, her eyebrows raised.

"Just a little," Quisenberry replied, offhand. "Do you have a phone I could use?"

"It's through there," she said, nodding, "on the other side of the door, to the left." She was pointing the way towards a set of doors that led to the front entrance and a sign that read: Toilets. "Can I get you anything?"

"Um…" He felt lost for words. It wasn't a tough question and he needed a drink, but he found it hard to give an answer. "Maybe when I get back… I really need to make a call first." Without engaging the barkeeper further, Quisenberry turned and set forth for the doors leading to the telephone.

Finding it easily, Quisenberry snatched up the black metal handset from the matching armoured body and found some loose change from a trouser pocket. Inserting a pound coin, he then punched in the eleven-digit mobile phone number that was burnt into his memory. The call connected with no ringing tone or pause for breath.

"*Hi, this is Gemma. I'm sorry, I can't get to the phone right now, but if you'd like to leave your name and number I'll get back to you…*"

Quisenberry pressed the cut-off button and held the handset close to his ear, hearing the dialling tone. He had hoped his girlfriend would pick up. He tried the number again.

"*Hi, this is Gemma. I'm sorry–*" Quisenberry hung up the phone with an embittered jab. *Oh God, no…* His mind was cast back to his office earlier that morning. General Makepeace's goons had just roughly pulled him from his chair. The scene played out vividly within his mind:

"*What about Gemma? Our baby is due any day now. She needs me! AARON needs me!*"

"*Is that your baby's name?*" The general had asked.

"*Yes,*" he had replied.

"*I'll make sure they are looked after,*" said Makepeace ominously.

"*Stay away from her!*" he had screamed. "*You won't get away with this!*" Then the two MPs had pulled him from the laboratory, kicking and screaming. "*I'm not the only one who knows!*"

Panicking, Quisenberry dialled an alternative number. Gemma's mother's mobile. The ringing tone sounded distant and continued for much longer than he was expecting. Just as he was about to give up, a small voice filled his ear.

"*Hello?*"

"Mrs Warren? It's James. Have you heard from Gemma? I've been trying to call her, but not getting any answer. I'm worried something might've happened to her." *Like she's been kidnapped... or worse.*

"*Oh, James, thank God you've called.*"

"What's happened? Is Gemma okay? They didn't get her, did they?"

"*Huh?*" Gemma's mother sounded puzzled. "*James, Gemma's fine. We're at the hospital.*"

"What?" alarm filled Quisenberry's mind. Usually, whenever you hear that a loved one is in hospital, it's not normally regarding something positive.

"*We're sorry you weren't here, but, James... the delivery was so fast. You're now a daddy! Baby Morton and Gemma are both doing well.*"

2

He was not surprised to find the front door to his house was busted open and his property mercilessly ransacked. The downstairs rooms had been tossed, with furniture upended, the television thrown aside, and drawers within the wall unit pulled free and emptied on the floor. Decorative prints and photographs had been torn from the wall and glass crunched underfoot as the doctor slowly walked through to the kitchen. The remains of his breakfast had ended up on the floor along with the overturned table.

A quick search of the whole semi-detached house revealed each room similarly tended, including the nursery that had been prepared for Morton's arrival upstairs; the cot had been smashed to pieces, the chest of drawers dumped of its contents into a corner, and a bookcase displaying cuddly toys had been broken into splinters, the heads ripped from the half a dozen teddy bear's bodies.

This was General Makepeace's doing, Quisenberry pondered. He fisted his hands blindly, fury building inside. Stepping into the wreckage of his bedroom, he found some clean clothing turned out onto the floor, though he had to hunt for a pair of boxer shorts that had been mixed in with his girlfriend's undergarments. Disposing of his soiled shoes and clothing, he took a quick shower and slipped into a pair of jeans, a Fred Perry polo shirt and a pair of trainers. From a hook on the back of a bedroom door, the geneticist snatched a black 'Universal Studios Florida' baseball cap and slipped it onto his head.

Refreshed – though the smell of the sewers still lingering in his nose – he exited the house via the same route taken that morning; through the French doors set into the side wall of the kitchen-diner. He slid it open a gap and stepped out apprehensively, keeping his head down. Then he skirted the house, hastily leaving his property and the devastation behind.

Quisenberry walked hurriedly to a bus stop on The Avenue and caught the number eleven, a single-decker that operated every twenty minutes with stops picking up and setting down travellers surely and frustratingly, every hundred yards, and which took a scenic tour through the centre of town before eventually terminating at Fulbarton General Hospital. Forty minutes later, and almost three hours after ending his call with Gemma's mother, he stepped off the green bus and jogged into the grounds of the hospital, zigzagging between moving traffic, entering a large and busy carpark.

The maternity wing was at the end of half-a-mile of corridor. Before climbing the stairs to the delivery ward where Gemma was currently placed, Quisenberry called into a small shop selling gifts and flowers situated close to the entrance – positioned to capitalise and exploit on last-minute visitations, with prices to match. Recoiling from the initial shock at the costs, he picked out a bouquet of flowers presented within decorative florist wrap and, whilst paying, bought a 'Congratulations' balloon prefilled with helium.

With growing excitement, he announced his arrival at the security intercom set at the entrance to the ward and was swiftly buzzed in. Almost skipping, he stepped up to the nurses' station. A small Filipino nurse was manning the desk. She looked up, seeing Quisenberry with the bouquet held in one hand and the helium balloon bobbing up and down close to his head in the other. "I'm here to see my partner, Gemma Warren… and our baby, Morton."

The nurse smiled. "Of course… you must be James," she said. Her NHS ID card clipped to the pocket of her light blue tunic revealed her name to be Sampaguita. "They're in ward three, along the corridor behind you."

"Thank you." Quisenberry followed the directions smoothly, mentally ticking off the ward numbers. One and two were immediately to his right. Further along the corridor was a breakout room with an arrangement of chairs focused on a large screen television placed in the corner. On a coffee table positioned in the centre of the room was a pile of magazines and a glass bowl piled high with fruit. A woman dressed in a satin red bathrobe was watching Deal or No Deal whilst breastfeeding her infant.

Quisenberry found himself momentarily watching. When the woman looked up and offered a smile, he turned away quickly, embarrassed.

The next door along was a utility cupboard and along the left side of the corridor opposite were toilets, bathing facilities and a birthing suite.

Ward three was at the end of the passage, situated in the corner. Quisenberry rapped a knock at the door and, without waiting to be summoned, entered.

She was lying in the bed and cradling a small form wrapped in a soft white blanket. Gemma looked tired but wore a radiant smile as her boyfriend stepped into the room.

"James…"

"Gemma!" Quisenberry flew across the room, sidestepping past Marion – Gemma's mother – and her father Derek, the balloon bouncing back and forth and batting his girlfriend's parents as he went. Unseen or completely ignored in the corner of the room were two others, a man and a woman, seated like spoilt children in attendance under protest. They watched on impassively, serious looks upon their faces.

"I'm sorry…" Gemma whispered. The geneticist didn't understand the meaning of her apology, thinking it likely aimed at his missing the birth of their son. He placed the bouquet of flowers next to her.

"And this is little Morton?" It came out as a question, but it was obvious to Quisenberry that the small child, quietly sleeping in his mother's arms, was his newborn son. His small, wrinkled face reminded him of an over-ripe peach, capped with a thick scruff of dark-brown hair.

"James Quisenberry?" said a male voice from the back of the room alerting the geneticist to his presence.

"Yes?" Quisenberry turned languidly, taking in the official-looking figures of Detective Inspector Baylem and his colleague, Detective Sergeant McCardle. Baylem stood up and approached with a considered step.

"I'm DI Baylem of Fulbarton C.I.D; this is DS McCardle." Baylem produced his warrant card, holding the leather case open to reveal his identification. "I know this is an especial occasion, the birth of your son an' all, and I take no pleasure in doing this, but... James Quisenberry... I need you to come with us."

"What?" the geneticist appeared confused. He turned back towards Gemma with a questioning look.

"I'm sorry, James," said Gemma miserably.

"Is this for real? You called the rozzers?"

"You weren't answering my calls and some strange men carrying guns showed up outside our house. I was scared. I thought the worst had happened to you. Then there are the fly attacks. One thing led to another; I didn't think I had a choice."

"James, you can come to the station willingly or you can come wearing cuffs. It's your choice."

"It's hardly a choice," said Quisenberry crestfallen. "Let's get on with it." He turned his face again to the woman lying in the bed. "Bye, Gemma." He pressed two fingers to his lips and transferred a kiss to Morton's forehead. "Whatever happens, I love you both."

CHAPTER EIGHTEEN

"T HROUGH HERE," SAID BAYLEM, STOPPING outside a doorway that opened into a large office. There were more than a dozen people moving around, some in police uniform, but most in plain clothes. He gestured for Quisenberry to enter. McCardle was standing behind the geneticist.

James Quisenberry was not certain and had no clue what was required of him. During the journey to Fulbarton Police HQ, sitting in the back of Baylem's car, Quisenberry had convinced himself that he was heading for a jail cell or a lengthy interrogation. He'd escaped from one prison only to end up in another one.

"Go in then," pressed McCardle, "we haven't all day."

Stepping over the threshold, Quisenberry quickly surveyed the walls and the layout of the room. Banks of desks embellished with computers, phones and a bounty of stationery filled one half of the room; five rows of chairs balanced it out, facing a screen positioned to the centre of a wall, with myriad photographs grouped together in a crude timeline representing five incidents under investigation. There were a dozen others yet to be verified.

"What is this place?" asked Quisenberry moving into the room and gravitating towards the first set of photographs. Sean Wallace deceased was well represented with over half a dozen prints Blu Tacked to the wall.

"Our hastily erected emergency operation room," replied McCardle, "dealing with the aftermath of your flies…"

A look flashed onto his face, a mix that conveyed unbridled horror, guilt and flagrant denial.

Baylem ambled smoothly to the other side of the geneticist. "Nine dead as of this morning… a young man in his bedroom," he walked a couple of feet to the next set of photos, "a couple in their forties and a child found in their basement. The Jessops." He sauntered, one by one, to each set of images, giving a brief outline respectively. "Justin Piper. He worked in insurance. Claims. It was his last shift… in the office and in life." Quisenberry followed the DI, closely tailed by McCardle. "This infant would've been the next victim if it hadn't been for his quick-thinking mother. Luckily for us, we got our first real close-up of what we are dealing with." An enhanced image of a fly captured Baylem's attention for a lingering moment. He swiped at it with the back of his hand, like he was dealing with the pest in the flesh. "Our murderer and his thousands of accomplices," he said. "The MP Edwin Carslake will not be standing for re-election now, unfortunately, though I'd never vote for him anyway; and the popstar, Makayla."

Quisenberry recoiled from the most recent set of photos, in part from embarrassment as the two victims were completely naked, but also from being overwhelmed by the grotesque nature of their deaths.

"My God…"

"Today, during a coordinated attack at lunchtime, reports were received indicating flies attacked a pizzeria in town killing four; a shopping centre, killing two; a tanning salon – three were killed trapped within sunbeds there; a small boy whilst in his bedroom playing; a dental surgery – the patient there went in for a routine check-up, came out dead and ended up with something more than just a filling in his mouth." Baylem spoke sardonically.

"I don't understand... my flies... they were all destroyed. Two months ago..."

"Evidently not, sir." Creeping up behind the trio was a smartly dressed man with white hair and a matching goatee beard. He held a laptop clamped under his right arm. Baylem recognised him from earlier as the forensic entomologist Floyd Hamilton had introduced to the enquiry. "I've cross-examined DNA profiling extracted from a number of specimens Dr Hamilton sent over from each incident and compared them with the data found within the thumb drive you gave me this afternoon, Detective Inspector.

"There's no doubt about it; these flies are germane to those created by Doctor Quisenberry, although some are fourth or fifth generation variants, with evidence of interspecies breeding."

Baylem looked confused.

"The flies we are dealing with are not *exactly* the same as those conceived within the Biomargent Sciences laboratory, but a relative of. My guess, one or a couple escaped into the natural environment, themselves relatively harmless. They interacted reproductively with a common blowfly, and began to produce greater numbers, creating a new hybrid.

"These hybrids have then gone on to mate very efficiently; they reproduce, mate, reproduce, mate and so on, and so forth, over and over. But, where one would expect characteristics to possibly weaken or diminish from generation to generation, the genetic alterations have been adopted and enhanced, evolving magnificently over a very short time." Dr Monroe Malhotra paused for breath. "You'll have to excuse my exuberance, but, it was a crazy idea, though executed most brilliantly."

"Thank you," answered Quisenberry automatically.

"Sorry, it wasn't meant as a compliment. When I said it was a crazy idea, I meant it was a recklessly stupid idea."

"Well, I'm sorry, but I make no apology for my experiments and scientific research," said Quisenberry, affronted by the entomologist's accusation.

"And this is the problem within the scientific community…" began Dr Malhotra. "You do things without considering the consequences." Before he could add further insult, Baylem interrupted.

"All right, knock it off. We're now at where we are, what's the conclusion, Doctor?"

The entomologist wore a vague, contemplative expression. Gloomily, he shook his head, drawing free the laptop from under his arm. "I've done some calculations and run some scenarios within a couple of prediction models using Dr Quisenberry's data," he said, placing the laptop on a table close to where they were standing. Opening it up, Malhotra tapped in a password and waited a moment. "This is all based on a single fly mutation escaping into the ecosystem exactly two months ago."

Baylem and McCardle stooped down to either side of the entomologist. To the left of the DI, Quisenberry stood watching, intrigued and fearful.

Malhotra keyed in some figures and hit enter. "A pair of flies can produce between 500 and 600 pupae over a period of a few days." A graphic appeared on the laptop: two flies faded into a large circle filled with countless others surrounding the number 500. "These pupae turn into maggots and, after six days, develop into flies. Assuming confidently that these flies went on to reproduce, and making allowances for a fifty/fifty split in male/female demographics, the population of this new species would turn into 150,000 within a short time." Again, the entomologist tapped the enter key on the keyboard and the graphic changed to illustrate the change.

"It stands to reason that this new generation of fly, with its inbuilt instinct to reproduce, would do just that once fully developed. Around thirty-six hours after complete metamorphosis, the females are receptive to mating. If, at a conservative guess, we follow the same belief that fifty percent of the 150,000 offspring are female, and all efficiently reproduce, that number soon becomes 37,500,000." Again, the graphic was altered to highlight the figures, if verbally it didn't sound significant enough.

McCardle blew out in exasperation.

"Four weeks after introduction, that number balloons to nine billion, three hundred and seventy thousand," continued the entomologist, doing the business with the laptop, "and in no time, the population swells into the trillions. Of course, the balmy weather is aiding their lifecycle, allowing them to live longer, so actual numbers could be much higher if you factor in the older populations with the newer ones."

"Jesus…" exclaimed Baylem, turning angrily towards Quisenberry. "What were you thinking?" The DI wanted to give him a slap.

Quisenberry looked down shamefully. "It wasn't my intention…" he muttered. Nobody seemed to hear him.

"Things don't make sense. Why are the flies attacking people, and if there's as many as you calculate, why have they only started striking now?" McCardle spoke pragmatically.

"Maybe someone pissed off one too many flies," suggested Baylem, his comment meant to be flippant.

"There may be truth in what you say," replied the entomologist seriously. "Or, it could just be down to lack of food, evolution and their fight to survive."

"It's not entirely evolution," said Quisenberry distantly. "We wired their brains differently, programmed them to kill indiscriminately; insects and animals for food; humans only on instruction. They were designed for military use and would have been deployed against our enemies during battle; except, during testing, the flies resisted our orders and killed two lab technicians.

That's when the fly programme was shut down... or not, so it seems."

"Whatever's happened has happened. That's in the past. We need to focus on the now and the future. These fly strikes are increasing exponentially and will continually worsen if we don't do something about it." Dr Malhotra sighed.

"How much worse can it get?" asked McCardle cynically.

"Oh, what's happened so far is nothing," said Malhotra. "I have fed the latest data into a different forecasting model. It's something used by the CDC for analysing worst-case scenarios whilst dealing with highly virulent disease epidemics; extinction-level threats, that sort of thing. I've slightly modified it. Here, take a look." The entomologist used a finger to move the mouse pointer to the bottom of the laptop's screen and double-tapped on an application icon.

Baylem, McCardle and Quisenberry pressed in for a closer look.

A new programme flashed up with a map of the UK. "Factoring in the flies' reproduction and population data together with everything else, we know this is what is likely to happen... if we don't come up with a plan to stop them." Malhotra pressed the start button and a small video began to play.

The image zoomed down towards East Anglia, honing in on an area that the spectators recognised was Fulbarton. Red dots appeared in order of recorded fly strike, randomly placed at first, but then becoming more concentrated factoring in the attacks from today, and significantly from lunchtime. "This brings us up to date. Now, if we set the parameters to look ahead." Red dots started popping up around the map whilst a clock fast-forwarded into time. Splashes of red sprung up all around existing dots and then began to spread all around the map. The clock sped through twelve hours, then eighteen and soon twenty-four. In forty-eight hours, the map of the town was almost completely red and the image panned out to reveal the UK as a whole once again, the coloured mark appearing as a ragged hole, like a bullet leaking blood.

The clock was now moving in twenty-four-hour increments, and the red began to expand, taking in neighbouring towns like Ipswich and Colchester, and spreading speedily up, down and across the country.

"Within a week, the whole of the UK will be infected, with outbreaks migrating to mainland Europe shortly after. Two weeks, the whole of Europe will succumb, followed by Russia, Asia and Africa. Over the course of a month, Australia and the Americas will become affected. Even the remotest islands will not be immune."

"Okay, Doctor Malhotra, thanks for predicting the end of humanity. What can we do about it?"

"Quarantine," said a voice from behind, jumping in before the entomologist could respond. Annabelle Herman walked ardently into the room clutching her mobile phone in one hand and holding a mug of coffee in the other. "We need to stop these flies from getting out."

"That's exactly what I was going to say," muttered Malhotra quietly.

"That's well and good. But how?" challenged DI Baylem, turning to face the auburn-haired woman. "We can hardly enforce a 'no fly zone'." The idea sounded absurd and Dr Malhotra laughed.

"We don't need to worry about them leaving just yet," said Quisenberry portentously. "Their programming prohibits them."

Baylem matched McCardle and Malhotra with a confused look. Annabelle Herman was cool and indifferent.

"Their edict is simple; to invade and conquer. They won't be going anywhere... not until the last person in Fulbarton is dead."

"O-kay..." said the DS with an elongated slur.

An ominous silence settled on the five of them, though Annabelle appeared to look like she knew more than she was letting on.

Before Baylem picked up on it, McCardle dared to speak: "What can we do? I don't think I'm speaking for myself when I say we can't let them win. I'm not ready to die just yet…"

Quisenberry cleared his throat to talk. "We kill them," he said perfunctorily. "It's them… or us, right?"

"How?" asked Baylem, hopeful.

"I have an idea…" before he had a chance to add detail, Chief Superintendent Mills burst into the incident room.

"Detective Inspector Baylem… there's rioting in the town centre! Plus, a primary school in Cherry Blossoms has been attacked by flies; three victims, two of whom are children. Things are beginning to turn ugly. I've instructed all our officers to attend, but what do you propose we do?"

DI Baylem turned to the Home Office Advisor. "Annabelle, I think we're going to need outsider help to contain this thing," he said reluctantly. "There must be some protocols or a contingency plan for something like this."

"What? An invasion of killer flies?" she spoke sarcastically.

"Civil disorder," replied Baylem. "We're a small town. We can't hope to handle the problem of the flies AND rioters. Can you liaise with the Home Office, see what's on offer or check with the prime minister?"

The DI was playing directly into her hands. "I'm already on it," she said eagerly.

2

DIs Randall and Hardy, along with their retinue of sergeants, constables and civilian support staff, were back in the incident room for the teatime briefing an hour later. Chief Superintendent Mills was conferring with Annabelle to the side of the room whilst Baylem was once again at the head, standing with the projector screen at his back. Sergeant McCardle was close-by for moral support, whilst James Quisenberry and Munroe Malhotra had vacated the room so not to distract the DI with his conference and also to begin work on a plan hatched only moments earlier.

"Fifteen people died during the lunchtime attacks," started Baylem solemnly, "and six others this afternoon." Whilst Dr Malhotra had been briefing Baylem, McCardle and Quisenberry with regards to forecasts and the predicted activity of the flies, there had been a further spate of attacks across the town, most devastatingly, a children's nursery at a local Primary school where two infants had died along with a teacher who had been trying to protect them.

"Furthermore, you are all aware of the civil unrest stirring in the town centre. Everyday townsfolk are gathering, protesting in a swell of numbers. They perceive a lack of response from the authorities. They are frightened and need to see action. Like our sun-scorched wheat fields, they're just a naked flame away from igniting." Baylem went quiet for a moment, as though grappling with his conscience, appearing to those who knew him to be tormented. He took a sip of water from a glass placed near to hand.

"This is an unprecedented position we're in. We are at a point where routine policing is no longer practicable or effective in dealing with the emergency affecting our town.

"Moreover, it's imperative that these invading insects do not set its sights on neighbouring societies. With reluctance, under the orders of Prime Minister Humphries, I've conceded control of policing the town to the military–"

Uproar broke out in amongst the audience, interrupting Baylem's scripted briefing. He held his hands up, urging calm.

"Listen to what he has to say," defended McCardle, stepping forward like a steward at a football match.

Slowly, order returned, but not without a few heckled

comments of "Shame on you," and "Judas!" mostly from rankled members of DI Randall's team.

"I like it as much as you do, but my hands are tied. This is for the protection and safety of our citizens, whilst we deal with and overcome the threat. The military will assume control of the town from eight p.m. this evening, and stay for as long as is necessary."

"What does that actually mean?" asked DI Hardy from the centre of the second row of chairs. She knew that, had she been in charge, no such authority would have been relinquished. "The military don't 'police', they 'enforce'." The woman drew a few 'here, here's' and gentle applause from a couple of her detective sergeants.

"It means, come eight o'clock, we'll have less rights than a stray dog shitting on a garden path," said DI Randall half in jest. Nervous laughter started but barely rose to an infectious level.

"Now's the time to make a run for it," suggested a small ferret-faced man in constable's uniform sitting in the back line of chairs. His eyes were close together giving him a less-than-trustworthy face. "Get out whilst we still can."

No one in the audience laughed, and most seemed to be contemplating it with an air of seriousness.

"I'm afraid that's not an option," spoke up Chief Superintendent Mills. "I have it on good authority that the roads leading in – and out – of Fulbarton are being blocked as I speak. No one is allowed in and nobody's allowed out. As of this moment, we are in total lockdown."

Disgruntled voices filled the room as DIs Randall and Hardy, and their team of subordinates began to vent their disagreements.

"By who?" piped up Randall belligerently.

"What about the flies?!" bellowed PC Anders loud enough to cut through the fog of noise. "What's going to keep THEM in?"

The audience quietened into total silence. It was a reasonable question and one which all ears in the vicinity felt a need to hear answered.

"We don't need to worry about that," said Baylem gloomily. "The flies won't leave..."

"And why not?" sniped Randall, sneering angrily towards Mills' stooge standing ahead of the projector screen.

"Because—" Baylem clawed for an easy answer. He settled for the truth. "—they won't leave. Not, that is... until we're all dead."

Cries of: "preposterous!" "you're havin' a laugh!" and "bollocks!" filled the room.

"Knowing this puts us at a great advantage," started the DI enthusiastically once the incident room settled again.

"Advantage? What advantage?" challenged DI Hardy fiercely. "How do you know that?"

"We have an idea which we are working on, but... you're going to like it even less than our decision to surrender policing to the army," replied Baylem contritely.

Chapter Nineteen

/

A CONVOY OF TWO DOZEN MILITARY vehicles rolled into Fulbarton from the west, deployed by order of Prime Minister Humphreys and under General Makepeace's command. Land Rover Wolfs, Pinzgauer cargo trucks and Land Rover 101 light utility vehicles brimming with combat equipment and armed personnel, all festooned in Nato green and wearing excited expressions. Based at neighbouring East Anglian town Colchester, the contingent was made up primarily of troops from the 16 Air Assault Brigade, Britain's rapid response formation.

Arriving by helicopter on the outskirts of town eight minutes earlier, the general stepped down from the Westland Lynx to greet the procession as it pulled in; a mobile phone was pressed up to his ear. "Phase one of Operation Remedy is ahead of schedule!" He shouted to be heard over the 'thwapp-thwapp-thwapp' sound of the helicopter rotor blades beating above his head, the downdraft buffeting his combat fatigues and ruffling his hair. He blinked fast against a cloud of dust swirling around him as he ran partway to the lead vehicle in the cavalcade. He watched a passenger climb out, though couldn't see who it was through the poor visibility. "How goes it your end?!"

General Makepeace turned his head away and pressed the phone tight to his ear. The line was terrible and the background noise made it almost impossible to hear the caller at the other end. He gave a response to what he thought he could understand.

"That's good! Pleased to hear it. As long as they understand, even though we're taking over from eight, the roads going in and out are now strictly off limit. Suitable force will be met out to any transgressors." The general concluded the call and returned the phone to a pocket in his uniform.

"General Makepeace," greeted the person who had stepped out of a Land Rover Wolf to meet with him. He was holding a local map opened out. Makepeace recognised him as Captain Dodd, one of his advisors from the four who had sat on his side of the table within Biomargent Sciences earlier that afternoon. "This here is our perimeter detachment…"

"Very good, Captain. Are they fully briefed on their role and responsibilities?" asked Makepeace soberly, feeling compelled to add: "Nothing in; nothing out."

"Fully, to the letter, sir." Dodd placed the map on the bonnet of the Land Rover and held it in place with the flat of one hand. The wind from the helicopter threatened to tear it from beneath his grip. Makepeace joined him at his side. "Squadrons one through to ten will be controlling the north and east of the town," Dodd jabbed a finger and drew a line within thin air, "eleven through to twenty-one the south and west." Red pen circled Fulbarton on the map and a dotted line had been marked at places where each jurisdiction started and ended. "I understand that any force deemed necessary is authorised."

"Hopefully it won't come to that, but yes. Fulbarton is to be contained… and handled like a hot zone. Think of it as a smaller version of Kandahar," said Makepeace jovially.

"Perhaps without the IEDs and the suicide bombers," suggested Dodd, half-smiling. Without warning, he snatched up the map and folded it with little care. "Leave it in my trust, sir. Nothing in; nothing out, you have my word." Turning to face the column of vehicles, he raised an arm and signalled for the troops to move ahead; a forward-facing waving movement above his head. Dodd's Land Rover Wolf drove forward five feet and mounted a verge bristling with tall grass and weeds, allowing room for the cavalcade to trundle by. "We'll have it locked up so tight; even Michael Scofield would fail to get out." Thinking the *Prison Break* reference was lost on the senior officer, he added: "It'll make Belmarsh look like a children's play centre for unruly kids by comparison."

"Okay. I get it. Just ensure it's done will you," grunted the general. "Inform me when the perimeter is in place." He turned his back on the captain and walked back towards the helicopter in a loping trot.

2

In synchronicity, the Westland Lynx helicopter landed smoothly on the road outside Fulbarton Police Head Quarters just as the first of a large host of military vehicles thundered along the road. Pedestrians and people in cars watched in fear and wonder at the arrival of the British Army. A crowd of reporters and paparazzi were camped on the steps leading up to the police building, including the BBC's John Harriman. Cameras and Video equipment were being turned towards the arriving spectacle.

The time on General Makepeace's watch was a couple of minutes shy of eight o'clock and he shifted eagerly in his seat, jabbing a button to release the belt strapping him in. The pilot in the cockpit was powering the helicopter down and the noise of the rotors above their heads were decreasing. "We'll take that building across the road for operation command," he spoke loudly to Major Broadbent sat next to him. The building he pointed to was a small office complex filling an old Victorian coach house replete with an arched entranceway leading into a courtyard to the rear where horses were once stabled. The courthouse was a little further along to its right. "You make the arrangements, I'll go meet with the peasantry."

Broadbent accepted the instruction with a nod and a curt acknowledging response of: "General."

Stepping down from the helicopter, Makepeace assessed the scene. Soldiers dressed in khaki combat clothing and Kevlar body armour and holding rifles in readiness streamed out of vehicles in a run. Some were heading his way, whilst others manoeuvred into places around the block, heading-off passers-by and ushering those already in the area towards a hastily erected cordoned zone – red and white hazard tape stretched tight between lampposts and buttressed by army vehicles – putting a secure boundary into effect. Of the soldiers heading towards the general, a dozen branched off towards the press and TV crews buzzing with excitement on the steps; flash photography splashed white light at them in staccato bursts whilst journalists yelled out demands to know what was going on.

Without warning or explanation, the soldiers rounded up the gathering with shouted orders and fiercely-aimed rifles, confiscating their photographic equipment and soon marching them off towards a single decker bus with impatient jabs and threats of violence. One brazen photographer rebuffed a verbal warning and received a swift smack to the side of the head with the buttstock of a soldier's rifle. John Harriman shouted pompously: "This is outrageous!" before cowering behind shielded hands from the threat of a pointed weapon.

"Shouldn't we try to keep this civil?" suggested Broadbent appearing at the general's side.

"Crowd control is your job, Major. It's nothing to do with

me…" Without further confab, Makepeace walked away towards the now-empty steps leading into the police building, an entourage of soldiers joining him at his flank.

Throwing the double-doors open forcefully, the general stepped into the police headquarters, startling the desk sergeant contained behind a toughened glass service hatch in the process. The grey-haired man knocked his cup of coffee over; liquid spilled across his Sudoku puzzle book and sloshed over the edge into his lap.

"Shit!" the sergeant cursed, patting a wad of tissues against the dampness of his trousers whilst standing upright like a rooster at a cockfight. "What's going on?!" the sergeant griped. "What's the meaning of bursting in like that?!"

"General Makepeace…" he introduced himself. "We're here to help with your bug problem." He spoke in a condescending manner and was in no mood to engage with someone at the low end of the food chain. "Be a good fellow and locate the person in charge; it's Chief Superintendent Mills, isn't it?"

The desk sergeant bristled at the general's tone of authority. He made no attempt at answering him. Wordlessly, he walked away from the desk and escaped out of the room with the air of someone in search of something long ago lost and now forgotten. A female officer made pretence of looking busy at the back of the office, riffling through papers, her back turned towards Makepeace, though he espied an occasional sideward glance in his direction.

A few moments passed and the desk sergeant returned. "Carol, can you man the desk," he said, pressing a button that emitted a protracted buzz and unlocking a door that led in from the waiting area. "I need to take the General here through." He walked up to the door, pulled it open and said as though addressing a prisoner: "This way."

Makepeace and his armed guard of four soldiers followed the desk sergeant deep into the building, through a system of corridors that eventually arrived at a room that was filled with a noise of activity and the appearance of a conclave. Saying nothing, the sergeant stepped aside and motioned with a pointed hand towards a senior officer sandwiched between a group of plain-clothed men and women standing at the front of the room ahead of five rows of empty chairs.

"Chief Superintendent," boomed Makepeace, marching into the incident room importantly. He quickly surveyed the walls as he passed, taking note of the many photographs, most grisly and stomach churning, and focusing especially on the blown-up one of the fly. "I'm General Makepeace. I gather you knew that I was coming."

"You don't waste any time, do you?" Mills' eyes had flitted over to the wall clock and noticed the sweeper hand glide past the topmost digit where the minute hand was settled; the hour hand was fixed on the eight.

"Not a minute early nor a minute late, that's my motto. Now, let's get down to business." Makepeace manoeuvred himself around the group of people, gravitating towards the front of the assembly. The four soldiers took up guard duty; two sentinels by the entrance door, the other two positioning themselves to either side of the general. They adopted a not-so-discrete gap at his back.

"General," greeted the Home Office advisor sticking out her hand, culminating the opportunity of introductions.

"Annabelle, always a pleasure," said Makepeace, taking her hand and giving it the gentlest of shakes.

"I thought you said you never knew him?" asked DI Baylem, raising an eyebrow and giving McCardle a wary look.

"Oh, me and Annabelle go way, way back," replied the general with no intent of explaining it, though hinting closeness in his manner.

"Um... a long time ago," she floundered, her cheeks turning bright red.

"Be a good girl and grab us a coffee, would you?" he said over-familiarly towards the auburn-haired woman, starting to smile.

"Still two sugars?"

"Yes… with only a little milk."

The Home Office advisor nodded her head obediently before heading towards the door. Before stepping through, she glanced at one of the two soldiers guarding the entrance and smiled, giving a nod in recognition. He returned her acknowledgement coyly with a slight drop of his head. He was dressed in standard military greens and wore the maroon beret of the Paras regiment, matching the other three soldiers in the room. The only difference was the sergeant's badge affixed to his sleeves. The name 'Pope' was stitched into the fabric at his chest.

"Lovely girl," Makepeace said whimsically, still smiling. He could have been attending a social banquet. Now, where were we? Ah, yes. The civil unrest and your fly problem…" Flippantly said, he could well have been making small talk about canapés.

"You mean YOUR fly problem?" volleyed back Baylem, thick with sarcasm.

Makepeace's composure shifted dangerously, the smile dropping from his lips. He raised an eyebrow, urging silently for the DI to continue.

"I know about your work with Biomargent Sciences and your association with James Quisenberry," continued Baylem. "It's my understanding you had Doctor Quisenberry arrested this morning," the DI accused, "in an attempt to cover things up, I'd wager."

"Now, now, Baylem" interjected Chief Superintendent Mills, "there's little need to throw accusations around."

The DI ignored his superior. "What is this, General? Damage control? An attempt to clean up the bloody mess?"

Makepeace sighed and allowed equanimity to return, partnered with a carefree, almost saccharine smile. "I saw you on the news this morning, Detective Inspector Baylem. Of course, you are completely misguided. Sure... I am here to help clean up the 'bloody mess' as you so eloquently put it, but it doesn't make me complicit. However, I'm not going to deny that I am on the board at Biomargent Sciences – I *am* – this is all public knowledge – I have an advisory role as part of the contract the Ministry of Defence has with them. Plus, I am there as an obligation to Prime Minister Humphreys – but, what you said about me and James creating the flies... that's all nonsense." The general chuckled, as though the mere suggestion was a silly joke and an absurd one at that.

"I'm glad it amuses you, General," spat Baylem.

Makepeace shook his head, slowly removing his smile. "James Quisenberry is a brilliant man; one of the best geneticists of his generation, but he's only one of many we have working at Biomargent. I am just a stakeholder, a mere silent partner, privy to just the barest details of what research is being conducted.

"Sure, we knew him as the bug person. But, creating a hybrid-fly of some sort...? That's all news to me." The general was looking down, avoiding eye contact, a clear sign, Baylem noted, that the man wasn't being totally honest.

"What about the failed demonstration the other month," Baylem coached, "at the labs, in front of a hundred or so witnesses? You were there, weren't you?" Quisenberry's file had detailed the failed presentation, highlighting the outline of the experiment, the flies' behaviour and the fatal outcome. It also listed the names of those in attendance; General Makepeace was right at the top of it.

There was even a video file of the episode, downloaded from CCTV footage obtained from inside the laboratory. A short time earlier, Baylem and McCardle had viewed it in silent horror, watching the flies descend upon one of the two lab technicians before they turned their attention to the woman. Before the flies had completed their attack, the detectives watched gas being pumped into the room through sprinkler heads set into the ceiling.

"Okay. You got me. I was there ONLY as an observer. But then you should also know that I ordered an end to the madness," replied Makepeace firmly. "I had been promised a demo of a weaponised insect, capable of delivering undetectable human devastation, fully compliant and completely under Quisenberry's control. On the surface, what he promised offered to revolutionise modern warfare. What I got instead was a front row seat to an execution.

"I should have had Quisenberry arrested then and there. Instead, we are... where we are..."

Without forewarning, the overhead lights, the computers, the projector, the phone lines and all electrics into the room cut out. A ruckus outside of the room revealed the issue was station-wide.

"Oh bugger it, all we need is a power cut," grumbled Mills.

"What's going on?" asked McCardle, instinctively turning towards the general.

"That's phase two of my orders," replied Makepeace soberly. "The power has been cut across Fulbarton entirely, severing ties with the rest of the world. It's to ensure there's no widespread panic whilst we deal with this... emergency. We're just taking precautions."

"Sergeant... look..." Baylem held up his mobile phone. The screen displayed the usual arrangement of apps, icons and symbols with the exception of the service signal, which was now devoid of any strength bars. The words: NO SIGNAL flashed at the top of the screen.

General Makepeace creased his face, appearing to be conflicted. "I'm afraid the signal tower has been switched off too."

"So we've no way to communicate with anyone inside or outside the town?" asked Mills, a worried look taking over his face.

"You'll still be able to use your terrestrial trunk radios for communication amongst yourselves; but with Joe Public, that's an affirmative." Terrestrial trunk radios, or TETRA, was the name of the two-way radio system used by the police, emergency services and other government agencies.

"Well, that would be great… if we had a power supply," griped Baylem.

As though a higher being was answering Baylem's wishes, the lights, computers and myriad devices requiring an alternating current throughout Fulbarton Police HQ flickered, clattered or buzzed into operation. It suddenly dawned on the DI how normal everyday sounds made so much noise, and only noticeable in the absence of it.

"The emergency power system has just kicked in," said Mills. "Obviously not a permanent solution, but will keep us functioning in some shape or form for the next thirty-six hours."

"It should all be over with by then," predicted the general confidently.

"I gather you have a plan?" asked Baylem.

"Not completely," said Makepeace hazily. "First and foremost, we need to safeguard the population. The best way we can do this will be to gather them altogether and keep them contained."

"What like a quarantine?" Baylem repeated the suggestion made by Annabelle earlier that afternoon. It was an idea which Dr Malhotra had agreed wholeheartedly with, and which the DI had already proposed to the investigation team in the teatime briefing he had already held.

"Well… it's more like protective confinement. Tell me, what's the population of Fulbarton?"

"Thirty thousand… approx.," replied the Chief Superintendent.

"So… with those numbers, any suggestions where we could hold so many people and which'll allow us to provide adequate protection?" The general didn't need any recommendations; he'd seen it from the helicopter on the way in, but believed it good for relationship and trust building.

"Way ahead of you, General," replied Baylem. "We came to a similar conclusion. Fulbarton Town Football Club has plenty of space. We've already alerted groundsmen to make preparations."

Makepeace smiled. *This is going to be easier than I thought*, he reflected. "Sounds perfect."

"We also thought it might act as an unorthodox trap for the flies. Doctor Quisenberry had an idea on how to kill them all. With the populace all in one place, we can use them as bait."

The plan was not dissimilar to the general's but he didn't hear anything beyond the mention of the geneticist's name. "Quisenberry?" It echoed inside his head. "You have him here?" Makepeace spoke with a combination of excitement and trepidation. "How? Where?"

"He voluntarily handed himself into custody this afternoon," McCardle lied, foregoing mention of catching him at the hospital visiting Gemma and their newborn son, Morton. "He admitted his part in proceedings and gave us his research. Charges will be brought against him when the emergency is over, but for now, Doctor Quisenberry is currently working with an eminent entomologist to fashion a means to combat the flies."

"We're not going to have a problem here, are we General?" asked Baylem challengingly.

"Problem? There's no problem. I'm going to want a chat with Doctor Quisenberry before this is all over, but... for now... there are more pressing matters to see to."

Annabelle Herman stepped back into the room carrying a steaming mug of coffee. "Sorry it took so long. Bloody power cut whilst I was boiling the kettle. Then I had to track down some sugar," she griped. "Here."

General Makepeace accepted it with a forced smile. "Thank you." He turned back to Chief Superintendent Mills. "I take it you'll help with rounding up the citizens? The quicker we have you on board, the better. Who's to know when the flies are going to attack next?"

"You have our full cooperation," replied Mills sincerely. "Just tell us when you propose to start."

"Start? My dear fellow, things have been underway since my arrival." Makepeace lifted the mug up to his lips and sipped at its contents. "Mmmm. Nice coffee that, Annabelle," he said, receiving a look of satisfaction in return.

3

Exiting the police building, General Makepeace was quietly impressed with the efficiency and effectiveness of his plan, helped enormously by the local police department. Busses, commandeered by army personnel, slowly trundled by with armed foot soldiers taking big strides alongside. Military vehicles and lorries moved purposefully in all directions, and platoons of soldiers marched hither and thither, executing their orders.

The evening sun was warm and shining beatifically. Closing his eyes, Makepeace could easily forget where he was and conjure images of serenity and relaxation, or a holiday in the Maldives. The illusion was shattered when DI Baylem crept up from behind and took up some space next to him.

"Remember, these are good people, General. Treat them with care and dignity," said the policeman.

"We may be the army, Detective Inspector, but we're still British. We're here to protect our kinsmen, not persecute them."

Flying in the face of Baylem's request and the general's assurances, a soldier could be seen dragging a woman kicking and screaming from a building by her hair. Another soldier arrived in front of her and planted a kick to her midriff.

"A strange way of showing it," said Baylem, miffed. He charged down the steps towards the struggling woman, shouting: "Hey! Set her down at once!"

Gunshots in the distance sounded surreally ominous and hung in the air like rolling thunder. As though responding to a mating call, crackles of gunfire echoed from districts all around Fulbarton.

Baylem threw an anxious glance back at General Makepeace who was casually walking across the road towards him.

"Don't get your knickers in a twist, Detective Inspector. They're likely warning shots. They're under orders not to engage the locals…"

"That better be the case!" Baylem warned forcefully as he wrested the woman from the soldier's clutches, helping her to her feet. "Are you all right?" The woman began to complain about her treatment between racking sobs.

"If you'll excuse me," said the general, "I've got to update the prime minister and an operation to manage." Taking large strides, he walked towards the Victorian coach house earlier earmarked for tactical use.

"Don't you want to know what Doctor Quisenberry's plan is?" Baylem called after the general.

Makepeace didn't reply. Instead, he waved his hand dismissively behind him.

CHAPTER TWENTY

/

THE PROCESS OF EVACUATING THE streets and houses of residents was a timely and arduous one. The population of Fulbarton was recorded as 30,311 at last count – a figure obtained from the Office of National Statistics. With the clock striking eight o'clock, army vehicles rumbled noisily into the town from the blockaded access points in their hundreds, filling the warm evening air with thick clouds of diesel, whilst troops of seven thousand soldiers marched in on foot like they were invading Basra, rifles held at the ready and patrol packs strapped heavily to their backs, an impressive and ominous sight.

With fear levels already heightened in communities owing to the fly strikes and the rioting, the arrival of the army was first viewed as a welcome sight. However, with electrical power being cut and the mobile telephone network shutdown, alarm and fear began to fill the citizens, compounded when groups of two or three soldiers started kicking in the doors to their homes and barking orders as they entered forcefully.

"Everybody out!" a soldier shouted, setting the standard; the demand would be repeated from door to door and street to street all across Fulbarton. It didn't matter that they were fellow British citizens. The oppression started at the outskirts and worked steadily inwards. Operation Remedy was in full swing. "No packing. Bring only what is essential!"

Inhabitants began to congregate to the sides of the road, herded together, reminiscent to scenes viewed in old films re-enacting Nazi roundups in occupied Poland or Germany during the Second World War. Red double-decker buses, expropriated from a local public transport authority, pulled up with doors already open. "In!" ordered the driver wearing the Nato green of the army.

Men, women and children – young and old alike – trudged confused and scared onto buses. Some voiced complaint in angry tones, most demanded to know what was going on more civilly, whilst others cried or pleaded. It was a simple ask, but the British were famous the world over for their complaining. Today, for once it seemed justified.

"It's for your safety," said a sympathetic soldier, his rifle flung behind his shoulder. He offered steadying hands to those stepping up. "All will become clear when you get there."

"Get there? Where we going?" queried an elderly woman.

"The football ground," replied the soldier. "You heard the saying 'safety in numbers'? There's truth in that... now, move along."

2

PCs Anders and Manning, the odd ones out dressed in black uniform amongst the army of olive green, approached each house with reluctance, trepidation and dismay. Initially, they had protested against the assignment, not agreeing with the action, but the Chief Superintendent had addressed them all, trying to lay away their fears. Even so, the orders given were less about serving and protecting Fulbarton, and more like enforcing a dictate that revoked liberty and independence, a right everyone in the western world took for granted.

If a door went unanswered, the burly soldier – identified as a sergeant – accompanying them would muscle in ahead and kick the door in. If anyone refused to leave, a posse of armed men physically removed them, not shy in using whatever force deemed appropriate.

"Hello? It's the police… don't be afraid… we're coming in."

House after house was emptied and, within fifteen minutes, the first street was cleared, the inhabitants loaded up onto the buses and driven out.

"Next road…" enthused the soldier wearing the stripes of sergeant. Soldiers swarming around had referred to him as Pope. Though one or two knew him as John. He took the lead with a squad of men following close at his heels. PCs Anders and Manning hurried after them warily.

"I don't think I can do this for much longer," complained Manning after an hour. The stress of extracting families from their homes, of ignoring their pleas and cries, of witnessing the brutality occasionally met out by the military personnel; it was all getting too much for the constable.

"I don't think there are many streets left now," pacified Anders, "and we don't have much choice. We'll be clocking off soon." Prophetically, he turned out to be right.

After the next road, which was equally exhausting and traumatic to evacuate, they turned on to a street PC Louise Manning recognised. At the other end, they could see another attachment of soldiers joining the task. She reckoned they would likely meet up somewhere in the middle.

"We were here yesterday," said Anders conversationally. "It's where we found those three bodies… the Jessops. I'll never forget the way they looked…"

"I wouldn't know," replied Manning, "you stopped me from going in, remember?"

"Oh, yea... I spared you from it; it was horrible," he recalled, his thoughts lingering on the child. A girl. They still had no idea who she was... and probably never would. "On the bright side, all I have to do is think on what I found and it puts things into perspective. What we are doing... here," Anders inclined his head towards a young, dejected-looking family – a mother, a father cradling a sleeping baby and two young children (a boy and a girl) – being marched towards a stationary bus, "tells me we are doing right by these people. It might not feel like it, but... better this than what was down there in that basement. It's for the greater good."

PC Manning would never forget it either, but for entirely different reasons. It had been the first time she had come into contact with the flies, abundant in their numbers, but dead, scattered all over that house like black tic tacs.

Number sixty-three Claringdon Street.

She could see the house from where she was standing, completely in darkness. The fact they knew it was empty made no difference. Every house was to be checked.

"I hope you are right," she said.

When the last of the residents reluctantly climbed aboard the red double-decker, the sergeant who had been coordinating the gathering stepped over to the fatigued police officers. He backhanded sweat from his brow and took a deep breath. "Our work is nearly done," he said cordially. He stifled a yawn as he slapped the side of the bus, giving the signal for it to leave. "Excuse me," he apologised.

"Are we okay to return to police headquarters?" asked Anders hopefully. "That is, if our work is now done."

"*Nearly* done," the soldier known as Pope corrected. "We've been ordered to make sure the Grey Friars development area is clear. There are reports that some homeless, drug dependents and other undesirables have a tendency to shelter there from time to time...

our surveillance drone picked up some heat signatures therein which we're to check out. Should be a quick one and done…"

"Okay," sighed Anders sullenly. He had occasioned on a few vagrants living rough there from time to time. It was also notorious for drug ODs.

"Once all the stragglers are taken care of, then we can call it a night."

3

The Grey Friars development was named after a medieval friary that had stood on the site between 1253 and the dissolution of the monasteries in 1538. Although the priory had been demolished and the site levelled with countless redevelopments since, it never completely shook off its heritage, retaining the street names 'Grey Friars' and 'Friars Bridge Road' running parallel to the front and one side of the now abandoned building site. Building work had begun in the mid-2000s, but with the financial downturn of 2008, construction ground to a halt and the developer ran out of money. Now the Grey Friars development stood like a ten-storey concrete wine rack on the outskirts of the town centre, a derelict framework of an apartment block that had promised affordable housing but, instead, stood as an ugly reminder of how fragile ambitions and dreams invariably were.

"We need to search all the floors… if it's possible." Sergeant Pope quickly assessed, noting that parts of the construction looked inaccessible – the topmost levels appeared to be designed much like a house of cards, with floors and walls but with no means of getting up to them. He was addressing a crowd of soldiers, together with half a dozen police constables, of which PC Anders and PC Manning were standing closest. "Our orders are unchanged: clear the building using whatever force necessary. Let's do this double time and spread out..."

It was now after ten and the sky was that dull grey-blue that prefaced night. Efficiently, all personnel disbursed and started forward towards boarding covered in graffiti that faked an appearance of security, but which proved utterly useless when two of 16 Air Assault Brigade's finest pulled it down without contracting a single muscle. In clusters of three and four, soldiers and police officers charged into the grounds, the blue 'safety helmets must be worn at all times' sign ignored. No one was wearing helmets, and not all of the soldiers were wearing the maroon regimental berets either. They all carried powerful torches, splashing brightness in a cuneated shaft of white light, and weapons at the ready. Joining the search party were a couple of soldiers brandishing what appeared to be hosepipes attached to two gas canisters strapped to their backs.

Before either Anders or Manning could question the sergeant, the commanding soldier stepped up to them.

"You two, you're with me," said Pope. "We'll take the lower level and work our way up."

If the outside looked bad, nothing prepared the constables for what waited inside. Almost instantly, the smell of death and decay hit them, comingled with piss and faeces. Manning clapped a hand across her mouth and nose and felt vomit rise at the back of her throat.

Pope, moving ahead, shifted his torch back and forth to reveal puddles of liquid and lumps of dark stuff collected in corners or splashed up concrete pillars and weight-bearing walls. Evidence of other uses was clear to see. Hypodermic needles were scattered around, broken bottles crunched under foot, scrunched up beer cans were strewn all over, and used condoms, condom wrappers, take-out food cartons, empty wallets, and a variation of discarded junk items that had no discernible appearance littered the floor.

"Hey! Over here!" A soldier searching the far side of the same level shouted towards them, obscured behind a number of concrete pillars, but his light wasn't. He swung his torch like a beacon to attract their attention.

Pope jogged towards the light, his own torchlight bouncing around the walls and columns throwing up curious shadows that more than once startled Manning into thinking that they weren't alone.

"What is it?" asked the sergeant, moving out of PC Anders' view for a moment. He quickly rectified that, stepping around a pillar into an area that had been earmarked as a kitchen or bathroom. Pipework jutted up from the floor and the world's filthiest toilet – looking out of place – was plumbed in at the side of the room; a thick, dark sludge of unimaginable origin overflowed its rim and spread in a pool around the base.

It wasn't the rancid smell assaulting their senses, or the sight of the toilet that the soldier was alerting them to, but the huddled forms slumped over each other in a corner. There were four of them, all lifeless; three young men and a woman sandwiched between. She looked to be seven months pregnant.

Unable to spare PC Manning from this sight, Anders stepped aside to allow his partner a better view. She tentatively walked to where the discoverer was standing; his torch was now directed on the closely snuggled forms and soon joined by hers. The double illumination left nothing to the imagination.

"Drugs?" enquired Anders. There was plenty of evidence to suggest this. Needles, spoons, BIC cigarette lighters and some suspicious packets of white powder were strewn close to where the bodies lay.

"No," said Manning, hunkering down by the woman. She was shabbily dressed in soiled sweatpants that her swollen stomach overhung and a red LYCRA boob tube that just contained her breasts and looked overtly slutty. "Point your torch towards her head." The constable set her own Maglite down for a moment to slip into latex gloves. "They've taken drugs… but it wasn't that which killed them."

PC Anders, Sergeant Pope and the soldier trained their light beams onto the dead woman's face as Manning gently prized open blue, lifeless lips.

"What the fuck…" exclaimed Pope.

A steady torrent of what looked like raisins fell onto the pregnant woman's bump and distributed aimlessly to her legs and onto those of the two dead men either side of her.

"Flies killed them," stated Manning emotionlessly. "The same way as the others… and not long ago either I should think."

"Doesn't look like there was much of a struggle," proclaimed Anders with a hint of grief.

"Probably stoned out of their wits," said Pope apathetically. "Doubt they even realise that they're now dead."

"Uh! Shit!" yelped the soldier, his torch arcing to and fro. "I saw something!"

"What was it?" Pope's torch joined the soldiers, swishing back and forth across the floor.

"There!" bellowed the soldier.

"I see it," said Anders.

All eyes focused on the bluebottle which had landed on the furthest man and was crawling across his cheek in a zigzag.

"Is it the same as the ones that did this?" asked Anders, using his torch to indicate the four decedents.

Manning located a small sample bottle from within her uniform, one-handedly popped its lid and quickly used it to trap the fly.

The bluebottle buzzed about agitatedly, cracking wildly against the translucent tube.

PC Manning deftly replaced the lid on the sample bottle and tucked it away.

Sergeant Pope unclipped his radio handset from his belt and

raised it to the side of his head. "Control... this is Pope. Do you copy?"

"*This is control,*" replied a tinny voice after an audible click. "*What's your position, Sergeant Pope?*"

"We're in the Grey Friars development. Got ourselves four stiffs, still warm, on ground zero. Evidence suggests a fly strike... quite recent too. Do you still have the surveillance bird up in the sky?"

"*That's an affirmative. We're using the infrared to coordinate sweep-up crews. Picking up stragglers roundup teams have missed.*"

"That's good. Any chance you could use it to check something for me?"

Control offered no response, confirmation or otherwise.

"Can you check the area," Pope persevered, "grid reference: two-nine-six-six-four, one-one-eight-five-nine, and surrounding locations? I don't much fancy coming up close and personal with any of those flies. Over."

"*Give me a minute, Sergeant Pope, and I'll get back to you. Over.*"

The sound of breaking glass from across the building alerted Pope, the soldier and the two police constables.

Instinctively, Pope's hand dropped to the weapon holstered at his waist but didn't draw it.

Manning casually gravitated into a position behind the army sergeant and allowed the other soldier to add an additional barrier ahead of her. PC Anders was standing next to Pope and discovered he was glued to the spot. Frozen in fear, he couldn't move even if he wanted to.

"Yo, Pope... you in here?" A torch beam flickered into view beyond a concrete pillar. Something metal clanged as though kicked into touch and more glass crunched and smashed.

"Novak? That you? Over here!" Pope relaxed.

Mark Novak leading two other soldiers walked across the ground floor and came into prominence. "Oh, Jesus," he exclaimed, his torchlight landing on the four bodies propped up against a wall. "Not more."

"You found others?" asked PC Anders.

"A couple on the second floor... another one on the fourth. We found a survivor on the third floor... an old fella stoked on crystal meth; there was also a kid on the fifth floor, but he did a runner. Matthis and Renleigh have gone after him."

"Is the building clear?" asked Pope hopefully.

"Nah, not quite, but almost. A couple of patrols together with the bobbies managed to get up to the seventh and eighth floors. Once they've finished, we're done. The top two floors are inaccessible... unless you're Spiderman."

The radio in Pope's hand made a crackle and bleep sound. "*Sergeant Pope, this is control, do you copy?*"

"I copy."

"*Sergeant. I don't want to panic you... but you all need to get out of there. Quick sharp!*"

"Control? What's happening?"

"*GET OUT NOW! THAT'S AN ORDER!*"

From above their heads, a commotion of shouts and screams, closely matched by two long bursts of gunfire:

Tat-a-tat-a-tat-a-tat!! Tat-a-tat-a-tat-a-tat!!!!

More shouts, followed by an elongated shriek that sounded distant at first but gradually grew in pitch and echoed, accompanied by a blur of movement towards the other end of the building, and a meaty thud from outside.

"What was that?" asked PC Anders.

"Let's not dwell on it," said Pope, not wanting to consider the answer.

Pop! Pop! Pop!

Handguns were discharged, followed by more rifle-fire and then a low, whooshing, roaring sound, akin to the noise made by a burner in a hot air balloon.

Flamethrowers.

That was the strange hosepipe contraptions being held by those two soldiers seen at the gathering in front of the building.

"Come on, let's get out of here; that's not a request!" ordered Pope, setting forward at a trot. Anders and Manning followed by his side, with Mark Novak close behind.

Piling down the stairs were police officers and soldiers. No one stopped to acknowledge each other, the expressions on the faces of those from the upper levels looked fraught with fear. Steadfast, they exited the building, with one of the men wielding a flamethrower taking up the rear, setting off jets of fire thirty feet towards the way they had come.

Crossing to the opposite side of Grey Friars Bridge Road, edging around to the far side of the army vehicles lined up waiting, PC Anders stopped to look back at the shell of the building. Orange flames could be seen licking out through its side.

Unprompted, a young soldier with angular features and sallow complexion spoke up hysterically. "Flies... all over the place; never have seen anything like it. Bloody thousands of them... may be millions!"

The last to leave; flamethrower soldier backed out of the building obliquely, shooting bursts of searing orange and yellow fire after him.

"Is the building clear?" asked Pope urgently, watching the flames licking the building's opening and conflagrate deep within.

Calls of: "Yea" and "Think so," were repeated amongst the forlorn figures that huddled together or sat crestfallen on the pavement.

"Except Hansen... they got him, sir. Took us by surprise..."

Hansen had been the youngest in the troop and, like an eager puppy, had charged ahead of his search party full of spunk and bravado. The only thing faster than his legs had been his mouth, which he'd used actively to voice his opinions on everything from the flies to everyday matters. When the flies attacked, they sprung up like a snagged trip wire, killing the soldier efficiently, as though they had been waiting in ambush; probably to shut him up, a few colleagues had thought but considered ill to speak.

"And Botwright," piped up a police constable, referring to a uniformed colleague. "He jumped from the eighth floor. Guess he thought it a better way to die…"

The sergeant took a moment to process this before raising his radio to the side of his face. "Control… this is Sergeant Pope. We're down two men, but the evacuation is complete… as instructed."

"*Copy that.*"

"Control… it might be proactive to target the building with an air-to-surface missile; take the host out whilst we have a fixed location for them."

"*That's a negative, sergeant. It's chump change. What you've just encountered is nothing more than a splinter group; a small one at that.*"

"A small one? What the fuck… my men–"

"*Your men have done you proud,*" interrupted a different voice over the radio. "*Sergeant Pope… this is Makepeace. Your job is done. Your orders are now to return to base, over and out.*"

CHAPTER TWENTY-ONE

/

"**Y**OUR MUNROE MALHOTRA APPEARS TO be worth his weight in gold," said DI Baylem while walking fully into the mortuary that was located within the basement of Fulbarton General Hospital. Dr Hamilton was working on one of that afternoon's many victims. A naked woman lay on a metal table with her chest and stomach flayed open to reveal her internal organs. There were other bodies placed on the other four tables within the room, concealed beneath surgical sheets.

"I'd say he'd need to lose a few stone before I'd value him at that," replied the police pathologist, half-smiling. He continued with his work, despite the intrusion.

Baylem ignored the witty riposte. Instead, he asked: "I thought the hospital was to be evacuated by ten tonight?"

"It is, and all but the infirm and those who are unlikely to survive removal have already gone. But I've been given a little latitude and freedom to conclude my work... well, for a few more hours at any rate." Information had dribbled down to him that all remaining staff – including those staying behind within ICU and within wards caring for the remaining patients – had to leave no later than six a.m. the following morning. The backup electric generator would likely run out of fuel long before then.

"Sounds like similar instructions to that received by the constabulary." He didn't feel it worth mentioning that the entire police force had been transferred to the football ground already, and that only he, DS McCardle and a handful of constables were still free to roam the streets. Unlike the hospital, his orders were to be at the stadium no later than nine a.m.

"At least the fly strikes have petered out," said Hamilton appreciatively.

"There has been another incident," stated Baylem, "for the record."

"Oh?"

"The Grey Friars development." News had filtered through to the DI a short time earlier with regards to the deaths of a soldier and a police constable, both searching the building as part of the roundup of citizens operation. "Two dead... their bodies have yet to be recovered. At least they should be the last. Hopefully."

"Yes, well, in theory. Of course, with the population now all in one place, it should help keep an eye on things. But, don't you *worry* that it makes it easier for the flies to knock us all off at once? They don't say 'don't put all your eggs in one basket' for nothing!"

"We're banking on the flies believing that; it's the only sure way to guarantee getting all the flies in the same place at the same time. I just hope that Doctor Quisenberry and your friend Malhotra will have created a way to destroy them by then."

"And what if they don't?"

Baylem's shoulder slumped in resignation, as though the outcome was more than likely. "Then I dread to think what will be worse: The flies attacking thirty thousand people in a confined space or what General Makepeace has up his sleeve in dealing with it."

Despite numerous attempts in soliciting information with regards to what the military leader and his battalion had planned, nothing had been revealed.

CHAPTER TWENTY-TWO

/

THE FOLLOWING MORNING WAS BRIGHT and sunny. At eight a.m., thermal pictures from the surveillance drone confirmed that the whole town, with the exception of eight patients within Fulbarton General Hospital too sick to move, had been evacuated and were now confined within the football stadium.

The military leaders had convened for a meeting over breakfast and were seated within the backroom of the old Victorian coach house across the square from Fulbarton's vacated Police Headquarters. Coffee was flowing freely and a plate of croissants was set in the centre of the table.

Tim Howlett, who enjoyed eating pastries of any variety, was tucking into a chocolate and hazelnut croissant.

Switching from thermal to visual radio wave mode, the flat screen monitor screwed into the wall flickered as it transformed the landscape from black with a kaleidoscope of colours (representative of hot and cold signatures), into dark-grey with light grey outlines. Splashes of red were dotted around in fewer places than before, with one giant formation close to the Grey Friars development, the final place checked by soldiers the night before.

As General Makepeace watched, the drone picked up movement of one of the smaller red splodges. He tracked it flying as a solid unit across the town's sky from the east, merging with the multitude being tracked.

"It looks like they're still gathering their numbers," said Major Broadbent sitting beside the general.

"Yes… it's what they've been doing," confirmed Makepeace. He was tired and holding a cup of coffee which he took a sip from, trying to keep himself awake. He hadn't slept in over twenty-six hours. "But not many left… just a few pockets here and there. I doubt it'll be long now."

"Any further attacks since the Grey Friars incident?" asked a lieutenant from the other side of the table.

"A patrol unit came in contact with a contingent shortly before midnight, but nothing which a flamethrower couldn't handle. Don't think they knew what hit them," replied Makepeace with a chuckle. *If they didn't then, they soon will*, he further mused.

"And, the next phase of Operation Remedy?" asked Broadbent. "Is everything ready?"

"The trap has been set, yes. RAF Marham is on standby with a Tornado prepped and ready for deployment. Coordinates have already been supplied for the Storm Shadow missile."

"Jesus… I can't believe we're going through with this. Does the prime minister truly understand what's at stake here? Thirty thousand innocent lives…" The CEO of Biomargent Sciences sat within the committee at General Makepeace's insistence. The flies had originated from his laboratory facilities after all. He shook his head dismally.

"You're a civilian; I don't expect you to have the stomach for this sort of thing. Humphries knows what's at stake, Tim," maintained Makepeace. "He even suggested that we blow Fulbarton off the map if need be; but I assured him that wasn't going to be necessary; just the football ground… which won't be missed… they're a tin pot team anyway. When it's gone, I suggest they stick a carpark there in its place. But, as a precaution, I propose we move troops and operational command out beyond the town's borders. Not only do I not want to get caught up in the crossfire, I fear we are vulnerable to a fly strike ourselves. Look at how organised they are…"

The screen on the wall continued to broadcast radio wave imagery from the MQ9-Reaper. Compounding the general's rationale, another red blob could be seen moving across the sky, this time from the right of the screen towards the centre, stopping at an unidentified location.

"That's the hospital, isn't it?" ventured the lieutenant.

"Yes," confirmed Makepeace in a grunt.

"Those poor bastards," uttered the lieutenant, thinking of those who couldn't be moved and the doctor who had stayed behind.

"When do we leave, General?" pressed Broadbent with a little urgency.

"Just as soon as I've spoken to Annabelle Herman, Major… and finished my coffee, of course," he replied.

CHAPTER TWENTY-THREE

1

THE SENIOR NURSE, CATHERINE POWERS, had begged Dr Pam Edvardsen to leave the eight patients and just go when it came to vacate the hospital. Four soldiers had arrived shortly before six a.m. to collect them, but the duty doctor had pointedly refused to leave. "Who's going to care for these people?" she had asked firmly, sweeping strands of blonde hair away from her eyes. "Look at them!"

The patients had been squeezed into a ward designed to hold only four beds – usually two on either side of the long side walls – but which now each accommodated four in an attempt to preserve power from the generator which was outlasting everyone's estimation (including Floyd Hamilton's the evening before) by at least four hours. For how much longer was anyone's guess.

"Ma'am, we have orders to move you to the stadium," said Sergeant Cooper, sounding American despite being raised in Northumberland, lifting his rifle dangerously. He was one of those people who pronounced 'water' *war-dar*.

"Are you going to shoot me if I refuse?"

Catherine had stepped in front of the soldier, coming between the two in an attempt to head-off any hostility. "Please, Pam…

just think about your son. He'll be at the football ground right now, likely scared. He needs his mother… and John needs you too." John was the doctor's husband.

"Matthew will be fine and his father can take care of himself. These people here need me more. Without me, who's going to monitor their vitals? Administer their medication, ensure their oxygen tanks aren't empty or tend their hourly needs?"

"But, Pam," Catherine implored in a quiet, desperate tone.

"Let's go, people," ordered Cooper impatiently, making a grab for the doctor.

"No!" shouted Edvardsen, shrugging free from the soldier's reach. "I won't!"

"Fine," said the sergeant abruptly, out of patience. He stepped back. "Suit yourself. She stays. Everyone else… out!"

Jostled from behind, Catherine was manipulated towards the room's exit by one of the soldiers. "Pam!" Catherine looked imploringly over her shoulder as she was marched towards the exit.

"I'll be all right," she said defiantly, crossing her arms in a show of confidence and unquestionable authority.

"Don't bet on it," countered Cooper as he left, the double-doors swinging closed behind him.

2

The overhead lights flickered on and off a couple of times, then settled on off for a time, worrying Dr Edvardsen that the generator was about to pack up or was now out of fuel, but after a protracted moment of darkness, the fluorescent tubes came on and stayed on.

Around the room, the eight patients lay in beds unconscious and barely alive, connected to life-support machines and ventilators that wheezed and groaned and bleeped and clicked, with IV drips hooked up on stands providing a combination of liquid sustenance and vital medication.

A glance at the stainless steel fob watch clipped to her pocket informed her that two hours had passed since Catherine and the rest of the nursing staff had been forced to leave. "Doesn't time fly…" she spoke to no one in particular, but a young woman – Molly – in an induced coma was closest. As expected, she gave no reply or signs of hearing her. The doctor worked to change a saline drip which was near to empty.

The patient was in her early twenties and had been knocked off her bicycle, receiving substantial head injuries and multiple bone fractures. She was a fifty/fifty for survival.

Across the ward, a small electronic alarm began to resonate. Pam glanced towards an elderly man and saw the infusion pump monitor flashing red numerals next to him. "Okay, okay… I'm on it." He had Alzheimer's and a rare form of bone cancer that had spread to multiple organs, including his lungs. He wasn't expected to survive his illness, but his son had Power of Attorney and insisted that everything be done to keep the man alive for as long as could be, no matter how much he suffered or how much it cost the NHS.

Edvardsen crossed the ward and turned off the noisy monitor and removed the fluid bag from the drip chamber connected to the long, flexible IV tubing. She then tugged it down from the stand and disposed of the empty fluid pouch in a yellow medical waste bin standing next to the bed. The doctor then crossed to a tall refrigerator in the corner of the ward, unlocked it with a key attached to an elastic fob clipped to a belt loop at her waist and pulled out another bag, clearly marked for use with this patient.

Dead centre of the room, fitted within the ceiling, was a white air con vent placed subtly among matching tiles, pumping cool sterile air into the ward. The low 'whoosh' and 'hum' of the unit was drowned out by the dissonance of the medical paraphernalia connected at various points to each of the eight patients lying unconscious to either side of the room. Pam Edvardsen was used to the noise, but to any visitors, the sound was enough to give even the deafest person a headache.

"Okay, Kenny," said the doctor as she returned to the patient, "last bag for today." Speaking aloud made her feel less alone. She pushed the bag onto a hook on the IV stand and then swept up the clear plastic reservoir of the drip chamber, dragging the flexible tubing with it. The effect caused a slight tugging at the taped needle attached to Kenny's hand. With practiced dexterity, she attached the medicine bag and then turned on the infusion regulator, tapping in the delivery rate and countdown time with a couple of flicks of an index finger.

A small ball of sweat had formed on the doctor's forehead. Despite the air con, the room felt stuffy and warm.

"I think I'll just open one of these windows a crack," she muttered conversationally, turning her attention to the double glazing behind Kenny's bed. Twisting a small handle, Edvardsen unlocked the window and then pushed it out an inch.

Behind the doctor, a bloated fly squeezed through the vented air con grill, cautiously moving around the slats, avoiding the draught of air that poured through and ruffled the micro-hairs covering its small legs and body. As it arrived at the edge, it surveyed the room, watched the doctor changing the IV bag and continued to scrutinise her movements as she carried out what were considered by the medical profession as 'nursing duties'.

After a minute, the fly had cased out the ward, identified that the humans in the beds posed little or no danger, and the doctor caring for them the only potential threat, was on her own.

In a single thought, the fly telepathically communicated the status quo and followed it with a basic command:

Attack!

Using multiple points of entry, the flies crawled and wriggled into the ward. Drifting down from the air con vent in clusters; spitting up from the waste pipe in the sink in bursts of one or two at a time; flies scrabbled through the small gaps to the sides of the fluorescent lighting – of which there were twelve fixed within the ceiling – and more found a way in through the three-pin plug sockets. Steadily, the numbers swelled from a dozen, to a couple of hundred, then into several thousand, all in less than a matter of minutes.

Obliviously, Dr Edvardsen continued to care for the patients, her attention now moving onto a man in his mid-twenties. He was not unconscious but paralysed from the neck down, a result of being struck by lightning whilst trying to adjust a TV aerial during a thunderstorm. A stupid act, but the man believed it was worth it. Man United were playing Borussia Dortmund in a crucial European Cup game. The Reds lost, adding salt to the injuries.

"Now, Toby... your turn." The doctor retrieved the man's chart from the end of the bed and quickly scanned it. Toby Harris was printed at the top of the page. Glancing at the vitals monitor affixed to the cantilever bracket above him, she noted down his current stats. "I'll just get your blood pressure," she said colloquially, manoeuvring a stand-mounted sphygmomanometer from behind her and bringing it up towards the head of Toby's bed.

Unable to turn his head, Toby's eyes fixed on the blonde-haired doctor as she walked into view. From the corners, he spotted a movement that he struggled to focus on. It was a black mass and spreading fluidly across the ceiling. He wanted to scream out in alarm but the endotracheal intubation tube prevented it. He tried to convey panic by forcing his eyelids wider, making his eyeballs almost protrude and close to popping out.

"No need to worry about this, Toby. You know we have to do it. It's just you're a high risk for hypertension," misinterpreted Edvardsen, stretching the short rubber tube from the sphygmoma-nometer and wrapping the cuff around the paralysed man's upper arm, securing it firmly with the big Velcro fastening. She then pressed a button on the electronic blood pressure machine, watching the cuff inflate around Toby's bicep and heard the familiar pattern of bleeps signifying diastolic and systolic blood flow was being measured, concluded with an elongated beep.

After pottering around rearranging equipment, the doctor returned her attention to the sphygmomanometer. "There... one hundred and thirty-eight over seventy-two; not too bad."

Behind her, Toby noticed the creeping patch of blackness drop from the ceiling as a solid, board-like shape and watched it hover noiselessly a short distance above and behind the doctor's head. In desperation, he willed Dr Pam Edvardsen to notice the fear and pleading in his eyes, and something extraordinary happened.

Toby felt his head move ever-so-slightly.

Dr Edvardsen flinched with an involuntary gasp. *Had Toby Harris just twitched?* This could be a miracle, she started thinking.

Before the excitement had a chance to manifest itself fully, the room suddenly swelled with the noise of sixty-thousand flies, the hum and drone reverberating off the sterile walls so deafeningly loud, the doctor was unable to hear the sound of the electronic medical equipment around her or the air con blowing out air above, or even the scream she knew escaped her lips.

The overhead lights appeared to go out, plunging the room into oppressive gloom as the thick cloud of insects blotted out the fluorescent luminance from the ceiling and made the room impenetrably dark.

Blindly, Edvardsen struggled to fight off the flies, backhanding the insects away from her face and pulling at them from her hair. She flapped at the air around her head frantically, finding her reactions were slow and ineffectual.

For every fly she repelled, five others replaced it. Sensing their intention, she dropped to her knees and crawled along the floor between Toby's bed and the cancer patient, thinking there was a good chance she might escape the nightmare.

Momentarily, she was released from the flies' attack whilst they regrouped and turned their focus on the easier prey.

Around the ward, the flies dropped onto the eight frail and vulnerable patients, covering their beds with a thick, moving counterpane that spread over their recumbent bodies and continued until consuming their faces.

Flies wriggled, jostled, squeezed and poked their way into mouths and nostrils; no orifice was impossible or impassable to penetrate. Where ventilators assisted with breathing, the flies sabotaged the equipment or used it to their advantage, infiltrating the machines. From inside, they accessed the artificial lung chambers and allowed pressurised oxygen to propel them into a patient's airway through intubated tubes. Once inside the larynx, the flies applied their 'well-practised' tactic, building an obstruction that eventually blocked-off the air supply.

Out of the eight ICU patients, only Toby Harris suffered. Despite losing all feeling throughout his body, he was fully conscious and aware of the flies as they entered his mouth, filled up his throat around the endotracheal intubation tube and jammed up the endpoint of the ventilation conduit so that oxygen no longer entered his lungs.

With the paralysis affecting his diaphragm and with the breathing machine effectively cut-off, Toby quietly – but agonisingly – asphyxiated, slowly blacked out, and died.

In spite of the reprieve afforded Dr Pam Edvardsen, the clemency was short lived. Hope of escape finally deserted her when she reached the double-doors and realised she would need to stand to open them. Before she was able to force herself into a stoop, the thick pulsating brume of flies descended upon her, cloaking her body from head to foot an inch deep in twitching insects.

Screaming and squirming, Edvardsen twisted and turned in a vain attempt to avoid contact with the bluebottles; with one hand, she tore a fistful of the small attackers clear from her face and with the other, she slapped and punched many others away, killing hundreds.

Undeterred, the flies continued with their assault. Buzzing louder and more determined, they fell on her in a heavy rainfall; bloated torrents of blood-thirsty flies began to weigh down her body.

Although many of the vile insects had accessed her mouth, found their way into the doctor's trachea, and began to build the blockade that would ultimately end her life, the flies had yet to gain a foothold to clog her airways entirely. Even so, oxygen depletion was notably obvious. The blonde-haired woman was now shuffling around like a shapeless monster within a blizzard of insects. Her breathing was becoming harder and more laboured.

Edvardsen knew it was hopeless. It was just a matter of time; maybe only a few more minutes.

She had read the news stories about the fly strikes over the previous few days, and even watched *This Morning* and the many news reports the day before, continuing to do so until the electricity had been cut off, isolating Fulbarton from the world outside.

The doctor wasn't ready to give up. The instinct to survive spurred her into making one last effort to escape. Summoning all her strength, she made herself run towards where she knew the window was. In full stride, she launched herself, trying to forget the moving mass of bugs clinging and concealing her entire body, many of which had started biting her in frustration.

OOOPH!

Almost blind, the doctor collided with the first intensive care bed within the ward, somersaulting over its side railings and landing hard and awkwardly on the other side, sandwiched between it and the next bed wedged in close. She tried struggling to her feet but found it difficult to lever herself into an easily mobile position.

Wasting no time, the remainder of the sixty thousand flies fell from the air precipitantly, as though exposed to gravity for the first time or abruptly losing the ability to fly.

Upon landing on the trapped doctor, the drone of the flies ceased. Focusing on the woman's face, the insects settled over her airways, layer after layer, creating an airtight barrier that she was weak and powerless to overcome.

This is it, she thought, *this is my time*. Pam Edvardsen allowed herself to think about her son, Matthew, only five years old. The small boy's face appeared inside her mind; his clipped short dark-blond hair, his misty-grey eyes and his sweet, bright smile; even the small scar on his forehead, just above his left eye. He was beautiful and looked so much like his father. She wished she'd listened to Catherine now and gone with her to the football stadium. Staying behind had been all for nothing. She made a silent prayer:

Please, God, don't let this happen to my son.

The pain of suffocation tore the final thoughts from her head and replaced it with sheer, agonising panic. For a long moment, she felt the burning sensation in her lungs as her body screamed for oxygen; she believed her chest was going to explode and her eyes would pop out of their sockets, absurdly remembering a scene in the film Total Recall, when Arnold Schwarzenegger found himself without oxygen on Mars, clawing and gasping for breath.

And then it was gone, the suffering was over.

Blank nothingness started to fill her mind. She thought she could see a light somewhere ahead; a small dot of white brightness in the distance that promised comfort and reassurance. She felt herself floating towards it, but the quicker she yielded and willed herself forward, the further the dot appeared to be, eventually disappearing altogether. Then the canvas became blank and all sense of being deserted her.

There was completely nothing.

3

Realising that the woman was dead beneath them, the flies surged back up into the air, filling the room with a deep, resonant humming sound that seemed less frenzied than before and more serene, almost jolly.

The flies circuited the room a dozen times, doing their customary victory lap, before making their exit. Very conveniently, Dr Edvardsen had opened a window a short time before the flies had struck, the slight movement of the vertical blinds highlighting the feature. In a shapeless form a meter wide and six meters long, the insects swooped, did a loop-the-loop, and then poured out through the crack of the window in a swirling mist, allowing a breeze to carry them gently up into the morning sky.

CHAPTER TWENTY-FOUR

"**D**ICHLORVUS**," SAID **MUNROE MALHOTRA**, THE entomologist. He was holding out a small test tube for the small gathering around the table in the makeshift laboratory that was set out in the hospitality suite of Fulbarton Town Football ground.

It was nine a.m. With the exception of eight hospital patients too ill to be moved and a doctor too stubborn to leave them, the whole town had been evacuated, the last of the ICU nurses having arrived within the containment facility shortly after six a.m. that morning.

DI Baylem, DS McCardle, Chief Superintendent Mills, DI's Randall and Hardy, James Quisenberry and the pathologist, Floyd Hamilton, stood around like an audience watching a street magician executing the three cup and ball trick. There was one other spectator standing to the back of the group. He looked odd and out of sorts, but the detectives assumed he was with the Chief Super and paid him no especial attention. This little assembly were the selected few invited into the spacious room overlooking the normally lush green of the football pitch, now teeming with thousands of people sitting, standing or milling around in confusion or fear.

"A commonplace and very effective insecticide used in agriculture and horticulture to control flies and other pests," explained the entomologist. "It's a formidable poison, and our best solution for dealing with these *Calliphoridae*. One hundred percent kill rate."

"Of course, that statistic is based on the fact we used it on our only living specimen," interposed Quisenberry nervously. They had used the straggler found at the Alexandra Hotel and Country Club discovered when Baylem and McCardle had attended the scene of Edwin Carslake's murder the day before.

"And countless studies by the manufacturer," replied Malhotra defensively.

"Sounds perfect," cut-in Baylem. "How soon can we get this…" the DI had forgotten what it was called.

"Dichlorvus," Malhotra finished for him.

"*Dichlorvus*," repeated Baylem, "and how do we administer it?"

"Getting it isn't a problem," said an unfamiliar voice from behind Baylem and McCardle. A man in his late-sixties stepped up, coming between the detectives. He had thinning white hair, a deep tan and a mouth almost empty of teeth. "I have gallons of the stuff out on Crawley farm. I even have a way to deliver it. An old Cessna 188 agricultural aircraft, fuelled and ready to take-off and at your service. I use it to dust my crops." The Crawley farm, to the east of the town, was a producer of rapeseed, onions and potatoes. There was also an orchard, but the apples weren't good for anything except cider. The farmer, Bill Crawley, was the odd man in the room. "It's the side effects that you need to be concerned about."

"Side effects?" queried Baylem.

"Aye, side effects," he repeated. "Dichlorvus is highly toxic to humans. Not only does it work on contact, it attacks the respiratory organs and the stomach. The National Poisons Unit has classified it as 'toxic if swallowed', 'very toxic if inhaled', and 'toxic in contact with skin'. It's a triple whammy." The farmer paused to see if his point had hit home. Vague expressions glared back at him. He sighed. "Put that into simple speak: it can lead to cancers, nerve damage, and even death; most likely death.

"Accidental exposure has resulted in more than a hundred fatalities since 1983; what you are proposing is using a high concentration of the stuff... deliberately... in a densely populated area. I don't think I can spell it out better than that."

"Oh crap," exclaimed McCardle succinctly.

"Then we can't possibly use it," said Dr Hamilton sensibly.

"What options are there?" asked Quisenberry with a note of desperation.

"Great. We die from the poison or we die from the flies. Perfect."

"I might have an idea," said Baylem, upbeat. "What about protective clothing and gas masks?"

"What?" Hardy sounded dumb and was ignored.

"That would work," replied Bill Crawley. "I use them all the time."

"But, where do we get enough for thirty thousand?" asked Chief Superintendent Mills who had been quietly contemplating their plight.

"I don't think there's enough time to obtain thirty thousand, sir; but I know where I can get five thousand." In the boot of Baylem's car were forensic coveralls, overshoes, latex gloves and half face masks combined with respiratory filters, all the protection needed against gas, chemical or other pollutants, normally for use when attending crime scenes. Plenty of stock was kept back at the police station.

This very equipment would provide ample defence from the use of Dichlorvus, thought the DI.

"What about the other twenty-five thousand?" beseeched DI

Randall, disdain for the idea clear from the look on his face. His nose was turned up and his lips were sneered. "We can't just leave them to die!"

"You're right," said McCardle. "These are our people, our friends... colleagues... family. We'll have to bring as many of them inside; into the rooms, bar areas, corridors, conference facilities, the basements, cupboards, even the toilets. It'll be tight... like sardines in a vacuum-packed wrapper. But we will make them all fit in. We'll seal all the doors, all the windows, and block up the air vents. We leave no crack or gap free for the poison to seep in or for a fly to squeeze through."

"How soon can we get everything in place?" asked Mills in anticipation.

"We can get to the station and back in twenty... maybe fifteen minutes," calculated Baylem. "Allow a further ten/twenty to go down to the storage room to find what we need and fetch it. Four of us should be able to get the job done in no time."

"Okay, Baylem. You and Randall go... take a couple of constables with you. DI Hardy... you and McCardle can set to work moving people into the stadium and making the rooms airtight."

"Okay," chimed McCardle and Hardy in unison.

"Doctor Malhotra... Quisenberry, and Mr Crawley... you are in charge of the Dichlo-poison-thingy... we need to be prepared for an imminent attack," continued Mills. "Since the town's people have been confined here, there's been no sign of the flies. I doubt it'll be long before that all changes."

"We'll need to get over to the farm at once," said Crawley, moving towards the geneticist and the entomologist. "The plane is fuelled, but the insecticide tanks need to be topped up."

"Everyone... grab a radio..." instructed Baylem. At the back of the room was a table filled with two-way TETRA handsets placed within charging stations. "Let's keep an open dialogue," he explained, turning his on. "I'll be on channel five." He turned to each of them, considering those around him earnestly. "If this is to work, we need to be in harmony."

As the small gathering began to disperse, Dr Hamilton stepped forward stating importantly in the absence of a defined role: "I'll coordinate with the medical team. We'll try to keep everyone calm and provide medicinal support to help us through to the end of this emergency." His mind flitted to thoughts of the ground's bar and alcoholic remedies.

Chief Superintendent Mills didn't argue with the pathologist. "You do that," he said pretentiously.

2

Before DI's Baylem and Randall, together with PCs Anders and Manning, stepped off the stairs that led up to the hospitality suite and to various exits out of the stadium, Annabelle Herman charged directly into their path.

"Baylem!" She sounded distressed.

"Annabelle, where've you been?" Baylem broke free from his group to shorten the gap between himself and the Home Office adviser arriving from the opposite direction. "Doesn't matter; we've got a plan."

"Hear me out first," she dismissed, a little out of breath. "You need to know something… we've got a big problem."

"What? What's wrong?"

"The general just gave me an order to leave. They have pulled back and camped outside Fulbarton. I'm to meet them at their base of operations." Fear filled her face whilst her voice raised an octave. "The flies… they're mobilising!"

"Are you saying the flies are getting ready to attack?"

DI Randall and the two constables crowded around to hear the whole conversation.

"Imminently it would seem, and the general is creaming

himself in anticipation." The truth was that General Makepeace was relishing the opportunity of a bit of action on home ground.

"What's he planning to do?" asked Randall.

Nervously, Annabelle answered. "When the flies attack, he plans to kill them all with a laser guided missile."

"What?!" chorused Anders and Manning.

"That's..." Randall shook his head in disbelief, his face draining of colour.

"I know," she said. "The bomb radius is around three hundred and fifty meters."

"Jeez... That's the stadium plus a good area outside of it..." said Baylem. "We've no chance."

"They're going to kill us all?" Manning's eyes misted over. "How can they get away with this? We're not in Aleppo, we're their people?! This is their country! The prime minister won't allow it."

"Shocking, isn't it. Worse still, the prime minister has given his blessing. The general called it an 'expendable outcome'," replied Annabelle laconically. "They seem to think it's a small price to pay in the bigger scheme of things. Keep it to yourselves. We don't want to cause a mass panic."

"Bloody hell," muttered Anders.

"Those flies won't stop at just Fulbarton; once done here, they'll move on to the next town... then the next. Look at it from the general's P.O.V; he doesn't think he has a choice." Annabelle allowed a long pause for the police officers to digest what she was saying. "Okay, so you've heard what the general has in store, now tell me what you have in mind."

Baylem spent the next two minutes giving Annabelle the outline of their plan, highlighting their mission and what they intended to do to protect the people contained within the stadium.

The PA system clicked on overhead, an imminent broadcast introduced by a loud siren that match day attendees would be familiar with. DS McCardle's voice immediately followed, echoing around the building:

"*PLEASE CAN I HAVE YOUR ATTENTION? CAN ALL WOMEN AND CHILDREN, AND MEN OVER THE AGE OF SIXTY... PLEASE MAKE YOUR WAY INTO THE STADIUM BUILDING AND AWAIT FURTHER INSTRUCTIONS. I REPEAT: CAN ALL WOMEN AND CHILDREN, AND MEN OVER THE AGE OF SIXTY PLEASE MAKE YOUR WAY INTO THE STADIUM BUILDING... EVERYBODY ELSE, YOU ARE TO AWAIT FURTHER INSTRUCTION...*"

"Your plan could work," said Annabelle, tinged with pity. "But... you may be too late."

"We need to try," asserted Baylem.

"Okay. I will speak to the general."

"You do that; tell him we have things under control." He turned to go, the action prompting Randall and the two constables to follow suit.

"Wait! Not that way. The doors are all chained locked from the outside. There's currently only one exit left open. It's this way, follow me." Annabelle led them away towards the centre of the stadium, through a network of gloomy corridors that provided various access points to lower level seating areas overlooking the football pitch, and off which metal staircases ascended beyond the ceiling, giving access to the upper reaches of the stadium. Signs with seat numbering and stand names were placed every so many meters, with warnings that fans were required to have their tickets on them at all times.

"DI Baylem!" Sounding panicked, Dr Munroe Malhotra appeared from a corridor behind them, followed by James Quisenberry and the farmer, Bill Crawley. "The doors! They're all locked and chained shut. We're trapped!"

"I know," replied the DI. "Annabelle knows of one which isn't. Come with us."

A minute later, the eight people stepped up to a turnstile that, on first glance, appeared locked like all the rest; Annabelle pushed a narrow door open. "They left this open for me. I'm supposed to lock it as well before I leave."

A flash of concern crossed Baylem's face.

"But I won't," she reassured.

Outside the stadium, bright sunlight blinded them. Baylem shielded his eyes with a cupped hand and scanned the area. The surroundings looked eerily empty except for a dozen cars and police vehicles; marked vans and cars were parked along one side of the road, with Baylem's Audi easily picked out ahead of a black SUV. It was deathly quiet, not even the sound of birds or insects filled the air.

"Where is everybody?" asked Quisenberry, walking out a little ahead of the detective inspector. The entomologist and the farmer fanned out beside him. In the foreground was a statue of a former footballing legend in a pose of celebration or defiance.

"Gone," replied Baylem. He turned to the geneticist who looked confused. "Don't ask," he said, "just get to the place and the insecticide and await further instructions."

Quisenberry nodded.

"Be ready for our signal... and use your radios... use channel five; keep in contact. No surprises, right."

In a swagger, Baylem led the way to the vehicles. At the Audi, he moved casually around to the driver's side of his Audi. PCs Anders and Manning passed him in a hurry, each taking a police van; Randall opted for a marked car, with Quisenberry, Malhotra, and Bill Crawley taking one of the others. Annabelle Herman made a beeline for the black SUV – a government issue – which she had rolled into Fulbarton only the day earlier.

In a scream of tyres, revving engines and a sudden burst of unnecessary siren sound from Anders', the vehicles began to pull out, driving to the end of the stadium road where Baylem led a small convoy of four vehicles west. Quisenberry turned a sharp right and Annabelle Herman crossed the road straight over, taking the route leading out of town.

The time on Baylem's watch was now 9:18 a.m.

3

With the roads entirely clear of traffic and Baylem pushing the speed of his Audi to fifty mph in a thirty mph zone, the convoy of police vehicles passed the front of Fulbarton Police Headquarters in a little over nine minutes.

"Seems so odd," the DI muttered under his breath. Yesterday, the place was teeming with military personnel and gridlocked with army vehicles. Now, like the rest of Fulbarton, it was completely empty and resembling a ghost town. A sideward glance towards the Victorian coach house, where General Makepeace had set up his base, appeared completely desolate and abandoned.

Baylem indicated left and followed the road round to the side of the large police building, taking the private road first on the left designated for 'authorised personnel only'. It led to the back entrance. The DI knew it would be closest to where the stores were situated, making it easier to locate and transfer the supplies they needed.

Baylem parked his car in a bay reserved for Chief Superintendent Mills, and the two vans and Randall's police car pulled in either side of him. Wasting no time, the DI exploded out of the Audi and charged up the ramp leading into the building. As expected, the double-doors were unlocked and Baylem pulled it open forcefully and bounded inside.

"He's keen," griped Randall, stepping away from his police car. With Manning and Anders, they hurried after Baylem.

The place was eerily quiet in the absence of staff and running electricity. The stores were down a flight of stairs found on the other side of the back office reception. There was a service lift, but without power, it was rendered completely useless. A serving desk partitioned the room and a dozen chairs were set out ahead of a designated waiting area.

At the bottom of a short flight of stairs, the basement branched off in two directions. To the left was the way towards a secure section where the cells could be seen through a steel prison gate; to the right at the end of a brief corridor was a door leading into the stores. Baylem was trying a number of different keys in the lock when Randall and the two constables caught him up.

"There," Baylem grunted in satisfaction. The door was unlocked on the seventh attempt. Allowing it to swing open, Baylem led his party in. Warm, stale air washed over them.

A quick survey revealed a large room with metal warehouse shelving lined row after row, from ceiling to floor, stocked with everything a police station would need; stationery, uniforms, helmets, handcuffs, two-way radios, cleaning products, torches, whistles, toilet rolls, liquid soap and sundry other things; all were clear to see. A walkway ran the length of the room off which were three reinforced steel doors evenly spaced out. Each was labelled with a sign, a hint as to what was contained behind them.

The first one stated: Evidence.

The second: Armament.

The third: Records Office.

Baylem paid them no interest. "What we want is at the back," he indicated, dragging a flatbed platform trolley out from one of the aisles between shelving. "Grab one of these and follow me."

As Baylem had stated, the protective clothing, latex gloves, face masks and shoe covers – ordinarily used for crime scene investigations – were found towards the back of the room, neatly boxed up on shelves clearly labelled.

"It's quite fortunate that this thing is happening now instead of last month," said Baylem casually, "we only replenished our stock two weeks ago."

"Lucky us," replied Randall sarcastically.

When Baylem had attached his timings for travelling to and from the police station, and collecting and loading the vehicles with the protective clothing, he hadn't factored in the short flight of stairs. After the maiden trip between store room and Anders' van, it was clearly going to take a lot longer than twenty minutes to complete the task.

It was decided to put in place a production line, which worked like this:

Baylem would load a trolley up; Randall and Manning would take said trolley to the bottom of the stairs and transfer the boxes to another trolley set at the top by lobbing them between themselves (whilst Baylem would hastily start filling up another). Once the trolley at the top of the stairs was full, PC Anders would then wheel it out of the police station, down the ramp and transfer the boxes into the back of a van.

After half an hour, Baylem loaded the last box onto his trolley and pushed it to where Randall was waiting. Dripping with sweat, the DI used the sleeve of his shirt to mop his brow. "Last one," he confirmed, out of breath.

"Good," wheezed Randall. "You can help get it up there."

Two minutes later, PC Anders closed the door of his van whilst Baylem waved Louise Manning and DI Randall off. When Anders was behind the wheel of his van and reversing out of the station's carpark, Baylem climbed into his Audi and keyed the ignition. With his two-way handset, he radioed back to base.

"McCardle, do you read me, over?"

"Loud and clear, Baylem... where are you? Annabelle has been trying to get hold of you; I'VE BEEN TRYING TO GET HOLD OF YOU! Why haven't you been answering your damn radio?!"

"I have been a little preoccupied," he replied testily. "But don't worry, we're just leaving HQ and on our way back."

"*Baylem, we don't have much time. The flies... Annabelle says they are becoming 'lively'. You need to get back here now. We are running out of time... Hurry!*"

CHAPTER TWENTY-FIVE

/

HELICOPTERS HAD TRANSPORTED THE GENERAL and his company out of Fulbarton, setting down on a clearing five minutes to the west of the town. A temporary barracks had been constructed, where lines of large dark-green tents, each big enough to sleep ten, plus a mobile command centre had been erected. Were it not for the armed men walking around in groups of three or four and the military vehicles parked haphazardly, it could easily have been mistaken for a country retreat campsite.

Makepeace had watched the flies descend upon the hospital through the lens of the overhead surveillance drone patrolling Fulbarton's skies. Alternating between infrared and radio wave viewing settings, the general had watched the insects first disappear into the building, and then efficiently snuff out the lives of the nine people left within.

First to go were the eight patients, clearly identified by their lack of movement.

Putting up more of a fight was a person Sergeant Cooper had helped identify. Dr Pam Edvardsen. Even so, resistance was ineffective and she was dead within a couple of minutes.

Now, two hours later, Makepeace was standing within a Portakabin surrounded by Tim Howlett and half a dozen military advisers. Within the makeshift room, there were others sitting behind desks wearing headsets and watching VDU and radar screens. On the wall behind the general were three large flat-screen televisions. Only one was on, broadcasting the landscape of Fulbarton from the MQ9-Reaper flying high above the sky.

"We have just seen the last of the splinter groups join up with the main horde, General," said Major Broadbent. "If you were asking me to stake my bet, I'd say an attack is imminent."

Makepeace was about to agree but was interrupted.

"Sir, there's movement outside the football ground," observed a female operator from the side of the room. She was wearing military uniform and a green beret. Others to the side of her – male and female – were similarly dressed.

"It's likely the Home Office advisor, Annabelle Harman, Alison," stated the general. "I called her a short while ago ordering her out."

"That could be it," conceded the woman hesitantly. "But, if that is the case… how many vehicles will she be driving?"

On the screen behind the general, the surveillance drone focused in on a line of four vehicles moving eastwards away from the football stadium. Two were easily identified as police vans. Makepeace turned around to consider the situation playing out. Another two cars were moving westwards in the opposite direction.

"I thought my orders were quite clear," griped the general to no one in particular.

"Should we intercept?" asked Captain Dodd keenly.

Makepeace turned about to watch the surveillance footage on the wall behind him. The air around him seemed to turn icy cold.

"Sir?" Dodd pressed for an answer. "I could send in a Lynx with a commando unit."

"No…" replied the general acerbically. He was conflicted.

"If the flies attack, I don't want any army personnel caught in the crossfire. We'll observe for now, see what they are up to; see what happens."

2

Fifteen minutes later, a soldier patrolling the border radioed into the command centre requesting clearance for a civilian.

"*She said you requested her to leave Fulbarton. The name she gave me was Annabelle Herman,*" said the voice through the speaker of the two-way communication device.

"Have her escorted in," replied Makepeace gruffly.

The Home Office adviser arrived with a Land Rover Wolf at her tail. The black SUV rolled to a stop towards a section of grass a stone's throw from the Portakabin and two car lengths from where a Westland Lynx helicopter was stationed.

The Wolf pulled up alongside the SUV and two soldiers leapt out, one rushing to the front of Annabelle's car, the other hanging back indifferently with no intention of further involvement. With little benevolence, the soldier at the front of the SUV opened the driver's door and moved aside, allowing space for the auburn-haired woman to climb out. "The general is this way," he said.

Confidently, Annabelle followed the soldier into the Portakabin, her handbag hanging loosely from her shoulder. Before acknowledgements or pleasantries could be shared, she launched into a rehearsed tirade:

"Damn it, Phil, what you are planning is preposterous!" she shouted, marching into the room. "When you suggested to me yesterday about containing everyone in one location, you misled me into believing it was for their protection... not so that you could use them as an enticement, and then go ahead and kill them. What you are doing is wrong... it's barbaric. It's genocide."

"Miss Herman," started the general, a look of annoyance flashing across his face. "When you address me whilst I'm in uniform, it's 'sir' or 'General', you got that! But, I don't think I need to remind you that you were invited to act as a 'go-between' and to be our 'eyes' and 'ears' inside the police department." He sighed, allowing his demeanour to soften. "For that, you have performed splendidly and I thank you.

"As to my alleged *misleading* you, I think you are mistaken," he spoke more calmly. "I don't recall ever setting forth my plans with you; besides, I don't need your permission. It's the prime minister I take orders from. Now, would you mind telling me why the hell we saw five vehicles in addition to yours moving away from the football ground a short time ago? And how was it that they got out in the first place? Only you knew which door remained unlocked."

"General. I think you should see this," interrupted Captain Dodd from the side of the room, reprieving the Home Office advisor from giving an immediate response. He was peering over the shoulder of one of the VDU operators closely monitoring surveillance footage.

"What is it?" Makepeace growled.

"The flies, sir... they're moving."

The image which Dodd was viewing flashed up onto the flat screen on the wall behind the general.

Where earlier there had been small patches of red dotted around the map in addition to the big mass identified near to the Grey Friars development site, there was now only the one.

And just as Captain Dodd had said, they were indeed moving, albeit slowly. Steadily, the patch of red began to swell and shift slightly eastwards, expanding on the screen like a plume of thick crimson smoke.

"Are they heading towards the football ground?" asked Makepeace warily.

"Looks that way, sir," replied Dodd vaguely. "Upwards and

eastwards. But to be sure..." He turned to the VDU operator sitting below him. "Can we zoom out to see the flies in correlation with the football ground?"

"Sure." The VDU operator tapped a few keys on the keyboard in front of him and the image on his screen began to pan out, mirrored on the flat screen attached to the wall. The whole of Fulbarton swam into shot; streets, roads and buildings in a patchwork of light-grey lines on a dark-grey background. "That's close to zero magnification." The football ground was one of the largest constructions within the town and easily identified.

Instead of shrinking to scale, the widening spread of flies grew larger still as they gathered like clouds in a thunderhead.

"My God," exclaimed Major Broadbent.

"Isn't it amazing?" admired Tim Howlett.

The general might have agreed once. When Dr Quisenberry had pitched his idea to him of an insect army, completely controlled and capable of causing absolute devastation, he had first laughed. When he had seen a video demo, he clapped his hands in glee and imagined a scene almost identical to that which currently played out, only over enemy lines. How opinions soon altered. "Captain... get me RAF Marham on the line. I think it's almost about time."

"General... you don't need to do this," implored Annabelle, desperation slipping into her voice. "There may be another way. You wanted to know about those five vehicles you saw. That was DI Baylem, James Quisenberry, Dr Munroe Malhotra, a civilian and three other police officers. We think we have a way to destroy the flies... without unnecessarily killing all those innocent people or destroying the stadium."

"Quisenberry? He's got a nerve!" The general actually spat on the floor. Saying the traitor's name left a sour taste in his mouth. "I'll be dealing with him later... if he isn't dead by then. But Annabelle, I don't have time for this bullshit. And I care even less."

"Hear me out," she pleaded. "The flies could be killed with an industrial strength insecticide that is a hundred percent effective. Quisenberry has confirmed that it should work; the flies were genetically altered, but not against pesticides." Annabelle thought she saw contemplation on the general's face which spurred her on to continue. "We'll use the people in the stadium like you planned, as bait for the flies. Then, when they attack, we drop gallons of the stuff on and around the stadium using an agricultural aircraft."

"Isn't that stuff lethal to people also?"

"Yes, but we figured out we could protect everyone from coming into contact with it. That's what Baylem is doing. He's going to the police headquarters for protective clothing and face masks; enough for everyone who will be exposed to the stuff."

General Makepeace sighed, as though conceding defeat. What he said next was completely surprising and made Annabelle involuntarily cry.

"All I heard was a load of 'shoulds', 'coulds' and 'maybes'... the bastard kids of mother fuck up. Sorry, Annabelle, we've passed the point of hare-brained ideas. Conclusive action and hard decisions are needed, that's why I'm here; why I'm in charge." Makepeace returned his attention towards Captain Dodd. "Do you have Marham yet?"

"Yes, General, they just confirmed the Tornado has taken off. All we need to do is give authorisation to fire."

"General... please don't," beseeched Annabelle, rubbing at her moist eyes. "You'll be killing children... women... babies." Her petition fell on deaf ears.

"I think you need to take a breather, Miss Herman. P'raps grab yourself a coffee and a bite to eat from the dining marquee. Lieutenant Clark... assist the private in removing Annabelle Herman from my sight. Stay with her; make sure she is escorted at all times..."

The lieutenant made to seize the woman by the arm. Annabelle retracted it sharply, a look of malevolence aimed towards him.

"Dodd, patch me into the Tornado's pilot when he's in firing range."

3

The two soldiers escorted Annabelle out of the Portakabin, one on either side of her.

"I just need to get my handbag," she said, nipping ahead and heading towards her SUV. Opening the door, she stretched in across the driver's seat and snatched up her handbag theatrically from the floor whilst discreetly slipping the two-way radio placed on the passenger seat into her hand. As she scooched out, she deposited the two-way into her bag and zipped it up. Closing the car door and locking it, the Home Office assistant smiled welcomingly, throwing the handbag onto her shoulder. "So, this dining marquee... does it serve alcohol? I could do with a stiff drink!"

Offering no endorsement, the lieutenant stepped towards the young woman intensely. "It's this way, miss..."

The sun was bright and the other soldier was shielding his eyes with a hand, like he was peering at something. As Annabelle accompanied Lieutenant Clark, he took up a position walking behind.

"Just point me in the right direction; I'm sure I can find the marquee on my own..."

"The general has given strict instruction not to leave you unattended." Now in the lead, Clark took the Home Office assistant along a path that weaved through an area designated as the sleeping section for the troops; row after row of large green tents had been hastily erected with just enough space to walk single file between each.

The sight more resembled a refugee camp, Annabelle thought. A radio played somewhere close, the sound of a long forgotten sixties song filled the air, something by Jefferson Airplane, though she didn't know its name.

"What about leaving? Can I go if I want?"

The lieutenant stopped and shrugged. "I'll have to check with the general... Shall we go back?"

They had been walking for two minutes and a sizeable distance had been wrought between them and the mobile command centre. "No... that's fine," she replied disheartened.

"Come on... it's this way, just out through there. You can just about see the white of the marquee."

Thirty seconds later and they walked out into a small clearing ahead of a large industrial marquee. Lines of trestle tables and benches stretched out ahead of it, with uniformed soldiers and civilians in short-sleeves and office attire sitting and eating or walking and talking.

"Are there... wash facilities?" Annabelle sounded embarrassed. Seeing the incomprehension on the lieutenant's face, she elaborated: "Toilets? I have a woman thing to deal with..."

"Oh... yes, of course. I'll take you to them."

Beside the large tent were thirty single-use chemical toilets placed neatly in a row, the type often hired for use during music festivals and summer fetes. They were all light blue.

"These are the men's," said Clark. "Bog-standard," he started to chuckle, "with no thrills and no running hot water; the ladies are over there next to them; delicately designed to cater for all women's necessities." Across from the last portable toilet was what appeared to be a large windowless dark-green caravan supported above the ground on jack legs and accessed via a set of rhino grating steel steps; a 'Ladies' sign had been affixed next to the door.

"Excuse me, gentlemen..." said Annabelle crisply. She clambered up the metal steps as the lieutenant and the soldier watched on.

Immediately ahead of the entrance into the ladies' toilet block were three boxed cubicles with lockable doors, currently open slightly ajar. To the right of the cubicles were two wash basins with soap dispensers affixed to the wall below a large wall-length pristine-clear mirror. Screwed onto the wall on the side were two air dryers. A washroom vending machine was in the corner, offering a range of feminine products, including tights, tampons, lip balm, headache pills, deodorants and even condoms, 'ribbed for *her* pleasure'.

Annabelle stepped into the furthest cubicle from the entranceway and locked the door behind her. She closed the lid on the toilet, slipped her handbag off her shoulder and sat down. Unzipping the bag, she reached in and retrieved the two-way radio, recalling Baylem's request to keep in contact.

Now was as good a time as any to update the detective inspector.

Considering the communication device in her hand for a moment, she fiddled with the channel knob, turning it to '5' and then pressing the talk button.

"Detective Inspector Baylem... do you copy?" She spoke in a hushed tone, worried that the soldiers outside might hear her. They didn't.

Adjusting the volume control, Annabelle heard a sharp static-crackle in response with a small amount of distant whistling. Counting twenty seconds in her head, she pressed the talk button again.

"DI Baylem? Are you there? It's urgent."

No reply.

"Shit," she cursed to herself.

"*Is that Annabelle Herman?*" A distinct female voice echoed through the two-way's speaker, the sound bouncing off the walls of the toilet cubicle.

"Yes." Annabelle sounded both relieved and startled. "Who is this?"

"*DS McCardle. Where are you?*"

"On the outskirts of town, but I really need to speak with Baylem. Is he back at the stadium?"

"*No. Not yet. Why? What's wrong?*"

"It's the flies… they're getting lively and are on the move."

McCardle didn't immediately react over the airways. Instead, she cursed only to herself and to those with her in the hospitality suite and VIP box overlooking the football pitch.

"Sergeant? Are you still there?"

"*I'm here. How long do we have?*"

"I don't know. Best guess is ten… maybe twenty minutes tops." Five minutes had already passed since she had left the general's command centre. Annabelle's voice became tense. "But that's not your main problem."

"*Main problem?*" McCardle chuckled humourlessly. There was always something worse to think on. "*What is it then, please do tell…*"

"When the flies attack, General Makepeace has been autho-rised to use an airstrike to obliterate them. I only found out this morning. Baylem already knows."

"*What?*" said McCardle traumatically.

"I thought I could change the general's mind and told the DI to keep it hush-hush. We didn't want to cause alarm. Unfortunately, I failed."

"*They can't… it's not possible, not without…*" killing everyone with them.

"Yep…" she didn't need to spell it out. "It's what the general calls 'decisive' action."

"*But that would need the prime minister to sign it off…*"

"Who else do you think authorised it?"

"*Fuck…*" It didn't seem real and the expletive hardly expressed her fear or the insurmountable anger building up within her. "*Remind me never, ever to vote for David Humphries,*" said McCardle deadpan. She sighed desperately. "*What do we do?*"

What DO we do? Annabelle pondered the question sitting there on the edge of the toilet seat. The situation appeared hopeless, but she didn't want to share that thought with the detective sergeant.

"Try and get hold of Baylem; find out what's taking him so long. You're running out of time.

"Otherwise, maybe you could evacuate the football stadium before the missile strikes."

"But... what about the flies?"

Annabelle didn't know what to suggest. Damned if you do and damned if you don't. Not offering any solution, she said: "It does seem to be a bit of a Morton's fork."

"You're not helping!" McCardle remonstrated, sounding desperate.

Annabelle exhaled heavily. The heat of the late morning confined within the tiny toilet cubicle felt almost as oppressive as the situation. "I know," she conceded dismally, "I will think of something. I promise. Carry on with the plan... I'll get back to you shortly."

CHAPTER TWENTY-SIX

"I ALWAYS WANTED TO BE A policeman," said Munroe Malhotra excitedly, "but I had neither the build nor the temperament." The entomologist looked small within the driving seat of the marked police car, a BMW 530D Touring. Gunning the engine, he navigated the vehicle in the opposite direction to that taken by Baylem, Randall and the two uniformed constables. He was closely following the auburn-haired woman in her SUV.

At the crossroads, Bill Crawley instructed them to take a right, losing Annabelle Herman who drove ahead towards the signposted A-road leading out of town.

"The farm is not far from here," stated the farmer in the back seat, "just ten or so minutes, likely quicker with the roads bein' empty an' all."

It seemed crazy to Quisenberry, sitting in the passenger seat of a police car on official business with a strange Indian man sitting next to him and an out-of-sorts farmer peering from behind between the gap of his and Malholtra's seat. The whole situation was surreal, like an extremely weird dream experienced prior to waking.

For the rest of the journey, the three travelled silently, contemplating their task. The more Quisenberry thought on what they were about to embark on, the more apprehensive and panicked he felt. So much was riding on their mission; it felt as though he was burdened with the weight of the world on his shoulders.

After ten minutes, land belonging to the farmer soon appeared.

Fields of yellow rapeseed yet to be harvested stretched into the distance on their left, and crops of potatoes and onions filled large squares of land on their right. Half a mile ahead, steel sheds, silos and farm buildings could be seen huddled together, shimmering and glinting brightly under the morning sun hanging indifferently halfway up the eastern sky.

"This here your farm?" asked Quisenberry pleasantly with a slight stammer, just for something to say, his nerves betraying him. He had half-turned so that he was facing the farmer.

"Aye, yes. Been in the family for four generations," replied Crawley, "though I'll likely be the last."

"Oh... you not married?" asked Malhotra intrigued and genuinely curious.

"Once," Crawley said gravely. "Betty died of cancer, back in two thousand and eleven."

"Oh. Sorry to hear that," replied Quisenberry sadly.

The farmer batted off the sympathy. "My daughter – Laura – upped and left shortly after that, went travelling around the world or joined the circus or some such; and we never had any sons. Plus, I was an only child."

Quisenberry said nothing and the car fell silent.

"The entrance is just up there," Crawley announced subdued, his eyes downcast. He shook the gloom from his mood and pointed animatedly ahead. "You'll need to follow the road round to the shed at the back. That's where I keep ol' Dusty."

"Dusty?" asked Quisenberry confused.

"Aye. The Cessna. Most people think it's named after what I use it for – dusting crops. Or a nod towards that cute animation film those folks at Disney did. But it's actually after Dusty Springfield.

"When I was young and stupid, I wanted to marry her. That was back in the seventies... I even met her once, that was in eighty-two," he started to laugh; the absence of teeth in his mouth gave him a sinister, carved pumpkin look. "She signed my LP and shook me by the hand."

Malhotra and Quisenberry rolled their eyes.

"From that moment, I was smitten," continued Crawley.

The entomologist steered the BMW through a marked entrance into the farm and then followed a dirt road that ran adjacent to the single carriageway on the opposite side of a thicket of blackberry bushes that bordered much of the farmland.

Two minutes later and the three men were walking towards a hangar that looked more like an old derelict barn missing its front doors.

Inside was Bill Crawley's old red Cessna188 plane, Dusty.

Stored alongside the aircraft were metal drums stacked five deep and twice as high. Each was clearly labelled: *Dichlorvus*, together with 'poison' and 'highly toxic' stickers. A small forklift was parked towards the rear of the room.

"It's a'ready fuelled for take-off. We jus' need ta fill up the liquid dispersal tank... which should-na take more than a couple of mins... that is, with your help... and then I'm good to go."

"*You're* good to go? We're not all coming?" Quisenberry didn't hide the relief from his voice.

"I'd like to know where ya think you'll be sitting... it's jus' a one seater. I can hardly 'ave you perched on me lap! But don't ya worry boys; you're not jus' here for spectating.

"Come, let's not tarry; you can drag over one of t'ose drums... be careful not to drop it!" Crawley crossed the shed to where an industrial hose pipe, wound into a coil, hung from a rusty iron wall bracket. He pulled it down and carried it over his shoulder to the rear of the Cessna.

2

"*James...? Munroe...? Are you there?*"

"We're here," replied Malhotra, lifting the two-way to the side of his head. He and Quisenberry were in Bill Crawley's conservatory annexed to the house, sitting in wicker armchairs and sipping ice-cold lemonade from tall glasses. From where they were sitting, they could see the rear of the small aircraft hangar and a number of outbuildings, mostly storage sheds. The farmer was somewhere else in the house changing into his 'flying clothes' and had likely just used a toilet, from the sound of flushing water and the banging of old pipes that filled the room. "Is that you, Detective Sergeant?"

"*Yes,*" McCardle replied abruptly. "*Listen, there's not much time. I've just received word that the flies are on the move. We think they are about to attack.*"

"Okay. We're ready... just give us the nod," said the entomologist casually, like they were preparing entertainment at a summer fete instead of carrying the fate of the town in their grasp.

"*Oh God!*" whimpered McCardle through the two-way. "*They're here. THEY'RE HERE!*"

"Say again, Sergeant?"

"*The flies... in the sky... so many of them... it's too late. Baylem is too late.*" From around McCardle, screaming sounds came through the two-way's speakers before abruptly cutting out.

"I think that was our nod," suggested Quisenberry.

"Sergeant McCardle?" Malhotra spoke urgently. "Sergeant McCardle?!"

At that moment, Bill Crawley stepped into the conservatory.

Despite the temperature edging into the high twenties and summer far from showing signs of abating, he appeared fancy dressed as Biggles; brown leather jacket with a shearling collar, a classic leather flying helmet and a pair of black Halcyon aviator goggles which were pushed up above his eyes across the front of his head. All he was missing was the big white scarf flapping to the side of his neck.

Quisenberry stifled laughter. Amusement twinkled in Malhotra's eyes but he showed no other signs of being affected.

"What?" asked the farmer self-consciously.

"I think it's time, *Johnny Johnson*," said Quisenberry mischievously.

"Huh?" The reference was totally lost on the farmer who had never heard of the British fighter pilot. Johnny Johnson had been the leading Allied air ace in Europe during World War 2, shooting down a total of thirty-eight German planes. "Is tha' your fancy way of sayin' I shoul' haul me-ass over to Dusty?"

"Uh, yes," replied Malhotra. "Yes, it is."

CHAPTER TWENTY-SEVEN

/

"THE FLIES... IN THE SKY... so many of them... it's too late. Baylem is too late." The two-way radio handset in which she had been talking to Dr Malhotra slipped from McCardle's fingers and clattered to the floor.

Men, women and children began screaming at the moving swell of insects that floated above the stadium, disc-shaped, like a flying saucer half a mile above their heads. Gradually, the swarm blotted out the sun and submerged the football arena under a cover of artificial darkness.

Dr Hamilton charged into the hospitality suite. "They're back!" he yelled excitedly. The police pathologist had been keeping an eye out through a window of the Centre Spot bar and restaurant, overlooking the exterior of the football ground. The vantage point provided ample view of the road which Baylem, and those assisting him, had taken.

"*Sergeant McCardle?*" The DS ignored the radio that was still on the floor and ran out of the room in a blur, skipping past women and children who congregated in packs along the corridor, and leaping down a flight of steps two at a time. She almost stumbled at the bottom. Regaining her feet, she navigated her way towards the only unlocked door within the building; a closely guarded secret; one that was watched strictly by a couple of uniformed constables.

"What kept you?!" McCardle shrieked as Baylem burst out of his Audi, having brought the vehicle to a sudden, screeching halt just ahead of where his subordinate had exited the stadium.

Parking up on the pavement nearby were the two police vans driven by Anders and Manning (manoeuvred so that the rears were positioned close to the door) and alongside them was Randall's police car. Baylem had been the last to arrive, boxing them in.

The DI ignored the question. Sighting the ominous black cloud floating in from the north of the town and hearing the growing, repetitive hum that filled the air, he believed his energies were better spent coordinating distribution of the protective clothing and masks rather than briefing out the derangement of his excursion. "Get as many people to assist with unloading these vans as you can. There's no time."

McCardle wheeled around and disappeared back into the stand. Barely a second had passed when she returned, closely followed by several groups of women and children. With the exception of a handful of police staff, the men were all out on the field, exposed to the massing insects droning eagerly above the stadium.

Randall, Anders and Manning had opened up the vans and were hastily pulling out boxes and piling them on the pavement. Baylem was then collecting them and promptly putting sets together for distribution. "Get these to the football pitch at once," he ordered. A woman police officer picked up a large box of coveralls; a young girl accepted two smaller ones containing latex gloves and half face masks, and an elderly woman took hold of a box of overshoes.

As one group of individuals withdrew into the stadium, another took their place, then another, the growing buzz of the flies around them competing with the excited voices of helpers working feverishly hard with their allocation duties; all the time, the lengthening shade of living cloud stretched across the foreground, spurring them to work desperately faster.

Through the PA system, Chief Superintendent Mills spoke loudly, his voice booming with authority inside – and outside – of the stadium, his message specifically for those fated to remain outside on the football pitch:

"*Gentlemen… collect your protective clothing in an orderly manner and proceed to completely cover yourselves at once… it is imperative that you do this as swiftly as possible…*"

People streamed out through the gap in the narrow doorway, and flowed ever-faster back in.

Keeping up with demand, the four police officers – Baylem, Randall, Manning and Anders – continued unloading the vans. It felt like a fight against time and, soon after, DS McCardle and Dr Floyd Hamilton had joined the fray.

Everyone worked at breakneck speed for a little over three minutes.

"That's the last of them," declared PC Anders, tossing a box of coveralls heavily over to Baylem which he then handed across to a pretty blonde woman in a flowing white dress that she wore with a black belt buckled around her waist. He gave her a warm smile which she returned before hurrying away.

"Okay… let's get in off the street." The DI looked up towards the black mass of insects hovering half a mile above his head; they seemed to be moving in an ominous whirl, like a forming twister. "Those flies could attack at any moment."

"How many do you think there are?" asked the DS following Randall, Anders and Manning into the stand. Baylem took up the rear position.

"Billions," he said quietly, closing the door behind him. "Billions and billions…"

McCardle locked the door and covered the cracks and gaps up around the frame with silver duct tape and then ran her fingers along the length of it, making sure it was smooth, securely fixed and sealing them in.

2

"DO NOT PANIC!!"

Chief Superintendent Mills was continuing to address the stadium through the PA system. It was, by now, so dark that the floodlighting – set atop towers of framework positioned in the four corners of the ground – had been switched on. Watching the flies begin their attack, the senior police officer started to wonder whether *that* had been a good idea, thinking that maybe the effulgent glow washing down across the pitch was attracting them.

In addition to seeing the flies dropping into the stadium in thick clumps of buzzing black death, Mills watched dozens of men – the ones last to receive their protective clothing – struggle frantically to slip into the over-garments, one tripping over thin air and falling to the floor in panic, another sticking his foot awkwardly into his coverall and ripping it into worthlessness in the process. Feeling hopeless, one man tossed his PVC clothing aside after balling it up in frustration, and sat on the tinder-dry grass accepting his fate. He crossed his arms and legs in defiance.

Sensing those without protection were the weakest, the flies attacked them first, focusing on faces and their vulnerabilities; the eyes, the ears, the nose and the mouth. Now well-practised, the flies brought grown men down to their knees in no time and suffocated them under three inches thick of compressed insect bodies, seemingly taking pleasure from each of their initial kills with exuberant, high-pitched buzzing.

The first to die was the man who'd ripped his coverall; initially, he had struggled, flapping aimlessly at the cluster of insects falling down on him like bloated raindrops, swatting at the many that attempted to land on his face, but it wasn't enough to make a difference. He then rolled around the patch of land he occupied as though he were on fire and was trying to extinguish the flames. Flies soon forced their way into his body via his nose, crawling and biting through the nasal cavity, burrowing along the linked air passages until eventually entering his oesophagus. The man's struggles ended abruptly as the flies successfully restricted his airways, cutting off his oxygen supply.

Dr Hamilton, standing at a window within the hospitality suite, watched the tussle on the football pitch between men and flies. He could just about see the melee, though visibility was reducing by the second as the heavy swarm of bluebottles settled into the football ground like a dense fog.

Mills was standing next to Hamilton, as were DI's Randall and Hardy. Each of them wore grim expressions and looked on helplessly.

The pathologist counted fifteen unprotected citizens struggling to fend off the insects, horrified and amazed in equal measure at how effortlessly the flies brought each victim down. Before the last of them had fallen, Hamilton's view was completely obstructed by the sheer volume of flying insects. Muffled screams and rebellious roars filled the stands normally associated with shouts of encouragement, cheers of celebration, or chants of: "The referee's a wanker!"

The entire football ground was a blur of throbbing dark movement. The floodlighting became subdued and less intense as insects carpeted the glowing beacons, sending the arena into gloomy chaos.

Baylem and McCardle ran into the room.

"Is it working?" the DI demanded to know, having to shout to be heard over the noise of droning insects. McCardle looked out apprehensively upon seeing – or not seeing – the pitch; so dark, she thought it looked similar to the contents of a mug of coffee. "Damn," she lamented in a whisper.

Hamilton shook his head unconsciously. "I don't know. There are so many, I can't see anything."

"We can't have much time." McCardle snatched up a two-way radio from the back of the room and turned it on. A squeal of static was released in protest.

"What do you mean?" not understanding, Baylem turned to face his partner, his back now to the pitch-side window. "The plan WILL work... have a little faith."

"It's not the plan that's the issue," said McCardle, "it's Makepeace."

"Makepeace?" Baylem looked confused.

"Annabelle told me about his plan. You know, about blowing us up!"

"Shit... I thought Annabelle was going to put a stop to that!"

Ignoring him, the DS spoke into the radio. "Doctor Malhotra? Are you there?"

"...*thank God!*" exclaimed the entomologist digitally through the built-in speaker of the communication device. "*Is everything all right...?*"

"Is the plane ready?"

"*Yes, but...*"

"No time to explain it, but we could do with Crawley doing a fly-over around about now."

"*He's on it.*" The sound of an engine began to chug over the airwaves, deep, growing in power, and then slowly beginning to fade.

The red Cessna 188 lurched forward out of the hangar and trundled sluggishly across a strip of asphalt that led towards a stretch of dusty land running the full length of one of Bill Crawley's fields; a makeshift, but adequate runway.

The pilot, Bill Crawley himself, stared through the side window of his single-seat aircraft and gave a small hand salute towards Quisenberry and Malhotra standing outside the building as he passed. He could see the entomologist speaking into a two-way radio.

Both Quisenberry and Malhotra acknowledged the farmer with a gentle wave, like they were seeing off a child on a pleasure trip, and watched as the red plane turned right off the asphalt and on to the runway. Without a pause, the Cessna began to accelerate, kicking up a cloud of dust and pollen in its wake which drifted across the farm in hazy patches.

"He's on it," said the entomologist into the radio. He turned to watch Crawley pilot the aircraft almost the entire length of runway before aerodynamics played their part, appearing to pluck it up into the air.

"*That's good. It might not be enough, though,*" replied McCardle amidst the sound of static, a low persistent hum, and the smattering of distant screams. She then proceeded to tell him what Annabelle Herman had found out about General Makepeace and his solution towards eradicating Quisenberry's genetically enhanced flies.

"Shit," exclaimed the geneticist listening close-by. "Despite our solution, Makepeace is going to blow up the stadium anyway?"

"*That's the cut and drift of it,*" said McCardle blithely, "*unless Annabelle finds a way to stop him.*"

Malhotra could think of nothing to say. His lips were moving but no sound came through them. His family was safe back in London but he couldn't help feeling terrible for the plight of the people he had been drafted in to help.

"I always knew he was an arsehole, but... this..." Quisenberry shook his head contemplatively, trying to get a grasp of what it was he wanted to say, "... this gives a whole new meaning to the word..." Then something alarming occurred to him: "Gemma!"

His girlfriend and their newborn son, Morton, were both in the stadium having been moved from the hospital along with most of the other patients, together with the rest of the town. He snatched the two-way radio off Malhotra and hurriedly spoke into it: "You've got to get Gemma and Morton out of there!"

McCardle recognised Quisenberry's voice. *"James... I can't. They'd be exposed. The flies are outside... it's too late... it would be worse than death."*

In Annabelle's experience, time usually sped up when you were up against it and needed it most, and slowed down when it unfailingly wasn't.

Today was no exception as the young Home Office assistant checked the time on her Swarovski watch, its fifty-six sparkling crystals embellishing the outermost edge of the white silver-tone sunray dial, glinted and reflected dots of prismed light onto the ceiling of the dining marquee.

The time was 10:48 a.m.

Standing close behind her in the queue were her chaperones; Lieutenant Clark and the fresh-faced private someone-or-other; both had been ordered to babysit her whilst she was on base. Ahead of her was the serving counter where coffee was being poured and plates of full English breakfasts were being dished out.

A few minutes earlier, after ending her radio communication with McCardle, she had stepped down from the mobile toilet facility, looking vitalised and showing no signs of the unease she actually felt. "I'm ready for that coffee now," she had said, still thinking that a stiff drink would be preferable. Together, they had walked round to the front of the white marquee and entered, joining an established queue. The thick aroma of bacon and burnt toast assailed their nostrils.

Now, five minutes later, they neared the front of the line.

"Next!" called out one of the four caterers standing behind the counter as the soldier immediately ahead moved away, collecting his hot drink and cooked meal as he went.

"Coffee, please... plenty of milk; semi-skimmed. And a bottle of Evian."

"I know that voice!" boomed someone to Annabelle's left. Instinctively, she turned as a familiar face bobbed through a small crowd and bounded towards her. She remembered him from the police station yesterday when he had accompanied General Makepeace to a meeting with Chief Superintendent Mills and DI Baylem. He had been standing at the door when the general had sent her off on a beverage run.

"Fancy seeing you here," said the newcomer appearing to push into the front of the queue. One or two soldiers hissed and moaned their dissent, but the newcomer was ranked higher than most in the marquee; but not the lieutenant standing behind Annabelle.

"Do you know Annabelle Herman, Sergeant Pope?" asked Clark casually, stepping out of the queue. The private behind reluctantly followed him.

"A long time ago," Pope answered. "We were at school together. West Mersey High."

Cognizant that they were in the way of the line of soldiers queuing for food and beverages, the quartet stepped a few feet to the right.

"I wondered if you remembered me!" said Annabelle enthusiastically. "I recognised you yesterday... at the station." The caterer across the counter handed over coffee in a disposable cup and the bottle of water. She accepted both with a nod and a smile.

"I saw you look at me funny, but I didn't recognise you at first..." he replied sheepishly. "I even heard the general call you Annabelle a few times, but it wasn't until later that it clicked; then I remembered who you were."

"We only sat next to each other for two years doing GCSE

Physics," she said with a nervous laugh. "AND... you asked me to Prom."

"Yea, well... you said no if I recall..."

"I'd promised Andrew Reeves already!"

"Anyway," he said nonchalant, "when it did occur to me who you were, I was busy orchestrating some roundups. When I got back, you weren't anywhere to be found."

"Too bad." Annabelle sounded disappointed.

"Yea, well... that's life. Fate is fickle. Maybe we could go for a drink sometime... when this is all over?"

"How about now?" she asked eagerly. "Though, I'm already fixed," she indicated her coffee. "I'm sure Lieutenant Clark here won't mind. I bet he's got plenty else to be doing..."

"Err..." dithered the lieutenant. Neurons appeared to fail to connect within his brain for an extended moment.

"I've got fifteen minutes spare. I can have her back with you in no time," volunteered Pope amiably. "Come on, Lieutenant... do me a solid?"

"Sure, okay," said Clark hesitantly. "I guess the general only said that you should be escorted at all times and not left unattended," he recalled. "He didn't say anything about who should be doing it."

"Yay," Annabelle half-celebrated, smiling.

"When you're done, sergeant, make sure you see Annabelle returned into my care. I don't need to remind you our rules with regards to civilians..."

The Cessna 188 ascended to a height of six thousand feet, just under half the maximum service ceiling for the aircraft, before slowly coming back down again as sight of Fulbarton Town Football stadium appeared in the distance.

Bill Crawley was seated snugly in the cockpit with a hand on the single thrust lever positioned between his legs. An arrangement of basic dials was set within the instrument panel ahead of him, most easy to identify; fuel gauge, airspeed, altimeter, attitude indicator (also known as the artificial horizon), turn coordinator, and clock, amongst others. To the right were rows of numbered buttons and electrical switches (some glowing white or red) and further on the right were various levers and other push and pull buttons, most required to fly the plane, but some related to crop dusting and the distribution of pesticides.

The smell of aviation fuel could be detected within the small cabin, with a hint of something else; a chemical scent often smelt within museums where curators use strips coated in Dichlorvus to fumigate exhibition rooms.

"*Bill... you there?*" James Quisenberry's voice filled the farmer's ears. Earphones were wrapped around the side of his head, connected to the radio fitted into a slot beneath the instrument panel on a coiled lead.

"Aye," he replied. "Where else d'you think I'd be? Disneyland?"

Quisenberry ignored the sarcasm. "*You need to hurry. We're running out of time.*"

"I know! Tie a knot in it, dear boy, I'm nearly there..." He was a mile from the stadium and had taken the Cessna down to two thousand feet. "Good God!" he exclaimed. Although Malhotra had relayed Sergeant McCardle's dire exhortations regarding the fly attack, nothing had prepared him for what he was now seeing. "Christ! Flies... millions of the little buggers!"

A strange thought occurred to Bill Crawley as he gradually closed-in; the stadium appeared to be caught within a black, shimmering bubble. It reminded him of one of those glass snow globes you could often get at tourist attractions or from the capitals of the world, when all shook up; except, instead of white flecks marring the scene, a frenzy of black specks filled the spheroid.

"Yea, well, it gets better. The army figures they have a better way to rid the town of its fly problem... only; there won't be anyone left to enjoy it."

"What?"

A booming, subsonic sound outside the aircraft addressed his question, amplifying above the six-cylinder engine that putted, bombinated and vibrated through every square inch of the Cessna, growing louder by the second.

Before the farmer had time to contemplate the direction it was coming, the RAF Tornado fighter plane thundered from ahead, causing a wave of turbulence to hit and unsettle the small agricultural craft.

Bill Crawley felt the Cessna drop ten feet and his stomach five feet further. The small plane lurched to one side, then rocked and juddered as he wrestled with the thrust lever and hit buttons in a random fashion, trying to regain control.

"They mean to blow them up...!"

Initially, Crawley didn't grasp what the man was saying. Then it snapped. "Not if I can help it. Over," he said, twisting his head around the cockpit for sight of the military aircraft whilst bringing the Cessna back level.

The Tornado was nowhere in sight, but he could still hear it, the roar of its engine like a rocket rumbling in the sky. The football ground and the billowing fog of flies were now less than a quarter of a mile away. The farmer pushed the small plane towards its maximum speed of 120 mph.

In the distance, the military aircraft was circling the town ominously, either for a second flyover or preparing to fire its missile.

Speaking to himself, Crawley began flicking switches. "Okay... turning on the distribution system..." He took the Cessna down five hundred feet, the aircraft now appearing low in the sky with the football ground almost directly below it. "Three... two... one..." The farmer pressed the red release button. "Bye bye."

Attached to the wings of the Cessna, a dozen nozzles began spraying a fine mist of liquid, producing a swirling white vapour trail in its wake that a gentle summer breeze helped disburse across the entire width of the stadium (and a hundred feet to either side). In a haze, the Dichlorvus fell softly, the effects of the pesticide fast acting.

Bill Crawley turned the Cessna around and repeated the process, peering down at the targeted area as he glided past.

The black cloud hanging around the stadium thinned out as flies succumbed to the poison, falling like the fighter planes shot down by Johnny Johnson during World War 2, the undulating drone of their buzz increasing in pitch as they fought desperately to live. The Dichlorvus destroyed the nervous systems of the insects, swiftly killing them.

"Wahoo! See them fall... Fuck yea!"

The farmer's celebration came to an abrupt and premature end as Quisenberry's voice sounded loud and desperate in his ears. "*Oh, Jesus... no, no, NO!*"

In the distance, Crawley saw the RAF Tornado doing a Top Gun manoeuvre and the flash of something surging through the sky away from it, and – more disturbingly – towards him, the sun glinting off its cylindrical surface. The missile's trajectory was shifting at a slightly downwards angle.

"Have they gone yet?" asked Annabelle discreetly, leaning across the table. Sergeant Pope was sitting opposite her in the mess hall, stirring sugar into his steaming cup of tea. A side plate to his left had a quintessentially English snack item – a scone with two small pots; one of cream, the other strawberry jam.

Directing his attention over the auburn-haired woman's shoulders, the soldier nodded. "They've just stepped out."

"Good. John, I need your help." It took the Home Office assistant less than a minute to explain the general's plan, the alternative solution that James Quisenberry and Munroe Malhotra had developed, and the plight facing the people of Fulbarton Town.

Pope slumped back into his seat. "Are you serious?" He sounded unconvinced. He started stirring his tea again.

"Why do you think Makepeace evacuated the military from the area?"

"But, even so; thirty thousand people? Sounds crazy." Pope was shaking his head, undecided.

"Desperation sometimes leads to bad decisions... You of all people know that. You need to trust me on this; we're running out of time. We need to stop the general... before it's too late."

John Pope continued to stir his tea; his eyes were focused on the concentric ripples caused by his spoon.

"John? Will you help me?"

He looked up, his eyes hard. "Yea, okay. I'll help. On condition that you agree to go to the Prom with me... or, should I say, dinner and perhaps a movie after?"

"Maybe," she said evasively, smiling. "Now, how do we stop the general?"

"I do have an idea." Sergeant Pope said slyly. He raised his cup of tea and took a deep mouthful. "Tell me, do you need that water?" He nodded towards Annabelle's bottle of Evian.

Three minutes later, they were standing in an area filled with army vehicles, hidden from clear view. Olive green Jeeps, Leyland DAF trucks and non-descript cars were parked in rows a short distance from where the Westland Lynx helicopter had been set down, their drivers nowhere to be found. The Portakabin was forty metres to their right and the silhouettes of General Makepeace and Major Broadbent could be made out through the slats of the venetian blinds half-drawn at one of the windows.

"Are you sure this will work?"

"Nothing's certain," replied Pope. "But, it's the best way to slow them down. I'm confident." He sounded it. "Wait here." Without further explanation, the sergeant loped off towards the rear of the mobile command centre, Annabelle's bottle of mineral water in his left hand. Shortly, he disappeared around the side of a Leyland truck, away from Annabelle's eyeline.

"What are you doing, Miss Herman? Where's Sergeant Pope?"

Lieutenant Jordan Clark had crept into view; instinctively, his hand had dropped to the gun holstered at his waist.

"He... ur..." Annabelle shrugged. "I don't know. He said he had somewhere else he needed to be," she replied impulsively. "He led me part of the way and I said I could find my way back for the rest. Looks like I found you... yay!"

"Come... this way."

Annabelle glanced to her right, focusing on the truck she had seen Pope vanish behind. With reluctance, she followed the lieutenant towards the mobile command centre, passing army vehicles and the front of the Lynx helicopter. The pilot was inside, busy with something.

As they entered the Portakabin, General Makepeace looked up firmly. "Annabelle, you're just in time for the main event." The earlier frostiness was gone from his voice, the woman's disapprovals forgotten.

"Oh great! It's not every day you get to witness the murder of thirty thousand people..."

Makepeace ignored the comment, instead, directing his attention to a voice that was amplified through radio equipment set up in the centre of the room. *"We are coming in hot and have visuals on the target... over."*

From outside, the roar of the fighter plane could be heard echoing all around, the subsonic speed causing an elongated booming sound above their heads and the ground to shake beneath their feet. On the large screen at the back of the room, live images were still being broadcast from the drone.

No longer set to radio wave frequency, the aerial picture showed Fulbarton in the regular hues of greens, greys, browns and technicolour beneath glorious July sunshine. The football stadium, needlessly highlighted with a computer-generated graphic ring around it, was a palpitating blur of evil blackness. The fly strike had taken place less than a minute earlier after circumnavigating the grounds to allow for the entire force to come together. It had flown in from the west.

"On my word, Flight Lieutenant," Makepeace directed his voice towards the radio equipment. "Open fire..."

"Copy that."

Makepeace turned to where Captain Dodd was peering over the shoulder of a VDU operator. "Dodd, are we satisfied the flies are all in there? Any stragglers, can you see?"

"They've committed their entire swarm," confirmed the captain confidently.

"Good, okay. Flight Lieutenant Higson," he directed his voice over towards the conference call microphone on the centre desk. "Fi–" *re.*

BANG!

The large screen on the back of the wall, all the VDUs around the room, the lights, the radio equipment, and everything else electrical flickered or crackled on and off and on again, before dying completely.

"WHAT THE HELL JUST HAPPENED!!" shouted Makepeace angrily.

"We've lost power," said Tim Howlett hapless and obviously. An idiot never needed encouragement to live up to expectations, and the CEO of Biomargent Sciences was proving the point.

"Must be the generators," suggested Captain Dodd. "I'll go take a look." The officer stepped away from the VDU operator and moved efficiently towards the command centre's exit.

"Seems like what you planned is over, General," said Annabelle stuffily. "Perhaps you'll now give Quisenberry's plan a chance."

"You!" Makepeace waggled an accusatory finger towards the Home Office assistant. "You've got something to do with this," he accused.

Looking pleased, Annabelle pulled her two-way radio from her handbag and turned a knob. "Sergeant McCardle, do you read me, over?"

Sneering, General Makepeace located his mobile phone, speed dialled a number, placed it against his ear and then waited for his call to connect. Scowling at the young woman, he just heard her two-way crackle in response when the small speaker of his phone began to speak. Allowing the recipient no room to talk beyond a pleasant greeting, Makepeace spoke brusquely: "This is General Makepeace. Our comms with Flight Lieutenant Higson have broken down. As a matter of urgency, can you relay this order: FIRE WHEN READY!"

"*Annabelle, it's working! The farmer has just flown over spraying the insecticide. You should see it! The flies... they're falling like flakes of black snow...*"

Huffishly, Annabelle spun around and hurried out of the Portakabin, thrusting the door wide with the flat of one hand. It smacked the outside wall with a crash.

"It's all for nothing," Annabelle bemoaned. Looking eastward, away from Fulbarton, she could just perceive the RAF Tornado in the distance, the noise of its flight booming around the cloudless sky. For a moment, the fighter plane seemed to just hang in the air, and then it was moving, shooting forward like a discharged bullet. A split-second later and an object came free beneath the aircraft, dropped a hundred feet and then blasted forward, racing ahead of the aircraft at an impressive speed. Having released its payload, the Tornado changed course, made a turn and then turbo-boosted heavenward.

Whooosshhh!!

The Storm Shadow missile tore through the azure sky smoothly as it headed towards the small town, its trajectory perfectly horizontal. The target predestined.

"I'm sorry," she said, wretchedly. "I've failed you all."

Around the back of the temporary construction were four diesel-powered generators interconnected and wired into a control box/outlet hook-up unit, feeding electricity into the Portakabin. With up to 18kW from each, there was more than enough power to run all the highly sensitive electronics and communications systems inside, with three of the units there mainly as a backup.

Pope checked the surrounding area, making sure no one was watching as he stepped over to the power generators; diesel engines rumbled quietly, housed within a 'silenced' weather-proof casing that produced just sixty-five decibels of noise each.

The smell of exhaust fumes was thick in the air and the sergeant pulled up the front of his shirt to cloak his mouth and nose so not to breathe it in.

Ropes of wires led from one generator to another, and continued into the back of the grey control box/hook-up unit. It was the size of a small square waste bin, staked into the ground just a metre from the back of the temporary building. Cables ran from the mobile command centre and ended in the front side of the grey box, plugged into four 32A straight plug sockets.

Moving casually, Pope drifted over to the grey control box, dropped down to a squat and considered the setup. The simplest way to disrupt power to the mobile command centre was to just pull out the plugs. But that would only be a temporary disruption, one which was easily and swiftly rectifiable.

He needed to do something elaborate, something that would scupper General Makepeace's plans and totally disable the command centre indefinitely, or for as long as can be devastatingly advantageous.

The solution had come to him back at the marquee.

Casually, Pope loosened the plugs halfway out of the sockets and then twisted off the blue lid from the bottle of Evian water. Holding the plastic bottle two-handed ahead of him, he carefully aimed, squeezing the water in a jet towards the four plug sockets.

Water and electricity is not a match made in heaven. Combining the two together themselves does not pose too much of an immediate problem; however, water – especially mineral water with all its latent contaminates – is very conductive. Pope knew this, and he knew something else; squirting the water at such an angle so as to strike the half-exposed plug connectors all at the same time would cause the current to increase and merge together.

The result was a small display of electrical sparks, some pops and fizzes, and some tiny flashes of lightning between each of the four sockets, reminding the sergeant of an old plasma globe his dad used to have. When placing a hand on it, tendrils of ignited plasma would dance and stretch within the ball in response, providing hours of mesmerised amusement.

BANG!

Waking him from pleasant thoughts, the control/outlet hook-up box blew up with a sound reminiscent to a firecracker inside a tin dustbin. A small orange flame appeared from one of the sockets and a wisp of black smoke fanned out towards the sky from one of the others.

Wasting no time, the sergeant took a few backward steps and retraced the way back to the transitory carpark, hunkering down low as he passed the Lynx helicopter and running close to a sprint to where he had left Annabelle just a few minutes earlier.

Arriving at the exact spot, short of breath, two emotions wrestled for greater attention; relief and a nagging fear.

He was relieved to make it back undetected. But where was Annabelle?

The roar of the RAF Tornado tearing through the sky drew his attention momentarily away from the matter of Annabelle's absence. Looking up, his eyes fell upon the warplane at the exact moment Flight Lieutenant Higson received the relayed order from RAF Marham to fire the missile.

It was then that Pope realised that his great idea had failed. Not only had he let Annabelle Herman down, his actions had fallen disastrously short in delivering the townspeople of Fulbarton from an unjust and horrifying death.

9

"I see him!" announced Dr Hamilton, staring through the windows looking out of the stadium. Although the vast swarm of flies had blotted out the sun on the pitch-side of the stand, sunlight and plenty of sky could be seen from the other side. Bill Crawley's red Cessna 188 was descending from the sky fast. Because of the drone from the flies, its six-cylinder engine could not be heard over the din.

"In the nick of time, I imagine," said Baylem soberly. Sergeant McCardle smiled, overcome with joy and relief. The horror would soon be over and life could return back to normal.

Even before the small aircraft was overhead, the farmer proceeded with the spraying of the Dichlorvus insecticide. A fine drizzle of liquid cascaded from twelve nozzles affixed to the underside of the plane's wings, producing a misty-white vapour that washed over the neighbouring streets and buildings, raining down on the parked vehicles and beginning to splash and spatter the stadium's external windows. A summer breeze aided the disbursement of the insecticide, blowing it over a wide area, ensuring the entire width of the stadium, and a good area beyond it, was covered. In a smoky, steamy haze, the Dichlorvus cascaded in waves, the effects of the poison rapid.

"He's gone the full length of the pitch," asserted Hamilton excitedly. "He's now coming back. Looks to be giving it the 'twice over'."

Bill Crawley turned the Cessna around, descended a couple of dozen feet and repeated the process having already delivered half the tank's contents.

The black cloud of murderous flies succumbed to the effects of the poison. Before they could communicate alarm, warning or the simple order to retreat, the damage was done. Though they fought desperately to live, abandoning their attack mid-flow, the flies died instantaneously, dropping from the sky like obsidian hailstones or flecks of charcoal.

"*Sergeant McCardle, do you read me, over?*"

"Annabelle, it's working! The farmer has just flown over spraying the insecticide. You should see it! The flies... they're falling like flakes of black snow..."

Whoops of joy, cries of relief and yells of triumph filled the rooms and halls of the stadium. High fives were being shared between children and adults alike. Even Chief Superintendent Mills was celebrating by shaking the hands of councillors and other local dignitaries. The mayor, Dennis Matthews, was beaming with pride and relief.

"*It's all for nothing*," lamented Annabelle through McCardle's two-way radio. She sounded distraught and defeated.

From the east side of the town, the sound of the RAF Tornado became audible now that the constant hum of flies had subsided and almost ceased, its subsonic boom echoing ominously, like an approaching storm within the ghost town.

"*I'm sorry*," Annabelle added, wretchedly. "*I've failed you all.*"

A distant 'POP!' followed by a faint 'WHOOSH!' accompanied the crack and rumble of the fighter jet flying in the distance.

The radio slipped free from the DS's hand and a small whimper escaped her lips. "It wasn't enough," she cried, turning towards the windows facing out of the stadium and slowly walking towards them. Baylem was already there, together with DIs Randall and Hardy and others, mostly women.

A glint of metal sparkled in the sky, shimmering beneath the late-morning sun. They could all see that it was a missile, and it was heading towards them.

"But we won," asserted Chief Superintendent Mills incredulously. "The flies are dead."

Floyd Hamilton said nothing. In his hand was a bottle of whiskey, half-empty, and the cap not-so-long lost. The pathologist made no apology as he raised the bottle to his lips and poured the fiery liquid into his mouth.

Detective Sergeant McCardle slipped her right hand into Baylem's left and squeezed it. "Hold me, Baylem. I don't want to die alone."

With the Storm Shadow missile fast approaching, DI Baylem turned to face his sergeant. Despite what faced them, he was coolly-defiant and serenely composed. He wrapped his arms around her slender shoulders and drew her near, almost lovingly. "Close your eyes," he said softly, as though coaxing a small child to face her fears, "and count to ten. It'll soon be over. We won't feel a thing."

"I love you," she said, burying her head into his chest. It felt unnatural and strange, but nice and exciting at the same time. Under different circumstances, she expected she might have enjoyed it.

"Shhh," Baylem soothed, one of his hands stroking through the back of her blonde hair and brushing the nape of her neck. Without thinking, he kissed the back of her head. "I love you too," he whispered.

The missile looked like a long, thin airplane with narrow wings at its centre and a combination of fins (dorsal and ventral) at its rear. Travelling at a speed upwards of 1,000 km/h, the Storm Shadow was approaching at a terrifying rate; the descent to its optimal altitude of thirty metres was gradual as it closed in on its target.

10

"*Oh, Jesus... no, no, NO!*" Quisenberry's cries almost filled the cockpit.

"Sweet mother in heaven." He had clocked the cruise missile heading towards him. Now, flying the Cessna 188 past the football ground, Crawley turned off the insecticide sprayer with a flick of a button and turned on the mic of his radio. "Gentlemen... find my daughter. Find Laura. Tell her what I did today. Tell her to do what she wants with the farm; I am at peace with what she decides. But mostly, tell her that I love her."

The red aeroplane turned sharply and set off away from Fulbarton Town Football ground, heading towards the cruise missile surging through the sky, less than quarter of a mile east.

"*What's that, Bill?*" asked Munroe Malhotra having taken the radio off James Quisenberry who was inconsolable and crying in the background.

Smoothly, Crawley flicked a couple of switches and took hold of the throttle lever, steering the plane directly into the path of the Storm Shadow missile, meeting it head-on above a residential area a safe distance from the stadium. "Over and out," he replied, not elaborating. Switching off the microphone; he removed the earphones and tossed them behind him. "Goodbye, world... you bastard!"

The explosion was intense and loud and sent shockwaves through the air, causing windows and greenhouses to shatter for more than a square mile and the earth to quake violently, felt in neighbouring villages and within the temporary basecamp where General Makepeace stood gloating satisfactorily.

Debris and fire rained down, thick oily-black smoke filled the sky, and the smell of aviation fuel, burning metal, smouldering rubber and something like brimstone, filled the air.

//

The windows of the Centre Spot bar and restaurant shattered under the thermal impact of the explosion which had been deafening and sounded close, but not as close as everyone had been expecting. Shards of glass rained in over the cowering figures of policemen and women and civilians alike, bladed-edges causing lacerations and pricking flesh.

Recovering from the ringing in her ears, McCardle lifted her head up. "Did it miss?" she asked jubilantly, a look of relief spread across her face. She was lying on the floor, DI Baylem pressed on top of her, using his body to shield her. Despite the protection, glass fragments fell from her hair.

"Not exactly," said the DI. He had watched the whole thing, and what he had seen hadn't quite sunk in yet. First, the missile was coming towards the football ground, its trajectory unlikely to miss; then Bill Crawley's red Cessna 188 circumnavigated in from the right having deposited the Dichlorvus around the stadium, swooping down in front of the building blocking the DI's view, before flying headlong, kamikaze-style, into it. "We're alive. That's all that matters," he said solemnly.

EPILOGUE

/

NORMALITY RETURNED ALMOST IMMEDIATELY AFTER
the state of emergency had been lifted some twelve
hours after the Dichlorvus had been sprayed.

Around midnight, electricity supplies and all forms of
communication into (and out of) the town were restored. A legion
of journalists, paparazzi, TV crews, and media types, excitedly
arrived in their droves despite the late hour, joining those who
had been rounded up and detained against their wishes, now back
to not only report on, but be part of the unfolding news story.

The all-clear had been given once the council's environmental
health and safety officer had done a risk assessment, checking the
air quality for pollutants and reviewing the threat-level posed by
the invading flies. For the most part, all were passed; the danger
perceived to be over (except for within the immediate vicinity of
the football ground).

Policing Fulbarton was reinstated to the town, with the army
withdrawing from the outskirts in a convoy of vehicles with little
fuss and barely a murmur.

With his tail between his legs, General Makepeace was
summoned to Whitehall where the prime minister, heading a

COBRA meeting with ministers and other high-ranking officials, demanded answers from the most senior officer in the army.

The home secretary, seated alongside David Humphries, read out a statement put together by Annabelle Herman, presenting the fact that the general had blindsided the government with regards to the 'alternative' with dealing with the fly problem. Rather, he favoured military intervention that came with a heavy cost in human life and which was narrowly averted, if not for the brave actions of a local farmer who sacrificed his own life to save thirty thousand others.

People returned to their homes, their unfinished dinners, and comfortable beds, picking up their lives from the moment when soldiers had incongruously come calling the night before, flexing their military muscles and rounding up citizens like they were escaped animals or common criminals; like something seen in an old war film or in the headlines from faraway places like Iraq or Africa.

Although the effects of the fly attack would cause sleepless nights for many, and the news companies – locally and internationally – would run stories regarding the incident with a myriad of eyewitness accounts – some true, but most fabricated – throughout the rest of the month, people gradually moved on. British communities were resilient and life in Fulbarton swiftly returned to humdrum ordinariness.

2

DI Baylem was standing in McCardle's kitchen, her cat brushing up against his legs, throwing a hopeful look up at him that he easily interpreted as: Feed me!

McCardle was emptying a tin of cat food into a ceramic bowl decorated with red and orange fish under a glazed finish. She was next to the sink. "Here you go, buster," she placed it down on the floor with a clink. No longer interested in Baylem, the cat sauntered off to the offering and buried its head in the bowl, eating with vigour. "Would you like a drink? A gin or vodka? Both? I have some wine also; I could open a bottle of red. It's been one of those days," she laughed, sounding somewhat nervous.

"Jayne? Things between us… about earlier… will we be okay?" Baylem spoke with a note of apprehension; like he was afraid to raise the subject or scared to hear the answer. "We can draw a line underneath it… if you like. We were both under a lot of stress…"

The DS smiled reassuringly, "Do you want to?" Before Baylem could reply, she continued. "Of course we'll be okay, why not? We're adults." She had opened a floor-to-ceiling cupboard and reached for a bottle of Pinot Noir.

"In that moment, when death was closing in on us, I realised something… something important. It was like having an epiphany. I made a promise there and then… that if I got out of this alive, I would do things differently."

McCardle carried the bottle of wine over to a table and set it down. She walked slowly towards her superior saying nothing, but the expression she wore spoke volumes; her eyes were imploring. She was biting her lip. Resting her hands against her legs, she clasped and unclasped them nervously.

"I realised that life is too short to just live it. I don't want to be one of those people who just exist for existing's sake; plodding their way through every day and detail until the final breath. I want to do something extraordinary, be something I am currently not; become someone other than just a DI in a mediocre town where crime rates are low and IQs even lower."

"Oh," McCardle uttered, masking her disappointment by turning her attention to the bottle of Pinot Noir and twisting the cap free. She poured good measures of wine into two glasses.

Appearing not to see the distress in his subordinate's

expression, Baylem continued, "That's why I've decided to tend my resignation tomorrow so that I can start afresh. Take a long vacation and enjoy myself a bit. I've always fancied the Caribbean or Hawaii."

"Oh," The DS repeated, turning back to face Baylem. "Here," she handed him a glass a little too forceful. Liquid sloshed over the lip and splashed over Baylem's hand. "I guess we have something to toast: your new start and vacation," she said icily.

"OUR new start…" he replied softly, placing the glass down and cleaning the wine from the back of his hand with his lips. "I was rather hoping you'd come with me." Taking McCardle's glass and putting it side-by-side with his, he leaned in close and placed a gentle, probing kiss on her lips, in a way reminiscent to dipping a toe in a pool of water to test the temperature.

McCardle licked her lips, tasting a subtle hint of red wine. "Is that all you've got?" she asked, playfully.

3

A woman in her mid-twenties stepped into a hallway that ran eight feet in length and less than a metre wide. Her medium brown hair was long, parted in the middle and hanging behind her shoulders. She was strikingly good-looking and stick-thin, her pregnancy yet to show prominence. Clutching her purse, she nervously moved along, passing the staircase on her right and a door leading into a living room on her left.

The smashed remains of a telephone had been swept into one corner of the hallway, its electronic guts and a tangle of coiled wires clumped together in a disinterested mess. Amongst it were glass shards and some smaller fragments from a broken photo frame propped against the wall nearby. The woman recognised the picture within it and casually crossed over to pick it up.

It was of her and Sean whilst they were on holiday in Majorca the first year they started dating. That had been three years ago, she reflected; she was in a tiny barely-there-bikini whilst he was bare-chested. She noticed a small mark of dried blood marring the picture, smudged across Sean's face.

"Oh Sean," she whispered, brushing a finger over the man's half-concealed appearance, her lower eyelids welled up like twin reservoirs threatening to burst their banks.

"Francesca, are we clearing the whole house?" a man in a navy blue boiler suit stepped across the threshold. On his back was a cartoon picture of a house with arms, legs, and a happy face. A company name appeared above it: Clear/Removals. The young woman – former girlfriend to Sean – had hired him to clear the house in its entirety. "Did you want to collect anything first?"

"Take it all please, Andy, if you don't mind."

"This was that fella's house, weren't it? The one killed by them flies?" the house clearance guy spoke without restraint, just making conversation, sounding light-hearted and ignorant. "What's his name...? Sean something... *Don't tell me*... it's on the tip of my tongue."

Tears rolled down Francesca's cheeks freely, the banks overflowing. A small sob racked her chest which she managed to keep hidden from the removal man behind her. It had been two weeks since she received the call telling her that he was dead. It hardly seemed fair that for all the good times she had with him, the most vibrant memory she would ever recall would be of their final conversation; the argument over the telephone when she declared her love for someone else and announced her pregnancy.

It had all been a lie; an attempt to get Sean to fight for her, to woo her once again. She'd said hurtful, callous things, and now he was dead. The guilt and regret would haunt her for the rest of her life.

"Shaun-something-or-other... WALLACE!!" he exclaimed

excitedly. "That's it! He'll be dead famous now, won't he? Everyone always remembers the first ones, don't they? Neil Armstrong – first man on the moon; Margaret Thatcher – first woman prime minister; Barack Obama – first black president of the USA; Lynsey Adams – my first shag!" he started to laugh. "They'll likely write a Trivial Pursuit question about him or give him a mention on Who Wants to Be a Millionaire."

Francesca couldn't be bothered to tell him that the show was cancelled years earlier. "Yes... well... Sean was my first everything," she sniffed. "Even this," she rubbed her stomach gently before turning her attention to her face, using the back of the hand clutching the photo frame to wipe her eyes. "I've got to get going," she said abruptly. "If you can lock up once you're done. I'll stop by to collect the keys tomorrow."

"Don't sweat the sweet stuff, love," Andy replied, "me and Dave will crack on once we've had a cup of tea."

Francesca squeezed past the house clearance guy and exited fourteen Surbiton Close, scurrying down the garden path and out through the gates, ignoring Dave – Andy's colleague – stepping down from the cab of a 13.5 tonne Mercedes 1323 lorry.

Walking into the house, Dave found Andy in the kitchen filling up an electric kettle. "Semi-skimmed milk... fresh from Sainsbury's," he said, carrying in the pint carton of white liquid. "Saw the woman who hired us on the way out... seemed in a bit of a hurry."

"Yea, well... she was only here to unlock and leave us the keys. Don't think she's the small-talk-type."

"Where are the cups?" asked Dave. He placed the milk down on a worktop and started opening up wall units and built-in cupboards randomly, banging them shut after.

"Don't know. Tea's in that one, though," Andy pointed to a floor-to-ceiling cupboard in the corner of the room. He switched the kettle on. "There's a tin of Hobnobs and Garibaldis in there too," he added excitedly.

"Great!" replied Dave eagerly, dashing across to the cupboard. "The poor bugger who died here isn't going to eat them..." He pulled open the cupboard and reached in for the barrel biscuit tin decorated with photographs of the Duke and Duchess of Cambridge, Prince William and Princess Kate, commemorating their wedding day on 29 April 2011.

Disturbed by the movement, a single blowfly buzzed out from behind the biscuit tin and darted sluggishly around the room. It used height and the closeness to the ceiling to its advantage and for sanctuary.

"Ere, Dave... did that fly just come popping out of that cupboard?"

"I dunno," he mumbled through a mouthful of Hobnob, crumbs slipping from his lips. He was clutching the biscuit tin with his forearm against his stomach.

"It couldn't be one of them killing ones, could it?" queried Andy, following the fly with his eyes as it circled the room, watched it land on a spot of coving and then take off again.

"They were all killed, weren't they? Can't you remember, Andy? We were at the footie ground at the time..."

As if by magic, a second fly joined the first, racing it around the room like their lives depended on it, their buzzing in tandem, slightly amplified.

"I fucking hate flies," proclaimed Andy fiercely. From a pile of newspapers, the house clearance guy quickly fashioned a truncheon and strode towards the corner of the room where the flies were currently swooping about, brandishing it threateningly. "Which one of you wants to die first?" he asked merrily. "Eeny... meeny... miny... MOE!" Andy smacked the rolled up newspaper hard against a fly that had momentarily settled on the wall. Pulling the makeshift bat back revealed a black and bloody pulp and a couple of twitching legs. "Gotcha!"

The second fly whizzed around the room at breakneck speed, occasionally hitting the kitchen window, fooled into thinking it was a way out by its transparency.

"Perhaps we should add pest control to our repertoire of services," chuckled Dave, absently reaching into the biscuit tin he still embraced, picking out a Garibaldi. Slowly raising it to his lips, he just caught sight of movement.

The Garibaldi was covered with a layer of shifting flies.

"What the fuck!" Startled, Dave dropped the biscuit barrel with a clatter and tossed the Garibaldi away from him, jumping back.

In a puff, the flies from the biscuit barrel – at least a hundred of them – flew up into the air in a concentric ball, their drone filling the room, resembling that of an electric razor.

The sudden appearance of more flies galvanised Andy into frenetic motion, the rolled-up newspaper slicing the air ahead of him like it were a sword and he was D'Artagnan; although if asked, he would prefer to be likened to Zorro.

With each swipe or riposte, the newspaper connected with flies, knocking insects dead or stunned to the floor; for each felled or fallen, more mysteriously appeared. "Where in hell's arse-crack are they all coming from?!"

"I don't think I want to stop and find out," replied Dave, backing nervously across the kitchen towards the exit, hoping his slow, careful movement would not alert the bugs into noticing him.

"You poof," ridiculed Andy playfully, unperturbed or afraid of the flies whizzing about his head, gathering momentum as their numbers steadily swelled. "I could kill this lot with my eyes closed." To illustrate, he cockily closed both eyes and blindly wafted the newspaper baton about his head. "Come help me, it's quite satisfying," he laughed moronically. "We can then get on with our wor–*ERR-UKK*,"

A fly hurtled across the room, bypassed the rolled-up newspaper with a weave and a jounce. Acting independently, it plunged headlong into Andy's opening and closing mouth, scraping through the grit of his teeth and diving towards the back of his throat, getting caught up in phlegm and post-nasal drip.

Andy choked and tried hacking the fly up, an action that spurred other flies to take aim for his mouth and nasal passage. Demonstrating how close pain could follow pleasure, the house clearance guy started thrashing his fashioned truncheon desperately at the attacking swarm of insects. Reacting to the man's distress, the flies swiftly grouped and attacked in a tight phalanx projectile, hitting him hard in the mouth and entering like a bullet train bursting through a tunnel.

Wild and independently, Andy's eyes roved around the room, focusing on anything and everything at the same time, and then settling on Dave's face, full of pleading. The rolled-up paper slipped from his hand as he clawed critically at his mouth, attempting to clear his airway. Urgently needing air, he dug the fingers of both hands into the visible dip between his neck and collarbone; the suprasternal notch; that hollow at the top of the chest. With an unsound mind and urgent desire to live, he used his neck like it were a buttoned-up shirt, as though he was Clark Kent changing into Superman; except when he tore the flesh open, no famous symbol was revealed. Rather, just a geyser of blood sprayed across the room in thick crimson ribbons as he buried his fingers deep through sternocleidomastoid muscle and continued ripping through arteries, veins, and cartilage until he was probing his larynx and exposing his trachea.

When Andy collapsed in the centre of the kitchen and started convulsing, his body doing a spasmodic parody of a street dance against the bloodied black and white tiling (the only thing missing was a head spin), Dave turned away unable to watch his friend and colleague anymore. He ran out of the house, leaving the front door swinging behind him as he clattered through the gate, banging it hard against the abutting fence. His howls of distress and anguish bellowed ahead.

He continued at a sprint for half a block, when, with his body screaming for oxygen, he stopped and stooped over someone's front garden wall, using the brick barrier for support. On the other side was a border of bright flowers and a lush green lawn.

"Are you all right?" asked an old man with a gargled voice from the garden standing ten metres to his right. He was a young-looking seventy-year-old busy pruning a rosebush, snipping off dead heads and unwieldy branches. He wore a Havana sun hat, plaid short-sleeve shirt and tan trousers. Sandals were on his feet. "You look like you've seen a ghost."

Dave had no words to reply but heard himself say: "Flies." Immediately after, he threw up over the garden wall, long and hard, spoiling the pink and purple rhododendrons with a mixture of breakfast, biscuits, and gastric juices. He wished he could regurgitate memories as easily as his stomach contents.

The old man wore a look of disgust and shook his head angrily.

"Flies!" Dave repeated in a small but urgent voice, continuing to use the wall for stability. A fly buzzed about and landed brazenly on the back of Dave's hand. He recoiled, flicking his hand to destabilise the fly. "No," he said quietly, pushing himself away from the wall and beginning to lope off further down the road.

The old man sighed. He'd seen a lot of crazy shit throughout his life and the events of the past couple of weeks took some beating, but he wondered: when would things return to normal? He considered the puke dripping from the rhododendrons and uttered a curse under his breath, feeling nauseous himself. He didn't much fancy clearing it up.

The fly that had upset Dave moments earlier invaded the old man's space, buzzing around his face and landing on the back of his neck with a tickle. Without thought, he slapped the itch, taking the fly by surprise, squishing it between the flat of his compressed index and forefinger.

"Bastard flies," he grumbled, brushing the dead insect off against the leg of his trousers before returning to pruning his rosebush. "The world's going to shit!"

He barely noticed the smooth electric hum filling the air around him, dismissing it for the sound of a neighbour using a strimmer or a light aircraft gliding across the sky. It could even have been someone using a beard trimmer or a child playing with a remote control helicopter or one of those drone-contraptions that annoyingly hovered about. Maybe a low-cylinder moped even or a local woman with one of those popular 'massaging' devices. It didn't matter.

What he never considered, however, was the small oblique ball of flies hovering three metres above his house, a hazy fluctuating mass, bobbing up and down indecisively around the chimney and TV aerial, whilst his back turned towards them.

Slowly, the soft droning sound dissipated as the insects lost interest and drifted high into the sky, a gentle wind carrying them on an airstream away for many miles, away from Fulbarton and the scene of their failure.

They may have lost the first battle... but not the war. With more than seventeen quadrillion flies in the world at any given time, it didn't require a betting man to see that the odds were stacked in their favour.

They would learn and adapt, and in time, the flies would one day have their revolution.

Afterword

When Flies Strike started life as a short story. Originally titled *The Fly Revolution*, it was written back in October 1995 for my gran (who was a huge horror fan), and was less than 3,000 words in length. Only my gran and a handful of other people read it – including the person I've dedicated this book to, Jan Hackwith. The feedback received was encouraging, but my few readers wanted more. Admittedly, on its own it didn't feel complete and I always wanted to finish it, but for some reason or other I didn't feel ready to do it justice, so I put it away and forgot about it. After finishing *The Whisper of Persia*, which was exhilarating and exhausting, I felt the need to write something completely different; something for a mature audience and something personal to me.

It was on a crazy-hot day during 2016 when a fly began to harass and bother me in my living room (and which enticed me into acting out one of the early scenes in this book!). I'm not sure why – because I'd chased flies around the house many times before – but it reminded me of the story I had written more than twenty years earlier. It prompted me to dig it out from my archive. Reading it through, it brought back memories from my younger days, in much the same way as smells often evoked scenes of times forgotten. It got me excited and it got me thinking: what if flies did attack on a massive scale? Was it possible? How could it be possible? Of course in fiction, anything can happen and I got the itch to extend that short story, to give it life, and more importantly:

a beginning, middle and an end. With that in mind, what you've just read is the result, and I sincerely hope you enjoyed it.

As always, I am indebted to a number of people in bringing this book to fruition. At the forefront, my wife, Beth – as always – has been there to lend the emotional support needed to see this project through to its end (and to listen to my gripes during the times when things weren't going my way!). To Darren Staff who acted as a sounding-board for some of the attack scenes – some made it into the final cut – others didn't, but we had a lot of fun talking about them. To my test readers Paul and Lynne Cotton, once again the feedback given was invaluable and very much appreciated; without you a few mistakes would have slipped through.

Thanks go to Laura Wilkinson for answering the many queries with regards to her editing, and to Glendon Haddix at Streetlight Graphics for the cover designs and for tolerating the requests for revisions and putting up with my slow response times.

Finally, to those of you either returning after reading my previous books, or taken a chance and bought this book after seeing the cover, I hope you are not disappointed. I enjoy writing, but it's only worth it if it's being read and received well. Please feel free to tell me by dropping me a line or leaving feedback on *Goodreads*.com, (or any online forum for that matter). It's always appreciated!

Philip J Gould, Suffolk – 1 March 2018

ABOUT THE AUTHOR

PHILIP J GOULD was born in Ipswich in 1974, and still lives in Suffolk with his wife Beth, and three children, Rebecca, Sophie and Matthew. At an early age he discovered a vivid imagination and affection for the written word. Leaving school at sixteen, he went on to work in shipping, insurance, the NHS and is also a qualified personal fitness trainer. He quit the day job in 2012 to develop his career as an author and to spend more time with his family. His first book, *The Book of Alternative Records*, was published in 2004 by Metro Publishing Ltd.

Be the first to hear news and read exclusive content on the official website: www.philipjgould.com

 Join the official Facebook page:
www.facebook.com/philipjgouldbooks

 Follow Philip on Twitter @philipjgould